BODY
IN
THE ICE

Also by A. J. MacKenzie

The Body on the Doorstep

THE
BODY
IN
THE ICE

A. J. MACKENZIE

ZAFFRE

First published in Great Britain in 2017 by
ZAFFRE PUBLISHING
80–81 Wimpole St, London W1G 9RE
www.zaffrebooks.co.uk

Text copyright © A. J. MacKenzie, 2017

All rights reserved.
No part of this publication may be reproduced,
stored or transmitted in any form by any means,
electronic, mechanical, photocopying or otherwise, without the
prior written permission of the publisher.

The right of A. J. MacKenzie to be identified as Author of this
work has been asserted by them in accordance with
the Copyright, Designs and Patents Act, 1988

This is a work of fiction. Names, places, events and incidents
are either the products of the author's imagination or
used fictitiously. Any resemblance to actual persons,
living or dead, or actual events is purely coincidental.

A CIP catalogue record for this book is available from the British Library.

ISBN: 978-1-78576-123-2

Also available as an ebook

1 3 5 7 9 10 8 6 4 2

Typeset by IDSUK (Data Connection) Ltd.

Printed and bound by Clays Ltd, St Ives Plc

Zaffre Publishing is an imprint of Bonnier Zaffre,
a Bonnier Publishing company
www.bonnierzaffre.co.uk
www.bonnierpublishing.co.uk

To Cloudesley, Bertha and Refus, who made working on this book more difficult and more entertaining.

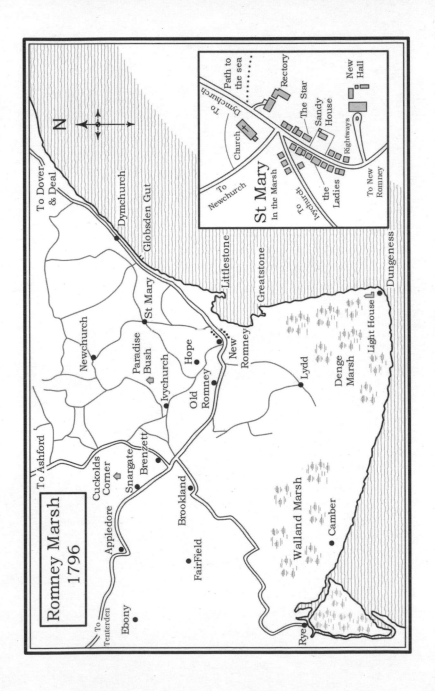

Romney Marsh
1796

To Dover
& Deal

To Ashford

To Tenterden

N

St Mary
In the Marsh

Path to
the sea

To Dymchurch

Rectory

Church

The Star

Sandy
House

New
Hall

To Newchurch

To Ivychurch

the
Ladies

Rightways

To New Romney

Dymchurch

Globsden Gut

Littlestone

Greatstone

Dungeness

Newchurch

St Mary

Paradise
Bush

Ivychurch

Hope

Old
Romney

New Romney

Light House

Lydd

Denge
Marsh

Cuckolds
Corner

Snargate

Brenzett

Brookland

Appledore

Ebony

FairField

Walland Marsh

Camber

Rye

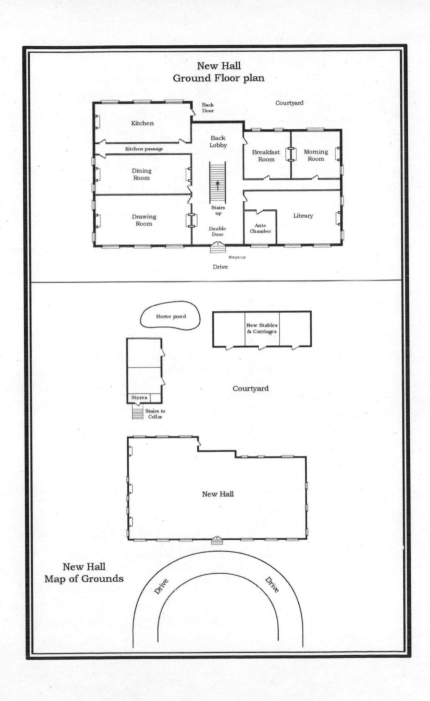

Rossiter Family Tree

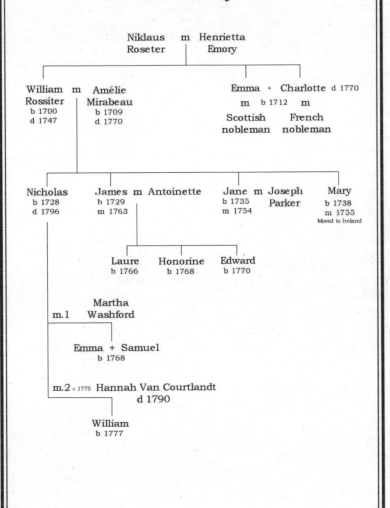

Niklaus
Roseter
m
Henrietta
Emory

William m Amélie
Rossiter   Mirabeau
b 1700   b 1709
d 1747   d 1770

Emma + Charlotte d 1770
   m b 1712 m
Scottish   French
nobleman   nobleman

Nicholas
b 1728
d 1796

James m Antoinette
b 1729
m 1763

Jane m Joseph
b 1735   Parker
m 1754

Mary
b 1738
m 1755
Moved to Ireland

Laure   Honorine   Edward
b 1766   b 1768   b 1770

m.1
Martha
Washford

Emma + Samuel
   b 1768

m.2 c.1775 Hannah Van Courtlandt
              d 1790

William
b 1777

Chapter 1

An Indigestible Christmas

Amelia Chaytor looked at the table in consternation, and made a swift survey of the room for places of concealment. Heavens above, she thought. I knew Christmas dinner would be an ordeal, but my imagination never prepared me for this. For what we are about to receive, may the Lord make us truly thankful . . .

She had accepted the invitation to spend this Christmas Day of 1796 with her friends Miss Godfrey and Miss Roper with some reluctance; only her genuine affection for the ladies had overcome her experience of their cooking. She just hoped that their servant had been able to make some of the food, and at least part of the meal would be as enjoyable as the ladies' company. If not; well, she had spotted several handy pots and a vase which might serve as receptacles for the more inedible items.

A groaning board is not usually a literal statement, she thought, as she studied the elderly, sloping dining table. She moved quickly towards the uphill end of the board and chose a seat as close as was polite to the struggling fire. Miss Roper's two nieces followed her, wrapping their shawls more tightly across their shoulders as they entered the room. Both had recently returned to England after several years in India; one was a widow whose husband had died in Calcutta, the other had returned in advance of her husband, who had been posted back to the East India Company's offices in London. Both felt the winter weather keenly.

Their hostesses fluttered in after them, Miss Roper moving to stand at the higher end of the table and Miss Godfrey at the lower. Mrs Chaytor wondered if the more robust Miss Godfrey had chosen this place in order to catch anything that slid off the table.

A tureen of soup, redolent of burnt onions, stood at the higher end of the board. The other end was occupied by a fish covered in green artificial scales and surrounded by what looked like seaweed. Various things encased in pastry marched down each side of the table, its centre commanded by a boar's head – more likely, that of a pig – whose rather collapsed visage was crowned with holly, ivy and crab-apples.

'How festive it all looks,' exclaimed one of the nieces. The other guests murmured similar sentiments, gazing at the quantities of greenery and ribbon festooning the pictures and hanging perilously close to burning candles.

'We do like to decorate for Christmas,' said Miss Roper, 'and of course everything stays up until Twelfth Night so we have a lovely long time to enjoy our festive house. So much more cheerful in winter; particularly with all the cold and ice. It has been a terrible winter, has it not?'

Everyone agreed. The winter had indeed been bitterly cold. Down here on Romney Marsh they had been largely free of the snow that lay thick and white on the downs further inland, but even at midday the land was still covered with ice and frost. 'We can be snug inside with reminders that the green leaves *will* come again in spring,' said Miss Godfrey. 'Reverend Braithwaite, who was with us here in St Mary in the Marsh before Reverend Hardcastle, said that our decorations were pagan, but we are pleased our present rector does not share such Quakerish views.'

'No one could accuse the rector of being Quakerish,' said Mrs Chaytor.

'And it is a very particular pleasure to have our dear visitors from the East Indies to share our celebrations,' said Miss Roper to her nieces. '*So* very different for you, my dears; we are eager to hear about what decorations and food you had for festivities in India. I suppose it must have been hot? How strange to have Christmas when it is warm; no snow and ice for you! And we have been truly grateful for your advising us about the *currey* sauce for the eggs. You must try some, Mrs Chaytor, for it is most delicious, and invigorating. We were quite surprised that we could obtain the necessary spices from Rye.'

'Perhaps we should be seated now, dear,' said Miss Godfrey, drily.

'Oh, yes, yes, we must have the soup before it cools or it will lose its savour.'

When tasted, the soup bore out all the promise of its odour. Mrs Chaytor drank the generous portion served by Miss Roper as quickly as possible, keen to move on to something more palatable. The fish, surprisingly, proved quite tasty once its dressings had been removed, and the eggs with *currey* sauce were also good, although Mrs Chaytor noticed Miss Godfrey's eyes water as she tasted them; chilli and Indian spices were a novelty here on Romney Marsh.

'To be sure,' said Mary, Miss Roper's younger niece, 'I have not cooked a *currey* sauce myself, but I had the receipt from our cook in Calcutta. Most of our servants there were so willing and helpful.'

Her remark sparked the inevitable discussion at all middle-class dinner tables about servants and the quality, or otherwise, of their work. The nieces told some amusing tales about the difficulty of directing servants when there is no common language, and Mrs Chaytor related some of her own experiences in managing diplomatic households in Paris and Rome. Despite the food, the evening was becoming enjoyable.

Miss Godfrey and Miss Roper praised the loyalty and hard work of their maid, Kate, and reminisced about the elderly gardener and general man-of-work whom they had suffered for many years until his death in the autumn. 'Our new lad is a great improvement,' said Miss Godfrey. 'He had been one of the Fanscombes' grooms, and came to us after old Albert died. Kate and he work together very well, and I must say that the garden is looking much better, even if we do have to check that he is digging up weeds and not plants. Still, he is a prodigious digger, and we shall set him to making a new sparrow-grass bed once the soil becomes workable.'

'Of course, he misses the horses he worked with up at New Hall,' said Miss Roper. 'Our poor old Nellie is no match for the magnificent beasts that the Fanscombes had in their stables.'

'Speaking of New Hall,' said Mrs Chaytor, 'is it true that the two men who came to the village the day before yesterday are living there?'

'Kate and the lad Jed assure us that they do indeed appear to be staying in the Hall,' replied Miss Godfrey. 'Their horses are in the stables, although the house is still shuttered, and smoke has been seen issuing from at least one of the chimneys.'

'It must be a bleak place to live, given that the house has lain empty for so many months,' observed Mrs Chaytor.

'We sent them a little note asking if they would like to join us for our Christmas feast,' said Miss Roper, 'for certain there cannot be much comfort at the Hall. There are no servants since that dreadful caretaker went off to Lydd on Friday past. But sadly we have had no reply from the gentlemen. We must hope that they have some food and warmth at the Hall.'

'Yes, indeed,' said Miss Godfrey, 'for this is surely not the winter to be without sufficient fuel. Our own supplies are growing a little low, although Kate assures us that there is plenty to be had outside, if you know where to look.'

Mrs Chaytor glanced at the small, struggling fire beside her and hoped that Kate did indeed know where to look, for there was hardly enough wood in the hearth to last until the end of the meal. 'It is rather puzzling that anyone should come down to New Hall at this season,' she said, 'especially with the caretaker having gone, and no one there to look after them.'

This line of conversation was interrupted as Kate and Jed, the latter in a badly fitting suit of black coat and baggy breeches, entered the dining room to remove the first course and then bring in the second. As they departed, Miss Godfrey asked Jed to bring more wood for the dying fire. The lad mumbled something that seemed to be agreement.

An enormous plum pudding with a large sprig of holly sprouting from its top was perhaps the most unsurprising, though still startling, element of the next course. A formidable rib of beef provided balance at the other end of the table, and the rest of the space was filled with jellies both savoury and sweet, coloured orange and red and green, and what Mrs Chaytor recognised as the ladies' attempt at a *croque-en-bouche*. Where, she wondered, had they encountered this quintessentially French sweet dish?

Conversation paused while everyone sorted out their selection of the delights on offer. The beef proved to be quite burnt on the outside and frequently raw on the inside, while the *croque-en-bouche* illustrated the ladies' usual heavy hand with pastry. The savoury jellies helped to disguise the rawness of the beef, however, and the sweet ones were unexceptionable. Those must have been made by Kate, thought Mrs Chaytor.

As the company dealt with their food choices the conversation turned once again, in that particularly English way, to a combination of the weather and gossip about their neighbours. 'I do hope that last night's thaw lasted long enough to make the rector's early morning journey to Ashford an easy one,' said

Miss Godfrey, 'for the cold has come down again this forenoon and it is frozen hard once more. For how long is he away, do you know, Mrs Chaytor?'

'For some days, I believe. I imagine he will return to St Mary to take service on Sunday morning.'

'Oh, I am certain that he will do that,' said Miss Roper. 'You know his strong views on rectors fobbing off awkward services onto poor curates, especially at this time of year.'

'He is pretty much alone in those views,' said Miss Godfrey, severely. 'The rector of Ivychurch has not taken a service in his parish for many, many months. That is why we churchgoers have to endure the vile odour of that old man from Brenzett, for he insists on what he calls a "proper priest" when he goes to church.'

'Well, at least he comes to church regularly, which is more than many do in St Mary,' said Miss Roper, ignoring the loud clearing of the throat from the opposite end of the table. 'Most only want the rector when there is someone to be buried, or to visit them when they are ill. Or, more rarely, to marry them or baptise their child; and they don't always wait for the marriage before having the baptism.'

'Not everyone who has faith chooses to go to church every Sunday, my dear,' said Miss Godfrey, gently but firmly.

Miss Roper looked up at Mrs Chaytor in sudden guilt. 'Oh, my dear Mrs Chaytor, I was not thinking of you at all! Please take no offence at my words. It is only that the rector has been so busy looking after people over the past month, making sure that no one goes cold or hungry. And then to have only six people at Christmas Eve midnight service! It did make me so cross on his behalf.'

'It was very cold, aunt,' one of her nieces murmured.

'Indeed it was,' said Mrs Chaytor, 'and Reverend Hardcastle appears to care little about the size of his congregation. I am certain that even if he found himself alone on Sunday, he would still say the services.'

'I am sure you are correct, Mrs Chaytor,' said Miss Godfrey. 'Mind, there have been times in the past when he did find it a struggle to concentrate on Sunday mornings, so bad was his head. But it seems to me that in recent months there has been less of that trouble.'

'Perhaps his new legal responsibilities have occasioned a more sober approach to life,' suggested Miss Roper. 'Being a justice of the peace is a serious matter.'

'I am not certain that Reverend Hardcastle's appointment as a temporary J. P. is the reason for his more measured manner of life,' said Mrs Chaytor, 'but whatever that reason may be, I think we must all agree that he is in much better health, despite the cold and the hard work he has been undertaking of late.'

'And I think we are very fortunate to have him,' said Miss Godfrey, firmly. 'After the events of last spring, it is good to know there is someone *reliable* looking after the affairs of the district.'

'I wonder if he has met the two gentlemen at New Hall,' said Miss Roper, returning to their earlier conversation. 'Has he said anything to you, Mrs Chaytor?'

Amelia shook her head. 'No. But then I have not seen the reverend except in passing for several days.'

One of the nieces sneezed. Miss Godfrey apologised for the chill in the room. 'I wonder what is taking Jed so long with that wood? Do you suppose that the fire in the drawing room will be any better? At least we can all sit closer to it. Shall we withdraw?'

As the noise of a banging door and running footsteps penetrated the room, she continued, 'Ah, perhaps we shall have some warmth at last,' but her words were cut off by loud cries from the corridor. The dining room door burst open and the maidservant tumbled in, staring in shock.

'Oh, oh, oh, Miss Godfrey! Miss Godfrey! I saw someone trapped in the ice up at New Hall stables! I think he might be dead! Jed says he is dead! He must be dead, to be frozen into the ice like that, face down. For certain, he must be dead!'

The man was indeed face down in the horse pond next to the stables behind New Hall, and he was certainly dead. Mrs Chaytor looked at the body in the dim light of the lantern, and shivered in her fur-lined cloak; not from the cold, but from pity and sorrow at the death of the unknown man before her. Lifting the lantern higher, she saw marks on the frozen ground that suggested he had crawled here from the direction of the house. No mercifully swift death then, but one filled with pain and fear. She shivered again.

New Hall was silent and dark. No flicker of light showed from its windows. There was no obvious trace of the other man who had ridden into St Mary's only two days ago. The silence around the house was complete.

Mrs Chaytor turned to Jed, who was standing and looking steadily at the body in the ice. He had said nothing since he and Kate burst into the dining room; Kate had done all the talking and exclaiming. 'Jed, we must get Mr Stemp to see to this.' Stemp was the parish constable, who would need to take charge until the rector's return. 'Please find him and bring him here as soon as you may.'

Miss Godfrey had insisted on accompanying Mrs Chaytor and Jed to New Hall. Now she put a gentle hand on the younger woman's shoulders and said softly: '*Lord, now lettest thou thy servant depart in peace according to thy word.* I hope that the poor soul has found peace in death, for his last moments cannot have been quiet.'

Chapter 2

The Body in the Ice

In the cold, grey light of a December morning the scene had nothing of last night's remembered horror, only a certain bleak tragedy. The body lay face down, the torso frozen into the ice of the pond, the legs and hips resting on hard ground. The man's arms, so far as could be seen in the ice, were twisted around his head. He wore an overcoat, beneath which were a pair of shabby black worsted breeches and thick stockings. One of his black half-boots had been wrenched off and lay on the frozen ground at the edge of the pond; the exposed stockinged foot was stiff and rimed with ice. He had, thought Mrs Chaytor irrelevantly, quite small feet.

The wind that whistled around the eaves of the stable block was strengthening; overhead, the weather vane clattered uneasily on its iron mount. The wind had a tang of iron, laced with salt. Joshua Stemp, the parish constable, rubbed his mittened hands together and scowled at the body. 'I wish that doctor would hurry up.'

Mrs Chaytor turned to look at the house behind them. 'The caretaker has not returned?'

'He has family down in Lydd, ma'am,' said Stemp. 'He'll have gone down there for Christmas.'

His companion, a fisherman named Jack Hoad, grunted. 'If that's so, he'll be blind drunk 'til New Year and beyond.'

'We'll go down and drag him back, you and me.'

Mrs Chaytor held up a hand. 'I think that may be the doctor.'

They heard the sound of a pony and cart, clopping hooves and iron-rimmed wheels rattling against the hard ground, turning off the main New Romney road and up the drive to the house.

A moment later the cart pulled up in the yard behind New Hall and halted, the pony shaking itself and blowing steam from its nostrils. Mrs Chaytor walked to meet the doctor as he stepped carefully down from the box, the yard icy beneath his feet.

'Dr Mackay. It is good of you to come out. I trust we have not ruined your Christmas.'

'Not at all,' said the doctor, bowing. He was a short, stocky Scot, heavily muffled like them all against the wind. He looked at the two men standing by the frozen horse pond, and then back to Mrs Chaytor. They were not well acquainted, but the doctor knew her for an unusual and intelligent person. 'Where is the body, then?'

She pointed, and turned to walk with him towards the horse pond. 'I imagined you would need help in moving him, so I have summoned the parish constable. I have also sent my groom to fetch Reverend Hardcastle from Ashford. I should think he will return directly, tomorrow or even tonight.'

'Hardcastle is in Ashford? I didn't know the man travelled any-where. He's as sedentary as a mollusc.'

'He went to spend Christmas with an old friend,' said Mrs Chaytor, patiently.

'Didn't know he had friends, either. Right, what have we here?'

The other three waited while the doctor circled the body, test-ing the ice once or twice with his boot. 'Frozen solid,' he said. 'Not surprised, given the cold last night. Any ideas as to who he might be?'

'We think he might be one of two men who arrived at the house three days ago,' said Mrs Chaytor. 'There is no sign of the other man,' she added, 'and their horses are missing from the stables.' She pointed to the stable doors, hanging open and swinging uneasily in the wind.

'Ah,' said the doctor. 'Intriguing.' He looked down at the body. 'Well, we'll need to cut him out of the ice, and then get him onto a table so I can examine him. Somewhere out of this blasted wind, for preference. Is there a place where we can take him?'

Hoad jerked his thumb at the house. 'The doors are locked,' said Mrs Chaytor. 'All of them. I have tried them,' she added.

The men looked at her, then back at the body at their feet. 'Tim Luckhurst at the Star will have empty storerooms,' said Stemp. 'We could use one of those,' and he shot Mrs Chaytor a meaningful look.

She sighed inwardly, knowing she was not wanted. 'I will go and ask him,' she said.

'Thank you indeed, Mrs Chaytor,' said the doctor. 'Stemp, there should be axes in the wood store. Fetch a couple, and let's cut this fellow out.'

She heard the sound of axes splintering the ice around the body as she walked down the drive, and shivered again; this time, she told herself firmly, it really was the cold. As she turned towards the village the wind increased again, keening over the flat Marsh and tugging at her hood and overcoat. Its cold hardness made her eyes water, and her nose was streaming by the time she reached the Star.

Luckhurst the landlord came out from the back, his eyebrows rising slightly at the sight of Mrs Chaytor; ordinarily she was not a frequenter of public houses. She explained her errand briefly in her light, slightly drawling voice, and his expression changed. He knew about the body, of course. Everyone in the village must know by now, or at least everyone who was awake; gossip was Kate's one great talent in life, and she exercised it ceaselessly.

'Of course, there are storerooms we use only at certain times,' Luckhurst said guilelessly. 'I'll show them into one of those. Here, you are shivering, Mrs Chaytor! Sit you down by the fire and get warm. Bessie! Bring a cup of that coffee for the lady.'

Then there was nothing to do but sit and wait. Bessie, the land-lord's daughter, a lively and intelligent girl of sixteen, brought coffee and Mrs Chaytor thanked her with a smile; she knew Bessie well, and sometimes employed her as an extra maidservant.

'How convenient that your father has an empty storeroom,' she said drily. That prompted a conspiratorial laugh. Some of Luckhurst's storerooms, as they both knew, were only in use on certain nights around the new moon, when boats came gliding over the sea from France thirty miles away, landing illicit cargos of gin and brandy and wine, silk and scent, lace and tobacco. Those cargoes had many resting places before they continued their journey to the markets of London; the cellars and store-rooms of the Star were one such place.

She heard the men arriving outside with the body. After what seemed a very long time, Dr Mackay came into the common room, blowing on his fingers. 'That is the coldest work I have done in many a day,' he said, sitting down. 'Is that coffee? Bring me a cup, girl, and put some rum in it, if you have any. No? Brandy will do, then. Don't tell me you haven't any brandy,' he added with a heavy attempt at humour.

'What did you find?' Mrs Chaytor asked directly.

'Well, there's a thing,' said the doctor. He paused for a moment, looking into the flickering flames of the fire, and blew on his fingers again. 'Or rather, there's two things,' he amended. 'First, when we got him out of the ice, we found he was an African man.'

'A black man?' Mrs Chaytor raised her eyebrows. 'How unu-sual. At least, how unusual for St Mary in the Marsh. Where do you suppose he came from? A sailor, perhaps, off a ship from Rye, or Deal?' But even as she spoke she knew she was wrong; no sailor would ever have worn boots like those.

'He was not a sailor,' said Mackay. He glanced at Bessie, hovering behind the bar and eavesdropping shamelessly. Then

Stemp and Hoad entered, and she moved away reluctantly to serve them. 'No, not a sailor,' the doctor repeated. 'You see, Mrs Chaytor, when I examined the body more closely – I don't quite know how to put this – I discovered *he* was not a *he* at all. The body we pulled from the ice was that of a woman.'

Very rarely was Amelia Chaytor lost for words. She was now. She stared at the doctor for a long time, her eyes an intense blue as she considered the news. 'That explains the feet,' she said finally.

'I beg your pardon?'

'When I looked at the body, I thought the feet were quite small, for a man. Now I see why.' She looked up at Mackay. 'How did the poor thing die?' she asked.

Mackay regarded her as if he was not sure how much was appropriate to tell her. 'The cause of death was drowning,' he said finally. 'But she had also been struck a very heavy blow on the head. That blow fractured her skull, and I suspect also damaged the brain. It is possible that this blow might have proved fatal.'

'Then how on earth did she come to drown?'

'I cannot answer that, I am afraid. She either found her way to the pond, or was taken there. There was open water; I saw signs that someone had broken the ice earlier in the day, perhaps to water the horses. That is where she met her end.'

'You mean she fell in the water when she was stunned and could not move? Or someone took her to the water and held her under?' Her voice was grave, but quite calm. Mackay looked at her, thinking again what an unusual woman she was. 'It could be either of those things,' he said at last, 'though I found no injuries on the body itself. Other, that is, than the blow to the head.'

He finished his coffee and rose to his feet. 'Apart from that, I fear there is little I can tell you. You may inform Reverend Hard-castle when he returns that I shall write a report in my capacity as assistant coroner, and forward it to the coroner's office in Maidstone. And of course, I shall send a copy to him.'

'Thank you, doctor.' Mrs Chaytor sat listening to the doctor's footsteps as he walked out into the cold road, and then the sound of hooves and rattling wheels fading away. It needed little effort to imagine those final moments; the woman stumbling and falling, or being pushed into the icy water and drowning. Was she aware, as she fell, that she was dying? One hoped that the blow had stunned her so thoroughly that she was oblivious; the fear was that it had not.

'What a terrible way for the poor soul to die,' she said to herself.

'It surely is, ma'am,' said Bessie beside her, refilling her coffee cup.

'What would a woman be doing dressed as a man?' Mrs Chaytor wondered.

'Well, ma'am; she must have wanted to escape notice. She might have had a secret errand, or,' and Bessie, who had a fine ear for drama and romance, paused significantly, 'she might have been meeting a lover. New Hall is quiet and out of the way. It'd be a perfect place for a lover's tryst.'

'Bessie,' said Mrs Chaytor briskly, 'you have a very vivid imagination.' But, she thought, that did not necessarily mean the girl was wrong. The same thought had already occurred to her.

The Reverend Marcus Aurelius Hardcastle, rector of St Mary in the Marsh and justice of the peace, returned home late that afternoon, as a winter dusk began to fall over the frozen Marsh. He was cold, tired from travelling on icy roads, and in a foul mood. He shouted for his housekeeper as he entered the hall of the rectory, throwing down his hat and stick on a side table, and she came out of the kitchens and snapped back at him. He glared at her, and demanded a pot of hot coffee.

'Coffee?' asked the housekeeper, with pretend incredulity. 'Not port?'

'When I desire port, Mrs Kemp, I shall inform you. Once you have made the coffee, send John to find Joshua Stemp. Tell him I wish to see him as soon as possible.'

In his study, the rector removed the guard from the fire and blew on the embers, then added a fresh log. Little flames rose up at once, crackling, and the rector bent over them to warm his numbed hands. The journey down from Ashford, exposed to the freezing wind on the seat of a creaking dogcart, had been every bit as hellish as he had expected it would be; but it had been impossible to ignore the urgency in Mrs Chaytor's letter. He would go and see her, he thought, as soon as he had heard Stemp's report.

Straightening from the fire, he looked up to see his own reflection in a mirror, and scowled. He saw a thickset man of about forty with the beginnings of jowls, sandy hair that was growing thin on top, and features that were not much improved by his current glowering expression. Ignoring the mirror, he looked around the room, gazing at the bookshelves and worn carpet and noting that two of the chairs needed upholstering. Everything is shabby and falling to bits, he thought, rather like me. He glanced at the mahogany cabinet where, he knew, several bottles of extremely potable cognac rested among his account books, and looked away again.

The parish constable appeared half an hour later, just as the rector was finishing the last of his coffee. He was a small man with a face badly pitted by smallpox and bright, inquiring eyes. Standing before the desk he gave a stiff little bow and said, 'Sorry if I'm late, reverend.'

'Sit down,' said Hardcastle. 'Do you want some coffee? I can send for Mrs Kemp.'

'Don't trouble her on my account, reverend.'

'Very well,' said the rector, leaning back in his chair. 'Now, tell me exactly what has happened.'

He listened in silence to the story of the discovery of the body, its removal to the Star and its examination by Dr Mackay. Only upon hearing that the body was that of a woman did his face change a little. Mrs Chaytor had not mentioned that; but of course, when she wrote to him, she had not known herself.

'What about the other man who was at New Hall?' he asked at the end.

'No sign of him, reverend, and both horses are missing. I've spent most of the day knocking on doors up and down the roads to Dymchurch and New Romney, asking if anyone had seen a man with two horses go past yesterday evening.'

'And had they?'

'Nah,' said Stemp with mild contempt. 'It was Christmas Day. By evening most people were blind drunk, even the children. When I talked to them this afternoon, most were still so hungover they couldn't remember their own names, let alone what might or might not have happened yesterday.'

Hardcastle frowned. 'We need a description if we are to establish a search for this man. Did anyone see them the day they arrived? I suppose it is too much to hope that someone saw their faces.'

Stemp shook his head. 'They arrived after dark, remember, and it was colder than charity. Not many folk were about, and those that were saw two cloaked-up figures on horseback, nothing more. They'd have been muffled up to the eyes anyway, in this weather.'

'Where is the body now?'

Stemp reached into his pocket and produced a key.

'Very well,' said the rector, rising to his feet. 'Let us go and take a look at her.'

The Star was quiet, most of the village still recovering in one way or another from Christmas. Stemp, carrying a lantern, let them into the storeroom and they approached the body lying on the plain oak table. Joshua Stemp was a kind man, and he had covered the body decently; now, he held up the lantern and pulled the covering sheet away just enough to allow the rector to see the head and face. 'Here's the wound where she was hit, reverend,' he said, gently lifting the dead woman's head with his free hand.

The rector nodded absently. He looked down to see curling black hair matted with dried blood and some splinters which might have been wood but, by their shape, were more likely to be bone. Any blunt object, wielded with sufficient force, could have cracked her skull. As to what else might have been done to the body; well, Dr Mackay's report would tell him that in due course.

He stood for a while longer, looking at the dead woman. Her face was swollen and the skin dark and blotchy. 'In what position was the body when she was found?'

'Face down,' said Stemp, 'with her arms stretched forward.'

That explained the blotchiness; the rector had learned enough anatomy to know that when the heart stops beating, blood settles in the lower reaches of the body, however it is lying. He pulled the blanket back a little and saw similar swelling and dark blotches on her shoulders. Where the blood had not settled, her skin was a gentle brown, not particularly dark.

He studied the face again. Beneath the swelling she had high, rather prominent cheekbones and full lips; the eyebrows over closed eyes were two fine arches. A young woman, he thought, perhaps five-and-twenty, no more. Where was she from? How had she come to meet her death here in the frozen wastes of Romney Marsh? How? How and why? There was nothing noble about her clothes, piled neatly on a bench at one side of the room. The rector examined these quickly. Worsted breeches and stockings, a man's coat and waistcoat, both of which he thought were rather too large for her, a thick overcoat which unlike the rest of her garments looked to be quite new, though sadly stained with dried blood down the back; a woman's small clothes, thin and worn from long use. The clothes told him nothing; as the doctor had discovered earlier, the pockets were empty save for a few coins, and there was not a single mark or clue to reveal the dead woman's identity.

Outside in the yard, Stemp locked the door once more. The body would need to remain there until the ground thawed enough for a grave to be dug.

'Out of curiosity,' said the rector, 'what were Miss Godfrey and Miss Roper's servants doing up at New Hall?'

'Raiding the woodshed or the coal store, I expect,' said Stemp, cheerfully. 'Nothing new there. People have been doing it ever since the autumn. The caretaker never notices.'

The caretaker, a one-armed alcoholic former sailor named Beazley, probably never looked out of the windows. 'And you have been turning a blind eye to this,' said the rector.

'House is empty, and has been for months. No one will miss a little wood or coal.' Stemp motioned towards the common room. 'I'm popping in for a glass, reverend. Care to join me?'

'No, but thank you.' The rector reached into his pocket for money, which he pressed into Stemp's hand. 'Have one on me. Buy one for Jack too, if he's there, and thank him for his assistance this morning. You did well today, Joshua. I know this is not exactly the job you signed up for.'

'Makes a change from the usual, sir,' said Stemp, and he grinned and walked off towards the common room.

The usual, for a local constable, consisted of catching stray dogs and rounding up vagrants. The former were returned to their owners in exchange for a small fine; the latter, in accordance with long-standing national practice, were hustled over the boundary into the next parish where they would become someone else's problem, although the rector – to the vehement disapproval of both Stemp and his housekeeper – made sure the vagrants had a hot meal before they took their involuntary departure from St Mary in the Marsh. Stemp insisted that such charity merely encouraged such people to come back. The rector thought he was probably right.

Stemp's duties as constable took up only a small amount of his time, leaving him free to carry on his other trades: by day an honest fisherman, on dark nights he transformed into Yorkshire Tom, leader of the smugglers in this part of Romney Marsh. The rector knew this; Stemp knew that he knew it, and that knowledge remained their shared, unspoken secret.

Hardcastle had appointed Stemp as parish constable on the same day that he had reluctantly accepted the post of justice of the peace. The act was an inspired one. On the one hand he gained a loyal lieutenant; a man who had his ear to the ground and knew what was going on, not just in St Mary in the Marsh but up and down the coast. On the other, the local free-traders were reassured that he did not intend to inquire too closely into their activities. There were already two preventive services – the Customs and the Excise – dedicated to the suppression of smuggling, and the rector judged them perfectly capable of carrying on their efforts without his assistance. He reasoned that his tasks as both rector and magistrate would be made much easier if he did not stand in the smugglers' way; and to those who reproached him for not joining in the fight against the smugglers, he gave the official's standard excuse: *not my department*.

Stemp would do his duty well, so long as it did not clash with his other interests, and with that Hardcastle was perfectly satisfied. He went to pay his call on Amelia Chaytor.

He knocked at the door of Sandy House, her home. Lucy, the young housekeeper, admitted him at once, shutting the door behind him against the chilly blast of the wind.

'Mrs Chaytor's not in, reverend,' she said. 'She was waiting for you to call. When you didn't come she got impatient and went looking for you. She said she would wait for you at the rectory.'

I can guess what is coming, thought the rector, walking home bent against the wind, the freezing air singing in his ears. Mrs Chaytor had been one of the first to see the body, and now she won't rest until the killer of the young woman is found. She'll poke her nose into an official investigation and make her views plain to everyone, whether they want to hear them or not. She'll go ferreting around looking for information, and likely as not will get into trouble.

He found he was smiling.

Amelia Chaytor was waiting for him in his study, seated in one of the chairs before the fire with her hands clasped primly in her lap. She wore a dark gown of fine wool, rather severe in its cut as became a still-young widow. He had never asked her age but guessed she was about thirty. Her dark brown hair was curled loosely under a white bonnet, and she had blue eyes with long, fine lashes, eyes which could grow rather intense when she was deep in thought. She had about her the kind of poise which, as a younger man, the rector had much admired in women; both her carriage and her voice suggested that she once moved in fashionable circles, if not absolutely one of the *ton* then perhaps on its fringes.

She said in her light voice, 'You have rearranged your books.'

The room was full of books, many of them, like the furniture, worn from long usage. 'The fading relics of my past intellectual pretensions,' he said, sitting down opposite her and looking at his bookshelves. 'Yes, I have put them in some sort of order at last. I began rereading Gibbon, and discovered half the volumes were missing. Tracking them down involved taking practically every book off the shelves. I decided I might as well put them back in order.'

'*The Decline and Fall of the Roman Empire*? Not exactly a cheerful subject for winter evenings.'

'Decline and fall have been much on my mind of late,' he said. 'We heard more bad news in Ashford. Lord Malmesbury's peace mission to Paris has failed; the Directory will not even receive him. The Austrians have been beaten in Italy, again. The embers of revolt still glow in Ireland, and French ships have been sighted off the coasts, preparing, it is said, to land troops to support the rebels. France grows daily stronger, and we, it seems, grow weaker.' He sighed and changed the subject. 'Has Mrs Kemp offered you refreshment?'

'I am perfectly content, thank you.'

He regarded her, quietly. 'This is a very bad business,' he said at length. 'I was persuaded to become a justice of the peace against my better judgement. More than ever, I am regretting that decision.'

'To be honest, I have never been entirely certain why you agreed.'

'After the events of last June, Lord Clavertye needed someone he could trust. *A steady hand on the tiller*, was how he put it. He was extremely pressing.'

'I am sure he was. But in my experience, you seldom care what Lord Clavertye thinks, and are even less likely to do what he wants.'

Lord Clavertye, the deputy lord lieutenant of Kent, was an old acquaintance of Hardcastle's from Cambridge; these days, he thought, Clavertye respects rather than likes me. 'I suppose I realised he was right,' he said. 'Someone had to take this duty, if only to restore some trust in the law after Fanscombe's disgrace. I was the only logical choice at the time. And, I do owe Clavertye a great deal. He is the patron of this parish, and it was he who found me this living after my own . . . disgrace.'

She nodded. 'What do you intend to do about the murder of the young woman?' she asked.

He frowned, staring into the fire. 'Let us take stock of the situation,' he said finally. 'New Hall has been standing empty since June. Then, on the twenty-third of December, two unknown people arrived at the house and gained entry. They apparently spent two nights there. At some point on Christmas Day the woman received a savage blow to the back of the head, then shortly afterwards drowned in the horse pond. The other member of the party has disappeared, locking the house and taking both horses with him.'

'Just a moment. You said, "him". Why do we assume the other person was a man? If one was a woman dressed as a man, why not the other?'

'It is possible,' he conceded. 'But I suspect it was a man because of the severity of the blow the woman received. Not many women are strong enough to strike a blow of such power. Also . . . one can conceive of reasons why a man might take a woman in disguise alone to a remote house. It is a little harder to imagine a motive for another woman doing so.'

'But it is possible,' she said, echoing him. 'I am not saying you are wrong, merely that we need to keep an open mind.'

'I yield the point. I have laid out what we do know. Let us now turn to the list of things we do *not* know. We do not know who the dead woman is, where she comes from or why she was here. We do not know the identity of the other person, or where this other person might now be. Most of all, we do not know why he – for the moment, I shall continue to say he – attacked the dead woman.'

'But you have a theory,' she said, and waited.

'I know how it appears,' Hardcastle said. 'The woman was enticed to the house, and the man killed her. There might be several motives: a fit of sudden anger, a quarrel, a disagreement over money, or sex. Perhaps the woman knew something, or had something the man wanted, but refused to divulge it. He attacked her out of spite, or in an attempt to beat a confession from her. The assistant coroner's report will tell us whether there were any other marks on her body.'

'All of that is certainly quite possible,' she said. 'But there is something particular that bothers me.'

'What is it?'

'The boot. One of her boots had been pulled off and was lying near the body. Why?'

'Might it have fallen off?'

'They were half-boots, and snugly fitting. It would have taken an effort to pull it off.' He remembered the boots and nodded agreement. 'I think someone tried to pull her from the pond,' Mrs Chaytor said, 'and seized her by one leg, and the boot then came away in the other person's hand. That person then dropped the boot and left the scene.'

'But who could that person be? The killer? Why would the killer smash her skull, push her into the water and drown her, and then try to pull her out again?'

'To hide the body?' she asked.

'Then why not go ahead and hide it? Why give up on the attempt, drop the boot and leave the body where it was?'

'Perhaps the killer then heard someone coming, and fled the scene,' she said.

'It was Christmas Day, and bitterly cold. No one would be out and about . . . except perhaps for some of our neighbours coming to take wood from the woodshed, of course. But Joshua has spoken to every household in the parish. No one admits to going to New Hall that day save for the ladies' two servants.'

'Very well. You have rebutted my arguments. Now advance some of your own, so that I may destroy them in turn.'

He smiled a little. 'I admit it is mysterious, and I have no better explanation to offer. In fact, for the moment there are really only two things to be done. I can write to Lord Clavertye and ask him to instigate a wider search for the man who fled New Hall, on the grounds that he is suspected of murder. And, we must of course search the house and grounds for clues as soon as it is light . . .'

The rector paused, staring into the fire again. 'Why *that* house?' he said, half to himself. 'Why of all the remote places to carry a woman to, why choose that ill-starred place? There are plenty of empty houses on Romney Marsh, many even more remote than this. There were only two of them; why did they choose a house so large? Or *did* they choose it? Did they perhaps stumble upon it by accident?'

'They chose it,' she said, 'or one of them did. They had keys to unlock and lock the doors.'

'Of course, of course. Where would they have got the keys?'

'From Mrs Fanscombe, after she left? Might there be some connection to her?'

'You are forgetting that the Fanscombes only leased New Hall,' he reminded her. 'Eugénie Fanscombe terminated the lease when she departed after her husband's death. She was unlikely to keep any reminders of her unhappy time in that house. The keys would likely have been returned to the owners' solicitor . . .'

The rector stopped for a moment, still staring into the fire. Then he rose and went to his desk, unlocked it and pulled out a letter, which he carried across to Mrs Chaytor and handed to her. She took it, noting the large and ornate seal, of a kind which meant the writer was either a self-important solicitor or a particularly prosperous cheesemonger. She took the letter and read.

ANTHONY JESSINGTON, ESQ
LINCOLN'S INN
LONDON
1st September, 1796.

The Reverend M. A. Hardcastle
The Rectory
St Mary in the Marsh
Kent

The Reverend Hardcastle, Sir,

In the wake of the unhappy events lately occurred involving the last tenant of New Hall, St Mary in the Marsh, it is my duty to resolve certain issues regarding the said estate. I would very much welcome your assistance in this matter.

I have been, in name, legal advisor to the Rossiter family, the owners of New Hall, these past two years or more. During that time I have, to the best of my professional ability, endeavoured to manage the family's estate in this country carefully and with probity, so you may imagine my dismay on being informed of the activities of the late tenant, Mr Fanscombe. I am duty bound to inform the owners of what has transpired, but I have had no fortune in contacting any member of the Rossiter family, who, as I was informed upon taking over their affairs, are currently residing in unknown parts of the Americas. I feel it my duty to attempt to contact interested members of the family, and, as it is not currently within my power to come myself to St Mary in the Marsh due to an indisposition which makes travel inadvisable, I am therefore communicating with your good self.

It is my devout hope that you shall be able to shed some light on any other members of the Rossiter family who are likely to be extant. For example, there might be a junior branch of the family whose names do not appear in my records. I should be very grateful if you could consult any records of baptism, marriage or death that you have, so that I might compare them with my own records to check the accuracy of the latter.

I should also be most grateful if you felt able to provide any further information as to the whereabouts of those family members who went to America. While I have a distaste for what might be described as 'gossip' or 'tittle-tattle', I am hopeful that some of the family may have been in informal communication with persons local to their estate. It is my hope that you, as rector, may be able to gather relevant information in a discreet manner, so as not to arouse any vulgar curiosity in the locale.

I include for your elucidation a list of the family members as I was passed them upon my acquisition of the Rossiter family affairs.

Your faithful servant,

ANTHONY JESSINGTON

'Dear, dear,' said Mrs Chaytor, clicking her tongue. 'Clearly Mr Jessington is not in favour of using one word where ten will do.' She folded the letter and returned it to Hardcastle. 'He wants you to find the Rossiters for him.'

'Which I have absolutely no intention of doing,' said the rector, returning the letter to his desk. 'I have enough on my plate without acting as a solicitor's runner as well. In any case, there is nothing I could do even were I so inclined. I did consult the registers, and it so happens that there is an Amélie Rossiter buried in the churchyard, but she died more than a quarter of a century ago. Apart from that, there is nothing.'

'But there is a connection between this letter and the murder,' she said.

He looked at her. 'What makes you say that? Woman's intuition?'

Her eyebrows rose a little. 'You must be feeling better,' she said. 'You are attempting humour. Your sudden recollection of the letter is reason enough to suggest a connection. Have you heard anything further from Anthony Jessington "Esk"?'

The rector shook his head.

'Suppose he did make contact with the Rossiters after the date of this letter,' she said, 'and informed them that their tenants have gone and New Hall is standing empty. And then suppose someone – a member of the family, a friend of the family – decided that a deserted house on Romney Marsh would make an ideal place to bring a woman for a little Christmas sport. And then, because he was angry with her, or tired of her, or because that is what gives him pleasure, he killed her.'

Amelia Chaytor's eyes, as she looked back at the rector, were steady and brilliant blue. 'Which means, so long as he is free, he is likely to attack again,' she said.

Chapter 3

Unlawful Killing

THE RECTORY, ST MARY IN THE MARSH, KENT.
26th December, 1796.

My lord,

It is my unpleasant duty to inform you of an event which took place in St Mary on Christmas Day. Briefly, the body of a young black woman was found dead in the grounds of New Hall. I have yet to receive the report of the assistant coroner, but judging by the condition of the body there seems little doubt that she was murdered. I am confident that the coroner will bring in a verdict of unlawful killing, and have begun my own investigation accordingly.

It would appear that the woman was enticed or taken to New Hall by a man, who has since disappeared. It is quite likely that this man is the murderer, and I believe it is urgent that we apprehend him, for he represents a clear danger to the public order. I urge you, therefore, to take all possible steps to track this man down as soon as you may.

We have no description of this man, nor any clues as to his identity. We know only that he left New Hall, with two horses, at some time on Christmas Day. I regret to say also that we have no information as to the identity of the victim.

Yr very obedient servant,

HARDCASTLE

The Rectory, St Mary in the Marsh, Kent.
27th December, 1796.

My dear Mr Jessington,

I am writing to inform you of an incident that took place at New Hall, St Mary in the Marsh, two days ago. The body of a young black woman was found in the grounds of the house, apparently murdered. We have, as yet, no information as to the woman's identity. As you are the legal representative of the owners of New Hall, I felt it only right and proper you should be informed.

As justice of the peace for the district, it falls to me to conduct an inquiry into this affair. I hope you will forgive me if, acting in that capacity, I put several questions to you.

Firstly, with reference to your letter of 1st September last, have you been able to contact the Rossiter family since that time? Have you located their whereabouts in the Americas, or have you unearthed any further family members in this country? If so, I should very much like to be put in contact with them.

On a related matter, can you also inform me as to whether anyone has made inquiries of you about New Hall in recent weeks? It would appear that the murdered woman, and presumably also her killer, gained access to New Hall by the use of keys. It would therefore greatly assist my inquiries if you could confirm the whereabouts of all known sets of keys to the house.

I look forward to your soonest reply,

Yr very obedient servant,

REV. M. A. HARDCASTLE, J. P.

New Hall, on a cold misty morning, loomed darkly through the trees. Brick-built with a handsome portico and four curving Dutch gables, it had an air of lost prosperity. Its builders had been people of substance and property. Walking up the drive with Stemp, his breath steaming in the cold, Hardcastle wondered what had led the Rossiters to abandon New Hall and seek a new life in the Americas. He had heard little of the family or its history during his years in the parish.

Mrs Chaytor was waiting by the door, cloaked and muffled like them all. 'Good morning,' she said calmly.

Stemp looked at the rector. 'Are you certain you want to do this?' the rector asked her. 'We do not know what we may find.'

'We may find nothing.'

Half a dozen steps led up to the front door. They knocked several times, hoping the caretaker might have returned, but were met with silence. They began by searching the stables. Two horses had clearly been stabled there, but all their tack had gone with them. A bag of oats, partly full, hung from a nail on one wall. The woodshed was half full of corded wood; there was nothing to be seen there.

An unlocked door at the end of the stable nearest the house revealed a stair going down. They descended carefully and found a range of cellars running underneath the kitchen wing of the house, musty and freezing cold. They were also surprisingly large; there were five rooms in all, each well-built and lined with brick. Apart from two hogsheads and a rack for wine bottles, the cellars were entirely empty.

They returned to the front door of the house. They had no keys, but Stemp produced two bits of metal from his pocket and waggled them in the keyhole. After a while there was a metallic click and the door groaned open. They walked quietly into the dusty shadows of the hall, doors leading off to left and right, a dark oak staircase in front of them sweeping up to a small gallery. To either side of the stair were passages to the rear of the house. There was a strong smell of damp.

Stemp held up his lantern. Shadows ran up the stairs and along the gallery, fleeing silently. Hardcastle remembered the treason and death that had been plotted in this house not so very long ago, and wondered what fresh secrets it was hiding.

'Let us begin,' he said.

They found the blood almost at once, at the foot of the stair. Two days old now, it was dried black, a pooled stain like an old inkblot on the floor. They looked at this for a while in the wavering light of the lantern, and Mrs Chaytor was conscious once again of the chill in the air.

'What do you think?' she asked quietly. 'How was it done?'

The rector frowned. 'I think she was going upstairs,' he said finally, 'and was struck from behind on about the third step.

Mrs Chaytor went up to the third step and stopped. 'About here?'

'Yes,' said the rector. 'He could easily have struck her from below. Hold up the lantern . . . yes, there. See the blood marks on the rail, and on the stairs themselves? Then, I think she fell to the bottom of the stairs, where she lay bleeding on the floor.'

'Not much blood where she fell,' commented Stemp.

'No. Which could indicate that she did not lie there for very long, perhaps only a few minutes. Joshua, the lantern, if you please.'

Holding the lantern low over the floor, the rector quartered the hall between the foot of the stairs and the back of the hall, pausing every so often to point to dark marks on the parquet. 'Drops of blood,' he said. 'She was still bleeding heavily, but most of it ran down the back of her coat; I remember the fabric was stiff with blood. That would mean that she was walking upright when she crossed this floor. If she had been dragged or carried, one would expect to see a trail of blood.'

'Badly injured as she was, she regained consciousness and got to her feet,' said Mrs Chaytor, and she shivered again. 'She must have been very strong; strong of mind, as well as body.'

'So, she stumbled outside and across the yard,' said Stemp. 'And fell into the pond.'

'Or was pushed,' said Mrs Chaytor. She had a vision in her head of the dazed, bleeding woman staggering in the cold wind, pursued by her tormentor like a cat playing with a mouse.

'She might not have been pushed, ma'am. If she was dazed, she wouldn't have been able to see proper. She could have stumbled into the pond without realising, or slipped on the ice and fallen into the water. If there was no one there to help her ...' Stemp spread his hands.

'But there *was* someone else,' said Mrs Chaytor. 'Remember the boot.'

'Ah, yes, the boot,' said the rector, holding up the lantern once more. 'Every theory we devise eventually shipwrecks itself on that blasted boot. Very well, let us carry on searching. We are looking for anything that might help us to establish the identity of either the woman or the killer. And also, keep an eye out for anything that might have been used as a weapon.'

They searched the house room by room, beginning with the drawing room to the left of the front door. The left-hand passage beside the stairs led to the dining room and then beyond to the kitchen, where they found the first signs of occupation: the remains of food; not much, a few crusts of bread and the rind of a cheese, both already worried by mice. The hearth in the kitchen had been used recently; there were fresh ashes on the grate, stirring a little in the draught from the chimney.

A connecting passage behind the stairs led to the breakfast room and then the morning room, all silent with the furniture covered by dustsheets. As they had in other rooms, they lifted the sheets to make certain there were no further grisly surprises. Across the passage, on the front corner of the house opposite the drawing room, was the library. A little surprisingly, there were no books. A few of Fanscombe's hunting prints still hung on the wall, frosted with dust. There was nothing else to be seen.

'Upstairs,' Hardcastle said quietly.

Warily, their footfalls ringing on the fatal stairs, they went up to the landing. Two more passageways led to the bedrooms. One bed had been used, though not made up; a rough woollen blanket had been flung over the mattress. Using the tip of his walking stick, the rector lifted the blanket gingerly, but to their relief there was nothing unpleasant under it, only the mattress itself, spotted with mildew.

They retreated to the landing and found the servants' stairs, narrow and plain. This led them to the attic, lit dimly by windows in the gables. Here they found boxrooms, full of dust that made Hardcastle sneeze, and quarters for the domestic staff. The caretaker's lodging was here, easy to identify; the room smelled of stale bedding and was littered with empty rum bottles. The rest of the rooms were undisturbed, save for one of the maid's; here, too, the bed had been slept in, but there were no other signs of occupation.

'Well,' said Mrs Chaytor. 'Whatever they were here for, it wasn't sex.' Stemp gave her an appalled look.

'You were right,' the rector said. 'We have found nothing.'

'We now know where the young woman was clubbed, reverend,' Stemp pointed out.

'Yes,' said the rector gloomily, 'but we are not a jot closer to knowing why. Nor has there been any sign of a weapon.'

'He might have used a poker from the fire,' said Mrs Chaytor, 'and then cleaned it and replaced it.'

'There was no evidence of that in the wound. And if he is the kind of cold-hearted brute we think he is, he might have carried a handy little truncheon in his pocket, and taken it away with him . . . Whoever he was, he has left very little evidence of his time here. The blanket upstairs and those scraps of food and the ashes in the grate; apart from those, you would never know that anyone had been.'

'Just a moment,' said Mrs Chaytor. 'What about the caretaker? He too is missing. Might he have returned, for whatever reason, found our woman in the house, and lashed out at her? I believe he carries a rather stout walking stick.'

Stemp frowned. 'Beazley is a cantankerous old cuss, but I don't think he'd do harm to anyone. Unless he was in his cups, of course.'

'Which he is most of the time,' said the rector, thinking of the man's fondness for brandy. Beazley might only have one fist, but he was very handy with it, and he had twice been hauled up before the rector during his brief term in office as justice of the peace. 'I agree, Joshua, I don't see Beazley as a killer, but we had better talk to him. Go down to Lydd and find him.'

Stemp nodded. 'What do we do now?'

'We'll interview Beazley, as I say, but I doubt he knows very much. Otherwise, we wait, and hope that Mr Jessington is able to offer us some useful information.'

'And meanwhile we do nothing?'

'My dear Mrs Chaytor, if you have any suggestions, please do feel free to offer them. I am stymied.'

'So am I,' she said angrily. 'And I hate the fact that this man is still free and at large among us, probably sizing up his next victim.'

She bit her lip and fell silent, and the rector watched her, wondering. She was, he knew, as tenacious as she was elegant; she tended to sink her teeth bulldog-fashion into a problem, and not let go until it was resolved.

WADSCOMBE HALL, TENTERDEN.
28th December, 1796.

My dear Hardcastle,

Thank you for your letter of yesterday's date.

I understand from the coroner that you have referred this matter to him and asked for an inquest. That is of course right and proper. Beyond that, however, I am afraid there is very little to be done. Searching for this man now would be rather like looking for the proverbial needle in the haystack. Given the present state of crisis in the country, I certainly cannot countenance diverting resources from the volunteers or the militia to undertake a search.

It is very likely that the woman was a vagrant, or a runaway servant, perhaps. In which case, she is of little account. Put the matter by, and try to enjoy what remains of the festive season.

Yr very obedient servant,

CLAVERTYE

Stemp went down to Lydd, returning late in the day with the news they had all expected. 'I found old Beazley, tight as a tick as you might expect. I got him sobered up after a while, enough to talk to. He left on the twenty-third to see his auntie in Lydd, and has been there ever since. His auntie vouched for him, and said he hadn't left her company since he arrived.'

'Was the lady really his aunt, do you think?'

Stemp made a derisive noise. 'Not unless aunts can be hired by the hour.' Hardcastle nodded, mentally writing off another lead. It had never been a strong possibility, but now they had virtually nothing to go on.

On 30th December, the coroner journeyed down from Maidstone through lashing rain and sleet to convene an inquest in the common room of the Star. Dr Stackpole had been appointed just a few months ago after his predecessor had been dismissed for corruption. He was tall and thin with a dark, gloomy voice and sunken cheeks below a frayed white wig. 'Looks like he should be carrying out an inquest on himself,' young Bessie Luckhurst murmured to the rector.

The common room was crowded; the entire parish had turned out in hopes that they might learn something new about the mysterious woman and her death. Hardcastle saw Mrs Chaytor enter and take a seat along with Miss Godfrey and Miss Roper and some of the other women. He knew most of them, but several were unfamiliar; he realised that the death of the young woman had touched a nerve with many women in the area. 'Bad news travels quickly,' he observed to his parish constable, 'and news of an unnatural death most quickly of all.'

Stemp rubbed his nose. 'It's mid-winter, reverend. Folk haven't much to do, especially with this cold. They're hoping for a bit of scandal. And, of course, some of 'em are worried.'

'Worried? About what?'

'Last time, this fellow killed a stranger. Next time it might be one of them. That's what some folk are thinking.'

Stemp was right, Hardcastle thought. Fear came easily in winter when the days were cold and the nights were long; the notion that the shadows might be harbouring a killer come to prey on them was a natural one.

To the disappointment of the common room, the proceedings were brief. The sole purpose of the inquest was to identify the cause of death; any question of responsibility or guilt was a matter for the magistrate. And the cause of death had already been made very clear in Dr Mackay's report. Mackay himself was the first witness, enlarging on aspects of the report while the coroner's clerk took notes with a spluttering quill. There followed a long technical discussion of the symptoms of drowning, during which the audience begin to shift restlessly. They perked up when the coroner asked whether there were any other injuries to the body.

'None, sir. Apart from the blow to the head and the visible marks of drowning, the body was untouched.'

A sigh, composed of mingled relief and disappointment, ruffled across the room. Mackay stepped down, and the coroner asked who had discovered the body. The lad Jed was urged forward and took the stand. The coroner directed a series of questions to him, and Jed replied in mumbled monosyllables, which everyone strained to hear. Mrs Chaytor lost patience.

'Jed and the maidservant returned at once to the house and reported finding the body. I was one of the next people on the scene. Would it help, doctor, if I took the stand?'

The coroner's voice became more sepulchral than ever. 'It is not usual for a woman to give witness, ma'am.'

The rector raised his own voice. 'In this case, Dr Stackpole, I think you may permit it.'

Mrs Chaytor described, neatly and accurately, the position of the body as it had been found.

The coroner thanked her and then, astonishingly, made an attempt at gallantry. 'If all ladies were as observant and concise as yourself, ma'am, I am sure we should welcome hearing their evidence more often.'

The rector winced. 'And if all coroners were as free-thinking and liberal in their views as you, doctor,' said Mrs Chaytor, rising, 'I am sure we ladies would make it our business to discover corpses more frequently.' She resumed her seat beside Miss Roper, who was giggling behind her hand.

The coroner sat quietly for a moment, aware that he had been insulted but not quite certain how, and then asked the jury to come to a verdict. They looked at their foreman and nodded as one: *unlawful killing.*

As the crowd dispersed, the rector made his way across the room to the women. 'Miss Godfrey, Miss Roper,' he said, bowing. 'I trust you are well?'

'As well as we can be,' said Miss Godfrey acidly, 'given that there is a madman on the loose.'

'I am certain you have nothing to fear, Miss Godfrey.'

'Are you, reverend? Well, I am not. Who is to say that this fiend will not return one night, and murder us all in our beds?'

She had not troubled to lower her voice, and some of the other women looked at her nervously. 'Lord Clavertye must send the militia to protect us,' said Miss Godfrey. 'At once.'

The rector bowed again. 'You may rest assured, ladies, that Lord Clavertye is doing everything in his power. Mrs Chaytor, may I trouble you for a moment?'

He gave her his arm, and they walked out into the street. The rain had eased to an icy drizzle; the wind made ripples in the cold pools that lay among the mud. Before he could speak, she looked up at him from under the rim of her bonnet and said, 'Lord Clavertye will do nothing?'

She had read the irony in his voice, though thankfully the other women had not. 'He thinks our dead woman may have been a vagabond, or a runaway servant. Therefore, in his words, she is of little account; even less so in his eyes, given her colour. I am to forget her.'

There was a little pause. 'You won't, of course.'

'No, I won't. But I am still stymied.'

'Something will turn up,' she said confidently.

'I wish I shared your certainty . . . the truth is that Clavertye is quite right about one thing. Searching now for the man would be like looking for a needle in a haystack. He could have gone anywhere; to London, even beyond.' He looked at her. 'We shall bury her tomorrow. Will you come?'

'Of course.'

Though the weather was still bitter the following day, the ice had melted and the ground thawed enough so that the sexton could dig a grave. The rector stood robed at the lychgate of the church, waiting for the body to arrive. He remembered the burial of another unnamed victim of violence seven months earlier. On that occasion, he and Mrs Chaytor had persevered; they had learned the dead man's name and why he had been killed, even if the man who murdered him had in the end escaped justice. The young man had a headstone now, with his name, *Jacques Morel*, boldly inscribed on it. The gift of the headstone had been anonymous, although the rector knew very well who had paid for it.

The squat tower of St Mary the Virgin reared above the dark barren trees. Across the road stood the rectory, foursquare and brick, its garden dripping and colourless. To the south, stretched out along the New Romney road, lay the village, chimneys smoking; further on, the trees in the garden at New Hall stood black and skeletal against the clouds. He looked at those more distant trees and wondered again, *why? Why there, why that house?*

Beyond the churchyard wall Romney Marsh stretched empty and flat, the wind hissing over marsh and meadow, rustling the dry reeds in the sewers. East lay the dunes that marked the edge of the sea; west and northwest rose the hills of Kent, running from Appledore up to Hythe. In spring those meadows would be full of lambs and their dams, grazing peacefully and filling the air with their calls. But in winter, this was an empty, bleak and soulless land, cut off by sea and hills from the rest of the world. People came down here to hide from that world. And, sometimes, Hardcastle thought, they also came to die.

People arrived at the church in twos and threes, huddled against the wind, their faces full of sympathy. Death was familiar; people died every year, of drowning or marsh fever or some other nameless illness. A man could be crushed when a wagon's load slipped and fell on him, or have his neck broken in a brawl, or join the navy and die of yellow fever far away in the Indies. Women could, and too often did, die in childbirth, or in accidents in the house or fields. This woman was a stranger; yet still they came. Part of it was curiosity; part of it was genuine pity, for they knew she had been young and many of the women of the parish shared Mrs Chaytor's horror at the brutal manner of her death. Her very strangeness, too, was an attraction. And, as Stemp and Miss Godfrey had said, there was also fear. Those who were frightened by what had happened wanted to be close to their neighbours, and take comfort from their presence.

Hardcastle read the service well, his deep rich voice full of compassion. As ever, he was aware that his role now was to give comfort and strength to the living, not merely to commemorate the dead.

'*Remember thy servant, O Lord, according to the favour which thou bearest unto thy people, and grant that, increasing in knowledge and love of thee, she may go from strength to strength, in the life of perfect service, in thy heavenly kingdom . . . The Lord bless you and keep you. The Lord make his face to shine upon you, and be gracious unto you.*'

He was speaking to them, not just for the dead woman but for their own sakes in this troubled hour, and he saw in their faces that they knew it.

Later, as the congregation dispersed and the sexton and his assistant began to shovel muddy earth over the coffin, the rector shed his clerical robes in the vestry and put on his long cloak once more, before walking out to find Mrs Chaytor waiting for him.

'You did that very well, as always,' she said. 'Your eloquence was quite moving. Who knows? One day you may convert me.'

He smiled; both of them knew how unlikely that was. 'It is New Year's Eve,' she said. 'Have you plans?'

'I intend to sit by the fire with a glass of port and a volume of *Decline and Fall*, and then go to bed early.'

She raised her eyebrows. 'Only one glass? You really are being abstemious these days. Takings at the Star must be down considerably.'

He chuckled. 'I fear they may.'

'What has brought this about? Your new-found eminence as a magistrate?'

'I suspect that is partly the case, yes.'

'Laudable. But I had never heard that sobriety was expected of a magistrate. Quite the opposite, in my experience.'

He chuckled again. 'Mine also. But, in light of the responsibility I have accepted, I intend to try to keep a clear head.' Most of the time, he thought.

They walked on down the village street, passing the Star, where most of the congregation were now gathered, and on towards Sandy House. 'You have changed, since the events of last spring,' she observed.

'I know. Perhaps, after forty years on this earth, I am finally growing up.'

She laughed aloud at that. 'What can you mean?'

'My dear, I have spent most of my time playing at life. I have played at being a theologian, a scholar, a playwright, a duellist, a clergyman and a rake; often all at the same time. I have lived most of my life on a whim. The only serious decision I ever made, to come here to St Mary, was in fact thrust upon me: the choice given to me by the archbishop was this, or exile to the colonies. I have been self-indulgent, vain and foolish; even, at times, quite wicked. It is high time I began to live my life so that I may be of benefit to other people, not just myself.'

She listened to this speech with a smile still on her lips, rain dripping from the brim of her bonnet. 'You never cease to surprise me,' she said. 'You have written plays?'

'I have.'

'May I read them?'

'Absolutely you may not. I intend that every word I have ever written will go with me to my grave.'

'Then you will have very erudite worms,' she said. 'They will digest your plays, and then hold learned symposia over your bones, discussing your contribution to literature.'

They had reached the gates of Sandy House. 'Mrs Chaytor,' he said as they stopped. 'You are being positively whimsical. May I ask why?'

'I feel oddly light-hearted,' she said. 'I know one shouldn't, after a funeral. But I found your service quite uplifting. It offered hope, and I have had so little of it . . . And there is the new year. Perhaps, perhaps, this year things will be different. Perhaps I will learn to feel once more.'

It had been three years since her husband had died, and Hardcastle knew the rage and pain were still very close to the surface within her. 'I hope so, for your sake,' he said softly. 'If you will permit me, I shall pray for your happiness.'

'I cannot see that it will do any harm.' She smiled at him again. 'Happy New Year.'

He bowed and kissed her gloved fingers, gently, and then stood and watched her walk into the house, waiting until the door had closed behind her before turning to walk back up the muddy road towards the rectory.

That afternoon, as the rector sat in his study, a book face down on his lap as he dozed by the embers of the fire, there came to his ears the sound of horses and carriage wheels. The sound grew nearer, and he heard the carriage slow and turn into the rectory drive. He sat up and rubbed his eyes, wondering who the visitor could be. His first thought was that it might be Lord Clavertye; there came the sudden unreasonable hope that his lordship had changed his mind, and come down to see what assistance he could offer the investigation.

He heard the knock at the door, and Mrs Kemp the house-keeper moving to answer it, and then heard a man's rather quer-ulous voice outside, asking if this was the rectory. He sighed; it was not Clavertye. Then who the devil was it, come to disturb his tranquillity at this hour on New Year's Eve?

The housekeeper opened the study door and marched up to his chair, her face set and grim. Mrs Kemp did not approve of strangers in general; it was clear from the compression of her

THE BODY IN THE ICE | 44

lips that she disapproved of this one more than most. He took the plain, undecorated card from the silver salver she held out and read, to his considerable surprise:

ANTHONY JESSINGTON, ESQ
LINCOLN'S INN

Something will turn up, Mrs Chaytor had predicted the previous day. And now it had. 'Show him in, Mrs Kemp,' said the rector, 'and lay another place for dinner. And, given the hour, I think you had better make up a bed.'

Chapter 4

The Lawyer's Tale

Mr Jessington was miserable as only a Londoner could be when forced out of the city and into the wild, forbidding hinterlands, far from urban comforts. The roof of his hired carriage had leaked, dripping water down his back; at Ashford he had been forced to get out and stand in the rain while a wheel was mended; the cold wind was utterly enervating, and he had hardly the strength to stand. He could do nothing, he declared, until he first had a hot bath and a change of clothes.

Mrs Kemp was summoned and ordered to prepare a bath. She stared at the rector, her lined face incredulous. 'A bath? At this hour?'

'If you please, Mrs Kemp.'

The housekeeper stamped away to the kitchen. Soon after, they heard a violent clashing of pots. Moved by Mr Jessington's dejection, the rector unlocked the mahogany cabinet where he kept his cognac and poured out a small measure for his guest, adding after a moment a slightly larger measure for himself. Mr Jessington took a sip and choked, setting down his glass and wiping his eyes.

'What is this stuff?'

'French brandy, sir.'

'French,' said Mr Jessington. His tone suggested that everything bad in the world came from France.

Sometime later, warmed by a bath and dressed in dry clothes, the solicitor returned to the study and apologised for his earlier conduct. 'I fear I was not myself when I arrived. I have a weak constitution, you see. The motion of the coach has brought on my dyspepsia, and this vile weather has been quite dreadful for my liver.'

'It is quite all right,' said the rector, who had spent the last hour wondering what had possessed Mr Jessington to travel from London to Romney Marsh in mid-winter, rather than staying snugly at home in comfort and writing a letter. He gazed expectantly at his guest.

Stripped of his bulky overcoat and scarves, Mr Jessington was revealed as a small man, very neat and precise in manner; he reminded the rector of a mouse. On first glance the rector had thought him about fifty, but seen now in the firelight he proved to be rather younger than the rector himself, probably not more than thirty. His manner and the old-fashioned severity of his clothes, black apart from his white lace stock and his wig, made him appear older. He fidgeted constantly, plucking at his cuffs, fiddling with his stock, taking out a handkerchief to wipe his streaming nose.

'Before we begin, will you permit me – ah-*choo!* – to ask a question? What is the current condition of New Hall? Has this unfortunate incident resulted in any damage to the house?'

'None whatsoever.' The rector explained that, in the absence of the caretaker, he had let himself into the house to conduct an investigation. 'Apart from mildew and damp, and some staining to the front hall and the stairs, the house is in the same condition as when Mrs Fanscombe took her leave.'

'Mildew,' said Jessington gloomily. 'Ah-*choo!* Damp. One shudders to think what damage has been done to the fabric . . . And, you have not been able to identify the . . . the murdered woman?'

'No.'

'Permit me to ask you a question. Was she a black woman?'

The rector stared at him. 'How on earth did you know that?'

'It was reported in the *Kentish Gazette* – ah-*choo!* – but the details of press reports cannot always be relied upon. Did you not see the report?' Mr Jessington blew his nose with a delicate honk. The rector, who read no newspaper other than the *Morning Post*, shook his head.

'I had best come to the point,' said Mr Jessington. 'You will recall that I wrote to you in September asking if you possessed any information about the Rossiter family, the owners of New Hall.'

'Of course.'

'I should begin by explaining that I have only been responsible for the affairs of the Rossiter family for the past two years. Before that, their affairs were handled by the late Mr Joseph Parker, the well-known and much esteemed solicitor of Lincoln's Inn. You will have heard of him, I am sure.'

'I recollect the name. Pray continue.'

'I articled under Mr Parker, and he continued to show me many kindnesses after I left his service. His own son had migrated to the American colonies before the . . . recent unfortunate events, and joined the rebel cause. As a result of his doing so, Mr Parker broke off all contact with his son.'

The rector nodded; the rebellion in America had sundered many families. 'When Mr Parker died suddenly the winter before last,' said the solicitor, 'his chambers closed. His clerk asked me if, in light of my friendship with Mr Parker, I would take over the legal affairs of his clients. I said yes, of course.

'Needless to say, the Rossiters were among those clients. Upon examining their affairs, I discovered they had only a modest portfolio of property: New Hall, some houses in Maidstone and Canterbury and also some small properties in New Romney and elsewhere in this district, of little account. Then there is some land in Suffolk, and a few farms in Buckinghamshire. If I am honest, the entire estate does not amount to a great deal. The entire rent for all the properties, excluding New Hall, amounts to little more than eight hundred pounds per annum.'

It was a sum that might enable a man to live in reasonable comfort, but was far from vast wealth. And New Hall was doubtless expensive to maintain. Without enough land to support it, the house would be a drain on the pocket of its owner unless it could be rented or leased.

'New Hall is a rather large house for such a small estate,' said the rector, speculatively.

'From the papers connected with the estate, I deduce that there was once a great deal more land,' said Jessington. 'And I also recall Mr Parker saying once that the Rossiters had made a fortune in Ireland through estates there, but those had all gone. He did not explain why; he was a very discreet man, Mr Parker.'

The rector nodded again, thinking hard. 'So, the family fell on hard times,' he said, 'and went to America to recover their fortune.'

'That would be the logical conclusion,' said Mr Jessington, testily. This was his story, and he wanted to tell it his way. 'You will recall from the list of family members I sent you in September that Mr William Rossiter, deceased 1747, and his wife Amélie, deceased 1770 – the lady you identified as being buried in your churchyard – had issue, two sons and two daughters. Both sons, Nicholas and James, emigrated to the American colonies. The older daughter Jane,' said Mr Jessington, pausing significantly, 'married Mr Joseph Parker the younger, son of my old friend Mr Parker of Lincoln's Inn. Mr and Mrs Parker then migrated to Boston, in what was then the Massachusetts colony. Mary, the second sister, has dropped out of sight entirely; she may be in America, or she may still be in this country, I do not know which.'

'Mr Jessington,' said the rector, 'you promised you would get to the point.'

'I am coming to the point, sir, if you will allow me to do so in my way. The rebellion of the American colonists and their subsequent declaration of independence caused a good deal of disruption. My old friend Mr Parker, as I have said, broke off relations with his son when he joined the rebels. He had no further contact with Mr Parker junior or any of the Rossiter family. Although I have found no evidence of communication with any of the family for more than fifteen years, he continued to administer the estate in a conscientious manner. I myself have endeavoured to do the same, holding the estate in good trust until such time as they or their heirs should return. And now,' said Mr Jessington simply, 'they have returned.'

'They have?' The rector stared at him. 'When?'

'October last, not so very long after our correspondence. They came in the entourage of Mr Rufus King, the newly appointed American ambassador to the court of St James. Mr James Rossiter and his wife and two children, and Mr and Mrs Parker are all now in London. Mr Nicholas Rossiter, the elder brother, has sadly deceased, but his son Mr William is in London with the rest of the family. They have taken a house in a very fashionable district, and are much seen around town, if the newspapers are to be believed. They frequent the company of other Americans, of course, but they are popular in wider society too.'

Hardcastle had forgotten his earlier impatience. All of this was somehow significant, though he could not quite yet see why. 'What was their purpose in coming to England?'

'They did not fully divulge their reasons to me, I fear. I imagine there may be an element of nostalgia, wanting to see their homeland once again after so long a separation. But among other things, they wish young Mr William to inspect his inheritance in this country, or what remains of it. Now that we are fully at peace with the United States of America, there is no impediment to his doing so.'

'No, I should suppose not.' Only fourteen years had elapsed since the end of the war that brought the American colonies their independence. Bitterness still hung heavy in the air; but relations were improving. From the *Morning Post*, the rector knew about Rufus King's embassy, and knew too that one of Mr King's purposes was to conclude an alliance with America against Britain's common enemy, France. 'How old is young Mr William?' he asked.

'Nineteen. His uncle James is his guardian and acts for him, and Mr Parker the younger has charge of his legal interests. Shortly after their arrival, Mr Parker sought me out in my chambers and introduced himself. I was, as you can imagine, a little wary at this point, for I thought perhaps Mr Parker had come to challenge my right to have taken over his father's practice and demand I surrender it to him, even though everything had been done entirely according to the letter of the law—'

'Mr Jessington,' said the rector, gently.

'Yes, yes, of course. It transpired that Mr Parker had come merely to introduce himself and request that I hand over custody of young Mr William's estates to his uncle and guardian, James Rossiter. He had all the necessary papers, including, of course, the last will and testament of Nicholas Rossiter, signed and witnessed in New York in 1777. The will made the usual provisions for family members, including a handsome sum to his wife Hannah van Cortlandt, whom he had married two years earlier, but is now deceased. Beyond these bequests, the bulk of his possessions and estates were to go to his son William, who was at that time an infant. Those estates included all his lands and holdings in England and, of course, New Hall.'

'How did you respond to Mr Parker?'

'I did the proper thing, of course. The will had to go through probate, a process which took some weeks as there was a backlog in the courts, but the will was proved early in December. Mr William Rossiter now owns New Hall, though of course his guardian will continue to control the estate until he reaches his majority in two years' time.'

The rector's ears were tingling. 'And did you hand over the keys to New Hall to the Rossiters?'

'No.'

'No? Forgive me for asking, but why not?'

'The family did not want them. As Mr Parker himself told me, the house was large and in a remote and backward part of the country; his words, sir, not mine, I do assure you. They expressed more interest in the land and the town houses, which I was asked to inspect and value with a view to possible sale. They showed no interest whatever in New Hall or in finding a new tenant for it. I was merely asked to retain the keys for safekeeping.'

The rector nodded. 'Have you ever given, or lent, the keys of New Hall to anyone else?'

Mr Jessington flushed pale pink with anger. 'Reverend Hardcastle, I am astonished. Yes, sir, astonished, and gravely offended! The affairs of my clients are a sacred trust to me. I would never dream of doing anything so reprehensible! What sort of custodian of my clients' interests do you think I am?'

Hardcastle held up his hand. 'I apologise for any offence given, sir. But I must ask these questions. You, as a man of law, must understand that.'

Jessington subsided at once, looking more mouse-like than ever. 'Yes, yes, of course, of course. But rest assured, sir. Those keys have never left my strongbox since I took over from old Mr Parker two years ago. Indeed, they have been joined there by the keys passed to me by the wife of the late tenant. Now, if you will forgive me, I should like to continue my narrative. You see, the oddest thing of all then happened.'

'Go on,' said the rector, sinking back in his chair.

'Ten days ago, the twenty-first of December, I received a most unusual caller. He was a young black man, and I noted at once that he was dressed as a gentleman, though I would say that so far as fashion goes, he was sadly behind the times. To my astonishment, he gave his name as Samuel Rossiter, and claimed that he was the eldest son of the late Nicholas Rossiter.'

Hardcastle sat up straight.

'I assumed he was merely a by-blow,' said Jessington. 'But, to my further amazement, he produced several documents. The first certified the marriage of Nicholas Rossiter to one Martha Washford in New York in 1770, five years before his marriage to Hannah van Cortlandt. The second was a document registering the birth of twin children, named Samuel and Emma, in New York two years later, 1772. The third was another last will and testament by Nicholas Rossiter, made in March of this year, in

Montréal in Canada. This will recognised Samuel and Emma Rossiter as his legitimate children. It also disinherits William Rossiter, and states that all Mr Nicholas Rossiter's possessions including his lands and holdings here in England are instead to be divided between Samuel and Emma Rossiter. The fourth document was a notice of the death of Nicholas Rossiter a month later, also in Montréal.'

Hardcastle rose to his feet, moved to his desk and sat down. Pulling out a sheet of paper, he dipped his quill in the inkwell and began writing rapidly, making notes. 'What had happened to his mother?'

'She died a year after he and his sister were born. That is all he would say.'

'And Nicholas Rossiter remarried four years later. But if that first marriage was legal, then these two young people, not William Rossiter, are the rightful owners of New Hall. What did you say to him?'

'I explained about probate. This is of course a very complicated affair. Messages will have to be sent to Montréal to the solicitor there who drew up the will, asking him to verify its authenticity, and that will necessitate a long delay, as no ships will now sail for Canada until the spring. The certificate of marriage and those of their birth will have to be carefully examined and verified also.'

'Did you tell him this?' asked the rector.

'I did. He did not understand, or professed not to understand, about probate and hoped I would simply hand over the keys there and then. When I refused to do so, he became quite angry. I had to ask my clerk to escort him from the premises.'

'Did you explain about the other Rossiters, and the will favouring William?'

'Yes, but only in the most vague terms. It would have been most improper of me to discuss the affairs of a client with a complete stranger, let alone one whose motives I had begun to suspect.'

'Could you describe this man?'

Like most people when asked to describe someone, Mr Jessington became flustered. He waved his hands. 'About five-and-twenty. Of medium height. Dark-skinned, of course, but with features I would have said were more European than African. Black hair, quite tightly curled. He wore no wig.'

'And his sister? Was she there?'

'She did not enter the office, but he said that she was in London with him. After his departure, I looked from my window and saw him with a woman in the street. He was talking to her in an agitated fashion, and I saw her put her hand on his arm to restrain him. They moved off together around the square. Regrettably, she had her back to me all the time, and I did not see her face.'

'You said you had begun to suspect his motives,' said the rector. 'What do you mean by that?'

Jessington took out his handkerchief to wipe his nose again, and then looked directly at Hardcastle. 'Samuel Rossiter and his story may be entirely genuine,' he said, 'or they may not. It is not for me to judge. But until I can assure myself of their validity, the possibility exists that none of his documents is genuine, and Samuel Rossiter is attempting to defraud the Rossiter estate. My actions have been undertaken with that possibility in mind.' He paused. 'It is even possible that this man is not who he claims to be.'

'Please explain yourself, Mr Jessington.'

'It is not impossible that someone is passing himself off as the heir of Nicholas Rossiter in the hope of fraudulent gain. In which case the woman who accompanied him is also an impostor. Indeed, sir, it occurs to me that the murder is a case of falling out among thieves.'

'Why do you say so?'

'This man, Rossiter or whatever his name is, struck me as being a man of his hands. And when he left my office, he was angry and ready to lash out. I suspect that after our interview he came down here, to New Hall, perhaps in some misguided hope of seizing the house by *force majeure* and defying the law to remove him. He brought the woman with him. And then perhaps they had a quarrel; a falling-out among thieves, as I have said. I think it very likely, sir, that the body you found was that of the woman he called his sister, Emma Rossiter.'

They were summoned to dinner not long after. It was not a satisfactory meal. Mr Jessington ate sparingly of the sole and would not touch the beef or anything with pastry: 'They arouse my dyspepsia, you see.' He refused claret, asking instead for a little boiled water. The look on Mrs Kemp's face was more eloquent than words.

Equally disappointingly, the solicitor could not or would not shed any further light on what had happened at New Hall. Pressed for a more definite opinion as to whether Samuel and Emma Rossiter were genuine, he refused to give one. 'They might be brother and sister, or they might be criminals engaged in fraud. It makes no difference either way. The court has already proven the will of Nicholas Rossiter, and even if this new will is genuine, it will take a great deal to persuade the court to set the earlier will aside. There is still the question of validity of the marriage lines. If no marriage can be proven, then both children are illegitimate and cannot inherit.'

The solicitor retired early to bed. Hardcastle sat before the fire in his study, staring into the flames.

Jessington's account had been nothing if not comprehensive. But several things struck the rector as odd. First, if the second will really was genuine, this meant that Nicholas Rossiter had disinherited his own son. Relations between William Rossiter and his father had been ruptured; but why?

Second, why were Parker and the rest of the family apparently so uninterested in New Hall? It was the most important asset in the estate, and of course the childhood home of James and Jane. Surely they would want to see it restored, cleaned and leased out once more, so that at least it would return an income? Why were they content to let it stand empty?

Third, if Samuel and Emma Rossiter were not who they claimed to be – were, as Jessington suggested, criminals attempting to perpetuate a fraud – why would they not have been more thorough? Why had they not prepared proof that their documents were genuine? They could have hired a bent solicitor, and the Lord knew there were enough of those, to attest to the veracity of the documents. If this was a fraud, it looked a very amateur one.

Whether they were genuine or not, how did Samuel and Emma Rossiter – for on this matter the rector believed Jessington was right, that they were the people who had arrived at New Hall on the twenty-third; the timing fit, if nothing else – gain access to the house without keys? Why had Emma Rossiter chosen to disguise herself as a man? Why, if they were brother and sister, did one sleep in one of the main bedrooms and one in the servants' quarters in the attic? And finally, if Samuel Rossiter had indeed attacked his sister in a fit of anger and pushed her into the horse pond, why did he later try to pull her out, only to abandon the attempt once he had wrenched off her boot?

'That blasted boot,' said the rector quietly to himself. He sat thinking about all of these things for a long time, looking for answers to the questions and finding none, until the clock chimed over his head and the new year of 1797 ushered itself quietly in.

The next day, New Year's Day, was also a Sunday. Mr Jessington arose late and came downstairs neatly dressed and wearing his wig. The rector, who had been out for a walk despite the freezing rain, was tucking into a dish of eggs before crossing the road to the church and conducting matins. 'I fear I rise very early,' said the rector, 'and therefore have the habit of taking breakfast. Do you care to join me?'

Mr Jessington shuddered, dyspepsia no doubt rising. 'I should like to see the house, if I may, and assure myself that all is well. Will you be so kind as to guide me there?'

'We will go there directly after church,' said the rector, swallowing his coffee. 'Did you bring the keys?'

Nothing had changed at New Hall; it remained as bleak and damp and sad as always. The cold air and mildew made Mr Jessington sneeze. The rector showed him the patch of blood; the solicitor was surprisingly unmoved, and quite uninterested. He moved around the house, looking at the rooms with a professional's eye, much more interested in the peeling wallpaper in the drawing room and the loose tiles in the larder than he had been in the scene of a violent assault. He looked into the caretaker's stinking nest and drew back in horror.

'Where is Mr Beazley? Does anyone know?'

'He was last seen in the arms of an elderly prostitute in Lydd, where he has been since before Christmas.'

Jessington drew his nose down in disgust. They went outside, where the solicitor stood with his back to the horse pond and examined the roof for a long time. 'At least,' he said, 'the intruders did no damage. I was prepared for far worse.'

Light dawned on Hardcastle. 'Is that the reason you came down here in such haste? To inspect the house?'

'As I told you last night, I take my custodianship of my clients' interests very seriously. Had anything happened to the house, it would have been my responsibility.'

'So what will you tell the Rossiters?'

'Oh, I have not met the Rossiters. My only contact has been with Mr Parker, their legal representative.' He paused. 'Given that no real damage has been done, I think I shall bide my time about telling Mr Parker, at least until such time as the identity of the dead woman has been confirmed. And, I should like to complete my own investigations into the authenticity or otherwise of this second will. This, of course, will take some months.'

Hmm, thought the rector. Jessington suspects that Samuel Rossiter is a criminal and a murderer, but on the other hand he is hedging his bets. I wonder why? Probing, he said, 'What sort of man is Mr Parker?'

The solicitor wiped his nose, handkerchief in gloved hand, and then made a curious little *moue*. 'Mr Parker's father,' he said, still studying the roof, 'was a man of grace, courtesy and wit. Those qualities are signally absent in the son. I also formed the impression that he may not be entirely trustworthy.'

Interesting, thought the rector. This was the first indiscretion he had heard from the lawyer's lips. 'Why do you say that?'

'It is a feeling, nothing more. But understand me, sir. My duty is to see the estate well administered and passed in due course into the proper hands. That duty will always be my first care, and will always triumph over personal feelings.'

It was plain that he would say no more on the subject. Even though it was Sunday, having seen the house the lawyer could not wait to depart. He was off soon after, back to London in his leaking carriage with its wobbling wheel, leaving behind Mrs Kemp fulminating about baths and the size of the tip she had received, and the rector in some respects more perplexed than ever. Judging the hour to be sufficiently advanced, he walked through the village to Sandy House and knocked at the door. Lucy admitted him, and a moment later showed him into the morning room where Mrs Chaytor sat, quiet and pale, looking into the fire. He knelt down beside her chair, his eyes full of concern.

'My dear Amelia. What has happened?'

'Why, nothing, of course,' she said quietly without turning her head. 'Nothing has happened. Nothing has changed. Everything is the same.'

He rose and took a seat opposite her, watching her intently. 'I was so full of hope yesterday,' she said. 'I thought perhaps a new dawn, a new day, a new year . . . I went to my bed feeling so optimistic . . . I was almost happy. And then I woke this morning, alone. He is gone. He is gone, and he will never return.'

'Is there anything I can do?' Hardcastle asked, his voice gentle.

'No. There is nothing anyone can do.' She turned her head and looked at him. 'You promised to pray for my happiness. It does not seem to have worked.'

He had indeed prayed for her that morning, silently while standing in the pulpit and reciting the creed to his usual congregation of six, augmented by Mr Jessington, who had sat with his hands clasped and looking nervously about him like a man just landed on an island of cannibals. 'Not all prayers are answered,' he said.

'Why not? God is said to be omnipotent. Surely He could answer our prayers if He wanted to.'

'Sometimes, He chooses not to do so.'

'Then He has a great deal to be responsible for, don't you think? If He continues to allow so much suffering and misery in the world, then He cannot be very compassionate. Why do you put up with it? You are an intelligent man. Why do you worship a God who robs women of their husbands and condemns them to an aching eternity of loneliness?'

The rector spread his hands on his knees. 'I do not know why God allows suffering,' he said. 'Do you not think that I wrestle with this problem every day? Do you not think that very thought was uppermost in my mind as I gazed on the body of that poor dead woman? I don't know why God allowed her to die, Amelia, just as I don't know why He allowed your husband to die. But I have to believe in God. For without God, there is nothing in which to believe. And a world where there is nothing in which to believe, would be a bitter and evil place indeed.'

She looked at him, blue eyes full of pain. 'I am sorry,' she said. 'It is shockingly rude of me to berate you like this. You are a good man.'

'I am not. But it is kind of you to lie to me.'

The pain was still there, but the corners of her mouth twitched. 'Ring the bell, and I will ask Lucy to make some chocolate. Did you enjoy your port and Gibbon?'

'I never got to them. I had a visitor instead. That is my reason for calling on you today. You'll never guess who the visitor was: Mr Jessington.'

Her fine-lashed eyes opened wide. 'Anthony Jessington "Esk"? Goodness, whatever did he want?'

'To talk,' said the rector, 'which he did at great length.' He told her, as succinctly as he could, what Jessington had said, and Mrs Chaytor's blue eyes grew a little warmer and some colour came to her cheeks.

The chocolate came, and she took a sip. 'So, we have a name for our dead girl,' she said. 'Emma Rossiter.'

'And a possible killer,' said the rector, 'in the shape of her own brother.'

'I know. That is hideous, in quite a different way from what I had imagined. Poor Emma.'

'We don't know her name for certain yet,' he cautioned. 'Jessington thinks it possible that they were fraudulent. In which case they might have been using assumed names.'

'Oh, come. You don't believe that, do you? Petty criminals would hardly dare to take over a house like New Hall; what would they do with it? And more sophisticated villains would have come up with a better and more believable scheme. No, I think they were who they said they were. What their motives were, of course, is another matter.'

'Well, we may be able to find that out. On the basis of this new information, I intend to ask Lord Clavertye to undertake a search for Samuel Rossiter.'

'It is still a matter of a needle in a haystack,' said Mrs Chaytor dubiously. 'There are thousands of black people in London, and more in the ports around the coast. Samuel Rossiter could have gone to ground in any of those places.'

'But we have at least a rough description now. And if he did use his own name to book lodgings in London, the Bow Street Runners will find out where he stayed. They may turn up further clues as to where he has gone.' He hesitated, and then said gently, 'You see, there is hope.'

She disregarded this. 'Do you believe that Samuel Rossiter *is* the murderer?'

'It is a plausible theory. Certainly he is mixed up somehow in this affair. But we will know nothing for certain until we find him and talk to him.' The rector paused. 'I keep coming back to this,' he said. 'Why New Hall, and why now?'

Chapter 5

Things Fail to Add Up

THE RECTORY, ST MARY IN THE MARSH, KENT.
2nd January, 1797.

By express.

My lord,

Further information has come to light concerning the murder at New Hall on 25th December. It appears probable that the victim was one Emma Rossiter, and that she came from the Americas accompanied by her brother, Samuel. It is also quite likely that Samuel Rossiter is implicated in her death.

I believe that Samuel and Emma Rossiter came to New Hall on 23rd December. The livery stable in Ashford has confirmed that two horses were hired by travellers from London on that date, though no description of either has been forthcoming, and Roberts, the Ashford feed merchant, confirms the sale of a sack of oats on the same day. Both horses were subsequently returned, though the stable was unable to confirm the date; the season was, apparently, an unusually busy one despite the weather.

It now seems certain that, prior to the 23rd, both Rossiters were in London. May I ask your lordship to appeal to the chief magistrate of London and ask him to search for Samuel Rossiter and, if he is found, apprehend and hold him until I may come to London and interrogate him?

Rossiter, which may not be his real name, is a black man of about twenty-five years, of medium height with dark skin and dark curling hair, and with some non-African facial features. When last seen he was dressed as a gentleman, though not a fashionable one.

I should add that there may be a connection between this man and Mr James Rossiter, a member of the suite of the American ambassador. If possible, I wish to ensure that Mr James Rossiter does not come to know of this affair until such time as I have completed my inquiries.

Yr very obedient servant,

HARDCASTLE

Hardcastle looked at the last paragraph for a long time before he finally signed and sealed the letter. He was not entirely certain why he had added it. Clavertye, who had political ambitions, moved in fashionable circles in London and it was likely that at some point he would run across the Rossiters, if he had not done so already. But Clavertye, who had been one of the finest forensic barristers ever seen in the Middle Temple before his elevation to the peerage, would know better than to say anything indiscreet, to James Rossiter or anyone else.

No; what Hardcastle had written reflected as much as anything his own unease about some aspects of Jessington's story, and also his growing conviction that New Hall itself was important, that it had somehow played a role in Emma Rossiter's murder. In his mind he had begun to see New Hall as more than just a house. If I were still a playwright, he said to himself, I should cast New Hall as a character in its own right, with its own purpose and role to play . . .

He shook off the whimsy and concentrated on what he now knew. That the dead woman was Emma Rossiter seemed beyond doubt. Everything fit: the timing, the motivation for coming to Romney Marsh, her colour. Once Samuel Rossiter was found, they would know for certain. Either he or Clavertye would question the man until he told them everything he knew.

At this thought, the rector sighed. He hoped, very much, that Samuel Rossiter would prove to be innocent of his sister's killing. He had enough self-knowledge to understand why he felt this way; sororicide was a revolting crime. And, too, there was the problem of evil. Mrs Chaytor's grief-born jibe had unsettled him more than he let show.

But experience of the world told him that Rossiter's innocence was unlikely, and meanwhile he must do his duty, no matter how distasteful it was.

Days passed. Hardcastle presided over the magistrate's court at New Romney, sentencing the usual offenders; in the summer, cases mostly concerned trespass and sheep-stealing, but in winter when the nights were long, the days cold and gin in plentiful supply, the balance tipped towards wife-beating and violent affray. One of those appearing before him was Beazley, the caretaker at New Hall, who had finally straggled back from Lydd; a day later he had got roaring drunk at the Star and started to break up the furniture in the common room, until Bessie Luckhurst neatly cracked a bottle over his head. Beazley could not pay the fine imposed as he had spent all his money entertaining his 'auntie', so Hardcastle sentenced him instead to a week in cells. He then wrote another letter to Mr Jessington informing him of the caretaker's latest delinquencies, and the fact that New Hall was uninhabited once more. There was no reply.

Spiritual as well as temporal matters claimed his time. It was a busy season in the parish, for as well as the usual round of church services, January was when the cold and wind thinned out the ranks of the elderly and more vulnerable. There were three funerals to arrange in the first week after New Year; two of elderly men dead of pneumonia, the third of a girl of twelve who had fallen through the ice on a frozen sewer and drowned. The latter was particularly harrowing, and of course there was another inquest to be convened also.

Often on Romney Marsh, and particularly in bad weather, one could feel cut off from the rest of the world. Sometimes that could be comforting; one could sink into life here on the Marsh and let the rest of the world go hang. This year, though, the rest of the world refused to be shut out. The papers from up-country brought them news which grew worse by the day. The war with France, now in its fourth year, was going badly. All across the continent, the armies of Revolutionary France had triumphed. The British army and navy were stretched to breaking point; and the enemy coast was just thirty-five miles from Romney Marsh. On clear days, standing on the dunes above St Mary's Bay one could see the chalk cliffs of France shimmering in the distance. The cold north-easterly winds were redolent with menace.

For all of these reasons, the rector passed the first week of 1797 fighting off a deep and all-encompassing sense of gloom.

WADSCOMBE HALL, TENTERDEN.
9th January, 1797.

My dear Hardcastle,

This is to inform you that I have done as you asked and referred to the chief magistrate of London, asking for the services of the Bow Street Runners to track down Samuel Rossiter.

I can now report to you that the Runners found the lodgings of the Rossiters at a house in Marylebone. Their rooms were empty save for a few items of clothing and personal effects. The Runners questioned the landlord, who stated that the woman calling herself Emma Rossiter was last seen on 22nd December. He was vague about the details, but thinks he saw Samuel Rossiter a day later. Neither has definitely been seen since.

The chief magistrate has confirmed he will continue with efforts to trace Samuel Rossiter, but he has given his opinion that the man has probably left London. I am inclined to agree. After so long a time, it will be difficult if not impossible to trace him. I have nonetheless circulated the description you sent me to all magistrates in Kent, and asked them to instruct their constables to keep an eye out for this man. Let us hope that these enquiries will shortly yield results.

Your discretion concerning James Rossiter is appreciated. The man, who is known to me, has some very influential connections thanks to his closeness to the American ambassador. Tread warily in this matter.

Yr very obedient servant,

CLAVERTYE

The rector read the letter through and laid it down on his desk, thoughtfully.

Trust Clavertye, he thought; he wants me to steer clear of the Rossiters in case I start asking clumsy questions and offend an influential American diplomat. The trouble I create might rebound and land on his own head. Well, I have no intention of going anywhere near the Rossiters, although I am still puzzled by their attitude to New Hall.

The thing that nagged him about the letter was the dates. They had assumed from the beginning that Samuel and Emma Rossiter had arrived together at New Hall, that they were the two cloaked figures who arrived after dark on the 23rd. That still fit for Emma, who was believed to have left London on the 22nd. But Samuel was still in London the following day.

The rector considered the timings. It was about seventy miles from London to St Mary in the Marsh. Most travellers would take a couple of days to travel down from Town, posting or taking the mail coach to Canterbury or Ashford and staying overnight, then hiring a carriage or horses to bring them on the next day. Those who were in a hurry and who had means, like Jessington, could hire a carriage in London and drive straight through in a day, changing horses at posting stations. Or one could hire a post horse and ride, exchanging mounts along the way. The latter was a hard journey, but it was possible.

Suppose Emma Rossiter had left London without telling Samuel, and he did not at first discover she was missing. He could, in theory, have hired a horse early the following morning and ridden post-haste after her, overtaking her before they arrived at New Hall. Thus they could still have arrived together that night. It was possible.

But why, why? What was so important about New Hall that it led them to make such an arduous journey in the dead of winter? And why, *why* was Emma killed?

Still he had no answers.

Restless, he reached for the port bottle, then withdrew his hand. He put on his cloak and hat and boots and went out for a punishing three-hour walk, down to St Mary's Bay and then along the sea towards Dymchurch and back in the bitter, salt-laced wind. He returned home tired and frozen in body but with his mind churning as hard as ever. Over and over the pieces of the puzzle turned, but still no pattern emerged.

Turning back into the drive as dusk began to fall, he noticed a carriage in the yard. The rig was unfamiliar, a smart little gig whose cream and green paint was darkened with mud. His heart sank; he had no interest whatever in entertaining visitors, who-ever they might be. In the hall he found Mrs Kemp waiting for him, her wrinkled face even more forbidding than usual.

'What were you doing out in this weather?' she scolded. 'You'll catch your death.'

'Exercise is good for one, Mrs Kemp,' he said, taking off his sodden coat and handing it over. 'You should try getting some yourself.'

She sniffed. 'Exercise. Down at the Star again, more likely. Or was it the Ship in New Romney this time?'

'Mind your own affairs, you infernal old busybody. Whose carriage is that in the yard?'

'She is in the drawing room. She says she is your sister.'

In the middle of pulling off his gloves, he stopped and stared at her. 'My *sister*? Good God, which one?'

'As she has no distinguishing marks,' said Mrs Kemp in a voice oozing with satisfied sarcasm, 'I am unable to tell. I have brought her tea. But if she wants a bath at this hour of the day, she can jolly well draw it herself.'

Satisfied that she had emerged victorious from their latest skirmish, Mrs Kemp shuffled away. Cautiously, the rector opened the drawing room door and entered the room. A gush of sisterly affection washed over him.

'*Marcus!* My *dear* brother! How *wonderful* to see you!'

'Calpurnia,' said the rector. 'What a delightful surprise.'

The woman rising from the settee before him, face shining with smiles, was ten years his junior. She had a pleasantly round face with a long nose and dark eyes; her light brown hair was fashionably curled. Fashionable too was her day dress, of sensible wool for warmth but cut, he assumed, according to the latest mode, its lines emphasising her figure.

He thought of mentioning that she had put on weight. He restrained himself, and instead kissed her cheek and said, 'To what do I owe the pleasure of your company, dear sister?'

'Marcus. Do I need a reason? It has been three years since we last saw each other. Surely a lady does not need a reason to visit her dearest brother, and renew their fond acquaintance?'

'I am, of course, your only brother,' he muttered under his breath. Aloud he said, 'It is a vile time of the year for travelling. Should you not have waited until spring— What in the name of all that is holy is *that*?'

He had not at first noticed the thing lying before the hearth. Now, hearing voices, the thing stirred, opened its eyes, and then with a motion like Leviathan rising from the deep, clambered to its feet. Most of its long body was hidden beneath a coat of matted, curling hair, grey mottled with brown and black; it looked like an old mattress with the ticking torn away. A long-nosed head, framed by shaggy ears, swivelled round and looked at the rector. Its tail wagged hopefully.

'This is Rodolpho,' said his sister proudly. 'He is my constant companion. Aren't you, Rodolpho? Oh, good boy, good *boy*! Mumsy-wumsy wuvs you, *yes*!' She gave the dog a playful scratch behind the ears as he gently head-butted her. He was an Irish wolfhound, a big one at that, standing more than three feet at the shoulder.

'I named him after my first book,' Calpurnia said happily. When Hardcastle looked blank, she said, 'Oh, *you* remember, silly! *Rodolpho, A Tale of Love and Liberty.* My great triumph! You surely cannot have forgotten.'

The rector, who had read five pages of the book and been trying to forget ever since, forced a smile. 'Of course. You named your dog after your hero.'

'Oh, but *he* is my hero now. Aren't you, lovely poochy-woochy?' She bent and gave the dog a kiss on his hairy head.

Hardcastle thought the dog looked pained. He said, as he eased himself into a chair, 'Now tell me, Calpurnia: delightful though it is to see you, why are you really here?'

'Well,' said Calpurnia. She seated herself, arranged her skirts fussily, and then, when they were folded to her satisfaction, looked at him with bright eyes.

He knew that look of old, and distrusted it.

'The *truth* is, brother dear, that I need somewhere congenial to write.'

'You have a perfectly good house in Hampshire.'

'Oh, Rose Cottage is delightful. But therein lies the problem. My little home is, I fear, just a touch *too* comfortable. I need a location that will inspire me. I need a harsh and forbidding landscape peopled by stern yet homely characters; genuine people, but with just enough peculiarities to make them interesting. These are the materials from which I shall fashion my next book.'

At this the rector forgot himself. 'You want to set one of your infernal novels in St Mary?'

'Oh, no, certainly not. I always disguise any real people or places that appear in my books. Rest assured, I shall give them *quite* different names so that no one will recognise them. No, Marcus, it is the *feeling* that is important. I need to sniff the air, I need to feel the salt wind on my cheek, I need to hear the wild storms rage. I need to know that the people around me are enduring lives of great hardship, battling against the unfeeling elements and the cruelty of wind and wave, yet they are unbowed by the struggle, and their native nobility of character and beauty of spirit always shines through. I had thought of setting the story in a lighthouse. Is there a lighthouse nearby?'

'And how long,' said the rector heavily, 'do you intend to stay?'

'I don't know. Until I finish my book, certainly, but if there is material for more, then I may stay indefinitely. Isn't it wonderful?' At this she burst into laughter. 'Oh, Marcus, if only you could see the look on your face! You are afraid I will get underfoot, aren't you? Don't tell me you don't want my company!'

'I am rather set in my ways, Calpurnia, and I prefer my own—'

'Oh, you dry old stick, you've been living on your own for far too long. Look at this house; it is *far* too severe and masculine. It needs a feminine touch.' She looked around. 'This room wants redecorating, for a start.'

'Calpurnia!' he thundered. 'You will not interfere with my household! You will not change one single thing about this house! I forbid it!'

'Oh, stuff. I never paid any attention to your forbiddings when I was a girl, so I am hardly going to start now. Now, my bags are coming along from Ashford, with my girl looking after them. They will be here tomorrow, and then I can settle in properly. We will have a marvellous time, you and I and, of course, dear Rodolpho,' and she blew a kiss to the wolfhound.

'From now on,' said Calpurnia in a tone which accepted no argument, 'everything is going to be *lovely*.'

Wadscombe Hall, Tenterden.
10th January, 1797

My dear Hardcastle,

We have had a stroke of luck. I was in Appledore yesterday on business, and happened to speak to the ostler at the
Black Lion. He remembers a man fitting the description of
Samuel Rossiter, coming in on a tired horse late in the day
on the 28th December. The ostler recalled that the man
was muddy and wet from long riding. He dismounted,
handed over his horse and went into the inn.

I then spoke to the taproom staff and they too remembered the man, partly because of his colour, and partly
because he was very much interested in something
he read in the *Kentish Gazette*, a copy of which had
been left lying on a table. We can surmise, I think,
that what he read was the story of the murder, which
appeared in the paper about then. The staff recalled that
the man became visibly agitated for a moment, then
recollected himself, paid for his drink and walked out
of the room.

That was the last anyone saw of him. The ostler waited
two days then took the horse back to Ashford, where it had
been hired. I will make inquiries in Ashford, and will urge
the other magistrates and constables in this part of Kent to
be vigilant. We may yet find our man.

Yr very obedient servant,

CLAVERTYE

Calpurnia's baggage arrived late the next morning. There was a great deal of it. Accompanying the bags was the maid, a bright-eyed, red-haired Irish girl named Biddy, who marched beaming into the hall and dropped a curtsey to the rector before turning to the housekeeper. 'You must tell me how I can be useful, Mrs Kemp, and give me whatever tasks you like; I'll not shirk at any-thing. Only, let me watch you as you work sometimes. I'm still learning, you see, and I'm sure a wise lady like yourself has so much to teach me.'

She clearly meant every word of it. The rector's only pleasure that day was to watch Mrs Kemp struggle between her instinc-tive desire to be rude to the interloper, and the realisation that hurting this sweet creature would be like kicking a kitten. She hesitated, then temporised. 'Come along,' she said gruffly. 'I'll show you where to put your traps.'

The rector went back to his study, shutting the door firmly behind him. Sighing, he opened his desk, pulled out the bot-tle of port that he kept there, and poured himself a brimming glass. Then he sat down to read Lord Clavertye's letter again. If Samuel Rossiter had been spotted in Appledore three days after the murder, then it was quite possible he had remained in the district; indeed, he might still be somewhere close at hand.

Someone knocked at the front door; the housekeeper answered it, and a moment later Joshua Stemp was shown into the study. From overhead came a deep rumbling sound as heavy trunks were dragged across the floor. Stemp raised his eyebrows towards the ceiling. 'Problems, reverend?'

'Family,' said the rector without further explanation. 'What is it, Joshua?'

'Maybe nothing,' said Stemp frowning. 'Or maybe something. Bill Hayton says someone has been snooping around one of the lookers' huts.'

The rector looked up sharply at this. 'Has he seen anyone?'

'No, but he's seen footprints, several times over the past few days. He first thought it might be the Gentlemen, but there's no reason for them to be up there. It's a long time since the last run.'

'Have the smugglers ever used that particular hut?'

'Couldn't say for certain,' said Stemp solemnly, 'but I'd wager not. It's not on any of their usual routes. I suppose it might have been Preventive Men making a search,' he added doubtfully.

'Searching for what? Any cargoes from the last run will have been cleared out and taken up-country long since.'

'I thought the same,' Stemp said. 'And things being what they are, it seemed best if I came and told you.'

'Things being what they are,' the rector said grimly, 'you did right. Let us go and see for ourselves.'

The weather was a little brighter than in previous days, the clouds higher and less dark, but the air was still biting and raw. Hardcastle and Stemp turned up their collars and wrapped their scarves more tightly around their necks as they walked up the muddy track across the fields to the northwest. The Marsh around them lay flat and hissing in the wind and the steep hills to the northwest were dark against the dirty grey of the clouds. They crossed a sewer by means of a plank bridge and skirted a marsh fringed with dry bulrushes that rattled in the wind like a skeleton's bones.

Hayton was a grizzled man in his fifties who lived alone in a dilapidated cottage about a mile from St Mary. He suffered badly from marsh fever, the rector knew; he was shivering now, from fever or cold or both. He pointed with a crooked finger. 'That's the hut, reverend. There was more footprints there this morning. Three days running they been there now.'

'Thank you, Bill. We'll look into it.'

'If it ain't the free-traders, it must be Frenchies. Goddamned Frenchie spies snooping around. That's what it is.'

'If it is, Bill, we'll deal with them. Now, you go inside and get warm.'

'Think it's Frenchies, reverend?' asked Stemp as they walked across the squelching fields towards the hut.

In these times of alarm, people saw French spies behind every bush. 'Possibly. It is much more likely, however, that it is Samuel Rossiter.' The rector told Stemp Lord Clavertye's news.

Stemp rubbed his nose as he listened. 'But why is he still hanging around St Mary? If I'd dunted someone over the head and pushed 'em into a pond, I'd be hotfoot away and never come back. What's he doing here?'

'That,' said the rector, 'is a very excellent question.'

The lookers' hut was a small brick structure with a tile roof, a door and a single window. There were hundreds of these little buildings across the Marsh, all very much alike. Shepherds used them in summer for watching over their flocks; in winter, most were deserted. The rector and Stemp saw at once the marks of booted feet around the door of the hut. Most were older, partly washed away by yesterday's rain, but there was one set of new prints, which must have been made since the rain stopped, showing clear marks of someone going into the hut and then coming out again.

Hardcastle pushed on the wooden door, which yielded. Cautiously, they passed inside. The little room was plain and bare. There was a table, roughly made but solid, and a crude bench, a wooden bed frame with no mattress in one corner, and a brick hearth. The rector touched the chimney and found it cold; dust, rather than ash, lay on the hearth.

'No fires,' said Stemp. 'No bedding. No signs of food. Bit of mud on the floor; he'll have tracked that in on his boots. If he's holed up here, he must be mighty uncomfortable. It's colder in here than it is outside.'

'Yes,' the rector said slowly. His eye fell on something on the table, a scattering of small dark objects like grains of sand. He moistened the tip of his finger and touched some of the objects, then held them up to the light. 'What is it, reverend?' asked Stemp.

'Gunpowder,' said the rector.

Back at the rectory he retreated into his study, trying to ignore the sounds of trunks being unpacked in every room of the house; apart from his own room, he trusted, but had doubts even about that. The little Irish maid was singing as she worked, and it struck Hardcastle that she had quite a sweet voice. He wished she would stop.

When another knock came at the door, he groaned. 'What in God's name now?' he asked himself. But when Amelia Chaytor was shown into the study he looked at her with relief. He had not seen her for several days, and concern for her had been another thing plaguing his mind.

'How are you?' he asked gently.

'Resolved,' she said, and did not explain. She had shadows under her fine eyes, but otherwise she seemed well enough. She looked at the papers on his desk. 'Am I interrupting?'

'Ostensibly, I am writing next Sunday's sermon. In reality, I am worrying.' There came a thunderous crash from overhead as something large and heavy was dropped hard on the floorboards, and the rector pressed his hands to his temples. 'My sister has come to stay,' he said by way of explanation.

'My condolences.'

'I suspect your condolences are not sincere, but I thank you for them anyway. That is not what is worrying me. We have a definite sighting of Samuel Rossiter.' He told her quickly about Clavertye's letter and then about the lookers' hut, she listening intently. 'Gunpowder?' she asked at the end.

'It was priming powder, only a little. My guess is that it spilled from the priming pan of a pistol or musket left lying on the table. So, if this is Samuel Rossiter, then it would appear he is armed.'

'We saw no sign of a firearm at New Hall,' she said. 'No gunpowder or smells of smoke. And the victim was bludgeoned, not shot.'

'There could be any number of reasons for that. But Rossiter is clearly more dangerous than we suspected.'

She nodded. 'Do you think he has been hiding at the lookers' hut?'

'No, but he or someone has visited it repeatedly. It must be a meeting place; and if that is the case, then he must be meeting with someone, or expecting to meet with someone. Who, and why?'

'Find out why, and we will be closer to knowing who,' she suggested. 'What has drawn Samuel Rossiter back to the Marsh after apparently murdering his sister?'

'Apparently? It looks increasingly certain to me.'

'Why?' she challenged.

'Why else would he still be here, hanging around the Marsh?'

'But surely that makes him less likely to be our killer, not more. What sort of murderer risks detection by remaining near the scene of the crime?'

'Someone who has a pressing need to do so. Someone who has a secret to conceal, and is more afraid of that secret being revealed than he is of the gallows.'

'And what about the boot?' she asked.

'Oh, I know; the boot. Why hit her, push her into the water, then try to pull her out again, then stop halfway through? I agree, it makes no sense. But Rossiter is our only suspect, and we must pursue him. Even supposing he did not murder Emma himself, I am quite certain he knows who did.'

'So we come to your question, why?' she said. 'Why is he still here, hanging around the Marsh?'

'New Hall,' he said. 'It's that blasted house. It must be. It's the only thing that makes sense.'

'There we are in agreement, I think. What other interest could Samuel Rossiter possibly have in New Hall and Romney Marsh? We know he wanted access to the house. We know he became angry when Jessington refused. We believe he left London a day after Emma, and it appears he caught up with her and they came to New Hall together. That places him at the Hall when she was murdered. Both of them were fascinated by New Hall for some reason.'

'Well, that surely is obvious. They believe it to be theirs. If they are genuine, and the will is genuine, then they think themselves to be their father's rightful heirs.'

'And the secret you think Samuel Rossiter has killed to protect,' she said, her blue eyes suddenly intense, 'is connected with the inheritance.'

'It must be. Perhaps they quarrelled over that secret; perhaps that is why he killed her. Dear God.' The rector looked down at his hands in distaste. 'I hoped all along that this would not prove to be a case of sororicide. I fear my hopes are fading.'

A thought struck Mrs Chaytor; her lips parted suddenly, and she said, 'What about the other family?'

'You mean Nicholas's son, William? The other heir?'

'Yes. Here is a theory. Emma is the one truly obsessed by the house; that is why she sets off on her own. William, impatient to come into his inheritance and not trusting the courts to do the right thing, contacts Samuel and arranges to buy him off, pay him to go away and leave the original will uncontested. Samuel, who is less interested in the house, agrees, but Emma refuses. They quarrel, and he kills her. You will note that I have not mentioned the boot.'

Hardcastle mused on this for a moment. 'Jessington said that the family had shown no interest in New Hall, did not even ask for the keys. And he also said that he did not intend to tell the family about Samuel and Emma, at least not until this case was resolved.'

'Was he telling the truth?'

The pause this time was even longer. 'I believe he was,' the rector said. 'But the possibility that he was lying cannot be discounted. Nor can your theory that another member of the family was involved. I said I did not intend to go near the Rossiters. I may have to change my mind on that score.'

He showed her out himself, then returned to his study. Perhaps a minute elapsed before the door opened and Calpurnia came into the room, wiping her hands on an apron. Her eyes, button-bright, shone with unconcealed curiosity. 'Who was that lady, Marcus?'

'Do you never knock before entering a room, Calpurnia?'

'She was here for quite a time, was she not? And it was most unusual of her to come alone, without even a maidservant as chaperone.'

The rector drew breath. 'The lady is Mrs Chaytor, a respectable widow, and also one of my parishioners. She was here on a matter of business. If you must know, she is making a donation towards the repair of the church roof.'

'A widow? Well, she and I shall have something in common when we meet. Has she been widowed for long?'

'About three years, and she is still deeply stricken with grief. Please, for the love of God, do not allude to the matter in front of her.'

Calpurnia clicked her tongue. 'Really, Marcus. I am not *that* indiscreet, or that unfeeling. But I wonder if there was more to her visit than just a little donation to church funds. Surely that was business that could be concluded in a few minutes, and yet she stayed for half an hour.'

'Will you kindly keep your nose out of my affairs?'

'But someone needs to look after your affairs, brother dear. Charming widows are often on the lookout for male companions to ease their solitude.'

'You should know,' he said nastily.

She ignored him. 'I should like to meet her. Will you contrive an introduction between us?'

'I really am rather busy—'

'Or if you prefer, I will write to her directly.'

'Very well! I will introduce you at the first opportune moment. Now will you please go away?'

ANTHONY JESSINGTON, ESQ
LINCOLN'S INN
LONDON
12th January, 1797.

By express

The Reverend M.A. Hardcastle
The Rectory
St Mary in the Marsh
Kent

The Reverend Hardcastle, Sir,

I write with news, none of which I fear is happy. Yesterday afternoon, I received a caller at my chambers in the person of Joseph Parker the younger, in his capacity as solicitor to the Rossiter family. You will recall that he is the son of my esteemed former patron, and is married to Mr James Rossiter's sister Jane. He now resides in Boston, Massachusetts, and travelled to England in the retinue of Mr Rufus King, American ambassador to the Court of St James.

Having laid out his facts with lawyerly care and attention, Mr Jessington continued.

Somehow, by means I have not been able to determine, Mr Parker has learned of the presence in London of the persons calling themselves Samuel and Emma Rossiter. He also learned that Samuel Rossiter had called on me. He was very angry, and his language was most intemperate; indeed, he used words that I do not think one gentleman should ever use to another. It is only my poor health that prevented me from insisting that he give me satisfaction.

The substance of Mr Parker's complaint against me was an accusation that I had deliberately concealed the presence in London of Samuel and Emma Rossiter from himself and the rest of the family.

Well, thought the rector, but that is precisely what you did.

He denounced me for lack of honesty and integrity – as I said, had my dyspepsia not intervened, I should surely have called him out on this matter – and accused me of colluding with Samuel and Emma Rossiter to defraud the estate. In vain, I protested that I had done no such thing and had acted entirely in accordance with the law.

Mr Parker then demanded to see the will and other documents Mr Samuel Rossiter had lodged with me. When I refused, he flew into a great passion, and denounced Samuel Rossiter as a bastard and a fraud. He insisted that Mr Nicholas Rossiter had conducted an illicit affair – those were not his exact words, which were not fit for repetition – with a black maidservant, by whom he had two by-blow children, but there is no question of him ever having married the woman.

The children themselves had not been seen for many years until they reappeared in Boston the year before last, asking questions about their father. Mr Parker says he refused to allow them to meet the rest of the family, and sent them on their way.

Mr Parker expressed the view that the will and testament of Mr Nicholas Rossiter given in Montréal early last year is a forgery. I find myself less convinced by this, especially as Mr Parker has inadvertently confirmed that the man I saw was indeed the real Samuel Rossiter; his description of Samuel – such as could be gleaned from among his many expletives – fit very closely with the man I met. Therefore, Samuel Rossiter, and by extension his sister, would appear to be genuine.

The principal remaining issue remaining, then, is whether Mr Nicholas Rossiter and the maidservant were married, as Samuel claims, or not, as Mr Parker asserts. I will endeavour to find the truth, but as I have said, it will be spring before the Atlantic is clear of ice and storms and there is regular traffic with the Americas once more.

There is one final item of interest. Before he left, Mr Parker insisted I hand over the keys to New Hall. I was then given instructions to see the house opened and made ready for habitation. As matters stand, I have no legal justification for denying them access to the house. It is my understanding that the Rossiter family intend to come to New Hall in the near future.

Your faithful servant,

ANTHONY JESSINGTON

So, the Rossiters are coming here, the rector said to himself. He laid down the letter and stared into the fire, thinking. He wondered why they had suddenly changed their minds about New Hall. He wondered how much the American lawyer knew. He wondered when and how Parker had learned that Samuel and Emma Rossiter were in London, and if he had discovered where they were lodged in Marylebone. He wondered, finally and disturbingly, if Parker had known that Emma and then Samuel had left London with the intention of coming to Romney Marsh.

Blast this business! he thought. Every time I think we have a possible solution, something else comes up and muddies the waters. Will we *ever* learn the truth?

That was Saturday. The next day the rector's text for his sermon was the epistle of John the Apostle; appropriately enough its subject was brotherly love. After the service he stood at the church door as usual and said farewell to the verger, Misses Godfrey and Roper and the malodorous old man from Brenzett. After they had gone, he turned on impulse and walked across the damp churchyard to gaze out across the grey wastes of the Marsh towards the distant hills.

It was a cold morning but a bright one, the first such in a while, though the clouds promised more rain later. He glanced down at the grave beside him. It had a headstone, a simple slab already showing marks of weathering. Carved on its face was a simple inscription: *Amélie Rossiter, 1709-1770. Called unto God.*

Here in darkest mid-winter there were no flowers in bloom. But someone had cut two sprigs of holly, leaves deep green and berries rich and bright with the promise of regeneration, and laid them neatly in the shape of a cross on the earth at the head of the grave.

A thought struck him, with sudden, blinding force. He walked swiftly across the grass to the newly filled grave of Emma Rossiter. Wet earth lay in a dark mound, some of the soil washed down into the grass by the recent rains. There was of course no headstone. But lying on the earth, evidently placed with reverent care, was another bright cross of holly.

Chapter 6

The Rossiters

Excitement over the murder had barely died down when the arrival of the Rossiter family at New Hall created a fresh stir in the village. First to come on Tuesday the 17th were the house servants: three full carriages of them, agency staff sent ahead to open the house and make all ready. No sooner had they arrived than wagons and carts began rumbling in from New Romney and Rye and Dover, bringing provisions and furniture and carving deep ruts in the muddy roads.

Kate, Miss Godfrey and Miss Roper's maid, was predictably the first up to the hall to nose around. She reported back to the village that the new staff seemed quite friendly, 'with no stuck-up London airs about them'. Emboldened by this, a couple of village women went up to inquire about work in the kitchens, and to their surprise were hired on the spot. Lights burned late into the night at New Hall as the servants laboured to erase the marks of six months of emptiness and neglect.

On Wednesday, wagons laden with more furniture and baggage began to arrive, punishing the roads still further. Children stood with their mouths open by the side of the track watching the wagons pass. A dog barked furiously at each passing team.

'It would appear that they intend to live in state,' observed Mrs Chaytor, standing at the door of the rectory and watching another wagon roll down the road. 'They will put us all to shame.'

'Perhaps that is the idea,' said the rector. 'Have you received your invitation?'

'I have. I confess to being intrigued.' The invitations, printed and embossed, had arrived that morning by post from London: Mr William Rossiter hoped for the pleasure of their company on the afternoon of Saturday the 21st, three days hence.

'Come in out of the cold. Thank you for agreeing to meet her. She is curious about you, and until she satisfies that curiosity, I will have no peace.'

'It is my pleasure,' Amelia said as he took her cloak. 'How is Mrs Kemp bearing up?'

'She handed in her notice yesterday, declaring she would tolerate no further interference in her house. I refused to accept her notice, and we had a furious argument. That made her feel better for the moment, but I don't know how long it will last. Now, prepare yourself.'

He ushered Amelia into the drawing room and Calpurnia, her face smiling and her eyes sharp as a barrister's tongue, came forward to greet her. She was, the rector saw, assessing every detail of Mrs Chaytor including her bearing, her manner and her clothing, pricing the latter and, quite likely, arriving at a fair estimate of the other woman's income.

'Mrs Chaytor,' he said formally, 'my sister, Mrs Vane. Mrs Vane, my neighbour and parishioner, Mrs Chaytor.'

'I remember hearing your name,' said Calpurnia smiling innocently. 'I am sure you have mentioned her to me, Marcus. Something to do with the church roof, was it not?'

'Mrs Chaytor has been a most valued benefactor to our poor church,' said the rector, bowing.

'You attend services regularly, Mrs Chaytor?'

'No,' said Amelia honestly, 'but I do feel all churches should have a roof.'

They sat, Calpurnia slipping into the role of hostess and pouring tea with her own hand, 'for that is how they do things in Town nowadays. Do you ever get up to Town, Mrs Chaytor?'

'Very seldom, Mrs Vane.'

'That's surprising. Your clothes, if I may say, are quite beautiful. I assumed you must patronise some terribly fashionable dressmaker.'

'The woman who makes my clothes comes from Rye,' said Mrs Chaytor. 'I would be pleased to introduce you to her, if you wish.'

The preliminary skirmishes over, Calpurnia settled in for the main assault. Mrs Chaytor saw her open her mouth, and forestalled her. 'And Mr Vane? Is he here with you?'

'Oh, no,' said Calpurnia in surprise. 'Did Marcus not tell you? Like yourself, my dear, I am a widow. Marcus, I am surprised at you for not telling Mrs Chaytor of my sad condition.'

'It must have slipped my mind,' said the rector stonily. He was saved further scolding by the arrival of Rodolpho, who spotted the newcomer and lumbered over to her, laying his head on her knee and looking up at her with sad brown eyes. 'What a lovely dog,' said Mrs Chaytor.

Rodolpho responded with a wag of his tail that would have sent the sugar bowl spinning into the fireplace, had not Calpurnia lifted it neatly out of the way. 'What is his name, Mrs Vane?'

There followed a discussion of the dog's name, a long and detailed description of the plot, characters and main themes of *Rodolpho, A Tale of Love and Liberty* followed by that of another of her novels, *The House of the Lost Spirits*, and then an account of her late husband Captain Vane, R.N., sadly deceased of fever ten years hence, complete with full details of his looks (handsome), his manners (perfectly polished), his habits (those of a true gentleman in every respect) and his passion for fly-fishing, a sport at which he excelled even the renowned Izaak Walton. Mr Walton, Calpurnia explained, was the great master of the sport of fishing, author of the much respected book *The Compleat Angler*, and—

'I am acquainted with Izaak Walton's works,' interrupted Mrs Chaytor gently. 'My husband taught me to fish, and introduced me to *The Compleat Angler*.'

'Did he? Captain Vane never offered to teach me, but then I am sure he knew I was quite busy enough with my writing. But enough about me, my dear. I should like to know much more about you.'

There then followed an appalling interrogation concerning every detail of Amelia's private life, including her own marriage and widowhood, her background, her family, and the life in Paris and Rome and London that she had abandoned for solitude on the Marsh. Rodolpho sat all the while with his head on Mrs Chaytor's knee, occasionally giving her hand a gentle lick. No amount of significant looks from Calpurnia's brother could stem the flow of questions.

After inquiring as to whether Amelia had a dog of her own, and if not why not, Calpurnia finally fell silent. The rector, who had been sitting for several minutes with his eyes closed in pain, intervened. 'Dear sister, I think it is time we let Mrs Chaytor go, don't you?'

'Oh, but we were having such a lovely chat! Weren't we, my dear?'

'Delightful in every respect,' said Mrs Chaytor smiling. 'But I fear I really must go. Mrs Vane, I shall of course be delighted to return your hospitality as soon as possible. We may continue our conversation then, I am sure.'

'Oh, I should like that very much. I shall be most interested to see your house. I am sure it is full of lovely things. Mementoes of your time in Paris and Rome, perhaps? Dear Captain Vane used to send me souvenirs from every port where his ship touched. As he was on the Channel Blockade, I fear most of them came from Portsmouth.'

They rose and, after the two women curtseyed to each other and exchanged fond farewells, the rector walked Mrs Chaytor to the door.

'I am so very sorry,' he said, drawing her cloak about her shoulders.

'Do not be. She is quite artless. I was able to bat most of her questions away without her realising I had not answered them. And of course, I understand why she asked. Do you know she is fond of you?'

'The thought had not occurred to me.'

Mrs Chaytor smiled. 'There have been no further sightings of our man?'

'None. Stemp has been out every day, looking into possible hiding places, and I know the constables in the other parishes are doing the same. But, nothing. He has gone to earth; or, perhaps, seen sense and left the district.'

'While the family who disinherited him, at least in his eyes, arrive to take possession of his house? I think not. Whoever left the holly on the graves was doing more than making a memorial. They were sending a signal that they are here, and intend to stay.'

'I fear you may well be right. Let us take another tack.'

'What do you mean?'

'The Rossiters. I am glad you have been invited to this levee, because I want to know what you make of them. When we visit them, keep your eyes and ears open.'

'I had every intention of doing so,' she said, smiling.

To the disappointment of the parish, the carriages bringing the Rossiter family arrived after dark on Thursday, and thus no one was able to get a clear look at them. Friday passed quietly for the rector, who, after a morning walk through occasional showers of sleet, sat by the fire in his study with a reviving cup of coffee and read the letters and reports from his fellow magistrates concerning the hunt for Samuel Rossiter. There had been reported sightings of their man in Dover, Deal, Ashford, Chilham and Whitstable. In each case the magistrate had stated his firm opinion that the man spotted must be Samuel Rossiter, and then gone on to give a description.

The rector sipped his coffee, and winced. The beans were burnt; he would have to tell Mrs Kemp, and that would be the cue for another argument. Most of the people who had been spotted were very obviously not Samuel Rossiter. One had grey hair; one was described as stoop-shouldered with a furtive air; one had a wooden leg. The one in Deal was fairly obviously a sailor from one of the Royal Navy warships in the Downs – possibly a deserter, but that was not the rector's business – and the one in Whitstable was an itinerant pedlar selling brushes. The only thing they had in common was that they were all black men; that being enough, apparently, to identify them as Rossiter.

The rector pondered on the last sighting for quite a while. Whitstable was nearly forty miles away and it seemed unlikely, given his current theories, that Samuel would have gone so far from the Marsh. But his theories had already been exploded several times, and anything was possible. He wrote to the Whitstable magistrate, thanking him and asking for the brush-seller to be apprehended and his identity established if possible.

Saturday morning dawned bright and cold, the wind for once absent. Hoarfrost painted the rosebushes and hedges in the garden with silver-white rime. The rector put on his coat and hat and gloves to go for a walk and turned to find Rodolpho staring at him, beseeching eyes peering out from beneath the shaggy coat. The rector paused, and then snapped his fingers. 'Come on, boy.'

Rodolpho promptly bounded towards him, wagging his great tail and crashing against the furniture. 'Sit,' growled the rector, and the dog sat at once, looking up earnestly and waiting. The rector snapped his fingers again, and this time Rodolpho trotted meekly after him as they went out into the bright, cold morning.

They walked across the frosty meadows towards the sea. It was a beautiful morning; the sun was still a glowing promise below the horizon, streaking the sky with glowing red. The fields around were a marvel of feathery frost. Rodolpho scampered across them, bounding with puppyish energy. It came to Hardcastle that he had never once seen his sister walk the dog. Her usual routine was to rise around midday, spend several hours in the drawing room where she pretended (or so he strongly suspected) to write her new book, and then join him for dinner. After the meal he retreated to his study while she returned to the drawing room and amused herself most evenings by playing the fortepiano very badly. Rodolpho's only outings were brief ones into the garden to answer calls of nature.

Now, given his freedom, he bounded across the meadows barking with pleasure, a mass of half-coordinated shaggy limbs and flapping ears and tail. When there are sheep in these fields, Hardcastle thought, he will need to be kept on a lead; otherwise, every local shepherd will want to murder him.

When they reached the sea, the dog stopped dead on the crest of the dunes, eyeing the water with deep suspicion, before trotting warily down across the frozen sand to inspect it more closely. The rector followed after him, looking into the bright-ness of the dawn and seeing the black line of the enemy coast on the fiery horizon.

There was someone else on the beach: a woman in long cloak and bonnet gazing at the sunrise. Not wishing to intrude on her, Hardcastle called sharply to the dog; but at the sound of his voice she turned and waved, then walked along the sand towards him. Rodolpho saw her and rushed to meet her, jumping up and put-ting his great paws on her shoulders and licking her face. To the rector's considerable relief, the woman burst into peals of laughter.

'Down!' he snapped, and the dog subsided, still wagging his tail, sand flying in all directions. Hardcastle stepped for-ward, reaching into his pocket and holding out a handkerchief. 'Ma'am, I am extremely sorry.'

'Oh, please don't be. He was only being friendly, I am sure. He is a lovely dog.'

She was a tall woman, with a pleasant pale face and a deter-mined line to her chin and jaw. The hair that escaped from under her bonnet was fair, reddened by the sunrise. Her eyes, above cheeks flushed with cold, were sparkling green. 'Is it not the most glorious morning?' she asked. 'I saw the sunrise, and simply could not remain inside another moment.'

'You must be from New Hall,' he said, bowing. 'Permit me. I am the Reverend Hardcastle, rector of this parish.'

'My name is Laure Rossiter,' she said, smiling. Her voice was soft and rather gentle. 'My cousin William is the new owner of New Hall.'

That would make her the daughter of James Rossiter, William's uncle, Hardcastle reasoned. He guessed she was about thirty. 'I am pleased to make your acquaintance. Doubtless I shall see you later today at New Hall, and then someone can introduce us formally.'

She laughed at that. 'Yes, we are looking forward very much to meeting our new neighbours. Father has invited all the quality of the district, it seems.'

'You intend to stay in St Mary for long?'

'Who knows?' They had turned and walked up over the dunes, back towards the village where St Mary's church tower stood squat in the glowing light. 'It was a whim of Father's that we should come down here, and doubtless we shall stay as long as his whim keeps us here.'

They walked on in silence for a few minutes, Rodolpho frolicking around them, and then the young woman said, 'Tell me, Reverend Hardcastle: is it true that you are also the magistrate for this district?'

'I am.'

'Then may I ask you, while we are in private, whether any progress has been made in finding out who killed that poor girl? On Christmas Day?'

'Inquiries are ongoing,' he said. 'You must understand I can tell you no more. Does it distress you, living in a house where someone died in such a fashion?'

'No,' said Laure. 'I lived through the war, reverend. I was eight when Bunker Hill was fought, and I still remember seeing the dead and wounded brought back into the city after the battle. Death was all around us in those days, and it holds no terrors for me now. But I am concerned for justice.'

'Justice? Why? The young woman was surely a stranger to you.'

'We are all strangers to each other, Reverend Hardcastle. Who can say that they truly know their fellow men and women, even their own family? And yet at the same time, we are also linked by our common humanity. New Hall is the home of the Rossiter family, and as a member of that family I feel responsible for what happened. I should like to know the truth, should the truth ever come to light.' Her clear green eyes looked directly at the rector.

'When the truth is found, I shall be sure to tell you,' he said quietly. They walked on through the thin winter sunshine.

Just on the stroke of noon, a smartly handled carriage pulled up in the drive of the rectory. Lord Clavertye stepped out and banged on the front door. Mrs Kemp showed him into the rector's study.

'My lord,' said Hardcastle, 'this is a pleasant surprise. Mrs Kemp, the madeira, if you please.'

'I'm invited to this damned affair at New Hall,' said Clavertye briefly. 'Thought I'd call on you first. Don't want to go, of course. I can't abide these bloody rebels. But this particular rebel is important, and it would be best not to offend him.'

Clavertye was tall and patrician with commanding dark eyes and hair going silver at the temples. Dressed in fashionable style with boots whose mirrored finish did not betray the slightest speck of mud, he made the rector feel shabby and ungroomed beside him. That had been the case throughout their acquaintance, since they first met at Cambridge twenty years ago when one was studying divinity and the other law. They had been friends then; their relationship had cooled a little since, but there was still mutual respect. Clavertye knew the rector as an irascible, insubordinate and occasionally alcoholic clergyman who still possessed what a contemporary had called 'the finest mind in the Church of England'; the rector recognised that Clavertye was a lawyer turned ambitious politician who could be relied on utterly, except when his own interests were at stake. They made use of each other when needed, and for the most part got along well.

'Do you mean James Rossiter?' asked Hardcastle as the madeira was poured. 'What makes him important?'

'You'd never know there had been a war,' said Clavertye, whose brother had died at Yorktown and whose hatred of Americans had begun at that moment. 'Rossiter has managed to worm his way into every fashionable circle in London. Every time I turn around, there he is. He even has the interest of the home secretary, would you believe it?'

The home secretary, the Duke of Portland, was also leader of the moderate Whig faction of which Clavertye was an ambitious member; if there was one man in the kingdom Clavertye did not wish to offend, it was Portland. 'What did Rossiter do during the war?' asked the rector.

'Fought against us, of course. What else? Oh, to blazes with Rossiter. Have you any news about that other business?'

The rector told him about the footsteps at the lookers' hut and the gunpowder, the holly, and the brush-seller in Whitstable. 'I doubt very much that he is our man, but I have asked for inquiries to be made all the same. I am certain Samuel Rossiter is somewhere close by. The constables are looking out for him, but there is only so much they can do. Could the militia not be called upon to undertake a more thorough search?'

'The militia have gone north. They've been summoned to Derbyshire, to deal with the unrest up there.'

'Oh, of course,' said the rector sarcastically. 'A handful of striking millworkers and their wives are undoubtedly a greater threat to the realm than the French Army of the North. Is there now *any* military force protecting the coast of Kent?'

'There's the East Kent Volunteers. And the Customs and the Excise.' Clavertye raised his hand. 'Hardcastle, stop. I know what you are going to say. I have been lectured by you often enough about how our government and army are unprepared to meet a

French invasion. As it happens, I agree with you. As it also happens, there is not a damned thing I can do about it. Now, let's go and get this over with, shall we?'

In the drawing room of New Hall, now bright with candlelight and warm with fires, the air scented by candles, Mrs Chaytor watched them enter. A butler in periwig bowed and presented Lord Clavertye, the Reverend Hardcastle and Mrs Vane to their host, William Rossiter. Mrs Chaytor repressed a smile. There had been no mention of Calpurnia Vane in the rector's invitation.

William Rossiter was a tall, slender young man, with fair hair, a strong jaw reminiscent of his cousin Laure, and amiable hazel eyes. Flushed a little with excitement and responsibility, he bowed. 'Your servant, my lord; your servant, ma'am; your servant, reverend. May I present my uncle and guardian, Mr James Rossiter? His wife, my lady aunt, Mrs Antoinette Rossiter. My cousins, Mr Edward Rossiter and Miss Laure . . . Where the deuce has Laure got to? Oh, there she is.'

The rector turned his head and saw Laure by the window, talking with Mrs Chaytor. 'And my aunt, Mrs Jane Parker,' finished the young man, 'and her husband, Mr Joseph Parker.'

The men bowed; the ladies curtseyed. 'What a lovely house,' said Calpurnia before either the rector or Clavertye could get a word in. 'I do declare, Mr Rossiter, I did not know that there was a house of such state in St Mary, or indeed anywhere in Romney Marsh. And how beautifully you have furnished it! Those chairs are by Hepplewhite, are they not? So elegant. My late husband's family had a pair of Hepplewhite chairs that were the envy of the district. Oh, *canapés*! How delightful!'

By the window, Laure Rossiter watched the scene and turned back to Mrs Chaytor. 'What sort of man is the rector?' she asked.

Amelia Chaytor smiled. 'What a curious question,' she said. 'May I ask what prompts it?'

The other woman hesitated before answering. 'I met him this morning, when I was out walking by the sea. When I learned who he was, I am afraid I was rather forward. I asked him about the . . . thing that happened here. Afterwards, I began to worry that I might have been too bold. Should I seek him out and make my apologies?'

Mrs Chaytor smiled. 'He will certainly understand,' she said. 'He understands most things. I see you have heard about our tragic event.'

Laure Rossiter looked around to ensure there was no one within earshot. 'We all know what the report in the newspaper said, of course. But I cannot help thinking that this matter closely concerns our family.'

'Oh? What makes you say that?'

This time the hesitation was longer. Laure Rossiter flushed. 'I am sorry. I have only just met you, and here I am talking nonsense like a silly girl. Please forgive me, and I shall now remove myself from your company.'

'There is absolutely no need to apologise,' said Mrs Chaytor, softly. Over Laure's shoulder she saw Calpurnia Vane approaching. 'It is clear that something is troubling you.' She searched Laure's face. 'Will you call on me tomorrow afternoon, at two? Sometimes troubles are best shared.'

She saw the sudden leap of gratitude in Laure's eyes, and then Calpurnia descended on them.

'Mrs Chaytor, how delightful to see you again! Have you tried the *canapés*? They are delicious! Will you introduce me?'

'Miss Rossiter,' said Mrs Chaytor. 'This is Mrs Vane, Reverend Hardcastle's sister. She too is recently arrived in the parish.'

'And what brings you to St Mary, ma'am?' asked Laure as they curtseyed. 'Is this a family visit?'

'Oh, no, it is more than that. I am a writer, Miss Rossiter,' announced Calpurnia. 'As I tell everyone, I have come to Romney Marsh seeking inspiration for my new book.'

'A writer? How exciting! What do you write?'

'I write novels, Miss Rossiter. To be more specific, I write novels in what Lord Orford has called the *Gothic* style. It is the very latest thing, you know; all the fashionable people are reading Gothic novels now. Have you read any of mine, perchance? *Rodolpho, A Tale of Love and Liberty*? *The House of the Lost Spirits*? Or, *The Silent Sorcerer*? That was serialised in *The Lady's Magazine* earlier this year, and was *very* successful. No? You have not read it?'

Miss Rossiter looked helpless.

'Perhaps the periodicals are not so widely available in Boston,' suggested Mrs Chaytor.

'Then I shall send a copy around to you,' said Calpurnia. She held up a hand to halt a servant passing with a tray. 'These profiteroles are simply heavenly. Oh, dear, I fear that was the last one. Did anyone else . . . Oh, good, I am glad. Now, as I was saying, I will send you a copy of *The Silent Sorcerer* this very day, and you simply *must* read it and tell me what you think of it. I should value your opinion very highly.'

'What is the subject of the new book, ma'am?' asked Laure a little desperately.

Too late, she saw the trap beneath her feet. 'Well,' Calpurnia began, drawing a deep breath, 'I am thinking of setting it in a lighthouse—'

Ten years as a diplomat's wife had taught Amelia Chaytor how to stage a tactful rescue. She took Mrs Vane's arm gently.

'My dear, I am so sorry to interrupt. But I promised Mrs Parker to bring you to her as soon as possible. She and her nephew are considering refreshing the decoration of the morning room and I thought, given your excellent taste, you would be an ideal person to advise her. Would you be so kind?'

It worked like a charm; Calpurnia moved off happily with her. Amelia looked over her shoulder at Laure and saw gratitude in the green eyes. 'Tomorrow,' she mouthed.

The room was filling up. Hardcastle saw young William Rossiter talking with Mrs Merriwether, Amelia Chaytor's pretty, chatty friend from Rye. Morris, the magistrate from Lydd, nodded to the rector as he passed, deep in conversation with Parker and a couple of up-country gentlemen, Cranford from Warehorne and Maudsley who had an estate near Shadoxhurst; Dering, the former M. P. who owned land to the south, was there too along with Coates, the mayor of New Romney. Miss Godfrey and Miss Roper were also present, the latter already a little cheerful on the Rossiters' excellent sherry.

It was, Hardcastle thought, a very gracious, highly civilised gathering of a type that one saw very infrequently on the marsh. He wondered if the Rossiters were bringing change to St Mary, and if so, whether he would enjoy it. He doubted it. It was this manner of life, among other things, from which he had sought to escape.

'So,' said James Rossiter beside him. 'A man of God and a man of the law, combined in the same person. Is this a common practice in England now?'

'More so than you might think,' said the rector. 'There is a shortage in some parts of the country of educated men capable of acting as magistrates. Men like myself are drafted in to fill the lack.'

'And of course, clergymen are perceived as reliable,' said Rossiter, his eyes twinkling. He was a big man, fair and a little florid with the square jaw that seemed to run in the family and the same vivid green eyes as his daughter. He wore his white hair long but loose, brushed back from his forehead and falling down to his collar. His clothes were quietly expensive, and he leaned nonchalantly on a handsome ebony walking stick. A man who likes style, thought the rector; and also a man who has power, and knows it, and enjoys the use of it.

'Rightly or wrongly, they are,' the rector agreed. 'Are you enjoying your return to England, sir?'

'Indeed I am. We have been made most welcome wherever we go, in a truly warm and genuine way. Everyone has made it clear that bygones are bygones – or nearly everyone,' and his eyes strayed towards Clavertye across the room.

'You must forgive his lordship,' said Hardcastle. 'Did you know he lost his brother in the war?'

'I did not. Thank you for telling me,' said Rossiter and bowed a little, stiffly. He must be in his mid-sixties, the rector thought; he is hale and hearty, but there are marks of ill health in his face too. That leg must be paining him, but he refuses to show it.

'In that case, I understand his lordship's antipathy,' Rossiter went on. 'In his position, I should feel the same. Blood is usually thicker than water.'

'Indeed. But I do believe also that we must put the past behind us. We face a far greater enemy now.'

'Revolutionary France? I imagine you feel the threat quite deeply down here, so close to the enemy. And tell me, why is your government doing so little? Why are they not building forts and redoubts all along this coast? And where is your army? Why is it not down here defending the ports and beaches? Your Mr Pitt is a little complacent, would you not say?'

The rector stirred a little. It was one thing for himself to write thunderous letters to the *Morning Post* denouncing government inaction; it was quite another for a stranger and former rebel to criticise His Majesty's ministers. 'If you read the newspapers, Mr Rossiter, which I am certain you do, you will already know the answer to your questions. Our army is stretched to the limit in the Mediterranean and the Indies. There are no forts or redoubts because there is no money to build them, and because the merchants of England have refused to sanction further tax increases, just as they did during the war with your people. Had they done so then,' he added, 'the British army would have been immeasurably stronger, and I doubt very much if you would be enjoying your present independence.'

'On another occasion, I might give you an argument on that score,' said Rossiter, his eyes twinkling again. 'But please accept my apologies for my bad manners, reverend. I should not have spoken slightingly of your government. I've met many of your ministers, and they are good men, doing their best for their country in difficult times.'

Artfully said, the rector thought. 'Is it permitted to ask how the negotiations in London are progressing?'

'Of course. Mr King and Lord Grenville have met several times, and have already agreed in principle to a defensive alliance aimed at stopping the ravages of French privateers on our shipping. The details remain to be worked out, but I expect a full agreement will be ready for signature by spring.'

The rector nodded. 'That is certainly good news. And I am certain that you yourself have played an important role in these negotiations.'

Rossiter smiled. 'My role is quite simple,' he said. 'I am attached to the embassy because I have connections in this country, connections which my government and Mr King hoped would prove useful.'

'Ah,' said the rector. 'Connections such as the Duke of Portland?'

'You are well-informed, reverend. Yes, our families are distantly related by marriage. And truly His Grace has been most affable and afforded us every assistance. Meanwhile, while the politicians talk, I have leisure to reacquaint myself with my former homeland,' and he gestured around the room.

'It must have been some time since you last saw New Hall.'

'Longer than I care to think. Fifty years this year! It hardly seems credible to me. Mind you, I never saw much of New Hall and Romney Marsh. Father preferred our house in Buckinghamshire, that was always the family's main place in the country. And of course we spent much of our time in London. Mother liked the peace and privacy of St Mary, though. Of course, she is buried in your churchyard.'

The rector nodded in assent.

'Well, for that reason if no other, I have an affection for the old place,' James Rossiter continued. 'I am not sure all my family feel the same, though. Here, Edward. What do you think of New Hall?'

'Very pleasant, sir,' said his son, turning from a conversation with his mother and two local ladies by the fire. 'The countryside around is charming, and of course, the company is delightful. What more could one ask for?'

Edward Rossiter had inherited his father's strong jaw but the rest of his features came from his mother; he was small and neat like her. He too wore his hair, brown turning to red, long and brushed back from his face; his clothes were expensive but lacked his father's good taste. He wore a somewhat vulgar ruby ring on his little finger.

'And you, Mother, how do you like St Mary?' Edward asked.

'Everyone is most amiable,' said Mrs Rossiter. She had a strong French accent.

None of them has mentioned the murder, mused Hardcastle. Is this simply good manners, or are they pretending it has not happened?

'Also, it is good that the family is back in this house,' Mrs Rossiter added, looking over to the other hearth at the far end of the room where William, her nephew, stood talking earnestly to Mrs Chaytor and Mrs Merriwether.

'I too am glad to see the house occupied once more,' said the rector. 'After recent events, we wondered whether anyone would want to live here.'

They looked at him politely, smiling. 'What do you mean, sir?' asked James Rossiter.

Something stirred on the back of the rector's neck. 'It pains me to say it,' he said, 'but New Hall had developed an unsavoury reputation. Few people might wish to dwell in a house where not only has a young woman been murdered, but also, where treason has been plotted.'

'Ah,' said Rossiter, smiling still. 'Are you speaking of that business last spring? The events involving our tenant, the unfortunate Mr Fanscombe?'

'You know of that affair, sir?'

'I was told of it in London. The plotters were all arrested and hanged, I understand.'

'All save one, yes.' It was said in such a way that they had to respond.

'We heard something of this,' said Rossiter, 'but I confess I remember little of the detail of that affair.'

'The detail is most interesting. The man who escaped justice was a Frenchman named Foucarmont. He had killed two men in this parish, including one before my eyes. But despite numerous witnesses and the statements of his co-conspirators implicating him in the crime, Foucarmont escaped justice. At his trial, the judge ordered the jury to find him not guilty, and so he was set at liberty.'

Edward Rossiter made a gesture of dismissal. 'Someone bribed the judge.'

'Possibly. Or some other form of pressure was put upon him. Someone, somewhere, wanted Foucarmont freed, and had the power and influence to make it so.'

And where is this Foucarmont now?' asked Edward.

'He has disappeared. Despite his acquittal, his identity as an agent of the French republic was now well known. There are men in government service who would have executed their own justice on him, regardless of the law.' The rector could think of one in particular. 'Knowing this, Foucarmont made haste to depart the country. I should imagine that he is now in France.'

'Who is in France?' demanded another voice. 'Who are you discussing, if I may ask?'

This was Parker, the lawyer and brother-in-law, the man who had abused poor little Jessington; a hearty, slightly fleshy red-faced man, balding with hair tied back in a queue. He too wore several rings, including a large – and certainly expensive – antique cameo. His normally cheerful face was now sharp with inquiry.

'That business here last spring,' said James Rossiter easily. 'Do you recollect it, Joe? Some English Jacobins and French agents were rounded up and hanged. Reverend Hardcastle informs us that one of them got away.'

'*Sacré nom*,' said Mrs Rossiter. 'Do you think we are in danger from this man, reverend?'

The rector bowed. 'I think it highly unlikely, ma'am. People here know who he is and what he is. I do not think he would dare to return to St Mary.'

'Well, that's a relief,' said Edward Rossiter, and his eyes strayed to Parker.

The rector left soon after, finishing his madeira, making his excuses and collecting Calpurnia who was munching on one last *canapé*. Clavertye had already departed, Mrs Chaytor likewise. He walked his sister home through the falling winter dusk, ignoring her voice beside him as she chattered on about the clothes and the jewels and the fine house, thinking hard.

His sister was right. They were a charming family. Their taste was impeccable, their manners beautiful. They would undoubtedly be an ornament to the parish so long as they remained in residence.

And they stank like week-old fish.

Chapter 7

The Cardinal's Jewels

Sunday 22nd January dawned with a gale from the north-east and squalls of bitter rain sweeping over the Marsh. The sound of the sea pounding on the Dymchurch Wall could be heard even over the wind.

Shivering a little in the draughty vestry, the rector robed and walked out into the body of the church. Here he stopped in sudden surprise. His usual congregation were already seated: Miss Godfrey and Miss Roper smiling at him from under their fading bonnets, the aged verger sitting and mumbling to himself, the church warden already half asleep. But behind them, the Rossiter family were filing through the door into the nave: James and his wife, their son and daughter, young William, the Parkers, all in their Sunday best under dripping cloaks and hats and bonnets, inclining their heads to him as he bowed, and taking their seats in the box pews. Several of their servants followed, sitting down quietly at the back of the church. To Hardcastle's even greater surprise, Calpurnia slipped in quietly a moment later and took her seat beside the Rossiters.

At first all was well. Then, after a few seconds, their noses began to wrinkle. An alarmed whispering broke out. It was William who first identified the source of the smell: the old man from Brenzett, sitting placidly two rows behind them. More whispering, and the family rose hastily and retired a safe distance towards the rear of the church, seating themselves once more and trying not to look discomfited. Miss Godfrey and Miss Roper continued to smile.

When all were settled, the rector raised his arms. '*Oh, send out thy light and thy truth,*' he intoned in his rich voice, '*that they may lead me, and bring me unto thy holy hill, and thy dwelling place.*'

After the service he stood at the church door, and his congregants thanked him as they departed.

'That was a beautiful service, rector,' said Laure.

'You are most eloquent, *monsieur,*' said her mother, and Hardcastle bowed to her.

'Very fine,' said James Rossiter, who came last of all. 'It's a shame there were so few people to hear it.'

'My parishioners are good people,' said the rector, 'but public expression of religious feeling is not among their virtues. It does not matter. They know that when they need me, I am here.'

'Then you are a good man,' said Rossiter, and Hardcastle thought he detected a note of regret in the other man's voice.

Rossiter hesitated for a moment, leaning on his stick. The rest of the family had gone on ahead, hurrying home to get out of the cold.

'Reverend, might I ask for a moment of your time?' Rossiter glanced around the churchyard. 'Seeing as we are here.'

'You wish to see your mother's grave?' asked Hardcastle. 'Of course. Give me a moment.'

Changing out of his robes and pulling on his cloak and hat, he rejoined Rossiter and they walked together across the wet churchyard. The rain had stopped, but the dark bare trees dripped water on them as they passed. At the grave, Rossiter bowed his head and stood silent for a moment. If he noticed the two sprigs of holly, he did not show it.

'Dear old *maman,*' he said finally. 'She took it hard when Nick and I went off to America. She must have known she would never see us again.'

'You must have known it also.'

'I don't think I gave the matter much thought. I was young, only sixteen, and I was certain that I would make a fortune and come home rich as a nabob. It never occurred to me that I might end up staying in America.' He looked at the headstone again. '*Called unto God.* Does God really call us? I wonder. Or do we find our own time to go?'

'I think some people do choose their own time,' said the rector. 'Others are not so much called by God, as dispatched by the hand of man.'

'That's true enough.' The older man's face was sombre as he looked at Hardcastle, water dripping from the brim of his beaver hat. 'There's another matter I'd like to discuss with you, reverend, if this is a convenient moment?'

Hardcastle nodded and they turned and walked back across the churchyard, past the ancient yew tree and through the lych-gate and across the road to the rectory.

Settled by the fire in the study, Hardcastle rang the bell for Mrs Kemp, but it was Biddy the maid who appeared in the doorway, curtseying and smiling her bright smile.

'Please make us a couple of toddies,' the rector told her kindly.

Biddy sped away to her task. 'How may I be of service?' the rector asked his guest.

'May I talk to you in your capacity as justice of the peace, sir? It's about this affair at the house. Not last spring, that doesn't concern us at all. That matter is finished now, and in any case, we were all on the far side of the Atlantic when it happened. No, what gnaws at me is this business of the woman who was killed on Christmas Day. Have you had any fortune in identifying her?'

'We have not yet managed to identify her formally,' the rector said, and waited.

'But you have some notion?'

The rector nodded. 'What could she have been doing there?' Rossiter asked. 'The newspaper said she must have been a vagabond.'

'That is quite possible,' said the rector, and he waited again.

'I have spoken with the caretaker. He assured me there had never been a problem with vagrants before. Is that likely to be true?'

'I think so. My constable is very diligent when it comes to vagrants,' said Hardcastle drily. 'I confess I am curious to know what you have done with Beazley. I have seen nothing of him for some time. I assume you haven't kept him on at New Hall.'

Rossiter smiled. 'He's a bit of a rough fellow, isn't he? But don't worry, we've looked after him. We have some houses up in Buckinghamshire, and we found a post for him there.'

'That was very generous of you.'

'Why not? I don't blame him for this incident, and it has to be said that otherwise he did a good job of looking after the house ... Reverend, I wouldn't want you to break any confidences, or say anything that went against your duty. But within those limits, can you tell me whether you are making any progress in identifying the murderer?'

The toddies arrived, and Biddy dropped a curtsey and departed, closing the door softly behind her. Hardcastle rubbed his nose. 'We are making some progress,' he said. 'We have tested a number of theories about the identities of the victim and the killer, and the motive of the latter. Most of those theories have been discarded, but I regard that as progress. Each false lead that we discard brings us a little closer to the truth.' He looked Rossiter in the eye. 'I feel we are now on the right track.'

'I'm relieved to hear it.' Rossiter sipped his toddy. 'You must be asking yourself why this is so important to me,' he said. 'You see . . . I had hoped this visit to St Mary would be a happy time for us all. Seeing my nephew come into his inheritance; bringing my own children to visit their grandmother's grave; seeing once more the house where my sister and I used to play as children. But this affair has cast a shadow over our happiness. I suppose I am hoping once the killer is found and the mystery solved, that shadow will be lifted.'

'I am truly sorry to hear that you have been disturbed by these events,' said the rector. 'Let me assure you that I am resolved to find the killer and bring him to justice. And I will do so, no matter how long it takes.'

'I am absolutely sure you will,' said Rossiter, smiling, and he raised his glass. 'More power to your elbow. I do not know how long I will stay in St Mary, and I fear I will be called back to London sooner rather than later. However, I should like to hear as soon as you know anything definite about this poor girl and her killer. If I am in London, would you please write to me with any information that you may have?' He raised a hand. 'Once again, only if your duty permits you to tell me.'

'Your ward is the owner of the property where the murder took place. I think that gives him, and you, the right to know.'

'Thank you, sir. That is very understanding of you. Now, permit me to change the subject,' said Rossiter. 'You preached a very fine service, reverend. Would you, as a token of my esteem, allow me to make a small donation to church funds?'

Music was the refuge of Amelia Chaytor's soul. When she played the harpsichord, the world around her vanished. That afternoon her long fingers moved across the keyboard, filling the drawing room with a tumult of sound, passion and energy released, flowing in the air like invisible fire. So absorbed was she, indeed, that she did not hear the knock at the door, nor did she at first notice

Lucy enter the room. Lucy walked quietly, almost on tiptoes, as she always did when Mrs Chaytor was playing. Lucy had been her personal maid for several years, and had been her rock of strength during the terrible time after John died. Last autumn, when Mrs Chaytor's housekeeper had been forced by a bad back to retire, Lucy had volunteered to take on the additional role, and Mrs Chaytor had accepted gratefully. She relied on Lucy as she did on few others.

Still playing, she looked up. 'What is it?'

'Miss Rossiter from New Hall, ma'am. She says you are expecting her.'

Amelia sighed, and her fingers became still. 'Of course. Show her in, and then be a dear and make us some coffee. Hot and sweet, the Italian way.'

'Of course, ma'am.'

Laure Rossiter wore a dark-red gown that made her look rather stately. Her green eyes were wide with amazement. 'Forgive me, but I heard you playing while I was in the hall. It was marvellous! Was that Handel?'

'No,' said Mrs Chaytor, rising. 'That was Telemann, a cantata called the "Thunder Ode". I think it is perfect music for a stormy day.'

'It was marvellous,' repeated Miss Rossiter as they took seats by the fire. 'I wish I could play half so well as you.'

'You are fond of music?'

'Oh, Mrs Chaytor, I cannot tell you the joy music brings to me. And London for me is like paradise, for there is music everywhere! Why, in a few short weeks, I have heard music by Haydn and Mozart and Johann Christian Bach, and operas by Cherubini and Zingarelli; new music, such as had never reached my ears before, and all so full of excitement and promise! I feel as if I have been reborn.'

They talked about music until the coffee arrived and then, gently, Amelia took hold of the conversation and steered it.

'How are you enjoying *The Silent Sorcerer*?' she asked. 'I assume Mrs Vane was as good as her word.'

'The book arrived within an hour of her departure,' said Laure, smiling. 'Her writing is . . .'

'Not a word you say will leave this room.'

'Shall I then say that the writing is as enthusiastic as the lady herself?'

They giggled together for a moment. It struck Amelia that they must be about the same age, but there was a freshness and innocence about Laure Rossiter that made her seem much younger. Next to her I feel like a withered old crone, she thought.

'It was nonetheless a splendid party,' she said. 'My thanks again to your family for inviting me, and I look forward to repaying their hospitality. It was a particular pleasure to meet you, Miss Rossiter. I felt at once that we should have much in common.'

'So did I,' said Laure, shyly.

Amelia lowered her voice a little and leaned forward. 'As I said yesterday, it is clear that something is troubling you. As one, albeit new, friend to another, will you tell me what it is?'

Some of the light had gone out of Laure's eyes. 'I should not have spoken,' she said. 'And I certainly should not have bothered the rector with this matter. It is nothing, I am sure.'

'Perhaps you might permit me to be the judge of that,' said Amelia.

'There is an idea that has got into my head, and I cannot get it out. I cannot help thinking . . . Mrs Chaytor, I keep wondering whether the woman who was killed at New Hall was in fact my cousin.'

The first thought that flitted through Amelia's mind was, *that makes two of us.* 'If so, then I am most truly sorry for you. Is there something in particular that makes you think she was your cousin?'

'It would be dreadful. I don't want to think about it, but I cannot stop.'

Thinking hard, Mrs Chaytor lifted the silver coffee pot and refilled their cups. 'In my experience,' she said, 'talking to other people and sharing one's problems can help one find solace.' *Advice I ought to take myself,* she thought, *but probably never shall.* 'If you want to tell me about it, I am here to listen.'

There was a long pause. 'My Uncle Nicholas had two children from a liaison, before he married William's mother,' Laure said finally. 'None of us knew about them until they arrived in Boston, year before last, seeking us out. Only Uncle Joseph saw them; he handles all our legal affairs, you see. I'm afraid to say that he was quite unkind to them. He refused to acknowledge them as Uncle Nicholas's children, and forbade them to see or correspond with any others of the family.' She looked at Mrs Chaytor. 'Father supported him in this. I love my father and my uncle, but I thought that was mean-spirited of them both.'

'I suppose they were attempting to protect the family interests,' said Mrs Chaytor. 'These two could have been impostors.'

'Oh, they were definitely Uncle Nicholas's offspring. Uncle Joseph said so himself, although "offspring" is not the word he used. But there is more.'

Mrs Chaytor waited. 'They followed us to London,' said Laure. 'Or at least, they arrived in London not long after we did. I know, because I heard Father and Uncle Joseph arguing about it. Father wanted to pay them to go away, but Uncle Joseph said if we gave them money they would just come back later and demand more.'

'Do the rest of your family know about this?'

'I don't believe so. Father and Uncle Joseph didn't know I was listening, and they didn't tell any of the rest of the family what had happened. I am sure you are right; they are trying to protect us. But I still think they are being unkind.'

'But what makes you think the dead woman is your cousin? Her name was Emma, by the way.'

'Emma. That's a nice name,' Laure said wistfully. She did not ask how Mrs Chaytor knew this. 'It's the coincidence, I suppose, of both women being dark-skinned; my cousin, and the dead woman. She may have come to New Hall because of the connection with our family. Perhaps she just wanted to see the house, and imagine what it would be like to be part of our family. But why would anyone want to kill her?'

'Why, indeed?' said Amelia. 'That is what the rector is trying to discover.'

'Does he have any idea what might have happened?'

'My dear, what makes you think I might know?'

Laure blushed. 'I am so sorry. What must you think of me? I assumed . . . I thought perhaps that because you are friendly with his sister, that you might have heard something from her.'

'Mrs Vane is indiscreet,' said Amelia, 'but the rector is not. He does not gossip about investigations, not even to his sister.'

'I have said too much. I am sorry, I shall go.'

I'm losing her, Amelia thought, as the younger woman rose from her seat. I shall have to give something away. 'I said the rector does not gossip. I did not say that I don't know anything. Do sit down, my dear, please.'

Slowly, still pink with embarrassment, Laure sat, arranging her skirts.

Mrs Chaytor thought for a moment. 'I was one of the first to find the body,' she said, 'and therefore I am privy to a certain amount of information. Her identity is not yet generally known, but your theory that she was Emma Rossiter does not seem unlikely to me. As for the killer, it seems quite possible that he has remained in the district. If he has, then he will probably be found and caught quite soon.'

'Why did it happen at New Hall?'

'That too is an excellent question. When the killer is found, then hopefully we shall learn the answer.'

Laure asked the same question her mother had asked the rector. 'Mrs Chaytor, are we in any danger? My family, I mean? Will we be safe at New Hall?'

'I see absolutely no reason why not,' said Mrs Chaytor smiling. 'Far safer than London, with its footpads and highwaymen. We do have smugglers down here, of course, but they only work during the new moon, and they're mostly harmless so long as you stay out of their way. My dear, may I offer you some more coffee?'

'I invited her intending to pick her brain,' Mrs Chaytor told the rector later that afternoon, sitting in his study. 'Instead, I found my own brain being picked, quite skilfully.'

'What did you tell her?'

'There is a phrase they use at the Foreign Office: the truth, nothing but the truth, but not necessarily the whole truth.'

'What do you think she was after?' Hardcastle asked.

'Oh, information, of course. The real question is: why was she asking? Is she genuinely concerned for her family's safety? Does she really feel sympathy for these lost cousins? Or does she know more than she is letting on, and is trying to find out what *we* know?'

'I asked myself the same questions after speaking with Rossiter this morning,' said the rector. 'He too picked my brains. He even offered me a bribe if I would tell him what I knew about the case.'

'A bribe? How exciting. You don't like James Rossiter.'

'No. And I like Joseph Parker even less. And that is difficult, because I am in danger of allowing my dislike of them to cloud my judgement. But . . .'

'What is it?' she said. She felt tired, but also strangely exhilarated.

'They are very pleasant people. Their manners are impeccable. They go out of their way to be charming and agreeable to everyone. They even attended church this morning.'

'Gracious! They really must be rotters.'

'But Rossiter made a mistake today. He told me Beazley had been a good caretaker at the house. That is clear nonsense. We both saw what the house looked like under his care. And, Beazley went absent without leave and thus allowed two people to break into the house. Most landlords would dismiss a caretaker for such a dereliction. Instead, Rossiter has found him another post elsewhere.'

'So, he is a generous employer. They do exist, I am told.'

'But is he generous? Or has he sent Beazley to Buckinghamshire to get him out of the way? Does Beazley know something about the house or the family that Rossiter wishes kept quiet?'

'What might that be?'

'I do not know, but I am more certain than ever that the house itself is important. There is another thing, too. In conversation with the Rossiters at their party, I mentioned Foucarmont. From Parker's reaction, I am quite positive that he recognised the name.'

'Ah,' she said. She thought for a moment. 'He may have read accounts of the trial, and the scandal, since coming to England.'

'In that case, I would have expected him to ask questions, to want to know more. Instead, he became deeply uneasy and said nothing. I got the distinct impression that he did not care for that topic of conversation. And I would add that, for a lawyer, he is not especially good at schooling his face.'

'I too have begun to dislike Mr Parker,' said Mrs Chaytor, and she related her conversation with Laure.

The rector listened, rubbing his nose thoughtfully. 'Cases like this are not uncommon,' he said at the end. 'By-blows of a gentle family make themselves known to the heirs, and are offered a pension in exchange for waiving any claims on the estate. If in future they should become in any way objectionable, the pension ceases. Often these settlements are reached quite amicably by both parties. So, what Rossiter proposed was nothing out of the ordinary. Why then was Parker so against it?'

'From what Laure says, and from what Mr Jessington wrote to you, it would seem that Parker has a strong personal antipathy towards Samuel and Emma.'

'Why? Because of their race?' The rector made a gesture of distaste. 'If so, my dislike of Parker increases still further.'

'Then, while we are disliking Mr Parker, let us essay a new thought. Might his antipathy lead him to commit murder? Or commission someone else to do so?'

'It is possible,' said Hardcastle, considering this new thought. 'He might justify such an act by claiming that he was trying to keep the family "pure", to ward off the malign influences that might come from contact with members of the African race. Damn that man Blumenbach,' he added.

'I agree, that is certainly a possible reason for his strong dislike. *My* suspicions are running along different lines. I was thinking instead of the cardinal's jewels.'

The rector regarded her. 'You will have to enlighten me,' he said.

'During our time in Rome, there was a most sensational crime.'

'Only one?'

'*Touché*. The mistress of a cardinal was murdered by her brother, ostensibly because she had stained the family honour. The brother's body was found floating in the Tiber a day later, and it was believed that he had committed suicide in a fit of remorse.'

'That would seem to fit.'

'I didn't believe a word of it. I told John and anyone else who would listen that this was a matter of greed. And, I was proved right. It transpired that the cardinal had given his mistress a number of jewels, which her family wanted so they could pay their debts. When she refused to hand them over, the brother killed her and stole the jewels. He was then killed by the rest of the family when he tried to keep some of the jewels for himself.'

'Charming people, the Italians. I have always said so. What has this to do with our case?' Just then, a horse's hooves sounded in the drive. They heard the knock at the door, and Mrs Kemp shuffling to answer it.

'Greed,' Mrs Chaytor continued, in answer to Hardcastle's question. 'Parker, or someone else in the Rossiter family, wants something and is willing to kill to get it. And like you, I am willing to wager that whatever they want is connected in some way with New Hall.'

'Another theory,' he said, and groaned.

'And it still doesn't explain the boot,' she said.

'I knew you were going to say that . . . I'm sorry to say it, but your theory has a rather large hole in it. Parker and Rossiter are both well-off, if their clothes and that house are anything to go by. They have presumably made their fortunes in America. By contrast, the estates here in England are small, and New Hall is frankly an encumbrance. There is nothing of sufficient value to tempt either man to commit murder, or to countenance it.'

The front door closed and they heard the horse trotting back down the drive. 'Samuel and Emma, on the other hand, might not know this,' he continued. 'They might well think the estates are valuable. Hence their determination to get their hands on New Hall.'

'Very well, I concede the point,' she said glumly. 'Samuel Rossiter remains our most likely killer.'

'Unfortunately, I fear so. Parker and Rossiter are concealing something from us, of that I am quite convinced; but I don't think it is murder. Yes, Mrs Kemp, what is it?'

'A letter has come,' said Mrs Kemp, laying a sealed packet on the rector's desk.

'Thank you.' He opened the letter and read it, then looked up sharply at Mrs Chaytor.

'We will learn the truth very soon now,' he said. 'This is from Dobbs, the magistrate in Rye. He has arrested Samuel Rossiter.'

Chapter 8

Brother Against Brother

Dusk was already falling as the rector walked up New Romney high street and knocked at the door of the gaol. A short, square man with thinning grey hair admitted him. 'They've just arrived, reverend.'

'Good.' He was shown into an anteroom: bare walls with wooden floor and a small stove, radiating heat. Stemp and the parish constable of New Romney were already there, warming their hands.

'Did he give you any trouble?' asked Hardcastle.

'Came along meek as a lamb,' said Stemp. He reached into the inside pocket of his coat and drew out a sheaf of papers. 'These are from Mr Dobbs in Rye, reverend. He asks if you could be so good as to sign them and send them back with the prison van.'

Although only twelve miles away, Rye was in a different county; the lord lieutenant of Sussex as well as the local magistrates had to be notified of the transfer of any prisoner from one jurisdiction to another. Hardcastle read the papers through swiftly, took up the pen and ink the gaoler offered, and signed. 'Where is he?'

'This way, reverend.'

The cell was about ten feet square, with a cot, a small wooden table and a stool. The only light came from a single high barred window. The prisoner sat on the cot, rubbing his wrists, and Hardcastle saw they had been chafed raw by manacles.

'Stemp!' he called, raising his voice. 'Why was this man in irons?'

'He tried to run when they came to pick him up in Rye, reverend,' came the response. 'Mr Dobbs advised there was a chance he might try to escape during the journey here.'

The rector looked back at the prisoner. 'Is this true?'

The man looked up, face dark in shadow. 'When the men came for me in Rye, yes. I tried to get away.'

The prisoner spoke carefully, like a man who has good English but is perhaps unused to speaking it. 'Bring a light,' Hardcastle said to the gaoler.

Two tallow dips were brought and lit. In the smoky light the rector looked at the man on the cot. About middling height, he thought, though difficult to tell when he is sitting down. Dark skin; but not that much darker than that of a sailor or a Jamaica planter. Dark eyes, with surprisingly long lashes; densely curling dark hair, straight nose, firm mouth and just a hint of the strong Rossiter jaw. There was enough facial resemblance between this man and young William Rossiter to make the family connection beyond doubt.

He pulled out the stool and sat down, still in his cloak. 'What is your name?'

'Samuel Rossiter,' said the other man, his voice dull.

'I am the Reverend Hardcastle, justice of the peace. Do you know why you have been brought here?'

'No.'

'Have you a sister named Emma?'

'Yes.'

'I will make this simple,' said Hardcastle. 'Emma Rossiter was murdered on the twenty-fifth of December last, at New Hall in St Mary in the Marsh. I am charging you with her murder. What have you to say?'

'I have killed no one,' said the other man, a note of passion coming into his voice.

Hardcastle nodded. 'Where were you on the twenty-fifth of December?'

'I was in London.'

'Your landlord says he last saw you on the twenty-fourth, the day before. He did not see you again after that.'

'I cannot help that. I was in London. I was waiting for Emma.'

'Oh? Where was she?'

'I did not know. She had gone, and I was waiting for her to return.'

'You knew where she had gone, Samuel. You knew she had gone to New Hall. You went after her, didn't you? And you caught up with her somewhere along the way.'

'No.'

'You joined her, and the two of you travelled on together to New Hall. And there on Christmas Day, you quarrelled with her, and you killed her.'

'No.'

'You hit her over the head with a blunt object. She was stunned, but she was still alive. She staggered outside, and you took her to the horse pond, and there you pushed her into the water and let her drown. Or did you hold her head under, to make certain?'

'No! I have never been to New Hall! *And that was not my sister!*'

The prisoner sat, body tense as a coiled spring; he had clenched his fists, but had not otherwise moved. His eyes, burning, stared into the rector's face. Hardcastle stared back, waiting for the other man's gaze to drop. Eventually, he said, 'If you have never been to New Hall, how would you know whose the body was?'

'I read in the newspaper. It said the dead woman was of dark colour, like me.'

'So?'

'Emma is not dark. Her skin is pale. She can pass easily for a white person.'

The rector paused. It was possible. He knew little about race, apart from the detestable theories of Dr Blumenbach, the publication of which had nearly made him resign his membership of the Royal Society; but he knew of cases of siblings of mixed race where one inherited the skin colour of the mother and the other that of the father.

'If you did not kill Emma,' he said, 'then where is she now?'

'I don't know.'

'Why were you in Rye?'

Silence.

'Was it you who went to the lookers' hut? Were you meeting someone there?'

Silence.

'Did you put the holly on the graves at St Mary?'

Silence.

'Mr Rossiter,' said the rector, 'I have circumstantial evidence suggesting that, as I said, you went to New Hall with your sister, where you killed her in the manner I have described. You deny this. But if you are innocent, you will have to prove it. You must start by telling me: first, if your sister is still alive as you claim, where we might find her; second, what is your interest in New Hall; and third, why you have continued to loiter around the Marsh after the murder.'

Silence.

'If we can find Emma,' said the rector, 'then she can help you to prove your innocence. And if that happens, you will go free. Tell us where to find her.'

His voice had hardened a little; he had lost patience and that, he realised, was a mistake. Samuel Rossiter looked up, and the fire kindled in his eyes again. 'I would not tell you where to find her,' he said, 'even if I could.'

'Why not, man? Tell us where she is, and you will go free! But if you persist in silence, then there is an excellent chance that you will hang for murder.'

He had lost. Samuel lowered his eyes, and sank into silence once more. Leaving the lights burning, the rector rose and wrapped his coat around him and went out, pulling the cell door firmly shut behind him. In the anteroom he spoke to the gaoler.

'See that he has everything he needs, including lights. Give him some more blankets too, that cell is cold as a tomb, and make sure he has decent meals. Send the bills to me.' He laid a gold guinea on the table. 'And no one is to see him apart from myself. Understood?'

Gaolers were notorious for supplementing their income by allowing the curious to come and view their prisoners, some-times to mock them or taunt them, especially if they were in any way remarkable. But Hardcastle knew that such behaviour would simply drive Samuel Rossiter further inside himself. The only way I will ever get at the truth, the rector thought, is to convince him that he can trust me and that he will receive fair justice at my hands.

He walked outside with Stemp and the New Romney consta-ble. 'What was Rossiter doing in Rye?' he asked.

'Working as an ostler at the George,' said Stemp. 'That's what first roused suspicion; he'd claimed to have experience, but the other grooms realised he hardly knew one end of a horse from another. Then one of them remembered the description that had come around, and sent word to the magistrate.'

The rector nodded. 'Well done, both of you. Have a drink on me at the Ship.'

'That's kind of you, reverend. Sure you won't join us?'

Hardcastle thought about the cold drive to St Mary. He thought about his sister's prattling conversation at dinner, and Rodolpho knocking over the furniture. He thought too about the atmosphere of festering secrecy at New Hall.

He thought about the man in the cell; a fit, healthy young man who should have years of life left to him, and about the fact that it was his duty to gather evidence that would see that young man's life torn away by the hangman's noose. That the prisoner had *probably* deprived someone else of their life did not signify; the concept of an eye for an eye and a tooth for a tooth did not feature large in the rector's ideal of justice.

'Perhaps a small one,' he said.

THE RECTORY, ST MARY IN THE MARSH, KENT.
24th January, 1797.

My lord,

It is my pleasure to inform you that thanks to the good offices of Mr Dobbs, magistrate in Rye, Samuel Rossiter has been apprehended. Mr Dobbs was quite willing to hand him over to my custody, and Rossiter is now lodged in the gaol at New Romney.

I have interviewed him and, as one might expect, he denies committing murder and states his innocence. He also insists that the victim was not, as I believe, his sister Emma. More than this, he was not willing to say. I have left him to cool his heels for a time, and will interview him again at a later date.

His claim that the dead woman is not his sister may be fanciful, or a ruse to throw us off the scent. The fact remains, however, that *someone* was killed, and circumstances continue to suggest that Samuel Rossiter is the likely murderer.

That said, certain recent events raised some questions in my mind about the Rossiter family, and about New Hall. The possibility exists that a member of the Rossiter family might be involved in this affair, even if indirectly. I wonder if I might therefore ask your lordship to undertake some inquiries about them. Specifically, I should like to know the whereabouts of Mr James Rossiter and Mr Joseph Parker on the 24th and 25th of December last. Also, I should be grateful for any information you could garner about the business interests of either man in America. I assume they must have commercial relationships with the merchants of either London or Bristol.

I would be grateful for any information received.

Yr very obedient servant,

HARDCASTLE

'You were very late last night, Marcus,' observed Calpurnia.

'I had business to attend to in New Romney,' said Hardcastle shortly, carving a slice of ham. He had a headache, the product of last night's over-indulgence, and even a punishing morning walk along the dunes had failed to dispel it. He remembered once again why he disliked gin.

'If it was only New Romney, you might have sent word. I was worried when you did not return for dinner.'

'I apologise,' said the rector with his mouth full. 'I forget, often, that you are here. Are you joining me, Calpurnia, or did you come in here just to annoy me?'

The door slammed behind her. The rector continued with his cold collation in silence, eating and thinking about Samuel Rossiter. Five minutes later the door opened again.

'What is it now?'

'I forgot to tell you. Mrs Chaytor called around midday, while you were out for your walk. She said there was no message, and she would call again later.'

'Then why are you telling me now?'

'Mrs Chaytor visits you often, doesn't she? Is the church roof in such bad repair as all that?'

'Will you mind your own blasted business? For God's sake! It's like living with a nagging wife!'

'Perhaps a wife is just what you need,' she said, and slammed the door again. The rector swore, got to his feet, stamped into the hall to fetch his hat and coat, and went off to see Mrs Chaytor.

She received him in the drawing room at Sandy House, as ever, cool and composed. She noticed at once that he had been drinking again, and was sorry.

'What happened?'

He told her about his visit to the gaol. 'Apart from this claim that the dead girl is not Emma, there is nothing new. He asserts he was still in London on Christmas Day, but cannot prove it.'

'Nor can he prove his claim about Emma, of course. What did you make of him?'

He is concealing secrets, certainly. Why he is doing so is a matter for conjecture. It might be guilt. Or,' he continued, 'it might be fear.'

'Or it might be both,' she pointed out. 'When you go to see him again, might I accompany you? A woman's presence might encourage him to speak more freely.'

'It might,' he said, regarding her, 'or it might not.'

'If I find my presence inhibits him, then I will withdraw.'

'Very well. I suppose there is nothing to lose by the attempt.'

'You are welcome,' she said, smiling. 'Meanwhile, I have had a thought. It struck me that we have been concentrating on James Rossiter and Joseph Parker, and have been ignoring the rest of the family. So I invited Miss Rossiter, her mother and Mrs Parker to join me for coffee this morning.'

'What did you make of them?'

'Laure confirmed my earlier impressions of her. Sweet-natured, naïve about some things, intellectually curious, a blue-stocking whose passions are music and literature and art. As you know, I had some doubts about her, but after further acquaintance I *think* she is genuine. Her questions about the murder had no ill intent. She has a natural sympathy for other human beings that will always make her curious about them.'

'I would imagine she quite admires you,' the rector observed.

'I—' Amelia checked. 'It is possible. Antoinette, Mrs Rossiter, is French from Québec, which explains that peculiar accent. She met James in 1760, the year we took Canada from the French. He was an officer in the American militia, quartered in Montréal. The hostility between their nations did not prevent friendship from blossoming between them, and they were married five years later. I don't think she has ever forgiven the English for taking over her country. At all events, she does not like London, or England in general, and wants to go home.'

'Did she say so directly?'

'Frequently, and with emphasis.'

'Does she like New Hall?'

'Her disinterest in New Hall is quite profound. She leaves all decisions about the running of the household to her husband's sister, Mrs Parker.'

'And Mrs Parker?'

'Mrs Parker is trouble,' said Amelia dispassionately. 'She is quite a sweet little woman to look at, with those round apple cheeks and that pepper-and-salt hair, but she has the temperament of a firecracker with a lit fuse. She has an opinion on *everything*, and that opinion is seldom good. She makes poor Laure wince. However, she also gives away little of substance. About the only thing interesting I learned about her is that she and her husband are collectors.'

'Collectors? Of what?'

'Rare and valuable things. Cameos, ancient coins, Roman vases, Cellini bronzes, pictures by Tintoretto and Claude, terracottas by Della Robbia. She wore a set of cabochon rubies that she claimed had once belonged to Elizabeth the Winter Queen. For morning coffee!'

'All of which confirms my opinion that the family are well off.'

'They are, in the vulgar phrase, stinking rich. Edward and Laure both stand to inherit sizeable fortunes. I had a thought about young William. I wondered if being disinherited by his father might have made him resentful; perhaps *he* might be a suspect?'

The rector frowned. 'I hadn't thought of that. But I struggle to see William Rossiter as a murderer, don't you?'

'William Rossiter is like Rodolpho: sweet and gangly and eager to please. When he introduced me to his family last week, he became quite tongue-tied and began to blush.'

'You often have that effect on men,' the rector observed.

'Hush. He is no more a murderer than you or I. Either that, or he is the greatest actor since Gentleman Smith. In any case, he broke with his father – or rather, his father broke with him – and James Rossiter has now adopted him as his son. He too will receive a share of the family fortune, far greater than this piffling inheritance from his own father. Mrs Rossiter was very keen to point this out to me.'

'Do we know what the break was about?'

'Politics. James and Parker supported the rebels, Nicholas the royalists. That is why Nicholas moved to Canada at the end of the war. William chose to side with his uncles against his father.'

'And I will set brother against brother,' the rector said quietly. 'Speaking of which, were you able to learn anything about Edward?'

'He is the apple of his parents' eyes. William idolises him. Aunt Jane dotes on him. He plans to join his Uncle Joseph in the practice of law in Boston.' She paused. 'His sister was not quite so quick to praise him as the others.'

'Sisters don't praise their brothers,' the rector grumbled. 'They knock lumps off them instead. Well done, my dear, for getting so much information out of them.'

'What will you do now?'

'Inform the Rossiters that we have arrested Samuel. They will hear eventually in any case; it is better if they hear first from me.'

The interview with James Rossiter and Joseph Parker took place in the library of New Hall. Its shelves had not yet been stocked with books, but at least the mildew-spotted hunting prints had gone. A huge fire roared in the grate, wood spent prodigiously. Outside the wind blew, moaning through the cold winter afternoon.

'Thank you for telling us this news, reverend,' said James Rossiter. He sat in a high-backed chair with his ebony stick leaning against one arm, flowing white hair reflecting the firelight. 'One of the kitchen girls reported a rumour to that effect this morning, but we were not sure whether to believe it. There is no doubt that this is the boy Samuel?'

'I am certain of it.'

'I've met him,' said Parker, standing by the hearth. The rings on his fingers flickered and sparkled in the light. The buttons on the waistcoat straining over his round belly were jewelled too. 'I can identify him, if need be.'

'Thank you, Mr Parker. If the question of his identity comes into doubt, I will be sure to call on you. For the moment, I am satisfied.'

'What happens next?' asked Rossiter.

'As yet, he has made only a partial statement. I shall continue to interrogate him over the next few days. Hopefully he will make a full confession. He will then be arraigned before a magistrate's court and held in custody until the next assize, where he will be tried.'

'And the victim? Did you discover her identity?'

There was no point in prevaricating any longer. 'It is probable that the victim was Emma Rossiter, his sister. I am sorry to be the bearer of such bad news. The young woman was your niece, even if she was born out of wedlock. This must be a time of grief for you.'

'Niece!' said Parker. 'I'll thank you not to describe her as such in my presence, sir! Those Negro bastards are no kin of ours!'

'Joe!' said Rossiter sharply. 'Lower your voice, for God's sake. And do not speak in such fashion to Reverend Hardcastle. He is only doing his duty.'

Muttering more abuse, Parker turned away and walked towards the window. 'I see I have intruded upon your sensibilities,' said the rector, rising. 'Permit me to take my leave.'

'A moment, reverend,' said the older man, picking up his stick and pulling himself to his feet. 'Let me walk you to the door.' In the hall, Rossiter waited while a white-wigged footman brought the rector's hat and cloak, and then said quietly, 'Joseph and I are old friends. But on the issue of race, we differ. I happen to believe that all men were created equal in the eyes of God, regardless of race. And you are right, those young people are our kith and kin, whether we like it or no.'

'If those are your true feelings,' said the rector directly, 'then why, when they approached your family, did you suggest paying them to go away?'

'Need you ask? I wanted William to come into his inheritance without trouble. But I am also a humane man, or so I like to think. We could have taken the matter to court, but the court would have found in our favour and young Samuel and Emma would then have lost everything. I felt it best to offer them a pension, something that would see them decently settled and comfortably off for the rest of their lives. For the sake of my brother, it was the least I could do.'

'But Mr Parker disagreed.'

'Yes. And to my lasting regret, I listened to him. Here's what bothers me, reverend. If I had pressed my case, and made young Samuel an offer he could accept, they would both now still be alive. Now the girl is dead, and the boy is likely to swing for her murder. That's not an easy thing to have on your conscience, reverend, not at all. I'll be haunted by that, to the end of my days.'

WADSCOMBE HALL, TENTERDEN.
26th January, 1797.

My dear Hardcastle,

I am in receipt of your letter of the 24th inst. Congratulations on apprehending Samuel Rossiter. I have no doubt that you are right and that he is your murderer. My clerk will inform you of the date of the next assize at Maidstone. It would be best if you can continue to hold the prisoner in New Romney if possible, for the gaol at Maidstone remains as overcrowded as ever.

As for your request that I conduct some sort of investigation into the activities and financial affairs of James Rossiter and his lawyer, I can only conclude that you have taken temporary leave of your senses. It is quite out of the question for me to do any such thing. In case I have not made this sufficiently clear already, Rossiter has interests greater than my own; he is untouchable. If you offend him, he will bring us both down.

You have your murderer. Follow the correct procedures according to law, and leave the Rossiters strictly alone.

Yr very obedient servant,

CLAVERTYE

It was one of those cold, hard days when it seemed winter would never end. The rector had been out since dawn. Old Mrs Pickney from Teal Farm had died; the event was not unexpected, but there were family to console and yet more funeral arrangements to be made. And Bill Hayton, the shepherd who had found the footprints at the lookers' hut, was ill; not mortally so, but unable to look after himself. He needed food and blankets and someone to sit with him until the fever passed. Arranging this had taken most of the afternoon, and Hardcastle was only able to spend a few minutes with Letty Murton, the blacksmith's wife, who had given birth to a daughter two days before.

'It's good of you to call round, reverend,' she said, propped up in a chair amid a nest of blankets before the fire, infant in her arms. 'I wanted to arrange the baptism with you, as soon as may be. It's our first, you see,' she said shyly. 'I'd like to see things done properly.'

The Murtons, like virtually all the parish, came to church on just three occasions: weddings, baptisms and funerals. Hardscastle's parishioners took it for granted that they would be available to perform these services for them, and otherwise went their own way. It was the same, he knew, in parishes up and down the land.

'I'd be honoured to baptise your daughter, Letty. Have you chosen a name?'

'We thought Mary, after my mother.'

'A good choice, for a little one to be baptised in Mary's church. Shall we say the fourth of next month?'

He struggled home through twilight and the endless biting wind, pleased that a new life had been called into the world but exhausted in body and spirit. On Monday there would be a magistrate's court, and he had to think further about Samuel Rossiter. Right at the moment, he did not want to think about anything. In his study, he opened the bottle of port that lay in his desk and poured a healthy measure, downed it and poured again. The knocker of the front door sounded, and he groaned and drained the second glass too.

He heard the cheery voice of Biddy answering the door. A moment later she came into the study, Biddy curtseying as she always did. 'Good evening, reverend, sir. Are you at home to Mr Stemp?'

'Certainly. Show him in.'

Stemp entered, pocked cheeks blue with cold. 'Evening, reverend. Sorry to intrude, but I've something to tell you from Jack Hoad. I reckoned you'd want to know right away.'

'What is it, then?'

'Jack was at the Ship in New Romney today, making arrangements for . . . Well, it doesn't matter. But there was a fellow there in the taproom, a stranger asking round for men who'd like to earn good money. Cash in hand, no questions asked. Won't be no trouble, he said, just quick in and out.'

The rector sat up sharply. 'What precisely did he want these men to do?'

Stemp cleared his throat. 'Break into New Romney gaol,' he said, 'and spring Samuel Rossiter.'

Chapter 9

The Frenchman Returns

The Rectory, St Mary in the Marsh, Kent.
27th January, 1797.

By express.

My lord,

I write to you with urgent news. Information has been laid before me which suggests that a person or persons unknown, may shortly attempt to liberate Samuel Rossiter from New Romney gaol.

The constable of New Romney has been warned, and I have sworn in several men of that parish to act as temporary constables. I must, however, emphasise that this is a temporary expedient only. These men cannot be expected to serve for more than a few days; nor am I entirely satisfied that they are reliable.

I have applied to Mr Cole of the Customs service and Mr Juddery of the Excise, asking if they will let me have a few of their men. Given that their services are already overstretched, I doubt they will be able to do so. Anticipating their refusal, I write now to ask you to send me a detachment of East Kent Volunteers. A sergeant and a file of men should suffice.

My warmest thanks for your consideration in this matter,

Yr very obedient servant,

HARDCASTLE

'I realise this is short notice,' said the rector to Mrs Chaytor, 'but I want to speak to him again and find out what lies behind this rescue attempt. Will you come with me?'

'Of course. Wait while I change into something warmer. Lucy! Ask Joseph to bring the gig around, as quickly as he can.'

A few minutes later they were driving down the muddy track to New Romney, the horse's reins resting lightly in Mrs Chaytor's gloved fingers. 'Did Jack Hoad give a description of the man?' she asked.

'"A rough bit of work", according to Stemp. Middle height, broken nose, wearing a fisherman's smock under an overcoat, duck trousers, boots. It could be anyone.' The rector changed the subject. 'We were right about Parker. His dislike of Samuel is based at least in part on the young man's race. He confirmed it himself, in no uncertain terms. Rossiter also told me that he wanted to reach a settlement with Samuel, but Parker opposed him because he objected to Samuel's colour.'

'And Rossiter let him have his way? I wonder why?'

'You are assuming that Rossiter was telling me the truth, which I doubt. "I'll be haunted by that, to the end of my days." Damn him for a hypocrite! He is not in the slightest bit sorry to see Samuel out of the way.' He brooded as the gig rolled along. 'I really do wonder how Rossiter made his money. There will be something wrong there, I'll wager my cellar on it.'

Across the street from the gaol, a man in a shabby overcoat leaned his shoulder on a brick wall, counting coins in his hand. He glanced incuriously at them as Hardcastle tethered the horse.

The gaoler admitted them, bobbing his head to Mrs Chaytor. 'There's a couple more in cells, reverend. There was a bit of an affray in the town last night. But I've kept your fellow on his own.'

'Thank you.' Hardcastle walked through to the cells, leaving Amelia in the anteroom.

Samuel Rossiter was lying on his bunk, hands behind his head, staring at the ceiling. In the cell opposite, two men sat slumped, staring at the rector with bloodshot eyes.

I'll have those two up before me on Monday, Hardcastle thought.

'I want to speak to the prisoner in private,' he said to the gaoler. 'Bring him out front, if you please.'

'As you wish, reverend. You want me to manacle him first?'

'Absolutely not. Bring him out to join the lady and me, and then make yourself scarce.'

Blinking, the gaoler complied. A few minutes later, Samuel Rossiter was ushered into the anteroom where Mrs Chaytor sat, gloved hands in her lap. The prisoner looked at her in surprise. Hardcastle pulled up a bench beside the stove.

'Be seated, if you please, Mr Rossiter. This is Mrs Chaytor.'

He made no further introduction. Rossiter sat slowly, dark eyes wary. He was uncertain as to what was going on, which was precisely what Hardcastle wanted.

'Your friends in this country must think quite highly of you, Mr Rossiter.'

'I have no friends in this country. Only Emma. Have you found her yet?'

'So highly,' said the rector, continuing as if the other man had not spoken, 'that they are offering money to people to break you out of this gaol. They will not succeed, of course, for the militia are coming to mount a strong guard. But it is surprising that anyone should be prepared to go to such lengths, is it not?'

Silence. Mrs Chaytor sat quietly, watching.

'Why would they do that?' the rector asked. 'What makes you so special that it is worth mounting a gaolbreak? That is a serious matter, for even if you were to escape, there would be a hue and cry for you throughout Kent, indeed throughout the country. Every road, every port would be watched. And anyone caught helping you would be liable to serious punishment, perhaps even transportation. Your friends must know that. Yet still they are prepared to take the risk. Why?'

Silence.

'Mr Rossiter,' said Mrs Chaytor softly, 'we can only help you if you tell us the truth.'

Slowly he turned his head towards her. 'I have told the truth,' he said.

'So far, you have told us nothing,' the rector said quietly. 'Mrs Chaytor is right, we must know what really happened. If you do not tell us, then you will hang.'

'I will hang anyway,' said Rossiter. 'A woman was killed, so someone must die. I am a convenient murderer. I am a stranger, and a black man. No one will miss me. Only Emma.' He stared at the rector. 'Where is Emma?'

'You tell me,' said Hardcastle.

'Are you looking for her? No, you are not, are you? *You don't believe me,*' Samuel said desperately. 'But why should you? I am a stranger and a black man. No one cares. Only Emma cares . . .'

For a moment he looked as if he was about to break down, but he mastered himself. 'I shall die here,' he said, half to himself, 'far from home, among strangers, a convicted criminal. And no one will care.'

'Mr Rossiter,' said Mrs Chaytor, her voice still soft, 'it is because we *do* care that we are here. An uncaring judge would leave you to your fate. Reverend Hardcastle is looking for the truth, because he knows that the truth about what occurred will save your life.'

He looked at her again, his dark eyes reading her face. 'The truth about what occurred,' he said after a while. 'How can I tell you, when I myself do not know?'

'Start by telling us what you *do* know,' said the rector. 'When did you leave London?'

'On the twenty-seventh of December. I would have gone sooner, but the mail coaches did not run on the twenty-fifth or sixth. The weather was bad, with snow on the hills. The coach travelled very slowly. I stayed overnight at an inn. The next morning I left the coach and hired a horse. I still travelled very slowly. I am not a very skilful rider.'

'Where did you go?'

'I went to a place called App-el-dore. There I stopped for food. I saw the newspaper . . . I knew at once it was not Emma. But I did not know where Emma was.'

'But you knew she might be in danger,' said Mrs Chaytor. Silence.

'You went to Rye,' she said, 'in hopes of hearing more news, and you took a job at an inn. That was clever of you. Inns are excellent places for hearing news from passers-by.'

'I was not very good at my job,' he said ruefully. 'That is why they caught me.'

'Why did you try to run when the magistrate's men came for you?' asked the rector.

'I was frightened. I did not know who they were. I thought they wanted to kill me, like they had killed that woman at New Hall.'

'Why would anyone want to kill you, Mr Rossiter?'
Silence.

'If the woman who was killed was not Emma, who might she have been?'

Silence.

'Where do you think Emma is now?'

Silence.

'Mr Rossiter, I will ask again. Who would want to rescue you from this gaol? And why? Why are you so important?'

Rossiter stirred slowly. 'I do not know,' he said. 'You said, the militia are coming?'

'They should be here very soon.'

Rossiter nodded once. 'May I warm my hands at the stove?' he asked politely. 'It is quite cold in the cell.'

'That was a damned waste of time,' said the rector as they drove back to St Mary in the Marsh.

'Language,' said Mrs Chaytor. 'I wouldn't say so. It ought to be possible to verify when he left London. The coach drivers and ostlers at Ashford would surely remember him.'

'He may have been trying to establish an alibi. There is nothing to prevent him from having left St Mary on Christmas Day after the murder, returning secretly to London late on the twenty-sixth, and then journeying openly back down to Appledore as he described, taking care to make sure that people noticed him along the way.'

'Is that what you think?'

'My dear Mrs Chaytor, that is what a jury will think. And that is all that matters.'

They crossed a muddy bridge over a sewer, water bubbling under the arch. All the drains on the Marsh were full to the brim from the recent rains. 'If we are to save this boy's life,' Mrs Chaytor said, 'we must find some means of compelling him to tell us all that he knows.'

'You now believe him to be innocent?'

'Whoever killed Emma Rossiter, it was not him. Think about it. He wouldn't have killed her, because she was all he had in the world. Even now, he desperately wants her to be alive. And that was fear we saw in his face, not guilt. He is terribly afraid.'

'Yes. I saw the fear, and also the relief in his face when he knew the militia were coming.'

'Exactly. He doesn't think the people planning the gaolbreak want to release him. He thinks they are coming to kill him.'

The East Kent Volunteers came the following afternoon, ten of them and a sergeant in sodden blanket coats over their red jackets and blue breeches. The rector breathed a sigh of relief, and sat down to write his sermon for the next day. Tonight, he remembered, was the new moon, and the wind had abated; tonight or tomorrow night, the boats would go over the Channel to France. That meant he would be without Stemp's services for a few days. His temporary constables in New Romney were likely to disappear too.

On Monday, at the New Romney magistrate's court, Samuel Rossiter would be arraigned for the murder of Emma Rossiter. The process would be a short one. He would read out the formal charge, and then ask Rossiter for his plea. The young man would of course plead not guilty, and Hardcastle would commit him for trial at the Maidstone Assizes on 15th March. There, unless he could mount a strong defence, he would be found guilty on the basis of circumstantial evidence, and soon after he would be taken out to Penenden Heath and hanged.

'Damn,' said the rector slowly. 'Damn, damn.'

Everything Samuel Rossiter had done – his journey to Romney Marsh, his behaviour at Appledore, his hiding at Rye and, especially, his attempt to flee from the Rye magistrate's men – could be construed as suspicious; and, thought Hardcastle, that is exactly how a prosecuting barrister *will* construe it. Samuel's only defence was his own testimony. But the jury would view him as a murderer and a sororicide, and race would doubtless enter the picture too; nothing he said in his own defence would be believed. Samuel was indeed a convenient murderer, as he himself had acknowledged. The only thing that might save him would be verifiable proof that Emma Rossiter was not dead; but even then, there was still a dead young woman buried in his churchyard, and someone must have killed her.

But the rector believed beyond doubt that the woman in the ground in St Mary's churchyard *was* Emma Rossiter. He put no faith in Samuel's statement that Emma was so fair she could pass for white; she was lighter skinned than Samuel himself, that was all. Everything else they knew, including the timing of her departure from London, pointed to her being the woman who was killed at New Hall.

He looked at the port bottle, and looked away again. This was not a time to hide from the world.

Hardcastle took the service on Sunday as usual. The Rossiter family and servants came, listened politely, put money in the collection plate and departed with gracious words of thanks for another fine sermon. James Rossiter lingered.

'Is there any further news?'

'The affair is all but done. He still has not confessed, though I hope to make him do so. But the evidence is strong enough to hang him, I fear.'

'This is a truly tragic affair,' said Rossiter quietly. 'Thank you, reverend, for handling it in such a sensitive manner. I am grateful to you.' He departed, limping on his ebony stick. Hardcastle watched his retreating back.

He was in the habit of taking tea with Miss Godfrey and Miss Roper, his most loyal parishioners, once every month or so, and that afternoon he called around at their tumbledown cottage near the southern end of the village. They were alone, their two nieces having left them shortly after New Year. They welcomed him in with pleasure, Miss Godfrey fussing and Miss Roper twittering, and served him tea spiked with a large quantity of brandy and ginger cake so over-baked that it crumbled into dust in his fingers. Then they sat and gossiped, he listening with half his mind while the other half thought about tomorrow.

Something they said made him sit up a little. 'Old Mrs Rossiter? You mean, Mrs Amélie Rossiter, James Rossiter's mother who is buried in the churchyard? I did not know you knew her.'

'Oh, yes,' said Miss Godfrey, pouring more brandy into the teapot. The bottle glugged in her hand. 'We moved to St Mary in the Marsh not long before she died. Let me see, Clara, was it 'sixty-seven, or 'sixty-eight?'

'I feel quite certain it was 'sixty-eight,' said Miss Roper. 'It was the summer we had those frightful thunderstorms; do you remember, Rosannah?'

'That was definitely in 'sixty-seven,' said Miss Godfrey. 'I cannot say that we knew Mrs Rossiter well, but we called on her a few times, and she on us before her illness made her too infirm to go out. She was very amiable, very pleasant. She was French, you know, from a Huguenot family, the Mirabeaus. The men of New Hall seem to make a habit of marrying French women,' she went on thoughtfully, as if not at all certain this was a good thing.

'Was she then a widow?'

'Oh, yes, and had been for many years. Her husband died not long after all that unpleasantness in 'forty-five. The family were very down at the heels by the time we came here. New Hall was *quite* shabby, and one got the feeling there was very little money about.'

The rector frowned. 'How strange. Did her sons not support her?'

'Well, you see, both boys had gone to America,' said Miss Godfrey. 'I think she may have received a little money from time to time from the older son, Mr Nicholas. She never spoke of Mr James, did she, Clara?'

'Not at all, in my hearing,' said Miss Roper. 'I think there must have been a falling out between them, don't you?'

This was proving to be a richer seam of information about the family than any he had struck so far. He wondered why he had not thought of talking to Miss Godfrey and Miss Roper before now. 'Were there any other children, or family?'

'Let me see,' said Miss Godfrey. 'It was such a long time ago. There were two daughters, sisters of Mr Nicholas and Mr James. Jane married Mr Parker, of course, and there was another: Martha? Mary?'

'I feel quite certain it was Martha,' said Miss Roper, pouring more tea.

'Then it was undoubtedly Mary,' said Miss Godfrey firmly. 'She married, I think perhaps not very well, and moved to Ireland. My memory is that Mrs Rossiter was unhappy with both her daughters' marriages. Well, one can see why, what with Jane marrying the son of the family solicitor. It was hardly what she would have had in mind for her eldest daughter.'

'Was that the whole of the family?' asked the rector.

'Oh, no. Amélie's husband had siblings too. There was a brother who I seem to recall died childless, and there were twin sisters. Now that I think of it, one of them married a Frenchman too.'

'Heavens above!' exclaimed Miss Roper. 'What *is* this fascination with the French?'

'It is said that the French make love beautifully,' commented Miss Godfrey.

'Then make love with them by all means, but don't *marry* them! What are these women thinking of?'

A combination of brandy and rapidly assimilated information was making the rector's head whirl.

'Ladies,' he said, 'I am indebted to you. And now I fear I must take my leave, as I have many affairs to attend to. Your company, as always, has been most charming.'

The arraignment took place the following day, Monday 30th January. The hearing lasted for two minutes. The clerk of the court read out the charge; Samuel Rossiter entered a plea of not guilty in a quiet, steady voice, and was returned to his cell. Hardcastle, in a foul temper, continued with the business of the court. He handed out swingeing fines to the two men guilty of affray, fined another man for allowing his dogs to run loose, and then examined a case of attempted sheep stealing. There was not enough evidence to secure a conviction, but Hardcastle warned the defendant that if he was caught a second time he would be transported to Botany Bay.

Old Lottie Strange was brought before him, charged with intoxication and bad behaviour in a public place. 'Why pick on me?' shouted Lottie, her one remaining front tooth shining yellow in the light. 'Every bugger in the town was drunk that night! 'Course they were, there was a run on! People were pissing gin!'

'Don't answer back to the magistrate,' warned the clerk of the court.

'You can fuck off and all!' snapped Lottie.

'Silence!' roared the rector. 'Mrs Strange, you are in contempt of court. I sentence you to one day's imprisonment. And if you repeat the offence, I will have you flogged down the high street! Do I make myself clear?'

Afterwards he was ashamed of himself. He knew he would never have carried out the threat; he abhorred the practice of publicly flogging women, which all too often turned into a spectator sport with unpleasant sexual overtones. Lottie was always rude, to everyone – that was why she had so few teeth – and losing his temper with her was pointless. He knew he would not have done so, were it not for Samuel Rossiter.

Driving back to St Mary, the rector turned in at the Star. The common room was empty, for it was still only mid-afternoon. 'Strong ale,' he said to the landlord.

'Coming up, reverend.' Luckhurst pushed the tankard across the bar and took Hardcastle's money. 'Bad day?' he asked.

'Yes.'

'About that young fellow, is it? They say he killed his sister and all. Even so, Josh says he's quite a well-mannered lad.'

Everyone knew that today was the day of the arraignment; everyone knew everything in St Mary. 'He is,' said the rector. 'However, it is out of my hands now.'

It was indeed out of his hands, and had been since the arraignment was concluded. In early March a prison van would arrive to take Samuel Rossiter to Maidstone, and the chapter would be closed. Time to get on with our lives, the rector thought.

The door opened and Joshua Stemp came in. He looked weather-beaten and tired, his pockmarked cheeks a little sunken. 'I've got some bad news, reverend,' he said quietly.

The rector motioned him away from the bar and they went and sat down next to the fire. 'There was a run night before last,' Stemp said directly. 'The lads went over to France as usual and met with the other side near Wee Meroo. The Frenchies were nervous as cats when they arrived. The lads didn't take any notice at first, they thought the Frenchies were just worried about the Mary Josies.'

The *maréchaussées* were the French constables; *gendarmes*, the Republican government now called them. Their duties included the prevention of smuggling, a task at which they were about as successful as the Customs and the Excise services; which was to say, not at all. 'Go on,' said the rector.

Stemp sipped the gin the rector had bought him. 'But that wasn't it at all. Bertrand, the leader of the Frenchies, started talking to some of the lads while the boats were loading. He said they'd had to make a run of their own earlier this month, a special one, not a regular thing. Some big bastard from Paris showed up with a warrant to commandeer two boats for a trip across the Channel. When one of the lugger captains refused, the fellow from Paris had him shot on the spot. Killed him dead. He had a wife and kiddies, too.'

'Revolutionary justice,' said the rector. 'What were they ferrying across the Channel to England?'

'French spies,' said Stemp.

Preoccupied as he was by the matter of Samuel Rossiter, the rector did not at first take in what Stemp had said. Then he stared at his constable. '*What?*'

'Eight of them, four in each boat. The big fellow was in Bertrand's boat. Landed each group in a different destination; he wouldn't tell us where. They were scared to death. There was a half moon, and the boats were visible out on the water like it was daylight, and there were two of our brigs upwind, riding off Dover. How they weren't spotted, he said he'd never know.'

Eight of them; four in each boat. In a small corner of his mind, the rector wondered if Stemp had noticed his earlier slip of the tongue. The rest of him was concentrating on this new emergency. 'Half moon? Waxing or waning?'

'Waxing. Don't you remember, we had a couple of clear nights, around the seventh and eighth, before the weather drew in again.'

'That was three weeks ago,' said the rector, low-voiced. '*Eight French agents*. My God, they could be anywhere.'

Stemp shook his head. 'Looks like old Bill Haytor might have been right after all. About that lookers' hut.'

'You said the French smugglers were still nervous. Why?'

'The big fellow said this was just the beginning. More agents were coming, and the French captains would be obliged to take them across the Channel too. Bertrand and his lads don't like running spies, you see, neither side does. It's risky, and there's no profit in it.' Stemp looked at the rector. 'I've saved the best for last.'

'What is it?'

'Bertrand had seen the big bastard before, and knew his name. Care to guess what it is, reverend?'

'Foucarmont,' the rector said grimly. Now he had both murder and espionage on his hands.

Chapter 10

The Prisoner's Tale

One had to hand it to Clavertye, Hardcastle thought: when action was required, his lordship moved like a scalded cat.

Hardcastle's message, written in haste on the afternoon of the 30th, brought a swift response. Clavertye himself came sweeping down to the Marsh the following morning, riding his fastest horse; his carriage, with baggage, servants and secretary, was not far behind. Another column of East Kent Volunteers came quick-marching down the Ashford road, a full company this time, fife squealing and colours waving in the north wind. After establishing his headquarters in New Romney, astride the two most important roads in the Marsh, the deputy lord lieutenant sent messengers racing away to the north and west and south-west, summoning men to a council of war.

Hardcastle, filing into the common room of the Ship with Stemp behind him, saw that most of the others had already arrived. Coates, the mayor of New Romney, was there wearing his chain of office and a look of worry on his solemn face. A red-coated captain of volunteers stood leaning against the wall, smoking a cigar. Hardcastle saw several of his fellow magistrates, including Maudsley from up-country, and a group of men in working clothes, some of whom he recognised as parish constables from across the Marsh and the hills behind. Juddery of the Excise service and Cole, supervisor of the Customs men, stood on opposite sides of the room, ignoring each other in their normal way.

Half the men in this room probably have connections with smuggling, Hardcastle thought; Maudsley certainly does. And of course, the Customs and the Excise are notorious for their dislike of each other. It will be interesting to see whether Clavertye can get them all to work together.

Lord Clavertye stood facing them at one end of the room, tall and commanding, one hand tucked into his waistcoat. 'I expect you all know each other,' he said without preamble. 'Although some may not have met Captain Austen of the East Kent Volunteers.' Captain Austen removed the cigar from his mouth and bowed.

'I don't need to tell you how serious this matter is,' Clavertye continued. 'At least eight French agents were landed on this coast three weeks ago, and there may be others about whom we don't yet know. It is likely that an attempt will be made to land more agents in the near future. The leader of these men is Camille de Foucarmont, the French spy and murderer who, as I need hardly remind you, evaded our justice last year.'

A murmur rippled around the room at the name. 'What Foucarmont's intentions are, we can only surmise. He and his men may be intending to attack our installations, powder mills, or the navy yard at Deal. They may plan to incite the traitors and sympathisers among our own folk: members of the London Corresponding Society and the United Englishmen and that ilk. Or,' and he paused for emphasis, 'this may be the prelude to an invasion.

'Gentlemen: the nation is in peril. The storms at the turn of the year blew our ships off their blockade stations, and now a sizeable proportion of the French fleet has escaped from Brest and is at sea. They carry several thousand troops with them, and their destination is the British Isles. The Spanish fleet has also put to sea. The most likely prospect is that the enemy will try a landing in Ireland. In that event, the French will be looking to create distractions elsewhere – such as here, in Kent – that will tie down our own troops and force us to divert men and supplies from our army in Ireland.

'That must not happen. These agents must be found and rounded up, at once.'

Heads nodded around the room, serious and sober. Swiftly, Clavertye gave them their orders. 'Austen, your men will patrol the roads. Set up watch points at all key junctions; the local men will show you where. Search and interrogate *anyone* acting suspiciously. Juddery, Cole: we'll need some of your men for the watch points too. Take the rest and start searching the places where these men might hole up. Barns, lookers' huts, any isolated structures. Parish constables: you'll help guide these patrols, and I want a local man stationed at every watch point too. Your role is vital; you know the local people, know their names and faces, and can help identify strangers. This is far more important work than catching smugglers or petty local rivalries. We need to work together to catch these men who are aiming to destabilise our country and bring their foul revolution to our shores.

'Headquarters will be here, at the Ship, and I or one of my deputies will always be here. Inform me *immediately* of any developments, no matter what the time, day or night. Any questions? Then, gentlemen, to work.'

The gathering began to break up. Clavertye caught the rector's eye. 'Hardcastle, a moment, if you please.'

They walked into the parlour that Clavertye had taken over as his office; his secretary was there, unpacking his writing desk, while another servant pinned a map of Romney Marsh and the inland area to the wall. 'I've received some new information on your murderer,' said Clavertye directly. 'I'm afraid the matter is rather more serious than you or I suspected.'

'Oh? In what way, my lord?'

'It has become apparent that there is a connection between your Samuel Rossiter and Foucarmont. Accordingly, I am having Rossiter transported up to Maidstone tomorrow, under heavy escort in case his friends try again to rescue him. Once I have Foucarmont and his gang in custody, I'll interrogate Rossiter myself more fully.'

The rector rubbed his chin. 'Do I understand you correctly? You are seriously suggesting that Samuel Rossiter is in league with French agents? That he himself is a French spy?'

'Precisely. Does it not strike you as suspicious that he arrived on the Marsh just before the French agents were landed? And that he went straight to New Hall, where Foucarmont formerly had his lair? It was clearly a *rendezvous*, no doubt previously arranged, all parties secure in the knowledge that New Hall would be empty and there would be no witnesses. The caretaker, I've no doubt, was lured away.

'Frankly, Hardcastle, I am surprised you didn't think of all this before. However, we may still be in time. Whatever scheme Foucarmont may have in mind, we'll catch him.'

'May I ask what led your lordship to this conclusion?' asked Hardcastle.

'What does anyone know about Rossiter, before he turned up in Montréal two years ago?'

'Nothing. He has told us nothing.'

'Exactly. He could have been anywhere before that, couldn't he? Even in France itself, come to that. That's only speculation, of course. But we do know that when Rossiter arrived in London, he went straight to Marylebone, which has a large black population and also a large number of French *émigrés* living cheek by jowl. The French community is riddled with enemy spies. Foucarmont had lived there, did you know?'

'No, I did not.'

'And, the London Corresponding Society is prominent in Marylebone too. Mark this,' said Clavertye, raising a finger, 'the house where Rossiter and his sister stayed is owned by a prominent member of that Society. Did you know that?'

Hardcastle shook his head.

'The London Corresponding Society is a nest of vipers,' said Clavertye passionately. 'Recently, they've been recruiting members of the coloured community by pretending to support the abolitionist cause. There's a man who goes by the name of Olaudah Equiano, who campaigns against slavery but who is also a member of the Corresponding Society and encourages his fellow blacks to join. Oh, and he's a Methodist, of course. I need hardly add that Marylebone is also rotten with Methodism.'

'My lord; how do you know all this?'

'It is my duty to prepare the case against Samuel Rossiter. As part of that task, I inquired again of the chief magistrate of London and asked him to investigate Rossiter's connections there. It turns out Samuel Rossiter met Equiano several times, and other members of the Society too: Thelwall, Binns, Felix Vaughan, all of them suspect. If Rossiter wasn't already a French agent when he arrived, then he was almost certainly recruited into French service while in London.'

'Your lordship has been most diligent,' said Hardcastle, a dangerous note creeping into his voice. 'May I inquire as to why you did not see fit to pass this information on to me?'

'Because it was none of your damned business,' said Clavertye shortly. 'Your task was to investigate the circumstances of the murder and prepare the arraignment. You have done so. The matter is now in my hands.'

'But you have clearly been working on this for some time.'

'I set the investigation in motion some days ago, yes.'

'You deceived me!'

'Don't indulge in melodrama, Hardcastle. I have been doing my duty, just as you have been doing yours. What Rossiter did in London is outside your jurisdiction.'

'Damn all that! The murder took place in St Mary in the Marsh. That makes it my responsibility!'

'Yes, it was,' said Clavertye. 'It is no longer. Your role in this business is done. Look here, Hardcastle, don't take on about this. You've done very well. You did a splendid job in detecting that attempted gaolbreak and preventing it. Without your prompt action, Rossiter might be out consorting with his *sans-culotte* brethren even as we speak. But don't you see? The man who tried to organise that gaolbreak must have been one of Foucarmont's men.'

Anger still stirred blackly in the rector's mind, but it was anger at himself now, for being duped. 'It occurs to me,' said Clavertye, 'that given Foucarmont's connections with the place, you might care to warn the Rossiters at New Hall? I doubt he would try to harm them, but there is always a chance he or his men might come snooping around there again.'

'I did so before coming here,' Hardcastle said shortly. He had warned Mrs Chaytor, too, and Mrs Kemp; whatever business had brought Foucarmont back to New Hall might also include the settling of old scores. He himself carried his pistol, loaded and primed, in the pocket of his cloak. He said, 'Another thought occurs, my lord. If Samuel Rossiter is one of Foucarmont's men, perhaps we should interrogate him again, now, before he suspects that we know more of him. He might know something that will help us track Foucarmont down.'

Clavertye, examining the map on the wall, paused with his hand on his chin. 'Very good idea,' he said after a moment. 'Yes, let's do that.'

Frankly, my lord, I'm surprised you didn't think of this before, the rector thought sarcastically. 'Let me deal with him, my lord. I know the man better than you, and I think I know how to get him to open up.'

'Good, good. Carry on.'

The rector saw himself out. The common room was empty now, all the soldiers and constables and Preventive Men gone to their respective tasks. By now, Joshua Stemp would be on his way to alert the rest of St Mary in the Marsh and warn people to be on the lookout for strangers.

These are bleak times, the rector thought. *We suspect everyone; we see in every stranger's face the eyes of a traitor. Where there is no treason, we invent it; we spin ropes of conspiracy, and bind them around ourselves. We feed our fears with more fear. How much of Clavertye's web of treason, encompassing radical politics, French émigrés, Methodists and the poor folk of Marylebone, was real? How much was the product of imaginations fever-bright with speculation and fear as rumours of invasion grew?*

He stepped outside, turning up his collar. Across the street a man in a mud-splashed black cloak stood holding the reins of a horse, apparently waiting for someone. *That fellow had better watch it,* Hardcastle thought. *Standing in a public place will be a treasonable offence before long . . . Or is it me? Am I the naive one, the innocent? What if these conspiracies and fears are real? There* are *French agents working among us. Foucarmont* did *escape justice and has returned to haunt us.*

Then he stopped dead. *Why, if Samuel Rossiter was a French spy, would he murder his own sister? What had the two things to do with each other?*

And what about that damned boot? Why pull a boot from the foot of the sister you have murdered, and then leave it and her lying there? And why then put holly on her grave? Why? *Why?*

The gaoler admitted him, touching his forehead in salute. In his cell, Samuel Rossiter lay immobile on his cot, staring at the ceiling. Hardcastle unlocked the door and sat down on the wooden stool. 'Sit up,' he said.

Slowly Rossiter sat, swinging his legs to the floor, leaning forward with his elbows on his knees. In the dim light, his brown eyes watched the rector warily.

'This is your last chance,' the rector said. 'If you can convince me that you are innocent, then you might yet escape the gallows. Otherwise, death awaits you, as surely as night follows the sunset.'

'Why does this matter to you?' The question was put simply, almost innocently; there was not even a hint of challenge.

'Because I believe in justice,' Hardcastle said, 'and I want to see justice done. Yes, I believe you to be guilty. But you have asserted your innocence over and over again. Tell me now why I should believe you, rather than the evidence I have before me.'

Silence, while Rossiter stared at the floor. Then he raised his head again. 'Where do you wish me to begin?' he asked.

It was so unexpected that Hardcastle was caught off guard for a moment. 'Let us begin with where and when you were born, and to what parents.'

'I was born in the city of New York in the year 1772. My parents were Nicholas and Martha Rossiter. Emma is my twin sister, born a few minutes before me. That makes her my older sister.' A smile, the first the rector had ever seen from him, crossed his lips for a moment. 'She never lets me forget it.'

'Your mother was a slave?'

'She had been a slave, but she was set free. She was a free woman when she married our father.'

'What happened to her?' None of this was relevant, of course, but at least the young man was talking.

'She died. She was killed.' Rossiter paused, his eyes far away now. 'She had taken Emma and myself to visit her family, the Washburns, in Pennsylvania. They had opposed her marriage to my father, thinking that she should marry one of her own folk and not mix with white people. After our birth, she went to see them in hopes of making a reconciliation, and carried us with her. I remember none of this; we were not yet one year old, and so have no memories of our mother.'

'What happened?'

'The Shawnee attacked the settlement where the family lived. Martha, our mother, was killed along with others. The Shawnee warriors found Emma and me abandoned, and took us back to their tribe.'

The Shawnee were, presumably, some sort of American Indians. Suddenly fascinated in spite of himself, Hardcastle said, 'What then?'

'We were given to a woman who had lost her own children in a raid by Americans. She raised us as her own son and daughter. She herself had been at a mission for a time, and spoke English. She taught us the language, thinking we should be able to speak it and read it, as it was the language of our birth.' His face in the dim light was bleak with deep-wrought sorrow. 'Her name was Ahneewakee. She was the only mother I have ever known.'

Wherever this narrative was going, it must be allowed to continue to its end. Hardcastle waited in silence while the young man mastered his emotions.

'She died,' Rossiter continued, 'when we were eighteen years old. As she entered her final illness, she told us about who we were, and where we had been found. After her death, we mourned her. Then we consulted the other people of the tribe. We always knew that we were not a real part of the tribe. After much talk, they agreed that we should go back to our own folk. The Shawnee had been good friends to us, so it was not easy to go. But . . . we wanted family, and with Ahneewakee gone, there was no one to take her place.' Looking at the floor, he said, 'We wanted to belong.'

This time Hardcastle spoke. 'Did you find your mother's family?'

'We found our mother's sister, Aunt Rachel. She survived the raid that killed Martha. The settlement had been rebuilt, and she still lived there. She had thought we were dead, as everyone did. But she accepted us and said we must make our home now with her. She was a good woman, and she loved us very much, and we loved her too. We lived with her and worked the land alongside the other people of the settlement for . . . I must think. It would be about five years.

'It was Aunt Rachel who told us what our real names were, that we were called Samuel and Emma. Before then, we had only the names Ahneewakee had given us. From Aunt Rachel, too, we learned about our father. Emma was very curious about him; more curious than me. But Emma is always more curious, more questing. That is why she gets into trouble, and I have to come and rescue her. It was always the same, even when we were children.

'Then our aunt died. It has been our history; those whom we love, die.'

'I am sorry,' said Hardcastle gently.

'It is kind of you to say so. When Aunt Rachel died, we took what little money we had and went to New York to find our father. Of course, much had changed. There had been the great war, and now the Americans were independent. Many who did not support the new government had fled. Father was one of them. We did not know at first where he had gone, but we learned that our uncle and his family still lived in Boston. We went there to find them.'

'And did you?'

'Oh, it was quite easy. Mr James Rossiter, our uncle, is an important man. But we were not allowed to see him. Instead we saw Mr Parker, who was very rude to us and called us the horrible names that many white people use. He denied that our parents had married. He said that we were . . . bastards, and that we must keep away from the other Rossiters. But he also told us that Father was still alive and living in Montréal. So we decided to go there to find him. We walked much of the way.'

The rector's knowledge of American geography was hazy. 'That must have been a very long way.'

'It took us three weeks. It was not difficult. From our time among the Shawnee, we were used to walking. We came to Montréal, and there we found our father. He had made a new life for himself as a trader in furs, and he had prospered in Montréal. Indeed, it seemed he was now very wealthy.'

There was a long pause while the young man remembered. 'That was a happy time,' he said finally. 'Father welcomed us with tears of joy. All through the years, he had thought we were dead. But he recognised us at once. He said I looked very like our mother. And we could prove we were his children, for Emma had the earrings she had been given at her christening.

'He took us into his home and introduced us to everyone as his daughter and son. Despite our colour, people did not find this difficult to believe, as Emma looks very like him, and I have my father's chin.' This was said proudly. 'He loved us as Aunt Rachel had loved us, kindly and gently. I think . . . I think that we made his life complete again, after a long time of much sadness.

'He gave us presents, all the time. Almost every day, there was a new gift waiting for us. Sometimes, we were moved to protest at his generosity. "Father," we would say, "this book, this trinket, it is too much." "No," he would say, "this is my way of making up for the lost years."

'But Father was nearly seventy years old. His health was failing. When he knew the end was near, he called his lawyer and made a will. He had remarried after our mother died. This wife too was now dead, but there was a son from that second marriage. Father and his son William, our half-brother, had become estranged because of the war, and what happened after it. So, Father made a new will leaving everything to Emma and myself. We were uneasy about this, and felt it was not fair to William. But Father said he would be well provided for. Uncle James, Father's brother, would look after him. And then Father died.'

'Why did you decide to come to England?'

'Montréal was sad without Father. We did not know what to do. And with Father gone, people were . . . less kind to us. And also, there was curiosity. During his last weeks, Father talked often about the old days in England. I think he regretted coming to America, even though he became wealthy. He missed his home. He talked about New Hall sometimes, and he spoke of his mother, our grandmother, who had lived there. When we discovered he had left us the house in his will, we were intrigued.'

He was thinking hard now, remembering, and also still trying to hold back emotion. Often there were pauses between sentences.

'So we set out. We had money now, and could afford to travel in comfort. We booked passage on a ship, the *Esperance*. We had never before seen the sea . . . It was cold, and there were many storms, for it was late in the year. I remember being frightened by the first storm, for the waves were like moving mountains. Emma laughed at it all; she thought it was wonderful. After a while I became resigned to it.'

'When did you arrive?'

'In early November. We landed at Bristol, and took the coach from there to London. Father's will had instructed us to contact his lawyer Mr Parker, the father of that unpleasant man in Boston. We had an address for this Mr Parker in London, so we travelled there. A lady at an inn in Bristol had given us the address of a rooming house in Mary-le-bone, and we went there and rented rooms. I then set off to find Mr Parker in Lincoln's Inn. But a man there told me Mr Parker was dead.

'This was a setback,' Samuel said earnestly. 'We did not know what to do next. We did not understand how the law worked. We were afraid that with Mr Parker now dead, no one would know about the estate. But, at the same time, we were not unhappy. We had plenty of money, and London was interesting. We met many people, and most of them were kind to us.'

'Did you ever meet a man named Olaudah Equiano?' Hardcastle asked.

'Oh, yes,' Samuel said at once. 'He was very helpful to us, and introduced us to many of his friends. Mr Equiano is a great man. He was once a slave himself, and now he is fighting to free others from slavery. He argues for the abolition of the trade in slaves. Emma and I respect Mr Equiano very much.'

'And did he ever mention the London Corresponding Society to you? He, or any of the others you met?'

The young man's brow wrinkled. 'I do not recall the name.'

'It is not important. There are many French people living in Marylebone. Did you associate with them?'

'Oh, yes. They are poor people,' Samuel explained, the earnestness back. 'They were forced to flee from France when the Revolution broke out, just as Father was forced to flee from America. Often they have nothing but the clothes they wear, and sometimes they are even reduced to pawning their clothes, to raise money for food. It is very sad to see people in such misery.'

Clavertye, you are wrong, the rector told himself. This boy is no more a French spy than I am. 'What happened next?'

'Mr Equiano explained that when Mr Parker died, his affairs would have been taken over by another lawyer. He helped us to trace Mr Jessington. I went to see him, but learned from him that there was another will. The estate, the house, had all been given to our half-brother William, Father's estranged son. I protested that this was wrong. I fear I became angry. I know I should not have done so, for it was surely not Mr Jessington's fault. Emma and I then went back to Mr Equiano for advice, and he told us what we must do to challenge the other will in court, and prove our case.

'Then Mr Parker came, the Mr Parker we had met in Boston. He was rude to us once again, and accused us of following the family. Until then, we had not realised that our uncle and aunt and their family were in London at all. He warned that unless we dropped our claim to New Hall and the estate he would – what was the phrase? Darken our daylights. I was very angry, and we exchanged harsh words. He promised to make much trouble for us if we did not do as he said, and then went away.

'Then Emma disappeared. I waited for her all of Christmas Eve, and then it occurred to me she might have gone to New Hall. As I said to you before, I had to wait until the twenty-seventh to travel after her.'

'Can anyone, anyone at all, vouch for your presence in London on the twenty-fifth or sixth?'

Samuel frowned. 'I do not think so,' he said. 'I was on my own, and everyone was quite involved in celebrating Christmas.

There was much drinking. I do not think anyone paid any heed to me.'

'Why did you go to Rye? Why did you stay near the Marsh?'

'I was afraid for Emma. I wanted to be close, so that if she was in trouble, I could help her. I waited and waited for news.'

His eyes were large and dark with sorrow. 'Sir, tell me truly. Is my sister really dead?'

'I fear very much that she is, Samuel.'

'It is so. I feared it, but I did not want to believe it was true. The report in the newspaper gave me hope for a while, when it said she was a dark-skinned woman, but I think the report must have been wrong.'

'I saw the body, Samuel. She was much less dark-skinned than you.'

The young man gave a sudden slow sigh of pain. 'I must accept it,' he said. 'All those who love me, die. But if there is no Emma, then my heart's wish is to die too. She is my twin, the other half of my soul. Without her, there is no life.' He looked at the rector. 'So, you see, I do not mind what happens next.'

'Samuel,' the rector said desperately, 'do not give up hope. There is still the trial to come. We will ensure that you have a good barrister, the best in the country. Do not give up.'

'No,' said the young man softly. 'Do not trouble yourself, sir, I beg you. They may take me and hang me; I do not mind. I will go to the place of the spirits, and there I will find Emma, and we will be happy.

'Thank you for listening to me, sir. My tale was a long one; I hope it did not weary you.'

'Dear God in Heaven,' said the rector. 'He thanked me and apologised for taking up my time. He'll probably apologise to the blasted jury when they convict him, and thank the hangman for putting the noose around his neck.'

'Did you believe him?' asked Mrs Chaytor. They were sitting in her drawing room before the fire, glasses of madeira untouched before them.

'His is an astonishing and compelling story, like nothing I have ever heard. A good barrister could make something of it, I am certain. There is an honesty and intensity about him that will make any jury, no matter how biased, sit up and listen.'

'Marcus.' She knew he hated his name, and only used it in times of stress. 'Did you *believe* him?'

He thought about it for a long time, and then looked her in the eyes. 'Yes,' he said. 'I believed him. Lord Clavertye's accusation shook me, I admit. But I believed him.'

'Lord Clavertye's story is poppycock,' she said astringently. 'People like him see French spies under every bed. He's worse than Miss Roper.'

'Oh?'

'I had them around today, after Stemp called. They were adamant that the invasion would begin tomorrow, and they would then be ravished by hordes of hairy Frenchmen.'

'I am sorry they were so alarmed. I will call on them tomorrow, if I can.'

'I wouldn't say they were alarmed, exactly. More indignant, and in the case of Miss Roper, there was the faintest hint of excitement, too, if I'm not mistaken.' Then, looking at Hardcastle more closely, 'My dear man, you are exhausted.'

'It has been a trying day, one way and another. And I must of course attend on Lord Clavertye tomorrow.' He brooded. 'But this business will not let go of me.'

'Nor me. I suspect neither of us will get much sleep tonight. There is another thing we can do to help Samuel.'

'What is that?'

'Find out who really killed Emma,' said Mrs Chaytor. 'If we can do that, we can then prove his innocence. Forget what Clavertye said. If Samuel is proved innocent of Emma's murder, then this notion that he is a French spy will collapse like a house of cards.'

'And Samuel's assertion that he does not want to live without Emma? Do we respect that?'

'There is not much I do not know about grief. He may well feel that he wants to die; I did. But he will wake up one morning and find that the urge to live is stronger than he had thought. Our task,' said Mrs Chaytor, 'is to ensure that he survives long enough to reach that day.'

Chapter 11

Yorkshire Tom's Coup

Dragged from its winter solitude, Romney Marsh rumbled with activity. Patrols of East Kent Volunteers and Preventive Men tramped the high roads and byroads, backs bent against the north wind. More manned the watch points in the villages and along the roads, stopping and searching carts and wagons and scanning the faces of passers-by. Quiet parties of men swept over the Marsh, searching barns and huts and derelict buildings, looking for places where men on the run might hide.

Trouble began almost at once. The locals did not like strangers and they liked Preventive Men still less. Reactions to the patrols and searches ranged from sullen co-operation to more blatant hostility. By the morning of the first of February, a steady flow of angry people was making its way down New Romney's high street and into the Ship to confront Lord Clavertye. The deputy lord lieutenant had gone to Rye, to meet the authorities in East Sussex and enlist their support for his search; the task of dealing with the complaints and the outrage fell to Hardcastle.

All that morning he sat at a desk in the common room, listening patiently while Clavertye's clerk took notes. Someone complained that searchers had left a gate open so that sheep had escaped; an angry woman accused Preventive Men of stealing a mutton ham she had left hanging in the woodshed. Two men complained of being manhandled at watch points when they refused to be searched; another maintained that the sight of the red coats had frightened his donkey so badly that she had gone off her feed; a very angry man who claimed to have studied law at Oxford insisted that the use of volunteers to search civilian property was illegal under the terms of the Volunteer Act (1794). And so it went.

The most serious incident occurred just outside Dymchurch, when a volunteer pinched the bottom of a fishwife on her way to market and she laid him out cold with a straight right; a punch, reported Captain Austen admiringly, that would have done credit to Daniel Mendoza. The rector sighed.

'Does your man wish to press charges?' he asked.

The captain shook his head. He was a tall, likeable man in his late twenties with pink cheeks and dark cheerful eyes. 'He's too embarrassed. But I fear people are growing resentful of us.'

Hardcastle gestured to the queue of scowling and muttering people waiting to make their complaints. 'So I can see. Can you not compel your men to be more polite in their behaviour? People here are sensitive to grievance already. There is no need to give them provocation.'

'I've done my best, but my men aren't regular soldiers; they don't take kindly to discipline. To be honest, the ones the people really hate are the Preventives. Having them on the watch points is like waving a red flag in front of a bull. Can we at least find something for them to do that will keep them out of the public gaze?'

'I'll tell his lordship when he returns. But I doubt he'll listen.'

'He's more of a talker than a listener, isn't he? Tell me, why is he convinced the French are still here on the Marsh? After three weeks, they could be anywhere in the kingdom.'

'They could,' acknowledged Hardcastle. 'But Foucarmont knows the Marsh country well. His lordship is convinced he will make his base here, even if he sallies out to stir up mischief elsewhere. It is a sound theory.'

It was late before Clavertye returned. Dusk was already darkening the windows of the common room when he strode in, tossing his gloves onto a table and taking off his coat. 'Anything to report, Hardcastle?'

'Apart from a number of annoyed and offended citizens, my lord, no. I am afraid some of the searchers are trampling on people's sensibilities.'

Clavertye snapped his fingers at Mrs Spicer, the landlady, who hurried to pour rum into a glass and make a toddy, then nodded to Hardcastle to follow him into the private parlour that served as his office. Here he turned to the rector. 'To hell with their sensibilities,' he said. 'Do they think the French will respect their rights, or their property, if *they* come?' He sighed, for he was not at heart an unreasonable man. 'Ask the people to be patient. The sooner we find our quarry, the sooner it will be over and they can get on with their lives.'

'And Samuel Rossiter, my lord? You still intend to move him?'

'Yes,' said Clavertye sharply. 'It is too great a risk to keep him here. The prison van will arrive tomorrow. I take it nothing came of your interrogation of him?'

'He told me a great deal,' said the rector. 'Unfortunately, none of it would seem to confirm your theory about him. His connections in London appear to me to be entirely innocent.'

Clavertye regarded him with disfavour. 'I sometimes wonder if you are too soft for this job, Hardcastle,' he said. 'Ah, Mrs Spicer, thank you. This is capital. You will add it to my reckoning?' He sipped the steaming toddy as the landlady departed, and said to the rector, 'You want to believe there is good in everyone. That's your church training, I suppose.'

'And you want to believe that anyone is capable of being a criminal,' said Hardcastle. 'That's your legal training, I suppose.'

They stared at each other, and then Clavertye's face relaxed into a smile. 'And the truth, of course, is that we are both right,' he said. 'Don't worry, Hardcastle. He will have his day in court, his chance to tell his story, and he'll receive his fair portion of justice. You have my word on that.'

Hardcastle inclined his head. 'As for the searches, they must be kept up,' Clavertye went on. 'We're putting pressure on Foucarmont. We'll flush him out soon. I can feel it.'

He was right. The following day, 2nd February, opened with the news that fresh footprints had been found around the lookers' hut near Bill Hayton's cottage. Two more sets of footprints were spotted by a sharp-eyed watcher in the shingle near Dengemarsh, on the other side of Lydd. A farmwife reported seeing men lurking in the fields west of Brookland; there was another sighting at Fairfield. Excise men searching an old stone barn at Cuckold's Corner found the remains of a small fire, though it was clearly several days old; the fire might have been lit by vagabonds, or it might not. Clavertye marked each sighting on his map, nodding confidently.

'See the pattern of the sightings,' he said to his team. 'Notice how they're staying away from the main roads and larger villages. We need to step up our searches in the wilder areas.'

Cole of the Customs protested. 'We're short of men as it is, my lord. There's hundreds of lookers' huts and barns and sheds. It will take weeks to search them all.'

Clavertye turned on him. 'I'm not interested in excuses, Cole. Find Foucarmont. Those are my orders.'

They went, Cole still protesting. Outside, a thin drizzle had begun to fall, mixed with occasional bursts of sleet. Silence fell in the common room, broken only by the occasional crackle of the fire in the hearth. The weather had clearly deterred even the angriest citizens from airing their grievances in person today. The rector sat quietly by the fire, thinking of Samuel Rossiter. Dogs were barking in the distance. After a while he heard the squealing of an ungreased axle, and looked out of the window to see the prison van, a square box with a single barred window on its side, making its way slowly up the street.

The door of the common room slammed open. A messenger, a volunteer in mud-splattered overcoat and breeches, dripping water, stood breathless in the doorway.

'We've spotted two of them, sir! Along the drain between Brenzett and Snargate.'

Clavertye came out of his office at once, followed by his secretary. 'What happened?'

'They were working their way along the sewer, using the bank as cover. When they saw us, they dived into the water.'

'Comb the banks, both sides. They'll have to come out of the water somewhere; find out where.' He turned to the secretary. 'Have the bloodhounds arrived?'

'That's them you can hear, my lord. Also, the prison van has just arrived.'

'Damn! I had forgotten. That complicates matters.'

'What is it?' asked Hardcastle.

'This latest sighting is damned close to the Appledore road. It runs through Brenzett and Snargate, doesn't it? And that's the very route by which I had intended to send the prison van and escort. I'll lay money those fellows Austen's men spotted were waiting to ambush the van and spring Rossiter free. Well, by God, we'll turn the tables on them.'

Orders came quickly to Clavertye's lips, as they always did. He turned to his secretary. 'Tell the commander of the prison van escort to use the coast road. He can then take the turnpike from Dover to Maidstone. And tell him he is not to stop for anyone or anything. Those are my express orders, clear? Then, tell the keeper to take the dogs out to Brenzett.' He turned to the messenger. 'You'll go with the dogs, and relay my orders to Captain Austen. Search both banks of the sewer and find where the French came out of the water. Then get the dogs onto the scent. Off you go.'

Tension and excitement thrummed in the air. Hardcastle listened to the yelping of the dogs and watched Clavertye, his face hard and set, the lamplight glinting off the distinguished silver hair at his temples. He scents a triumph, the rector thought. He anticipates the successful capture of the spies, the stories in the newspapers lauding his skill and determination, the acclamation of society. All will be grist to his political mill.

But the dogs went out and hunted, and the searchers searched until a pink rain-washed sunset faded and twilight drew down. They found nothing.

The rector knocked at the door of New Hall. A footman, immaculate in blue livery and white wig, bowed and took his card, leaving Hardcastle standing in the hall. He waited, noting how completely the staff had managed to erase every trace of Emma Rossiter's blood from the stair. He thought of her brother, manacled and buffeted in the lurching prison van on his way to Maidstone gaol.

The footman returned, bowing. 'If you will follow me, sir?'

Parker, balding and round-bellied, was in the library, standing by the fire. He looked tense. There was no offer of refreshment. 'My apologies for calling unannounced,' said the rector. 'Is Mr Rossiter available?'

'He is resting, sir. May I be of assistance?'

'I have further information about the situation with regard to Foucarmont. Several of his men have been spotted in remote parts of the Marsh. A manhunt is underway, but so far we have failed to catch them. The hunt will be resumed at first light, of course, but in the meantime I advise you to take extra precautions. Do not go outside after dark, and ensure your servants remain indoors as well.'

Parker's eyes were sharp. 'Do you believe we are in danger, reverend?'

'Not directly. But these men are dangerous, and will surely kill anyone whom they perceive as a threat, or who gets in their way. I urge you to be cautious.'

'You may trust us to look after ourselves,' said Parker. He was standing close to the fire, and his bald head was faintly sheened with sweat. 'Is that all, sir?'

'For the moment. I hope to return tomorrow with news that these men have been caught, after which we can all breathe more easily.'

'To be sure.' Parker looked at the door. 'You're certain you are close to catching them?'

'They cannot hide forever,' said the rector. 'If not tomorrow, then the next day. You may be assured of that.'

'That is good news indeed,' said Parker. He smiled, but the smile did not touch his eyes. He rang the bell on the table by the fire, and very quickly the door opened and a servant entered, bowing. This was a different man, liveried and wigged like the footman but older, with a weather-beaten face and broken nose.

'Then I wish you a good evening, sir,' said Parker. 'Steele, you may show Reverend Hardcastle out.'

'Welcome to Fort Sandy House,' said Mrs Chaytor smiling. The sound of hammering came from the drawing room. 'We are wedging the shutters, and Jack Hoad very kindly came around today and fitted a new bar to the front door. We are completely secure.'

Hardcastle was not in a mood for levity. 'Several of Foucarmont's men have been spotted between here and Appledore, but they evaded our searchers and escaped under cover of darkness. Tell your servants not to go out until daylight, and don't answer the door to anyone who cannot identify themselves. What are you doing here?'

This last was directed at his sister, who came out of the library carrying a small hammer. 'Helping Mrs Chaytor,' was the cheerful response. 'Mrs Kemp and Biddy and I have already made the rectory tight as a drum, and besides, Rodolpho is there; no one would dare break into the rectory and face Rodolpho. So I went out this afternoon to lend Miss Godfrey and Miss Roper a hand, and then called in to see if Amelia needed assistance.' She beamed. 'Isn't it exciting? We are having such fun, aren't we, my dear?'

The shutters had not been closed at New Hall, nor had the doors been barred. 'Is there any news about Samuel?' asked Mrs Chaytor.

'They've taken him away to Maidstone,' the rector said heavily.

'Oh, dear,' said Calpurnia, before Mrs Chaytor could reply. 'That is bad news. Those gaols are horrid places, anything could happen to him there. Marcus, you must find out who really killed Emma. That's the only thing that can save him, isn't it?'

The rector stared at her. 'How in blazes do you know about this?'

'Miss Godfrey and Miss Roper told me. We had a long talk this afternoon. They don't think Samuel killed Emma either, and they think James Rossiter and Parker have swindled him out of his inheritance. It's such a sad and terrible story, isn't it? I was reminded at once of my novel, *The Lonely*—'

'Then how did Miss Godfrey and Miss Roper learn?'

'I told them some of it,' said Mrs Chaytor. 'Miss Godfrey was with me the night we found Emma, and I thought she had a right to know. The rest, I should imagine, is down to their fertile imaginations. What is wrong?'

She had noticed something deeper than Hardcastle's usual cross-grainedness. 'I went to New Hall just now to inform them of developments. I saw Parker on his own, and got the strong impression he is keeping me away from the rest of the family. What is more, he could not get rid of me fast enough. He practically threw me out of the house. And there's another thing. One of the house servants is a rather hard-looking man with a broken nose.'

Calpurnia looked from one to the other, uncomprehending.

'Parker wanted to break Samuel out of gaol,' said Mrs Chaytor slowly. 'And when Samuel learned about this, he was afraid. He thinks Parker wants him dead.'

She looked up sharply. 'He thinks Parker killed Emma.'

'We entertained that theory before,' said the rector. 'And we came unstuck over the problem of the cardinal's jewels. What would Parker have stood to gain by killing Emma?'

His sister could contain herself no longer. 'The cardinal's jewels?' she squeaked.

Mrs Chaytor explained. Halfway through the narrative Calpurnia begged her to wait, rushed from the room and came back with paper, ink and quill, with which she proceeded to take down the story. Then she sat nibbling on one end of the quill and staring into space. 'There is no motive we can ascribe to Parker,' the rector said. 'Greed makes no sense; the family already have money.'

'There is the question of racial hatred. That could lead a man to kill,' said Mrs Chaytor.

'That might lead to a sudden, unprovoked assault. But a planned killing like this? It seems hard to believe.'

'But what if,' said Calpurnia, thinking hard, 'what if there is something *more* than just the house itself. What if there is something *in* the house that everyone wants? Samuel, Emma, Joseph Parker, James Rossiter, perhaps even Edward and William and Laure.'

The rector looked at her. 'From which of your novels does this idea spring?'

'*The Ghost-Hunters of Mirador*, of course. If you had read them, you would not have to ask. I think,' said Calpurnia firmly, 'that there is a secret at New Hall, a secret that someone wants very much to *stay* secret. A secret so great that someone is willing to kill to protect it.'

'Who?' asked the rector, and 'What?' asked Mrs Chaytor, simultaneously.

'I don't know,' said Calpurnia simply. 'But we must find out.'

'Thank you for the statement of the blindingly obvious,' said the rector. He looked at Mrs Chaytor. 'We discussed this earlier too, if you recall? The possibility that Emma was killed because someone is trying to protect a secret at the house.'

'We did,' said Mrs Chaytor. 'We did not get very far. Are you proposing this as a line of inquiry?'

'As my sister has pointed out, it is about all we have,' the rector said. 'Let us start with Parker. We must look into him, somehow. But I have already asked Clavertye for help, and been rebuffed.'

'Perhaps I can help,' said Mrs Chaytor reluctantly. 'It means contacting some people from the old days.'

He heard the tone in her voice. 'Don't,' he said, 'if it will distress you.'

'Distress me?' She smiled a little. 'A man's life is in jeopardy, and a murderer is on the loose. My distress is not even a matter worth discussing. I will write in the morning.'

'If you are quite certain . . . I must take my leave. I suggest you join me, Calpurnia; it has grown dark, and there is no moon.' He had driven back from New Romney in a dim light that blurred the difference between land and sky, his hand on the butt of his pistol the entire way, listening for every small night noise in the fields around him.

'The search resumes tomorrow?'

'It does.' The rector sighed. 'I told Parker we were on the verge of capturing the French. In truth I am not so sure. The Marsh is large and we have too few men. Unless we have a stroke of luck, Foucarmont could evade us for weeks.'

Sandy House, St Mary in the Marsh, Kent.
3rd February, 1797.

My dear Willie,

It has been some time since we last corresponded, and I must apologise most sincerely for my silence. I fear I was never the most diligent of correspondents, and since coming to rusticate in the country I have become something of a stylite. One day I must descend from my pillar and come up to London and visit my old friends, before they forget me entirely.

Meanwhile, dear Willie, I have a favour to ask of you. Your present position will doubtless have led you to become acquainted with Mr James Rossiter, a member of the American embassy. Perhaps you also know Mr Joseph Parker, the eminent American lawyer who is married to Mr Rossiter's sister. By coincidence they are staying quite near me, at a house belonging to the Rossiter family.

The Rossiters are charming people and we all enjoy their company very much. They have done their utmost to make themselves agreeable. But we are all very curious to know more about the family and their background. Little is known of them in the neighbourhood, due, no doubt, to their long absence from the country.

Now, at this point, Willie dear, you are doubtless clutching at your head and exclaiming that you are a busy man who has no time for idle female gossip. I am sure you are very busy indeed, but do please humour me in this matter. There is a most particular reason why I should like to know more about the Rossiters, and especially about Mr Parker. I shall confide it to you when next we meet.

I thank you for this and your many other kindnesses, and remain your faithful friend,

AMELIA

P. S. Please convey my fond regards to Anne.

A stroke of luck was needed, and that night it came, in the form of a vicious easterly squall that caused ships in the Channel to put about sharply and run north to avoid the dangerous shoal known as the Varne Bank. Most succeeded, but one French lugger was taken aback with all sails set and driven onto the shoals. Morning found her fast aground on the Varne.

Three fishing boats from New Romney approached the stranded ship and, after a short argument punctuated with threats of violence, an agreement was reached. The boats kedged the lugger off the sand and then towed her, sails lowered, into Romney Haven where she dropped anchor in the shallow water behind Littlestone. Her crew and her unhappy passengers were taken ashore by the fishermen and marched up the beach to New Romney. Joshua Stemp watched them come, and rubbed his nose.

'What did you bring them here for?' he demanded of the leader of the fishermen.

'What the fuck were we supposed to do? You saw who it is, didn't you? We couldn't just leave them out there and let the navy find them. And if we'd helped them off and then let them go, all it would take is for some bugger to see us and inform the Preventives, and then we'd get our necks stretched.'

'All right, keep your hair on.' Stemp looked around. There was no one about. All the idlers in the village were presumably down the high street, watching affairs at the Ship. A thought came to him then, and he grinned and patted the fisherman on the shoulder. 'Can you keep your mouth shut about this?' he asked. 'And make sure the other lads do the same?'

'Of course. We're hardly going to go blabbing, are we?' The fisherman looked narrowly at Stemp. 'What have you got in mind, Josh?'

'I think I've just figured out a way we can all make a profit out of this,' said Stemp. 'All right; take them up to the gaol and bring them in through the back door. Keep the lads quiet, and if anyone asks about the lugger, tell 'em it was derelict when you found it. I'll go talk to him.'

'He's mad as hell. He didn't want to come with us, but I told him we'd leave him out there if he didn't agree to lower his sails and let us take him in tow. What the fuck was he doing out there, anyway?'

'I'll find out,' said Stemp.

Swiftly, he walked back to the high street and along to the Ship, where he found the New Romney constable. 'Is his lordship here? Or Reverend Hardcastle?'

'Clavertye's gone out to see what progress the dogs are making, and Hardcastle ain't here yet.'

'Good. If either asks for me during the next hour, say you haven't seen me.'

Back at the gaol, Stemp knocked and entered. 'Got 'em all locked up, George?'

'All safe,' said the gaoler. 'There's four crew; I put them in one cell, and the six passengers in the other. It's a bit tight for breathing room, and they're all complaining like mad in Frog-talk. What's going to happen to them?'

'That depends on whether they're prepared to be reasonable,' said Stemp. 'Bring the skipper out to me, George. And let me alone with him.'

'Is this regular, Josh?'

A coin spun from Stemp's fingers into the gaoler's hand. 'That regular enough for you?'

A few minutes later, the French smuggler who called himself Bertrand was ushered into the anteroom. The gaoler went out, closing the door behind him.

'Bonjewer, Bertie,' Stemp said cheerfully. 'Sa-va?'

The Frenchman, a lean, muscular man with face and hands hardened by the sea, turned and saw Stemp. He blinked in amazement. 'Yorkshire Tom! What are you doing here?'

'My job,' said Stemp.

'What do you mean?'

Stemp gestured the other man to a wooden stool, and sat down himself. 'Well, you see, Bertie, over here I'm a constable.' The Frenchman looked blank. 'A sort of Mary Josie,' Stemp explained.

Light dawned. 'Ah!' said Bertrand, and he tapped his nose. 'A smuggler who is also a *gendarme*. Very good. I admire.'

'It has its uses,' Stemp admitted.

'Then, for the sake of the God: use your job to get me out of this . . . this shithole, and give me back my boat!'

Stemp wagged a finger. 'Not so fast, Bertie. There's a few things me and you need to talk about first.'

Bertrand looked at him, wary. 'You're a damned lubber, getting yourself grounded on the Varne,' said Stemp. 'What were you doing?'

'The wind caught us aback, and the water was more shallow than I expected. It must have been the spring tide.'

'Spring tide was five days ago, you pillock. Come on, Bertie, you've been sailing these waters long enough to know where all the shoals are. And you know better than to have the Varne to leeward when there's an east wind blowing. What were you doing out there?'

'*Merde*. Those imbeciles my passengers. They wanted to land in a place, some horrible-sounding place call Gallops-deen Gout. I wanted to go about south of the Varne, but they said I had to steer a direct course. I say again, imbeciles!'

'Who are your passengers? Spies?'

'Of course. Will you shoot them? I don't care if you do. They are stupid. No one will miss them.'

'Dunno. That's not down to me.' Stemp leaned forward. 'I've got another problem on my hands,' he said, 'and I'm hoping you can help me with it. And if you help me, then maybe I can help you too. See what I mean?'

Bertrand stared at him. 'You want me to turn informer,' he said. '*Bon dieu!* Why don't you just shoot me now and have done with it? If it is found that I give you information, I am a dead man.'

'If you don't, you'll rot in an English prison. And we'll seize your boat.'

'Not my boat, no! Tom, that boat, she is all I have! I beg you, for the sake of our friendship! Give my boat to me, and let me go!'

'Now, we're not really friends though, are we, Bertie?' reproved Stemp. 'We're partners, engaged in a series o' mutually beneficial commercial transactions, that's all.'

The Frenchman sat, digesting and translating the series of polysyllables. 'Now, I'm going to be bloody straight with you,' Stemp went on. 'I can get you back your ship. But – and mark this, Bertie – *only* if you tell me where your passengers planned to go once they were ashore.'

Bertrand jerked his thumb towards the cells where the spies waited miserably. 'You could interrogate them. Force them to tell you what they know.'

'They might not tell. Or they might spin us a pack of lies to throw us off the scent. I don't trust them. But I trust you, Bertie.'

'I am fortunate,' muttered the Frenchman, his voice deep with sarcasm. 'What makes you think I know where they were going?'

'Bertie. Don't try my patience.'

The Frenchman threw up his hands. '*Bon dieu!* You hold my balls in your hand,' he said, 'and now you squeeze. All right. I tell you.' Stemp was listening carefully.

'Now you keep your side of the bargain,' said Bertrand.

'Do you doubt the pledged word of Yorkshire Tom? I'm surprised at you, Bertie. One more thing. We're sending those six spies back with you.'

'Ah, *mort-dieu!* It is bad enough that I have to carry them once; I will not do so again. Why don't you just shoot them? It would be much easier.'

'But before someone shot them, they might talk about how they were captured. And then someone would start looking for the boat, and they'd dig around and find out I met you and sent you home, and then they would shoot me too, you see. You're a good fellow, Bertie, and a very useful business connection, but I'm already sticking my neck out for you on this business, and I ain't sticking it out any further. You'll take those fellows home, like I told you.'

Stemp stood up and clapped the other man lightly on the shoulder. 'We'll keep you here 'til after dark, so no one will see you go. That will give me time to square things with Reverend Hardcastle.'

'Who is he?'

'My boss. He's the local magistrate.'

'You are a smuggler who is also a *gendarme*,' complained Bertrand. 'Your chief is a priest who is also a judge. What sort of country is this?'

'He gave up everything,' Stemp reported to the rector. 'He's a nosy bugger, old Bertie, and I knew he would eavesdrop on his passengers, and a lugger's so small there ain't no privacy. He was going to land them at Globsden Gut, just north of St Mary's Bay. That's where he put the last lot; the other party landed down near Dungeness. Once ashore, the Frenchies were to head inland to the lookers' hut, where they'd find a message telling them where to meet with the others. There's a series of meeting places all pre-arranged. The message would indicate which one was safe to use.'

'Did this man Bertrand know where the meeting places are?'

'He did. There's five of them. A fisherman's cottage near Camber. Another lookers' hut, west of Hope Church. A cottage out by the Paradise Bush. The old stone barn at Cuckold's Corner.' Stemp paused. 'And the cellars at New Hall,' he said.

'*What?* Are you certain?'

'Quite certain. I even made him repeat it.'

The rector rose, reaching for his hat and cloak. 'A moment, if you please, reverend,' Stemp said. 'I made a deal with Bertrand for the information. I said if he told us what he knew, we'd let him have his boat back and he and his crew could go.'

There was a long pause, during which Stemp gazed innocently at the rector, and the rector read his thoughts without difficulty. 'Who else knows about this?'

'The fisher boys who brought him in, and the gaoler. I've told them all to keep quiet. Others'll see the boat, of course, but they won't know we have the crew. We've put it about she's derelict.'

'Can the fishermen be trusted to keep their mouths shut?'

'Yes, and I've made sure they'll be well paid. I told Bertie that he had to send money across on the next run, to pay them off. He promised he would.' Stemp told the rector about the rest of the arrangement. 'I know we'll lose them other spies. But I reckoned it'll be worth it, if we can catch Foucarmont. The minnows don't matter if we get the big fish.'

The rector thought about this. 'Will Bertrand keep his word?'

'If he wants to do business on this side of the Channel again, he will.' He hesitated, looking around. They were alone in Clavertye's office in the Ship, but Stemp had the caution of a man with a lifetime of felony behind him. He lowered his voice to a murmur. 'I'll wait 'til midnight, then we'll let them out and get them down to the lugger. If the wind holds fair, they'll be back in Wee Meroo by dawn.'

There was silence again, and then the rector said, 'Make it so. You take care of that business, and I will get word to Clavertye. We will have to raid all these places.'

'Including New Hall?'

'Of course. You know the cellars; the entrance is outside, by the stables. And I – cleverly – told the Rossiters to keep everyone indoors last night. Foucarmont and his men could have crept in and out during the night, with no one in the house any the wiser. We might as well have sent them an engraved invitation.'

When Clavertye returned to New Romney half an hour later, Hardcastle sought him out at once. 'Stemp, my constable, has information. A derelict boat was found off the coast this morning. It looks like the crew got caught in the storm last night, and either abandoned her or, more likely, were swept overboard. But Stemp found a list of locations the French are using as meeting places.'

'Well done! Where are they?'

The rector named them. 'The Paradise Bush?' asked Clavertye.

'A whorehouse,' explained the rector.

'Right.' Clavertye was on his feet. 'Where's Austen? Ah, there you are, captain. Time for action, at last. Get together as many of your men as you can. Be ready to move in a quarter of an hour.' His face was alight with pleasure. 'We've got the bastards this time,' he said.

Chapter 12

The Captain's Tale

For a few hours that February day, war came to Romney Marsh. The lanes and meadows were full of hurrying men. Pale low sunlight shone on swift red-coated columns and gleamed off browned steel musket barrels and the long spikes of bayonets.

The conflict was sporadic and brief. At Cuckold's Corner, the two men hiding in the old stone barn looked up sharply as they heard the tramp of marching feet. The sound drew closer. Seizing their weapons and scrambling to their feet, they ran out, and almost crashed into a line of Excise men, deployed silently there a few minutes earlier. Juddery, the Excise chief, shouted at them to surrender; instead the Frenchman drew their swords, and a few moments later both died in a hail of short-range pistol fire.

At the looker's hut west of Hope Church, two more men huddled, shivering. Still wet from their swim the previous day, they had spent a miserable night. Although the freezing weather had passed, it was still a long way from spring, and with the pursuit all around them they had not dared make a fire. The mutton ham they had purloined from a woodshed a few days earlier had been gnawed down to the bone, and they had eaten nothing since the previous day. They heard Cole and his armed Customs officers encircle the hut and then turn inward, tightening the noose, but they were too cold and dispirited to resist. Hands securely bound, they were dispatched under escort to New Romney.

Up at the Paradise Bush, a rambling house lying alongside the track between Ivychurch and Newchurch, Hardcastle and Captain Austen waited while the latter's men took up their positions. There were several buildings here: the house itself, a big stone barn and beyond that a low thatched cottage. The volunteers circled quietly around the cottage, muskets at the ready.

Hardcastle knocked at the door of the larger house. A moment later he heard the sound of the door being unbarred, and then it swung open. A woman, a gently faded blonde in an open robe over a purple corset, surveyed them, taking in the captain's red coat.

'It is always a pleasure to entertain officers of the law and the clergy, gentlemen. But we do not usually open for business 'til the evening.'

The rector was conscious of other interested faces peering over the woman's shoulder. 'We shall not detain you for long,' he said. 'We have come to ask for the key to your cottage.'

'The cottage?' The woman looked surprised. 'Why ever for?'

'So that we may search it,' the rector said patiently.

'Oh! Elise, fetch the key, if you please. Are the gentlemen not there?'

'What gentlemen?'

'Two gentlemen from London, who rented it three weeks ago. They were down for the wildfowling, their letter said.'

'Have you seen much of them since they arrived?' asked the rector.

'Nothing at all. They booked by post, paying in advance, and I left the key in the lock for them. That's how they wanted it. I have not set eyes on them. But of course, if they were here for the shooting, they would be keeping very different hours.'

The key arrived. The rector took it and nodded. 'Thank you,' he said. 'We will return this directly. Please stay indoors, and away from the windows.'

The cottage was silent, its windows shuttered on the inside. The volunteers waited in a circle around the house. Austen fitted the key to the door and turned it, but the door did not budge. 'Barred on the inside,' he said.

The rector nodded again, and raised his deep voice. '*Vous êtes encirclé, monsieur. On ne peut échapper.*'

The response was a pistol shot, fired in despair and anger, that splintered the door and flew between himself, Hardcastle and Austen. At a gesture from the captain, two of his men fired their muskets back through the door.

'*Sortir!*' commanded the rector.

A moment passed and they heard the sound of a bar being drawn back. A man in a weather-worn hat and cloak stumbled out and fell to his knees, clasping his hands behind his head. 'Got to hand it to the Frogs,' said Austen's corporal, levelling his bayonet at the man's throat, 'they surely know how to surrender.'

The rector walked past the kneeling man and into the cottage. It had only three rooms, bare and plainly furnished; there was a pack full of stale bread, and a few items of rank, soiled clothing. There was no sign of the other man.

'What have we here?' said Austen, holding up the contents of another pack: a worn map, a compass and a waterproof packet. This contained several sheets of paper, covered in dense writing. The rector glanced at these.

'Code of some sort,' he said.

'Definitely French spies then, it would seem? Do you reckon the ladies at the house knew?'

'I doubt it. They are not in the business of asking questions. Very well, we are finished here,' he said. 'Captain, assemble your volunteers, if you please. Detail four men to take the prisoner to New Romney. The rest will come with us to St Mary in the Marsh.'

They approached the village over the fields from the south-west, Austen sending his men out left and right to surround the grounds of New Hall. Two men who had earlier been posted on surreptitious watch signalled that all was clear.

'We shall need to be diplomatic here,' said the rector as he and the captain walked up the drive. 'The Rossiters are important people, and I am under direct orders from Lord Clavertye not to annoy them.'

'The Rossiters?' said Austen in surprise. 'Are some of the family living here once more?'

The rector glanced at him. 'It is not certain. That is, several of them arrived last month, but I do not know how long they intend to stay.'

At the house, he and Austen were shown at once into the drawing room. Most of the family were gathered here: Parker standing by the fire, Jane his wife and James Rossiter on a settee before it, Mrs Rossiter seated at her embroidery frame, Laure in a corner with a book in her lap, Edward and William playing cards. All looked up and then rose as the rector and Captain Austen were announced.

'Greetings, reverend and Captain Austen,' said Edward casually. 'Have you captured your Frenchman yet?'

'Not yet,' said the rector bowing, 'but we hope to do so very soon. Ladies, gentlemen, I do hope you will pardon this intrusion, and I shall make it as brief as possible. I must ask your permission to search the cellars of this house.'

Just for a heartbeat, there was silence. 'The cellars!' said Parker sharply. 'What for?'

'We have information that some of Foucarmont's men may have been using them as a hiding place,' said the rector.

'French spies, in our cellars?' Parker snorted. 'Ridiculous!'

'I agree the chances are slim. It is probable that your arrival here has caused Foucarmont to abandon any idea of using New Hall and to turn elsewhere. But we must be certain. Will you give me your permission?'

'Absolutely not!' said Parker. 'You cannot simply barge in here without notice and start rummaging around! I'll not have it! Lord Clavertye shall hear about this!'

'It is on his lordship's orders that we are here,' said the rector, bowing once more. 'Again, I am deeply sorry for intruding on you, but it is essential that we carry out this search. We will be brief, and not trouble anyone in the house.'

'I'll see you damned first,' said Parker. Once again, his bald head was shiny with sweat.

William Rossiter spoke up, his fair young face perplexed. 'Surely the reverend is just doing his duty, Uncle Joe,' he said. 'Why not let them look? I cannot see it will do any harm. I am happy for them to search if they have a need to do so.'

'Well said, cousin!' said Edward. 'Let us allow these gentlemen to do their duty. I'll even take them down to the cellars myself.'

'I agree,' said James Rossiter, and he stood up slowly, leaning on his stick. 'I understand your feelings, Joe, but the war is over. The British are our friends now.' He bowed to the rector. 'I concur with my nephew,' he said. 'Please conduct your search. And as he has volunteered, my son will go with you to assist you.'

'I shall join you also,' said William firmly.

Parker looked as if he had swallowed something unpleasant. 'This way, gentlemen, if you please,' said William.

The rector and Austen followed the two young men down the passage beside the staircase, through the rear door next to the kitchen, and thence out into the yard. Two grooms, who had clearly spotted the soldiers around the grounds, stood apprehensively by the stables. 'Fetch a lantern,' Edward called to them, and then led the way to the cellar door at the end of the stable block.

William drew out his keys and unlocked the door. One of the grooms brought the lantern and lit it, and Edward led the way downstairs. The cellar rooms were very much as the rector remembered. The two empty hogsheads had been removed and there were bottles now in the wine rack: port, madeira, Spanish wine. There were a couple of barrels of beer as well, and in another room several hams hung from the ceiling along with a brace of recently shot wild duck.

'Here you are,' said Edward cheerfully.

Austen looked around. 'The cellars are remarkably dry, given the house is in the middle of the Marsh,' he commented.

'They are, aren't they? Actually, if you care to notice, the house is on a little eminence of ground. Not much, just a few feet, but enough to lift the cellars out of the damp. I imagine the dry ground is one reason why the house was built where it is.'

'Has anything been disturbed since you were last here?' the rector asked.

'Well, I don't come down here often, of course. But all looks in order to me,' said Edward. 'Surely if anyone had been sneaking in here, they would have pinched some food and drink. It must be jolly cold, hiding out there on the Marsh.'

'And in any case, as you saw, the doors are always kept locked,' said William, holding up his keys.

Edward nodded. 'Well, gentlemen? Seen everything you need to see?'

'I think we have,' said the rector, nodding at William. 'Mr Rossiter, thank you very much for your time. Please convey my deep regret to the rest of your family for my intruding upon them, and for any alarm that has been caused.'

The afternoon was nearly done. At the end of the drive they halted, the windows of New Hall reflecting the watery late sunlight, the chimneys of St Mary smoking away to the right. Austen paused for a moment.

'Tell me, reverend; does Amelia Chaytor still live in St Mary in the Marsh?'

'She does,' said the rector. 'Do you know the lady?'

'Indeed I do. I went on the Grand Tour a few years ago, not long before the Revolution, and I met the Chaytors in Paris. They were very kind and generous to me, and I have always remembered them with great fondness.' He hesitated again. 'I have not seen her since her husband died. Would she mind if I called on her, do you think?'

Ordinarily Hardcastle would have spared Mrs Chaytor any contact with her past, but Austen's reaction to the news that the Rossiters were also in St Mary had intrigued him, and he wanted to explore it further. For that, he needed Amelia's help.

'I was about to call on her myself. Please do accompany me, if your duties can spare you.'

'That is kind of you.' Austen dismissed his men, sending them tramping back to their billets in New Romney. He and Hardcastle then walked into the village, the captain looking around curiously. He said nothing, but the rector could read the expression in his eyes: *whatever can have brought that elegant, fashionable woman to dwell in this Godforsaken part of the world?*

At Sandy House, Lucy admitted them. They found Mrs Chaytor in the drawing room reading a book, dressed in a simple white gown. She rose, and smiled at the sight of Edward Austen.

'My dear Mr Austen. What a delightful surprise.'

'Mrs Chaytor, it is a very great pleasure to see you again. I hope you will forgive me for not calling upon you sooner.'

'Not at all. The reverend had told me that you were here with the volunteers, and I am sure your duties have been keeping you very busy.'

'They have ... Mrs Chaytor, I was so sorry to hear about your husband. After all his kindness and generosity, and yours, towards myself in Paris ... Well, it was quite a dreadful blow to hear that he had gone. He was such a good man.'

'He was,' she said, her smile not quite reaching her eyes. 'Do sit. Lucy will bring us some sherry.'

They sat, the volunteer officer looking a little awkward; he was clearly wondering if he had made a mistake in accepting the rector's offer. While they waited for Lucy to return, Mrs Chaytor inquired politely after Austen's wife, and he spoke with pride of her and their rapidly growing family. They had recently moved into a large house at Godmersham, which he thought would suit them all very well.

The sherry arrived. 'Is there any news?' Mrs Chaytor asked Hardcastle, changing the subject with composure.

'Joshua Stemp has had a coup,' said the rector. 'He found a list of hiding places the French have been using, and we have been raiding them all afternoon. We caught one man, and I heard gunfire in the distance, so have hopes that we have taken or finished off a few others. And this will interest you, ma'am. One of the hiding places on the list is the cellars at New Hall.'

Mrs Chaytor raised her eyebrows. 'We've just been to take a look at them,' Austen explained. 'Everything seemed in order, though. We think Foucarmont must have sheered off when he realised the house was occupied once again.' He paused and said, 'They're a rum bunch, the Rossiters. Makes you wonder why they have returned to New Hall and the Marsh.'

There was a gentle silence, and then Mrs Chaytor smiled and sipped her sherry. 'That is a most enigmatic remark. You must enlighten us.'

'My word, you don't know about the Rossiters?'

'Only a little. We have met them a few times, that's all.'

'They're a rum bunch,' Austen repeated. 'They've a pretty interesting reputation, that's for certain. I was most interested to see the house. And the cellars.'

'I noticed that,' said the rector. 'Why so, if I may ask?'

'Well, there's a story that back in former times, the Rossiters were deeply involved in owling. Those cellars would seem to fit with the rumour. Very capacious and quite dry, and of course, close to the coast.

'Owling!' said Mrs Chaytor.

Smuggling was deep in the blood of Romney Marsh, but over the years the direction of the traffic had changed. Today it was brandy and tobacco from France and gin from Holland coming into the country; a century before, most of the smuggling trade was in untaxed wool going out. 'It's only a rumour,' said Austen, 'and anyway, it was a long time ago. No, what I've heard about the Rossiters concerns the present lot: James Rossiter and that fellow Parker, the unpleasant one we met just now.'

The rector felt the small hairs lifting on the back of his neck. 'Where did you learn about them?' asked Mrs Chaytor. Her blue-eyed gaze had intensified.

'From my aunt. Well, she's not really an aunt, sort of an adopted aunt. My family is a bit complicated,' the young officer said. 'She's a Knatchbull from the branch of the family that went out to America way back when. In 'seventy-five they sided with the Royalists, and came back to England at the end of the war. But they were in Boston before and during the war, and knew all about the Rossiters.'

The rector stirred. 'Did your aunt know why Rossiter and Parker came to America?' he asked.

'Not really. There was a rumour the family had fallen on hard times, and another that they were on the wrong side of politics back in 'forty-five, but there was nothing of substance. What is certain is that James Rossiter and Parker were mixed up in rebel politics, right from the beginning. They were Sons of Liberty, alongside Warren and Revere and that lot, plotting revolution and looking for any excuse to start a war. And of course they got it, at Lexington.'

Austen sipped his sherry. 'Once the war broke out, Rossiter and Parker rose to high rank in the rebel army. Rossiter was colonel of a militia regiment, with Parker as his second-in-command. After Saratoga, though, they changed course. According to Aunt Knatchbull, they were mixed up in some very dirty business. They started off hunting down British spies, and they weren't too particular about the methods they used. From there they went on to identifying and tracking down royalist sympathisers. The property of anyone deemed to be a royalist was confiscated by the new government, but much of the money seems to have stuck to the fingers of Messrs Parker and Rossiter. However it happened, they were absolutely swimming in lard by the end of the war.'

'Not very pleasant people, then,' said Mrs Chaytor with distaste.

'Quite so, ma'am. Aunt Knatchbull says even some of the other rebels were pretty sickened by them. But they had powerful protectors in high places in the Continental Army, and amongst Lafayette and the French commanders when they arrived too, so nothing was ever done.'

Austen finished his sherry. 'Rossiter was known as the smooth one, the plotter and planner, who made things happen but didn't get his hands dirty,' he said. 'Parker was the one who wielded the bludgeon, or pulled the trigger.'

The rector decided he could entirely believe this. The clock chimed, and the captain looked around. 'Is that the time? I'm afraid I must be thinking about getting back to my men.'

'Of course,' said Mrs Chaytor kindly. 'But thank you for telling us a most interesting story. The Rossiters seemed such pleasant people. Strange to think of all this lying behind their *façade.*'

'Yes, they all appear quite civilised, don't they? With the exception perhaps of Mr Parker. But I'll tell you another thing Aunt Knatchbull said about them. There was a saying in Boston even before the war: if you shake hands with a Rossiter, count your fingers afterwards.'

Hardcastle returned home early for the first time in several days, and so could not avoid dining with his sister. Calpurnia demanded details of the day's events, which the rector gave in edited fashion. 'And did you call on Mrs Chaytor?' she asked.

'Briefly. I encountered an old friend of hers, who desired to renew their acquaintance, and took him to her.'

'Oh? And who was he, Marcus?'

'Captain Austen of the East Kent Volunteers. He knew Mrs Chaytor and her husband some years back.'

'Captain Austen?' Calpurnia's expression changed, from inquisitorial to surprised. 'Captain *Edward* Austen? Oh, I am sorry I was not there! I should have liked to meet Mr Austen once more.'

'You know him?' asked the rector, surprised in his turn.

'The family were practically our neighbours in Hampshire, do you not remember? He's the one that was adopted by the rich Knight family from Kent. No, of course, you were off to Cambridge by then. But I saw the Austens often, both before and after I married Captain Vane. Such a nice family.' She smiled fondly. 'I remember there was a dear little girl, Edward's youngest sister, who was simply *fascinated* by my writing. She used to ask me questions: you know, all the usual things, where does my inspiration come from, and do I have a favourite place to write, and are my characters based on real people, and so forth. I gave her a copy of *Rodolpho, A Tale of Love and Liberty*, and suggested she use that as a model. *That, my child, is the style you must adopt if you intend to write in a truly modern way,* I told her.'

The rector had largely stopped listening; his mind was busy analysing what Austen had said, ferreting out the bits of information that seemed relevant. The Rossiters had been involved in smuggling in years gone by. Well, that hardly mattered ... or did it? He heard again Edward Rossiter's voice: *I imagine the dry ground is one reason why the house was built where it is.* Of course, New Hall was the perfect place from which to run a wool-smuggling ring.

But that was old history. What mattered, here and now, was the cellars themselves. Foucarmont knew about the cellars already and had been planning to make use of them. Of course, Foucarmont would have seen the cellars himself during his visits to the house last year and the year before. But ... had he been aware of them *before* those visits? Was it those cellars, that convenient dry hiding place that had attracted him to New Hall in the first place, and led to his fatal attachment to the Fanscombe family?

Calpurnia was still talking, oblivious to his silence. Hardcastle suddenly recalled his sister saying, *What if there is something in the house that everyone wants?* Good God, was she actually starting to make sense? But what could that 'something' be, and where would it be? He, Stemp and Mrs Chaytor had been diligent in their search of the house. The cellars had been almost entirely empty then, their brick walls and floors sound and solid.

They rose from dinner. Still chewing over the events of the afternoon, he bowed to his sister and retreated to his study, leaving her to the drawing room and her music. Parker's behaviour requires further consideration, he thought, as he poured himself a glass of port. Whenever I come to New Hall, he grows nervous and uncomfortable. And the sight of Austen's uniform nearly made him jump out of his skin. Of course, for a former Son of Liberty, the appearance of a red coat might bring back bad memories; but, he thought, there is more to it than that. More significant is the servant with the broken nose, the one who tried to recruit men to liberate Samuel Rossiter.

A second glass of port slipped down, and then a third. Samuel Rossiter would be in Maidstone gaol by now, crammed into a cell with perhaps a dozen other men; murderers, rapists, thieves, all living in a fug of their own sweat and stench, waiting for the day of doom that would send them to the gallows or the transports. His mind full of disturbing images, he fell asleep in his chair, and dreamed unpleasant dreams.

Next morning, Hardcastle had a headache again. He gulped some coffee, put his pistol into the pocket of his cloak and took Rodolpho for a walk in the dim, grey light of dawn, and then drove off through a light chilly drizzle to New Romney.

At the Ship all was bustle; the secretary and servant were packing up and Clavertye was striding around the common room giving orders. 'Foucarmont,' he said tersely in answer to Hardcastle's question. 'We cornered him in the fisherman's hut near Camber.'

That hut, with its near proximity to the coast, had been identified as the most likely hiding place of Foucarmont himself, and Lord Clavertye had taken personal command of yesterday's raid on it. 'What happened?' Hardcastle asked.

'There was no cover around the hut, just open heath and shingle. He shot and wounded two of my men with that infernal rifle of his; that's how I know it was Foucarmont. We pulled back and waited for dark, and then moved in, only to find the damned house was empty.'

Hardcastle raised his eyebrows. 'There was a tunnel,' said Clavertye angrily. 'Trust Foucarmont to know the place was an old smuggler's haunt. He and his men escaped into the dunes. We brought up the dogs and tracked them across the river into Sussex. There were three of them, Foucarmont and two others.'

There was a short silence. 'What happens now?' the rector asked.

'I'm going after him, of course. I'm off to Rye, to co-ordinate the search with the magistrate there.'

'What about the others?'

'We've killed two and taken three, so apart from Foucarmont and his two, that wraps everything up. I've interrogated the three prisoners, but of course they don't know anything of importance. These people work like criminal gangs: the lower ranks are told no more than they need to know; only the lynchpin knows everything. That's why I am determined to take Foucarmont.'

On another day, Hardcastle would have volunteered to go along. Today, his head hurt. He nodded. 'I'm leaving you in charge,' the deputy lord lieutenant said. 'Take whatever measures you see fit, and keep me informed. I'll be at the George in Rye.'

Then Clavertye was away, vigorous as ever, galloping through the rain down the Appledore road, and the carriage for his baggage and attendants drew up at the door, preparing to follow. Captain Austen came to join Hardcastle. 'Any orders for my men, reverend?'

'If you are able to keep them here for a little longer, sir, I would be grateful. I'm not convinced this affair is over yet.' Foucarmont was on the run, but if he escaped Lord Clavertye, he would come back to the Marsh; of that, the rector was certain.

Austen bowed, and turned at a new commotion. 'What have we here?'

What they had was a messenger, pulling up a tired horse in the inn yard and jumping down from the saddle, shouting for a groom, then hurrying into the common room. He was wet and splashed with mud to his neck, breathing hard still from his ride. 'Lord Clavertye?' he gasped. 'Can anyone tell me where to find his lordship? I've urgent news for him.'

'You must have passed him on the road,' said the rector. 'My name is Hardcastle, I am the magistrate here. What is your message?'

'That prisoner they were taking to Maidstone, Rossiter. He's escaped!'

Chapter 13

Mr Parker Calls

The escort had underestimated Samuel Rossiter; they all had, it seemed. The usual practice when transporting a prisoner was for one guard to ride inside the van, but this was never a popular duty and most guards tried to avoid it if possible. On this occasion Rossiter had seemed quiet and biddable, so his escort remained outside, four guards marching in front of the van and two behind. Somewhere along the road, Rossiter managed to pry up some of the floorboards of the van; then, waiting until it was dark, dropped through the floor onto the road and rolled silently out of the way before the trailing guards came up. Not until the van reached Maidstone prison and was opened did anyone realise he was missing.

Mrs Chaytor had been right: Samuel Rossiter had woken up, and realised he wanted to live.

The rector turned to Austen. 'It appears I have some work for your men after all, captain. I should be obliged if you would send out details to search for the fugitive. I will inform the parish constables and ask them to lend you every assistance.'

Austen nodded. 'It shall be done. But it's a big task you've set us, sir. We struggled to find eight men, until we'd received sound information about their whereabouts. It will be harder still with just one.'

'Do your best. One more thing, captain: I want Rossiter alive and unharmed. If your men capture him, they are to use him kindly.'

Austen raised his eyebrows. 'He is wanted for murder.'

'Yes,' the rector said. 'All the same. I am quite serious about this. No harm must come to him.'

Austen bowed and departed, calling to his sergeant and corporal. The rector sighed again. 'Mrs Spicer,' he said to the landlady of the Ship, 'I would be obliged if you would bring me paper and ink and pen.'

THE SHIP INN, NEW ROMNEY, KENT.
4th February, 1797.

My lord,

The messenger who carries this letter will have informed you that Samuel Rossiter has escaped from custody while on his way to Maidstone gaol. Your other officials will doubtless make you aware of the details in due course. Anticipating that Rossiter might attempt to return once more to Romney Marsh, I have asked Captain Austen to undertake a thorough search of the area, and apprehend Rossiter if possible. I have no doubt that he will carry out this task to the very best of his ability.

I will inform you as soon as Rossiter is retaken, so that you make whatever arrangements you desire for his custody. I must inform you, however, that I have grave reservations about the case against him, both pertaining to the murder of his sister and his supposed association with Foucarmont. I should also warn you that I intend to reopen the case of the murder of Emma Rossiter.

With that end in mind, and so that I may better attend to my parochial duties, I am returning to St Mary in the Marsh. I would humbly request that you direct all correspondence to me there.

Yr very obedient servant,

HARDCASTLE

Back at St Mary in the Marsh, it felt a little as though a siege had been lifted. News of yesterday's events had already spread; now windows and doors were unbarred and people came out into the streets despite the cold. When the rector called in at the Star after the Murton baptism, he found the common room full of cheerful people come to wet the baby's head. The air was dense with tobacco smoke while his neighbours chewed over recent events and speculated about what the French might be up to. The rector drank three tankards of small beer, answered patiently as many questions as he could about Foucarmont's agents, and said nothing whatever about Samuel Rossiter.

The next day, Sunday, he conducted matins as usual. James Rossiter, his wife and their two children attended along with the young master of the house, but Parker and his wife were noticeably absent. The rector pondered on this, briefly.

That afternoon, for the first time in many weeks, he had no engagements and no demands on his time. He put on his cloak and, after a moment's pause, took the pistol from its pocket and replaced it in the usual drawer of his desk. Then he snapped his fingers and called for Rodolpho.

The weather had improved a little; the wind still had an icy edge, but the clouds had broken to reveal a pale sun hanging low in the south. Rodolpho, his shaggy coat impervious to the weather, bounded across the meadows, barking with pleasure. The rector realised that, although he still resented his sister's presence in the house, he had grown rather fond of Rodolpho. The dog was, he knew from Calpurnia, about two years old; he had been a stray when she found him, only a few months old, and she had taken him into her home, raised him and fed him, and made no attempt whatever to train him. The dog had no more self-discipline than his mistress, but Hardcastle found him rather endearing.

They walked down towards the sea, the rector's favourite destination, to the tiny indentation in the long strand of sand and shingle known as St Mary's Bay, and climbed up onto the dunes. There, pale in the distance, were the chalk cliffs of France, the water between them churned grey and shredded into white foam by the incessant wind. The rector gazed once more at the enemy coast, wondering again what Foucarmont had been planning and what had brought him back to the Marsh. The more he thought about it, the more certain he was that he was right. The Marsh held the key. More particularly, New Hall held the key.

Something had drawn back Foucarmont to New Hall. At about the same time, something also had prompted the Rossiters to come to New Hall.

What if it was the same thing?

The rector stood for a long time in the wind, unseeing, ignoring Rodolpho scrabbling in the sand not far away while he considered this. Was it likely?

On the surface, no. Foucarmont was an agent of the French Republic, intent on carrying the war into England. James Rossiter was an American diplomat; he had fought against the British in the past, yes, but he was now tasked with concluding an agreement by which Britain and America would join forces against the French. Joining forces with Foucarmont would be against the interests of both his British hosts and his own country, and that Rossiter would choose to do so seemed highly improbable.

Rodolpho had caught the scent of something and was now excavating a hole in the rear elevation of the dune, interrupting Hardcastle's thoughts. The dog's shaggy coat would be full of sand, which would get everywhere in the house; Mrs Kemp would be furious, and probably would hand in her notice again.

Of course, it need not be the case that the entire family is involved, thought Hardcastle. Maybe only one apple has been spoiled; the rest of the barrel might be perfectly sound. Mrs Rossiter, for example, seems little more than an appendage to her husband.

Of the younger generation, Mrs Chaytor's evaluation of Laure seems fair. But then there is Edward, of course; and young William, who did after all break with his father to join his uncles.

And, what of Parker? We know that he bullied and threatened Samuel and Emma on two occasions. Parker has been nervous and full of bluster each time I called at New Hall. Parker has something to hide; and I am willing to bet that Parker knows the secret of New Hall, whatever that may be. And if this new theory of mine is right, there is also some connection between Parker and Foucarmont.

Oh, yes. It was time, and past time, that he spoke to Parker.

A rabbit, aroused by the noise overhead, popped its head out of a hole ten yards from Rodolpho and stared. The wolfhound raised its head and spotted the rabbit, and gave a single high-pitched yelp. Then, gathering his long ungainly legs, he fled, bounding behind the rector and skidding to a halt. The rector, roused from his thoughts, looked down and patted the frightened dog on the head, reassuring him. Rodolpho gave his gloved hand a lick of gratitude.

'Home, boy,' said the rector with a touch of grimness in his voice. 'There's work to be done.'

Back at the house, Biddy the maidservant promised with her usual cheer to clean Rodolpho thoroughly before he was let loose in the house. Her mistress, she explained, was at work on her book and must not be disturbed on any account. Hardcastle went into his study, warmed himself by the fire while he drank a glass of port, and then sat down at his desk with pen and paper and ink and began to write.

THE RECTORY, ST MARY IN THE MARSH, KENT.
5th February, 1797.

My dear Mr Jessington,

I am writing to ask you for some additional information concerning the list of members of the Rossiter family, which you so kindly provided me with last year. I am particularly interested in Mrs Amélie Rossiter, late wife of Mr William Rossiter, deceased in 1770. I understand from your document that her maiden name was Mirabeau and that she was of French descent.

Are you able to tell me anything further about the lady and her antecedents? Any information you provide will be received gratefully, and, I need hardly add, treated in the strictest confidence.

I look forward to your soonest reply,

Yr very obedient servant,

REV. M. A. HARDCASTLE, J. P.

That same cold bright Sunday afternoon brought Laure to call upon Mrs Chaytor. Over the past couple of weeks the two women had become friends. Laure made no secret of her warm admiration of Mrs Chaytor, her appearance, her manner, her taste, her clothes and her fondness for books and music; for her part, Amelia, though occasionally embarrassed by the other woman's

shiny-eyed enthusiasm, could not help warming to Laure's honesty and innocence.

They sat before the fire in Mrs Chaytor's drawing room and
discussed current ideas, everything from steam engines to the
discovery of nitrogen, and it was clear that in most cases Laure
was rather better informed than her hostess.

'I fear I am a little behind the times when it comes to the
scientific papers,' Mrs Chaytor said. 'You, on the other hand, are
wonderfully well-informed. Your curiosity and interests seem to
know no bounds. That is commendable.'

'Yes. Well,' said Laure, going rather pink. 'I believe that women
should be educated, as much as possible. The only reason why
men are allowed to think that our sex is inferior to theirs is
because most women are not as well-educated as most men. That
makes the women look stupid. In fact, women are just as clever
as men, if not more so. They lack knowledge, not intelligence.'

'An interesting idea,' observed Mrs Chaytor.

'Oh, it is not my own. I read it in a most remarkable book,
The Vindication of the Rights of Women, by Miss Wollstonecraft.
You have not read it? Oh, I am astonished to hear it. I beg you to
read it, you will find it full of the most fascinating ideas; some of
them very radical. Miss Wollstonecraft is in favour of abolishing
the rite of marriage altogether.'

'Oh? And why?'

'Marriage, says Miss Wollstonecraft, is an institution dedicated
to keeping women in a position of servitude related to men.'

'In theory, that may be true,' observed Mrs Chaytor. 'In practice, it depends entirely on the man, and the woman. My own
marriage was entirely equal; whatever my husband did, I did
too, and I do not recall there ever being any discussion of the
matter between us.'

It was a measure of their friendship that she could speak
to this girl – and she continued to think of Laure as a girl

despite their similarity in age – about John without pain. Laure smiled. 'You were indeed truly fortunate,' she said. 'And you are right, of course, some marriages are very much equal. Indeed, I would say the marriage of my aunt and uncle is such a union.'

'Oh?'

'You might not think it to look at them, but they are very much suited to each other. They share the same tastes; literature and music and of course, the *objets* they collect. Aunt Jane was saying only yesterday that she cannot wait to go to Paris and Rome, to buy pictures and rare cameos. She was a little miffed when Uncle Joseph told her they must wait.'

'I suppose the diplomatic negotiations in London must be resolved before they can depart the embassy,' observed Mrs Chaytor.

'Oh, Uncle Joseph has nothing to do with the embassy. He is only here at Father's invitation. But you are right, the negotiations are pressing; Father received word on Friday that he is wanted back in London, and so he departs tomorrow. But the only thing keeping Uncle Joseph and Aunt Jane from travelling further is lack of money.'

Mrs Chaytor poured more chocolate with a steady hand. 'I am surprised at that. These days, surely, the better banks such as Hoares and Coutts can arrange a line of credit and allow Americans to draw on their funds back home.'

'That's just it; they have no funds back home. I love Uncle Joseph and Aunt Jane dearly, but even I must admit they are frightful spendthrifts. Every penny they have, they spend on ... things. Their house in Boston is like a magpie's nest, stuffed full of things that glitter. Father had to pay their fare to come to London, and put them up in our house. It is silly of them, but I don't expect they will ever change. It runs in the family,' explained Laure. 'Eddy, my brother, is just as bad.'

'Oh, dear,' said Mrs Chaytor smiling. 'Still, you seem to be immune.'

'My only vice is books,' said Laure, and they laughed together. The conversation drifted on to other things; they talked of Mrs Chaytor's time in Rome, and she related the story of the cardinal's jewels and they dissected the nature of human greed.

'Family, in the end, meant nothing to them,' said Laure a little sadly. 'They were willing to kill their own kin to get what they wanted.'

'And also, to avenge a betrayal,' said Mrs Chaytor. 'They killed the brother not just to get the jewels back, but to punish him for the theft.'

'Perhaps Miss Wollstonecraft was right,' observed Laure. 'Perhaps people shouldn't get married and have families at all. It seems only to increase the quantity of human misery.'

'That was not my experience,' said Mrs Chaytor. I wonder what her own experience of family life has been, she thought.

'Even though the ending brought you sorrow?'

'My dear, I had ten years of unclouded happiness. I will face a lifetime of sorrow, if need be, and still count myself blessed. That is why I go on,' she finished quietly.

'I think you are very brave to carry on as you do.'

'It is easy to be brave when there are no alternatives. Do I take it you yourself have abandoned the idea of marriage?'

'No . . . At least, I don't think so.'

'You do not sound certain.'

'My parents, especially Mother, have always encouraged me to marry. They have over the years proposed several arrangements. I have always said no, not because I am opposed to marriage in principle, like Mrs Wollstonecraft, but because the candidates who presented themselves had nothing to offer me. The men my father would have had me marry would have been useful to him. The men my mother wanted me to marry were very fashionable, but . . .' Laure paused, staring into the fire. 'Marriage should be an act that increases the store of love and happiness in the world, not one that detracts from it. Don't you think?'

'On that point, my dear,' said Mrs Chaytor, 'you and I are in complete agreement.'

THE GEORGE INN, RYE, SUSSEX.
5th February, 1797.

By express.

My dear Hardcastle,

Thank you for your letter of yesterday's date. This matter is an annoyance, but Rossiter cannot remain at large for very long. He was transported in manacles, and unless he manages to shed these, then he will be unable to travel far or help himself. Even if our men do not find him, cold and hunger will soon force him to turn himself in.

Most importantly, so long as he is cut off from his confederates, there is little he can do. Ask Austen to set men to watching all the roads and tracks running southwest into Sussex. If Rossiter should hear where Foucarmont has gone, he may try to join the Frenchman. That would be an excellent chance to lay them both by the heels.

Yr very obedient servant,

CLAVERTYE

The rector read through the express again, silently cursing Lord Clavertye. The letter contained no comment, not a single word of acknowledgement of Hardcastle's expressed doubts or his intention to reopen the Rossiter case.

That omission was, he knew from experience, entirely deliberate. Clavertye had his own firm view of this case, and was convinced he was right and Hardcastle was wrong. But his lordship also knew Hardcastle well enough to recognise that the rector would not change his mind unless incontrovertible evidence were placed before him. By remaining silent, Clavertye was allowing the rector to go ahead and attempt to prove his own case, while simultaneously distancing himself from the investigation in case anything went awry.

If he is right and I am wrong, the rector thought, he will get the credit and I the blame. If I am right and he is wrong, he will magnanimously acknowledge his debt to me and then claim the credit anyway. Damn all politicians!

He wondered how long it would take Jessington to respond to his letter. *There is work to be done*, he had said; but he could not really start that work until he had tested the notion that had come to him while walking on the beach. He remembered again Parker's voice, sharp and demanding: *who is in France? Who are you discussing, if I may ask?* and Edward Rossiter looking at him curiously. And Parker again, sweating with anxiety: *You're certain you are close to catching them?* And again: *You cannot simply barge in here without notice and start rummaging around!*

Of course, there were other explanations. Parker might have been trying to protect the Rossiters, as he had done before. Or he might have been genuinely afraid for his own safety, and that of the family. The rector did not believe it. Parker *was* frightened; but there was more than simple fear behind those sharp, dark eyes.

Let us hope, thought the rector, that Jessington's dislike of Parker prompts him to be thorough in his search. He went about his parochial duties in an absent-minded fashion, waiting for the little lawyer's reply.

Two days later, as the evening light was beginning to draw down across the Marsh, the letter came.

ANTHONY JESSINGTON, ESQ
LINCOLN'S INN
LONDON
7th February, 1797.

The Reverend Hardcastle, Sir,

I am in receipt of your letter of the 5th inst. I have looked through our records and found they contain very little information about the antecedents of the late Mrs Amélie Rossiter. Her family, the Mirabeaus, were Huguenots who fled France in the last century. Mrs Rossiter herself was born in London in 1709.

I did find one letter from the Mirabeau family's solicitor, indicating that the family had connections in France up to the time of Mrs Rossiter's marriage. Her sister-in-law, Mr William Rossiter's sister Charlotte, had made a most advantageous marriage to a French nobleman, the Baron de Foucarmont from Normandy. The Foucarmonts had come into some property formerly belonging to the Mirabeaus and were offering to sell it back to the original owners, and the Mirabeau solicitor hoped that some of this French land could form part of Charlotte's marriage portion. The offer was, I understand, refused.

I hope this information is of some use to you, and apologise for having nothing of greater substance to offer,

Your faithful servant,

ANTHONY JESSINGTON

The thing was so simple that he almost laughed aloud. The connection between the Rossiters and Foucarmont was a perfectly ordinary one; two families united by marriage a generation ago. Of course they would have kept in contact; they had shared commercial interests as well as family ties. Parker, as lawyer for the branch of the Rossiter family in Boston, would have known of this and might well have had his own correspondence with the Foucarmont family.

He sat up sharply as another memory came to him. At Foucarmont's trial the previous year – at which the rector had been a witness – it had emerged that the spy had served in the royal army before the French Revolution. He had been an officer in a regiment commanded by the Duc de Biron, and like Biron he had gone over to the Republican cause when the Revolution began. Biron was now dead, guillotined by his own revolutionary comrades; there had been a long article about him in the *Morning Post*, recalling how the duke had also led a regiment to fight against the British in America.

It was enough to begin. A grim little smile crossed his lips, and the rector dipped his pen in the inkwell and began to write.

THE RECTORY, ST MARY IN THE MARSH, KENT.
8th February, 1797.

My dear Mr Parker,

I trust you are well, and that you continue to find your stay with us in St Mary in the Marsh agreeable and amiable. I hope you will forgive the intrusion of this letter, but a matter of some importance has arisen, which concerns New Hall. I would be most grateful if you would consent to call on me at noon tomorrow, so that we may discuss the matter.

I look forward to the pleasure of your company,

Yr very obedient servant,

HARDCASTLE

The clock chimed noon. A polite interval of about a minute passed, and then Joseph Parker knocked at the rectory door. Biddy showed him into the study, the cameo rings on his fingers winking in the firelight. The diamonds on his watch fob flashed little rainbows each time he moved. Beneath the bald head, his face was sharp and his mouth set in a thin line.

'It is indeed a pleasure to see you again, Mr Parker,' the rector said. 'Will you take refreshment? I believe it is still rather cold out. Biddy, kindly ask Mrs Kemp to bring us two toddies.'

'I'll see to it myself, reverend,' said the little maid, bobbing a curtsey and skipping away.

Hardcastle turned back to Parker. 'Thank you for coming,' he said.

'You mean, for obeying your summons? I hope you have a good reason for dragging me over here.'

'Oh, I do, believe me. But let us wait until the refreshments come. Meanwhile, how do your affairs progress here in St Mary?'

'What affairs?'

The rector bowed. 'My apologies. I assumed you came to St Mary with some purpose in mind.'

'My nephew invited me. And, of course, my wife has some sentimental attachment to New Hall, which she remembers from her childhood. She wanted to see it again, that's all.'

'Of course. And do you plan to remain here for long?'

Parker gazed at him steadily. 'We have no fixed plans.'

Biddy returned with the toddies, served them quietly and without fuss, and slipped out again. 'Now, Major Parker,' said the rector, 'shall we get down to business?'

The other man's eyes grew suddenly sharp. 'What did you call me?'

'Forgive me, but I assumed that was your title. You were second-in-command of a regiment in the Continental Army, were you not? And I believe the holder of that post normally has the rank of major. My apologies if I am mistaken.'

'I have not used that rank for years,' said Parker slowly. 'How do you know my history?'

'You were also engaged in work of a confidential nature on behalf of the American government,' said the rector, ignoring the question. 'You worked *sub rosa*, of course, but I think we can safely say that you were involved in countering British attempts at espionage and identifying those who might be deemed traitors to the American cause. It must have been unpleasant work, at times. Though it also had its rewards, I am sure.'

'I will ask you again, Hardcastle. How do you know this?'

'Mr Parker, my time is valuable, and so, I am certain, is yours. If we are to go off on long digressions about *how* I know things, we shall be here forever. Shall we just take it for granted that I know them?'

Parker blinked. 'Very well. What is your point?'

'I have several points, which I shall come to in order. The first point is that you are, to put it bluntly, a man of your hands. You are a soldier, who has fought and killed for his country, and I am sure that you would not hesitate to use violence again, or to order others to do so, to achieve your ends.'

Parker said nothing. His face, his eyes, his entire manner was wary.

'For example, when you met Samuel Rossiter in London and he refused to stay away from your family or abandon his claim to New Hall, you threatened him. The phrase you used was "I will darken your daylights". Samuel had spent most of his life living among the Indians, and his grasp of English idiom is rather limited. You and I know that phrase implies the threat of violence, even death.'

'I threatened him, yes. I wanted to drive him away and thought I could frighten him off. Look here, Hardcastle, I was entirely in my rights to do so. Samuel Rossiter and his sister are bastards, no more. They had no claim on our family, none at all. Why my late brother-in-law chose to consort with some coloured whore I don't pretend to comprehend. But I'll not have his degenerate by-blows sniffing around the family. They contaminate the very air we breathe.'

'You feel contempt for Samuel and Emma, of course,' said the rector, nodding as if in approval. 'I understand that entirely. And you feel that as the family's legal advisor, it is down to you to protect the family and keep it free from . . . contamination, as you put it.'

'Exactly. You've no doubt read your Voltaire, reverend. You know as well as I that these . . . people don't belong among us. Hell, are they even people? It would be better if they disappeared off the face of the Earth, and I don't mind helping one or two of them disappear. I've done it before.'

Too late, Parker realised he had implicated himself. He could not have been a very good lawyer, the rector thought. Perhaps that was why he decided to go America. 'And in order to protect the family,' he said, 'you were willing to use any means that came to hand including, as I think we have now established, the threat of violence.

'Now, let us remind ourselves of a few facts. Just before Christmas, Samuel's sister Emma Rossiter travelled to New Hall. She obtained entrance to the house, by what means we do not yet know. She was dressed as a man, again for reasons we do not know. Someone struck her a terrible blow to the head, and shortly thereafter she drowned in the horse pond behind the stables. These details will already be familiar to you, of course.'

'Why are you raking this up again? You have your killer; or rather, you had him. I gather, that in a typical piece of British bungling, you have managed to let him escape.'

'Samuel Rossiter did not kill his sister,' said the rector. 'I intend to prove his innocence.'

'Good luck,' sneered Parker.

'I have had some luck already, but I have also used my wits to examine the evidence. Once we remove Samuel Rossiter from the list of suspects, Mr Parker, another name quickly climbs to the top of the list. Your own.'

For a fat man, Parker could move fast. He shot to his feet, his fist clenched. The rector rose too, watchfully, but the urge for violence passed as quickly as it arrived. Parker swallowed, slowly relaxing his hands. 'This is horseshit,' he said.

'You despise and dislike Samuel Rossiter. You knew his whereabouts in London; you knew he had visited Jessington, whom you also tried to bully. You had a watch set on his rooming house. When Emma, disguised as a man, left London to travel to New Hall, you followed her in the mistaken assumption that she was her brother. On Christmas Day, when she was alone in the house, you saw your chance to rid yourself of this nuisance for once and all. Still thinking she was Samuel, you killed her.'

'What a pack of lies! I was in London—'

'On the day when all mankind should set aside its differences and celebrate the feast of peace, Emma Rossiter died a horrible, lonely death,' the rector continued, ignoring the interruption. His deep voice had turned hard. 'She died because of your hatred of her mother's race, your belief that the colour of her skin makes her degenerate and less than human; and she died because of your greed, your unwillingness to share your family's fortune with someone who, by-blow or no, is your own kin. You sicken me, Parker; you and all men like you.'

'If you think you can make that charge stick, you are even more of a damned fool than I thought you were,' sneered Parker. 'God, what claptrap. For your information, Hardcastle, I never left London until we came down here last month. And on Christmas Day, me and my wife were guests at dinner at the house of the American ambassador, Mr King. He and thirty others will confirm this.'

'But of course,' said the rector, nodding. 'You would not be so careless as to be without an alibi for the time of the killing. But you are an officer. As I said earlier, you would not hesitate to use violence, *or order others to do so.* And that brings us to the servant, Steele. Tell me about Steele, Mr Parker. The man with the broken nose.'

'I know nothing of him. He's one of the agency staff my sister-in-law hired in London.'

'No, he is not. For one thing, he is far too old; agencies employ younger people, ones who have not yet found a place in regular service. Nor would an agency employ a man with such a rough face. Agencies find it bad policy to provide servants whose faces might frighten their wealthy and more sensitive clients. No, Steele has been in the service of your family for a long time. What is he: your valet?'

Parker said nothing, which was eloquent in itself. The rector nodded. 'I thought as much. A long-serving valet becomes close to his master, knows his secrets. I'll wager Steele does far more than just brush your coat and polish your boots. You might have sent him after Emma with orders to kill her, but of course, you will have an alibi for him too. What is incontrovertible is that shortly after Samuel Rossiter was arrested, Steele went around the inns and public houses in the area to recruit men to break him out of gaol. He surely did this at your request.'

'I don't have to listen to this—'

'I have a witness, and can certainly find more. And when I told Samuel Rossiter that someone wanted to break him out, he was terrified. He was quite certain that the men were coming, not to rescue him, but to kill him.'

'I had nothing to do with any of this.'

The rector raised his eyebrows. 'So Steele was acting on his own, and not at your orders? Interesting. But valets don't tend to go around assassinating people off their own bat, do they? They tend to be taking orders from *someone*. And if it was not you that gave the orders, Mr Parker, then another suspect's name comes to the top of the list.'

He waited. Parker was only human. 'Who?' he said, eventually.

'Let us go back a bit,' the rector said. 'One thing that puzzled me about this case from the beginning was, why New Hall? Why did the murder take place *there*, of all the houses on the Marsh? Eventually, I realised that the house itself must hold the key to the mystery. The house has a secret. You know what it is, and you would kill – have killed – to protect it. You, and others, think Samuel Rossiter knows that secret too. As a result, there have been two attempts on his life: one resulted in the death of his sister, the other was thwarted when I learned of it and placed a guard around the gaol.

'When I accused you just now of being motivated by racial hatred and greed, I was not telling the full truth. Both *are* motives, I am certain; but there is something at New Hall that runs deeper than hatred, deeper than greed. What is it, Parker? What are you afraid of, and so desperate to protect?'

'Now this really is moonshine,' said Parker. 'You know, Hard-castle, I've heard rumours that you're something of a tippler. Did you dream up all these fancy theories while you were foxed? That might explain it.'

There was a sneer in Parker's voice, but it was not real; he was labouring to keep up a pretence. Yes, thought the rector; not a very good lawyer at all.

'When you served in the continental army, Major Parker,' he said, 'you met a number of French officers. You know who I mean; the gentlemen who came over with Monsieur de Lafayette and Monsieur de Biron to help you win your freedom.'

Suddenly, there were beads of sweat on Parker's gleaming head. 'That is not true.'

'Mr Parker ... It really is not a good idea to lie to me. Have you visited France since the end of the war?'

'No.'

'Have you corresponded with any of these men?'

'No!'

The rector sighed. 'So you have never met or corresponded with a French army officer named Camille de Foucarmont?'

'*Foucarmont?*'

'Foucarmont served in America. Perhaps you met him there for the first time, or perhaps there was already an existing link; after all, your wife's family have French connections.'

Parker had gone pale. 'So what? Many families have relations in France.'

The rector nodded. 'Either way, you established a direct connection with him, and that leads us to the present moment. I think Foucarmont knows the secret of New Hall too. Because of that, he came back to Romney Marsh at almost exactly the same time you arrived. Now, that could be coincidence, but Mr Parker, I do not believe in coincidences.'

Hardcastle paused as Parker opened his mouth to speak, but closed it without saying a word. The American's breathing was shallow and fast, his fists clenching and unclenching. 'You are in league with him,' said the rector. 'You and he are here for the same purpose.'

'No!' shouted Parker suddenly. 'What purpose could the two of us possibly have?'

'I do not yet know what that purpose is, but I suspect it bodes no good for England. It has already led to one murder, and another attempted murder, and unless I can put a stop to your activities, there may be yet more killing. Mark my words, Parker, and listen to them well. I *will* stop you.'

Parker made one last attempt at bluster. 'You have a fine imagination, reverend, but I am still waiting for you to come up with any proof. And now, if you'll forgive me, I must take my leave. Too much time has been wasted on this nonsense.'

'Proof? I am braiding the rope of evidence even as we speak, and the day is not far off when I will place it around your neck. I will have justice for Emma Rossiter. You have my pledged word on that.'

*

'You look cold,' said Mrs Chaytor.

It was early evening on 9th February. A chill mist was falling, its umbrous shrouds trailing slowly over the flat Marsh.

'I went for a walk along the shore,' said the rector, 'and got caught in this accursed fog. I am cold to the bone.'

'Lucy will bring us some tea. Should you be out walking alone at the moment? Foucarmont is still at large. I hope at least you took Rodolpho with you.'

'I did; not that he would be much use. The dog is an utter coward.'

'Truly?' She stared at him.

'It is quite true. The other day down at the bay, he was terrified of a rabbit. And this afternoon as we were walking, a small field creature, a mouse or vole or some such, ran across the path in front of us, and I thought Rodolpho would jump out of his skin. He is surely the most timorous creature on four legs.'

'Poor Rodolpho,' said Mrs Chaytor, putting a hand to her mouth. 'Unless, perhaps, he is a Quaker? Dedicated to doing no harm?'

'A Quaker wolfhound? In this day and age, I suppose anything is possible.'

The tea arrived. Mrs Chaytor poured. 'And so,' she said expectantly as she picked up the sugar tongs, 'apart from Rodolpho's terrors, what have you come to tell me?'

'I had a theory about Parker. I decided to test it, the difficult way.'

He told her about the conversation earlier in the day, she watching him steadily. 'I thought I could crack him,' Hardcastle said. 'He is more resilient than I suspected. He is certainly guilty of *something*; his demeanour told me as much. But guilty of exactly what offence is not clear. I feel sure he had a hand in

poor Emma Rossiter's murder, and he certainly has some connection with Foucarmont. Emma was killed to stop the secret of
New Hall, whatever it is, from getting out. But it seemed to me
that he was more afraid of being linked with Foucarmont than
the accusation of murder.'

'Goodness,' Mrs Chaytor said, staring at him. 'Parker has a
connection with Foucarmont? Then you have made a substantial advance.'

'Have I? Parker is still at liberty, and for all my fine words
he will remain so until I can find evidence that will convince
Lord Clavertye of Parker's guilt. Indeed, I may have put myself
in jeopardy. Clavertye told me to stay away from the Rossiters,
and I am certain that Parker will now complain of my behaviour
to his London connections or to his lordship, or both. I should
do so, were I in his position. And until I can prove that Parker
was involved in the killing of Emma, I cannot prove the innocence of Samuel.'

'But the connection with Foucarmont is very serious,' said
Mrs Chaytor. 'Should you not lay that before Lord Clavertye?'

'I have no proof; it is only a theory. I do not *know* anything
for certain, merely that the man began to perspire like Niagara
as soon as I mentioned Foucarmont's name. So long as he has
the protection of the American ambassador, there is little to be
done except continue to probe.'

'The American ambassador may not be so closely involved
as you think,' she said. 'Laure told me yesterday that Parker
is only with the embassy as a guest of his brother-in-law,
James. He is the one with the official protection, not Parker.
Of course, James would have to be persuaded to cut his tie
with his sister's husband. But he might not be entirely averse
to doing so.'

'Oh?'

There was a noise at the front door, and they heard Lucy moving to answer it. 'Laure also told me that Parker and his wife have largely squandered their fortune. They have, in the fine old phrase, not got sixpence to scratch with. James paid their fares to come to England, which was generous of him. But would that generous, extremely rich brother also enable his sister to go travelling to France and Italy?'

'They want to go to France?' The rector stared.

'To buy antiquities and pictures, Laure said.'

'I would lay money there is more to it than that . . . And James will not lend them the money?'

'Laure did not say that. I inferred it . . . Yes, Lucy, who is it?'

'It's a lady, ma'am. She has no card, and will not give her name. She says she must see you urgently. It is about New Hall, she says.'

'About New Hall! Is it Miss Rossiter?'

'No, ma'am. It's no one I have seen before.'

'You had better show her in,' said Mrs Chaytor.

The woman who quietly entered the room a few moments later was young, perhaps in her mid-twenties, dressed in a dark grey gown of the sort that a prosperous merchant's wife might wear. She was on the tall side, about the same height as Mrs Chaytor, but broader in figure, with curling brown hair framing her face. *She is a pretty woman*, Amelia thought. *I could envy those deep brown eyes, and those full lips and that lustrous golden skin. She looks familiar, too; but I am sure we have not met.*

'Mrs Amelia Chaytor?' the other woman asked. She had a soft, well-modulated voice with a peculiar accent neither Mrs Chaytor nor the rector could place.

'I am she,' said Mrs Chaytor. 'This is the Reverend Hardcastle.'

'I recognise you both,' the other woman said, curtseying a little. 'I have seen you before. But I think you do not know me.'

'Then will you tell us your name?' asked Mrs Chaytor.

The young woman nodded. 'My name is Emma Rossiter,' she said.

Chapter 14

Death Comes to Hope

They stared at her, and for a fleeting moment both the rector and Mrs Chaytor wondered if they were seeing a ghost.

The rector cleared his throat. 'Emma Rossiter,' he said. 'Can you prove that you are she?'

The woman nodded again, a quick little motion of her head; she had anticipated the question. 'I have no documents to prove my name. But you may ask me any question you wish. I will answer you truthfully.'

She had something of Samuel's manner of speaking, the rector thought, though she spoke more quickly and with greater fluency, and she had the same firm jaw and chin common to the Rossiter family. My God; could she really be who she says she is?

Aloud, he said, 'If you really are Emma Rossiter, then start by telling us who died at New Hall on Christmas Day.'

An expression of pain crossed the young woman's face. 'Her name was Sarah Freebody,' she said. 'She was my servant. And I am responsible for her death.'

'I see,' said the rector, and he shot a glance at Mrs Chaytor. 'I should warn you at once that I am a justice of the peace, an officer of the law. Are you confessing to the murder of this woman?'

'No. I am responsible, for it was my actions that led to her death. But I did not kill her. She was a good woman, and innocent of any misdeed.'

'Do you know who did kill her? Did you see the murderer?'

'No. She was attacked while I was in the cellar of the house. I saw nothing at the time.'

'I think we should all sit down,' said Mrs Chaytor.

They sat. The young woman perched on the edge of a chair opposite them, her hands in her lap. She had strong, capable hands, the rector thought. There was a poise about her that was part natural grace, part something she had learned very recently, for she was still very conscious of her posture. She looked at them now with wide dark eyes, her face full of concern and . . . yes, there was fear too, but only a little.

'Let us begin at the beginning,' said the rector. 'You say your name is Emma Rossiter. Where were you born, and when?'

'I was born in the city of New York in 1772. My mother was Martha Rossiter, wife of Nicholas Rossiter.'

The story she told was identical in every respect to that he had heard from Samuel, except it was a little more detailed. When she spoke of their life among the Shawnee her face softened. 'Looking back on it now, I see our life was a hard one. The winters were cold, and sometimes when the settlers burned our crops there was hunger. But Ahneewakee always looked after us. She would go without food herself, so that we might eat. She gave us everything she had.'

'She sounds like a good woman,' said Mrs Chaytor gently.

'Yes. She was noble and generous. No mother could have done more for us. Her death was a great sorrow, the greatest I have known. Not even the death of Father affected me so much.'

She spoke also of the return to her mother's family in Pennsylvania and the welcome they received there; her story was more nuanced than the one Samuel had told. 'Aunt Rachel was very kind and good, and she loved us. Not all the family did, nor did others in the village. Some still disliked the fact that our mother had married Father. They did not think it was fitting. And because we were the product of that union, they disliked us too.'

'Racial prejudice goes both ways, it would seem,' said Mrs Chaytor.

'I had never heard of this idea of race before. Among the Shawnee, all were equal; our colour was hardly remarked upon. In Pennsylvania, Samuel was accepted more quickly than I, because he had our mother's colour. I inherited my skin colour from my father, and they disliked this. That has often been the case. To black people I am white, but to white people I am black.'

'What do *you* think you are?' the rector asked. The question slipped out almost before he was aware of it.

'I do not know. I seem to be neither one thing, nor another.' The young woman stared into the fire. 'I miss my childhood among the Shawnee,' she said. 'Life was hard, but I knew who I was. Ever since Ahneewakee died, I have been searching for a home. I thought I had one with Aunt Rachel, and then with Father, but they died too.'

Those whom we love, die, Samuel had said. 'Did you ever think of going back?' said Mrs Chaytor. 'Back to the Indians?'

The other woman smiled a little. 'Yes. But it would not have been the same. What I wanted was my childhood all over again. I wanted Ahneewakee's love. But, time will not run backwards.'

She told of their journey to New York and then to Boston, and their rough reception there by Parker, and then the walk to Montréal and the reunion with their father. 'When he died, we were once again alone,' she said simply. 'But Father gave us something to cling to. He gave us the idea of a home here in England. We knew nothing about England. But, the will said we owned New Hall, where Father had lived as a child and where our grandmother was buried. That, we thought, might be a home for us.'

'So, you came to London,' said the rector. 'What then?'

'We searched for Mr Parker, the lawyer who had charge of the estate, but were told he was dead. We were not sure what to do then.' She smiled a little. 'Life among the Shawnee taught us many things; I can trap and skin a rabbit, I can track a deer, I can grow corn, I can harvest wild fruits and live for days in the forest on my own. But it did not teach us how the laws worked, or what lawyers do. It was some time before we found a kind friend to give us advice and tell us what to do.'

'That would be Mr Equiano,' said the rector.

'Yes. Samuel has spoken of him to you, then. He has also told you of his visit to Mr Jessington?'

'Yes. And after that, Mr Parker came and threatened you.'

'I was not there when this happened; he spoke to Samuel only. I came back to find Samuel very distressed. He was ready to give up. "We cannot fight these other Rossiters," he said. "They are rich and powerful, and they have the law on their side. We should stay in London for the winter, and in spring when the ships are sailing we should return to Montréal and make our lives there."'

She paused; she was coming to the crux of the matter now, and her audience watched her gather her thoughts, painfully.

'I wanted to see New Hall,' she said. 'What is the word I want? Obsessed, that is it. I was obsessed by New Hall. Even before Father's will was unsealed and we learned that we owned it, I yearned to see it. I knew that Samuel was right, and the house would never be ours. But I thought, if only I could see it for a little while, I could pretend it was the home we have been seeking.'

She is holding something back, the rector thought. For the first time since she entered this room, she is not telling the whole truth. He waited.

'So, I did a bad thing,' the young woman said. 'I knew that if Samuel learned what I intended to do, he would talk me out of it. *We cannot go against the law*, he would say, *because the law is on their side.* So, I left secretly without telling him, and I journeyed with Sarah Freebody to New Hall. That was two days before Christmas.'

'A moment, if you please,' said the rector. 'Can you describe Miss Freebody to me?'

'I will try.' In fact, the description was remarkably accurate, and left the rector in no doubt as to the dead woman's identity. 'When did she come into your service?' he asked.

'Only the previous day, the twenty-second. She was a seamstress, but she did other work to make ends meet. She sometimes came to clean at the rooming house where Samuel and I lived. I wanted a companion to travel with, someone who understood England and English manners and customs better than I. Sarah was born in London and lived all her life there. So, I thought, she could be my guide, and asked if she would be willing to come with me. She had no family left, and nowhere to spend Christmas, so she agreed. If I had not hired her, she would still be alive. I cannot forgive myself for that.'

'And why dress in men's clothing?'

'I knew we would attract less attention that way. I often travel in men's dress when I am with Samuel. It is my colouring, you see. Not everyone likes to see a white woman, as I am often perceived, in the company of a black man. Sometimes he travels as my servant, but I detest that. To treat my brother as a servant, even as a subterfuge, seems wrong to me. So, I dress as a man. I am tall, and can easily play the part.'

The rector nodded. 'What else did your father tell you about New Hall?' he asked quietly.

The question caught her off guard, and it took her several seconds to respond. 'He told me the house had a secret,' she said finally. 'The secret lies in the cellars, he said. He would say no more. I begged him to tell me, but he just sat and watched me with his eyes twinkling. He was teasing me, of course. He loved to tease me, and he knows I am curious about things and cannot resist a puzzle. I knew it was a game ... but I convinced myself there really was a secret in the cellar. I made up stories for myself, about buried treasure, or old papers that would prove we were descended from kings; all kinds of things. As much as New Hall itself, I had to see the cellars.'

The cellars, thought the rector. *The cellars that Foucarmont knows of, and has used.* He sat forward a little, looking directly at the young woman.

'This is very important. You must tell me everything that happened from the moment you arrived at St Mary on the twenty-third of December.'

She paused again, thinking and remembering. 'The hour was late,' she said. 'It was nearly dark and quite cold. There were no people about. The house when we arrived was dark too, and I recall Sarah was a little afraid. She said we should not be able to gain entry, for there was bound to be a caretaker who would refuse us. I said all would be well. I would persuade the caretaker, or give him money, and he would let us in. In the end, it did not matter, for the caretaker was not there.'

'Then how did you gain entrance to the house?'

'That was easily done,' said Emma Rossiter. 'We have a key.'

Mrs Chaytor gave a little laugh. 'The simplest explanation,' she said, 'and we never thought of it. Your father left you a key in his will?'

'Yes. He took it with him when he left for America long ago, as a memento. He told us he had never intended to stay permanently; he always planned to return home. And New Hall was his mother's house, the home of his heart. That was why he kept the key.'

'Go on,' said the rector, but he said it gently.

'The house was very dark and cold, and smelled. Sarah was still afraid. She had lived all her life in the city, and she found this dark, silent countryside threatening; just as I had been shocked by the noise of the city. We made our way to the kitchen – I see very well in the darkness – and there we found candles and a tinderbox. We lit candles and explored the house, going through every room. I wanted to show Sarah there was nothing to fear, not here, not in my father's house. And also . . . it was like I was in a dream. I could feel my father's spirit in every room. It was as if he was present, there beside me.'

Mrs Chaytor, that most rational of women, gave a little shiver.

'Was there anything unusual about the house?' asked the rector. 'Anything that seemed untoward, or out of place?'

'There was very little in the house. Some furniture covered by sheets, beds and chairs, a few tables. Many rooms were entirely empty. Even so, the house seemed warm and welcoming to me . . . although there was something odd about the passage at the rear, behind the stairs. I did not like that passage; there was something there.'

'Something there? Do you mean, a presence?'

'A spirit from the afterlife? No, I do not think it was haunted. But I felt *something*. Apart from that, the only unpleasant thing was the room where the caretaker slept.' She wrinkled her nose. 'That was not nice.'

'No . . . What did you do next?'

'The hour was late, so we lit a fire in the kitchen. We had brought food from London, and we made a meal of bread and cheese, sitting together and talking. Then we went to bed. Sarah insisted on sleeping in the servants' quarters, even though I told her it was not necessary. I picked a room that I thought, I hoped, had once been Father's. I lay down in our father's bed with a blanket wrapped around me, and I slept and dreamed that I was home.

'Next morning was cold, and the pond outside was frozen. I found an axe and chopped a hole in the ice to draw water from the pond, for the well was frozen solid. We explored the outbuildings, and found the door to the cellar. Sarah did not want to go down; she said it would be full of dead spiders and cobwebs. I found a lantern in the stable, and lit it and went down by myself. I explored all the rooms, looked into some empty barrels, looked at all the walls and floors and ceilings, trying to find places where treasure or papers might be hidden. I found nothing. Father, I thought, you really did tease me; there is no secret here. But I knew I was wrong. Father would not simply make up a story like that. There *was* a secret; if only I could find it.

'Sarah spent the rest of the day cleaning the kitchen. She said she had to, the dirt and untidiness offended her. We had plenty of wood and water, though we had to keep chopping through the ice on the pond; the cold was such that the water froze in a few minutes. As for me, I had never lived here, of course, but I made up memories for myself, imagining what life would have been like here as a child. It was make-believe; I do not know this country or its people, and I have no idea what life is like here. But in my made-up memories I roamed the Marsh, watching birds and butterflies in summer, or walked along the edge of the sea, and even went swimming in the water. Or maybe I had a little boat and sailed on the sea. My memories were warm and beautiful, and I was as happy as I have been since before Ahnee-wakee died.'

She paused, and they waited, letting her remember. *I really must acknowledge*, Mrs Chaytor told herself fiercely, *that I have no monopoly on sorrow.*

'The next day,' said Emma, continuing with a visible effort, 'was Christmas. Sarah was very patient with me, for it cannot have been a very pleasant Christmas for her; but at least, she was not alone . . . She liked to organise things. She started moving furniture from other rooms into the morning room, to make it more comfortable. It was now quite cold. In the morning I chopped through the ice on the pond again to draw more water, but by early afternoon it had frozen over again and I had to cut a new hole. I spent the morning by the kitchen fire, thinking. My dreams were done now, and I knew I should have to leave this place and return to London, and confess to Samuel what I had done. I knew he would scold me for having done a wrong thing. I was thinking about how I would apologise to him.

'And then, quite suddenly, a different thought came to me. What if the secret of the cellars was a hidden door or passage that opened onto other, undiscovered rooms? Another mansion might exist below the house, an underground palace or castle. I thought of the rack for bottles. Perhaps it had a . . . mechanism of some sort that would open the invisible door. Father's desk in Montréal had a handle that, if turned, opened a secret compartment behind the others. Now I wondered if there might be something like it in the cellars.

'Sarah was upstairs. I lit a lantern and went out without telling her, into the cold afternoon. I went down to the cellars to test my theory. Again, I was obsessed. I tried every piece of the bottle rack to see if it would move. None did. Then I tested the walls and floors and ceilings again, looking for loose bricks or any sign of a hidden door.

'By the time my lantern went out it was late and growing dark. I climbed back up to the courtyard, and then I smelled it; the blood. I knew it was fresh, quite fresh, for it smelled warm against the cold air. I followed the scent, and came to the pond. I found the body face down in the water. It took me a moment to realise it was Sarah. Her feet were nearest me; I seized them and tried to pull her from the water, but her body was heavy and the ice had already started to form. One of her boots came away in my hand. I realised then that she must already be dead.

'Then I heard a noise behind me, near the front of the house. At once I thought, it is the killer. He is looking for me. He killed poor Sarah, now he is coming for me. I could do nothing to help Sarah, for she was beyond human aid, so I left her there.

'I ran back to the house. I know how to move silently and swiftly, and also how to fight, but even so I was afraid. When I entered the house I could hear someone moving around in the front rooms, so I went quietly up the back stairs and fetched my clothes and money. Then I came down and went out to the stables and saddled both horses. I put my baggage on one, and rode the other. I rode as quickly and quietly as I could, out of the yard and down to the gates, expecting to be pursued, but I was not.

'I kept going until I was well away from the village and up in the hills above the Marsh. I found a stand of trees, where I pick-eted the horses and slept for a while. Early next morning, I rode back to Ashford and returned the horses to the stable where I hired them. I had to wait a day at Ashford, as the weather was bad and no coaches were running. Then I returned to London and Samuel. But Samuel was gone.

'I realised he must have come after me, so I retraced my jour-ney. At Ashford, I learned he had hired a horse, but no one knew where he was now. I was very worried. I could think of no rea-son why anyone would want to kill Sarah. I thought at first that someone had killed her thinking she was me; but then I real-ised it was quite possible that in my man's clothes, someone had mistaken me for Samuel and it was he they wanted to kill.'

'Who do you think might want to kill Samuel?' the rector asked. 'Or yourself, come to that?' And when the young woman did not answer, he said, 'You have an idea, don't you?'

'Mr Parker hates us,' she said. 'He threatened Samuel.'

'A murder had been done. Your brother had disappeared. Parker had threatened you. Why did you not come to the authorities and inform them of all this?'

'I did not know who the authorities were,' she said simply. 'And even if I did, how did I know they would listen to me? We are strangers, and of a different race. We are not of your people. Why would you believe us, against one of your own?'

The rector had no answer to that. 'Go on,' he said. 'What did you do next?'

'I wanted to find Samuel, but I did not know where to look. And, I wanted to find out what had happened to poor Sarah. As I said, I was responsible for her death. So, I went to a town called Lydd, where I found a room in a house. I was still in men's clothes, and I used a man's name. I was nervous, as I expected people to ask what I was doing there, but no one did.'

Lydd was another smugglers' haunt, where people kept their business to themselves. Strangers, provided there was nothing suspicious about them, were ignored.

'I read the newspapers,' said Emma, 'and learned there would be an inquest. I came here and attended it, and learned that no one yet knew who Sarah was or who had killed her. I thought of speaking up then, and identifying her, but I knew that you and others would start asking questions. Then I might be in trouble, and I might never find Samuel.'

'You were at the inquest?' said Mrs Chaytor, and then she gave a little gasp. 'You were! You sat behind me.'

'I was dressed as a woman then,' said Emma, giving her a little nod. 'I used to leave the house in Lydd every morning and go to a little barn that no one used, and change my costume. Sometimes I went as a man, sometimes as a woman, each time appearing as a different person. That way no one would ask why I kept coming back to the same places. I went all over, looking for Samuel and listening for news of him. I came here to St Mary several times.'

'You left holly on your grandmother's grave,' said the rector. 'And on Sarah's.'

'It seemed the right thing to do,' she said simply. 'I do not know why. Then I heard Samuel had been arrested. I was terrified, not knowing what would happen to him. I went often to New Romney and watched the gaol, hoping to hear news. I saw you there several times,' she said to the rector.

Hardcastle remembered a young man counting coins, and another standing holding a horse. 'You are a master of disguise,' he said, and he smiled for the first time that evening. 'Of course, as we assumed you were dead, it never occurred to us to look for you. But did you not know that Samuel also thinks you are dead?'

'I did not think he would believe that,' said Emma emphatically. 'The newspaper described Sarah as having brown skin. I do not. He must have known I was still alive. He must!' There were sudden tears in her eyes. 'He must know!'

'I think he does know,' said Mrs Chaytor gently. 'I think that may be one of the reasons why he has now escaped. I think he is still looking for you, Emma.'

'*Koneskwa!*' They did not know what she meant, but there was no doubting that it was a cry from the heart. 'I have done wrong,' said Emma. 'All along, I have done wrong. I went to New Hall when I should have stayed away. I fled and left Sarah dead. I failed to go to the authorities and so Samuel was arrested for

Sarah's murder. Now he has escaped because of me, and is in danger once more. Oh, what have I done?'

'Do not be so harsh with yourself,' said the rector. 'From another perspective, you have done right most of the time. You could not have known that by going to New Hall, you were putting Miss Freebody in danger. Had you come forward sooner, Samuel would doubtless have been freed. And both of you would have been out in the open, and exposed to Parker's vengeance.

'No, Miss Rossiter; you were well hidden and Parker could not find you, and Samuel was safe in gaol where Parker could not touch him. You have put your brother through a certain amount of pain, but it is quite likely that you have also saved his life.'

'Why does Mr Parker hate us so?' Emma implored. 'We have done no harm to him, or any of his family. Is it because our mother was black, but we are of Rossiter blood? Is that why he wants us dead?'

'He hates you for those reasons, but that is not why he wants to kill you. Your father was quite right, Miss Rossiter. There *is* a secret at New Hall, and I am willing to bet that it is in the cellars. Parker knows what the secret is, and he is afraid that you know too. He knows you were at the house, and whether he knows it was you in disguise or still thinks it was Samuel no longer really matters.'

'But I do not know what the secret is. I searched and searched, but I found nothing.'

'It doesn't matter that you yourself do not know what the secret is. Parker *thinks* you do, and so long as he thinks that, you are dangerous to him.'

'We will tell him that we do not know.'

'He would not believe you. Parker is a man of violence,' said the rector, 'and thinks violence solves all problems. I'm afraid, my dear, that if you show yourselves in public, both you and Samuel will be very much in danger.'

In the end, Hardcastle left Miss Rossiter with Mrs Chaytor. It was the safest thing he could think of; Lucy the housekeeper was devoted to her mistress, and could be trusted. He did not want to send her back to Lydd; Parker, or Foucarmont, was more than capable of tracking her there, and she was lucky they had not found her already. By now they must certainly know she was not in London, and would assume she had come back to the Marsh to find her brother.

Samuel in his prison manacles was still out there in the dark and the cold. Emma had been surprisingly unconcerned about this; Samuel, she said, had grown up with the Shawnee and knew how to survive in far colder weather than this. What worried her was that he would do something foolish and show himself, and Parker would then find him and kill him. On this score the rector could offer her no reassurance. He could only look after her own safety, and in the capable hands of Mrs Chaytor she was as safe as she would be anywhere. He returned home late, his mind a whirl. Mrs Kemp scolded him for spoiling dinner, and he snapped at her. Calpurnia scolded him for snapping at Mrs Kemp, and he snarled at her too, at which point she threw down her fork and marched away into the drawing room. So absorbed was he in the problem that he did not hear her weeping.

Half the puzzle had been solved. They knew for certain who the murdered woman was, and it was not Emma Rossiter. That left the other half: who had killed Sarah Freebody and why, and what were they trying to protect?

It was possible, the rector reflected, that Emma Rossiter was lying; that it was she who had killed Sarah Freebody, or even Samuel and she in collusion. A good barrister – like Lord Clavertye – could still make a case, and a jury might believe it. What was the phrase Samuel had used? A convenient murderer. That could apply to Emma too.

It was possible that they were the killers, yes; but he did not believe it for a moment. Twenty years as a clergyman had taught him how to take the measure of people. Emma Rossiter was no murderer. She was a worried, even frightened young woman who had stumbled into something she did not understand. She needed help. And in any case, he was certain he had his killer – or one of them. That Parker was complicit in murder and collusion with Foucarmont, he knew beyond doubt.

The fog lingered all the following day, hanging chill and silent over the Marsh and blotting out the sun. The rector thought about Samuel Rossiter as he went about his duties, out there somewhere on the run, and shivered. His sister had seemed confident that he knew how to look after himself, but even if able to cope with the cold he would be tired and hungry. Perhaps Clavertye was right and he would turn himself in. That was now a thing devoutly to be hoped for. Joseph Parker was a frightened man. Despite his bluster, Parker knew full well that the case against him was building, and a little more pressure would break his resistance. If handled correctly, he would not only confess to his own role, but implicate his confederates as well. That would kill the murder case against Samuel; and the rector was confident now that he could persuade the deputy lord lieutenant to abandon the notion that Samuel was in league with Foucarmont.

At dinner he was silent and Calpurnia, still wounded by his behaviour the previous day, was quiet too. Rodolpho's snoring as he lay before the fire was the loudest noise in the room.

'You are very preoccupied, Marcus,' his sister said finally. 'Is there any news about Samuel Rossiter?'

'No,' said the rector. Not trusting her discretion, he had not told her about Emma.

'You are not very forthcoming, either. Never mind, I shall ask Mrs Chaytor. She will tell me, I am sure. *She* trusts me, you see.'

The rector ignored this. 'When are you seeing Mrs Chaytor?'

'This very evening. I promised to call around and read her the latest chapter from my book . . . What did you say? It sounded very much like blasphemy, Marcus. Not terribly becoming for a clergyman, is it?'

'I said, please don't go. Mrs Chaytor has a guest, a young cousin from up-country.' That was the story they had decided upon to explain the presence of the young woman in the house. So long as Parker was at liberty, Emma was in danger.

'But it is all arranged!' protested Calpurnia. 'If Mrs Chaytor wished me not to call on her, then I am sure she would have let me know it herself. I am going, Marcus, and there is an end to it.'

'All right! Peace, for the love of God. The night is very dark, so take Rodolpho with you. *He won't be of any use, but any vagabond won't know that.'

'Rodolpho will always protect me,' said Calpurnia firmly. 'Won't you, my lovely, lovely boy?' she crooned to the dog, who woke up and wagged his tail.

Muttering under his breath, the rector retired to the sanctuary of his study. A few minutes later he heard the sound of his sister and the dog departing. Silently, he thanked Mrs Chaytor for providing him with a quiet and peaceful evening in his own home.

On the heels of the thought came a knock at the front door, and he heard Biddy hurrying to open it. She came into the study a moment later and curtseyed.

'It's Mr Stemp, reverend,' she said, a little wide-eyed. 'For sure he says it's urgent.'

'I will come at once.'

Stemp was in the hallway, blowing on his mittened hands. 'Bad news, reverend,' he said. 'It's Mr Parker from up at New Hall.'

'What? What is wrong with him?'

'He's stiff as a board, that's what's wrong with him. He's at Hope, lying in the old church where the altar would have been, and the back of his head's been stove in. He's stone dead. I reckon he's been there for most of the day.'

Chapter 15

The Siege of Sandy House

Centuries before, Hope had been a thriving Marsh village and All Saint's Church had been the bustling heart of a community. Plague and fever had killed its people or driven them away, and now all that remained was the ruin of the church, its roof long since fallen in, its floor a bed of grass and moss. Lantern-light flickered around the nave, casting wavering shadows on stone walls, windows like eyeless sockets giving onto the night beyond.

Joseph Parker lay sprawled on his side, one hand flung out where he had clutched at the turf in a final spasm before he died. He had been struck a massive blow to the back of the head, shattering his skull. The lanterns showed a dark shadowy stain where his blood had poured out and soaked into the grass. The light showed also the jewelled buttons on his waistcoat and the glittering gem on his watch fob. The cameo rings were still on his fingers.

The rector knelt over the body, studying it. *Unless I stop you, there will be yet more killing*, he had said to Parker. And more killing there had been. But Hardcastle had not expected him to be the next victim.

'Has Dr Mackay been sent for?'

Stemp nodded. 'I sent the lad to fetch him.'

The corpse had been found by a boy from Old Romney, coming back from an evening's fishing. That was the story, at least; it might be true, but Hope Church was also a favourite rendezvous point for smugglers. Foucarmont knows this too, the rector thought. Parker was killed and his body left here to ensure he would be found.

'One thing's for certain, reverend,' said Stemp. 'This was no robbery.'

'No,' said the rector. 'This was a calculated killing.'

Foucarmont was back on the Marsh. And Clavertye was still hunting him far away among the downs of Sussex, looking in the wrong place.

'What do you reckon happened?' Stemp asked.

'I questioned Parker very closely yesterday. He did not admit anything, but he was a frightened man when he left me.' The rector walked slowly around the ruined nave, looking for any clues as to what had happened. He did not expect to find any; Foucarmont and his men were professionals. 'Parker must have met with Foucarmont after we talked. Foucarmont would have seen Parker was frightened, and might have thought he was wavering. Perhaps he feared Parker would offer a confession in exchange for lenient treatment? So, Foucarmont killed him before he could betray their secret.'

'Whatever they are hiding up there at New Hall must be juicy,' Stemp observed. 'What do you think it is? Money?'

'Perhaps . . . There is the doctor.'

Mackay, cloaked and booted and carrying his bag, walked into the nave followed by a groom carrying another lantern and a pistol. The rector nodded towards the weapon. 'A wise precaution,' he said. He had left his own pistol at home, and wished he hadn't.

'The entire Marsh seems full of maniacs bent on homicide,' the doctor said sourly. 'Very well, let's get to work. Hold up that lantern, Stemp, if you don't mind . . . Aye, well, this won't take long. Cause of death is plain as daylight.'

'Anything else? Any other marks on him?'

'No . . . Ah, wait a moment. His wrists have been bound. There's chafing all around them. Someone tied his hands with rope, I'd say. Before he was killed, too.' Mackay looked up, face shadowy under the brim of his hat. 'What do you think happened?'

'A falling out among criminals,' the rector said grimly. 'Doctor, would you be so kind as to carry on here, and see the body transported to New Romney? I must go and break the news to Mr Parker's wife. Joshua, when you have finished assisting Dr Mackay, find Captain Austen, give him my compliments and ask him to call on me as soon as he may.'

Parker had been dead for hours; Foucarmont and his men could be miles away by now. They would have to start a new search for them, and of course Lord Clavertye would have to be informed. That last thought cheered the rector a little, for he quite enjoyed the sight of Lord Clavertye in the wrong. But the cheerful thought did not last long, for another, deeply unhappy task lay ahead of him. He began to walk back to St Mary in the Marsh, leaving Hope Church with its flickering ghostly lanterns behind, rehearsing in his mind the words of consolation he would use and the questions he would have to ask.

Tendrils of fog snaked over the Marsh, blown on a faint fluttering breeze. Apart from this little wind, the night was utterly silent and still. He had just crossed the bridge over the New Sewer, St Mary in the Marsh about three-quarters of a mile away, when he stopped dead in his tracks. Booming in his ears, muffled and yet magnified by the fog, came the sound of a gunshot, followed swiftly by another.

At Sandy House, Mrs Chaytor and Miss Rossiter sat by the fire drinking tea. 'The night is very quiet,' observed the younger woman.

'The nights are often quiet here on the Marsh. It is a lonely place, and still.' Mrs Chaytor smiled. 'I expect you are used to loneliness and stillness after your time living in the forest.'

It was Emma's turn to smile. 'The first city I ever saw was New York. It was terrifying. There was noise all the time: horses, carriage wheels, whipcracks, building work, pedlars crying their wares. It seemed never to end. While living with Father in Montréal, I grew used to the noise. But sometimes I still miss the silence.' Her smile faded. 'Sarah, of course, was used to the noise; she found the Marsh too quiet.'

She looked at Mrs Chaytor with her steady brown eyes. 'Are you happy here?' she asked. 'Living in this place?'

Mrs Chaytor considered her answer. 'You said that you were searching for a home,' she said. 'I came here for the same reason. I think I may have found one.'

That did not answer the question, and Emma knew it. 'You are sad,' she observed.

'Yes.'

'You are sad for the same reason as I, are you not? Those you love have gone, and you cannot go back to them.'

'What you said about Ahneewakee moved me deeply,' said Mrs Chaytor quietly. 'I know the pain you spoke of.'

'What do you do now?'

'You mean, how do I fill my days? I play music. I walk on the Marsh. I wait.'

'For what?'

'Nothing. There is nothing to wait for. And yet, still I wait.'

'You think of yourself as empty,' said Emma.

Amelia forced a smile. 'You are very perceptive,' she said.

'But it is not so. You do not only sit and wait. You care enough about me to help me, to open your house to me. You care about Samuel too, I know. You are not empty. You are full of spirit and strength.' She wrinkled her brow. 'You said you came to the Marsh looking for a home. But I think you must have had a home before. Why really did you come?'

'You are right, of course,' said Amelia after a moment. 'I had a home, but it came to an end when my husband died, just as yours did when Ahneewakee was gone. I came to the Marsh because I wanted to detach myself from the world, to isolate myself from all that had gone before. But of course that is impossible. We cannot leave the world behind, not so long as we live and breathe, and think. The outer world is always there, and sometimes its call cannot be resisted.'

Emma nodded at this. 'I think my case is the opposite of yours,' she said. 'I am isolated from the world too, but I do not want to be. I wish to be part of the world, but I do not know how to do so.'

'What do you mean?'

'It is hard to find a place. Many people do not accept me. Even as Father's daughter in Montréal, doors were sometimes closed to me because of my colour. It is the same in London also. And should we go back to Montréal as Samuel wishes, without Father's protection, it will be worse.'

'My dear; the doors that are closed to you because of your colour are not ones you would care to walk through in any case. The people behind them are not worth knowing. But Samuel told the rector that you also had friends in London, who helped you. Mr Equiano and others like him.'

'Oh, yes,' said Emma with gentle vigour. 'That is quite so. They are good people, very good people, kind and noble of heart. They talk about things like liberty, which I do not fully understand. But they talk about ending the traffic in slaves, and that I do understand. Mother's family told us how slaves are taken from Africa, and how much they suffer. Many people we met in London told us similar stories, and I realised then how thousands of people have been taken and made slaves. I realised also how fortunate my mother was to have been freed, and how lucky Samuel and I are too. I thought that I might be able to help them.'

'The abolitionists?' The slave trade was an issue on which Mrs Chaytor had strong views, and she was in any case grateful for the change of subject. 'You are right, they are good people. Nor are they alone. Many oppose them, but they also have friends in very high places, including the prime minister himself. You could do good work, if you cared to join them, and you would make good friends too.'

'You support the abolitionists?'

'I give them money from time to time, yes.'

'It is as you said,' said Emma smiling. 'The outer world is always there, and sometimes its call cannot be resisted.'

'You are wicked to trap me with my own words,' said Amelia firmly. They both smiled, and then came the knock at the front door.

The first to enter the room a moment later was Rodolpho, who bounded in cheerfully waving his tail. He was followed by Calpurnia, carrying a bundle of papers tied with a ribbon and scolding the dog. 'My dear Mrs Chaytor, I am so sorry for Rodolpho's bad manners. I do hope you don't mind my bringing him. He cannot bear to be separated from me for long, you see, and he pines when I am not there.'

'Rodolpho is entirely welcome,' said Mrs Chaytor. Rodolpho swished his tail again, shaking his head and grinning at Emma, and then lay down before the hearth and fell fast asleep. 'May I present to you Miss Latimer, a cousin of mine from the West Country. She has come to stay with me for a few days. Miss Latimer, Mrs Vane, Reverend Hardcastle's sister.'

'I am very pleased to meet you,' said Calpurnia, eyes bright with curiosity. With some misgivings, Mrs Chaytor watched her study the other woman. Calpurnia might be flighty, but she was not unintelligent. Emma's clothes, made in Canada, were clearly not of English cut, and there were certain features of her hair and face that made her heritage apparent, if one were observant enough.

'And I am also pleased to meet you, Mrs Vane,' said Emma in her soft voice. 'Mrs Chaytor tells me that you write books.'

Bravo, thought Mrs Chaytor with approval, that will distract her. Calpurnia was off at once, describing her literary career while Mrs Chaytor sent Lucy for more tea and then directed her to check that all the shutters were closed; the night was cold and foggy, and she did not want the damp getting into the house. The three women settled by the fire, around Rodolpho, who had begun to snore.

'You asked if I would read you the latest chapter from my book,' Calpurnia said eagerly to Mrs Chaytor. 'May I do so?'

That was not exactly how the original conversation had gone, but Mrs Chaytor smiled. 'We should be delighted,' she said, arranging her skirts. 'Pray begin.'

Calpurnia untied the ribbon around her manuscript, cleared her throat, and began.

THE LIGHTHOUSE OF VAVASSAL
A ROMANCE BY MRS CORDELIA HARTBOURNE

('That is my *nom de plume*, you see. All the most fashionable writers use a *nom de plume*.')

CHAPTER XVIII

High atop the lighthouse tower, Emily surveyed the wild scene before her. To every horizon there stretched a rolling chaos of waves, majestic, grey in the shadow of the clouds, green-blue where the sun touched upon them, crested with white where the force of the wind caught them. Golden was the sand that girdled the island, green was the moss that clung to its storm-scoured stones. White were the seabirds that wheeled and called and cried, incessantly, endlessly as they rode the wild flanks of the wind. Looking out, Emily saw the full force and majesty of this wild world, and it thrilled her to the very floor of her soul. Her body tingled with excitement, and the blood ran hot in her veins.

Deeply moved by this magnificent vista, she nonetheless recalled her purpose in coming to this remote place. 'I must tell you now the reason why I undertook the perilous voyage to the Isle of Vavassal,' she said, gesturing around her. 'I am, as you may have begun to realise, no ordinary visitor.'

'I assumed as much,' said the count, turning his hawk-nosed face so that he stood profiled against the rolling sea. 'I assume further that it is myself whom you have come to seek, and that you have some vital message for me.'

'Indeed I do. The message, Señor de Lorca, comes from the Duchess of Barcalonga, your aunt.'

'Ah!' A change came over the man's dark, sinister visage. 'My aunt. How interesting. I have not had intercourse with my aunt for many long years. Why does she seek me out now, I wonder?'

'That you will hear, when I retail her entire message to you,' said Emily. 'Pray, now, let me continue. The Duchess, knowing of your deep distaste for herself, advised me that you would be unwilling to hear any report of her. But this concerns you, *Señor*, most closely. It concerns your fortune, and perhaps even your life.'

'I care nothing for my fortune,' sneered the count, 'and I care even less for my life—'

Emma held up a hand. 'What is it?' asked Mrs Chaytor.

'I thought I heard something.' The young woman was suddenly tense, but after a moment she relaxed. 'It is nothing,' she said. 'I am very sorry for interrupting you, Mrs Vane. Will you please continue?'

'Certainly.'

'—and I care even less for my life. You may inform the duchess as much.'

'You declare that you care nothing for your own life. What then of the life of Sevilla de Lancefortet, the woman you profess to love? Do you care nothing for her life, Señor?'

The count turned sharply. Towering over Emily, he glared down at her, passion raging in his single dark eye, the other of course being covered as always by a black silk eyepatch.

'Sevilla is dead!' he hissed, his voice full of dark fury. 'She died here, on the Isle of Vavassal, five years ago. Her spectre haunts this very lighthouse. Do you not know that is why I came here, to seek out her spirit and make contact with it if I can? To renew in the life of ghosts the love we once had in the real world? And now you taunt me with this fantasy she is alive! Curses be upon you—'

'There!' said Emma suddenly. 'Did you hear it?'

All three women strained their ears. The fire popped; Rodolpho gave a gentle snore; the clock ticked.

'There,' said Emma again, in a whisper this time. 'I heard it again. There is someone outside the house.'

'Where?'

'Moving outside the dining room. Wait. There is another near the front door.'

'Be very quiet,' commanded Mrs Chaytor. She rose and, gathering her skirts, ran through to the kitchen. 'Lucy!' she hissed. 'There may be intruders outside. Check the back door again, and make certain it is barred. Then stay here out of the way.'

'Yes, ma'am,' said the girl, startled.

Amelia herself could still hear nothing, but Emma's urgency had infected her. Hurrying back through the house, she glanced through the open door of the dining room. The room was dark, the candles snuffed after dinner, but there was enough light to see that the shutters of one window were open. Lucy must have forgotten to check them when she toured the house earlier. Clicking her tongue, she moved to the window: and then stopped, rigid with shock.

There was a face outside the window, the face of a man, glaring, broken-nosed and full of hate. For a split second the two faces looked into each other, separated only by the panes of glass.

Then the hammer in the man's hand swept up and broke the glass in a shower of flying splinters. Dropping the hammer, he reached inside. He was a fraction of a second too late. With all her strength, Mrs Chaytor hurled the shutters closed and slammed down the bar that held them in place. She heard the man swearing and beating on the other side, but the shutters were strong oak and proof against any hammer – for a while, at least. She seized two chairs and jammed them hard against the shutters, and then with desperate strength, pushed the heavy table against the chairs, reinforcing the barrier.

Darting into the hallway, she turned to the console table that stood next to the hatstand, opened the drawer and pulled out her pistol. Normally this was kept safely upstairs, but since the news of Foucarmont's return, she had left the weapon here in the hall, primed and loaded. Hearing another noise she turned to see Calpurnia and Emma coming out of the drawing room. Calpurnia gasped when she saw the pistol.

'Whatever is happening?'

'We are under attack,' said Mrs Chaytor tersely. 'Help me move this table.'

Emma hurried forward and together they pushed the console table against the front door, which was already barred. Rodolpho had woken and come out too; he stood now, his ears pricked in alarm. 'Mrs Vane, Miss Latimer, perhaps you would join Lucy in the kitchen. I think it is the safest place. Put anything heavy that you can against the door.'

Calpurnia was pale. Amelia realised she herself must be white as a sheet; she had not yet recovered from the shock in the dining room. 'I will leave you, Rodolpho,' said Calpurnia, retreating.

Emma Rossiter looked at Amelia. 'I can fight,' she said.

'I have only one pistol.'

'Have you knives?'

'There are carving knives in the dining room.'

Emma darted into the dining room and came out with her hands full of knives. She held one by the point, and from her years in Italy, Mrs Chaytor knew what that meant. She knew she ought to urge Emma to go to the kitchen and be safe; she also knew she was immensely relieved to have the other woman here beside her, facing whatever was coming.

It came. The door knocker sounded, rapping hard and peremptory. Mrs Chaytor motioned for silence and they crouched on either side of the hall behind the furniture, weapons in hand.

The knocker sounded again, harder. 'Open up!' commanded a voice.

'Who are you?' demanded Mrs Chaytor. 'Identify yourself, if you please.'

'Open the door,' said the voice, 'or we will smash it down.'

'The neighbours will hear you,' said Amelia, 'and come to aid us.'

'No one will hear anything. Your house is apart from others, and everyone is indoors with the shutters closed. You are alone and isolated, and there are many of us. Open the door, Mrs Chaytor, and let us in.'

'No. Get yourselves gone.'

'Mrs Chaytor,' said the voice, soft with menace, 'you are women alone in a house. If I have to force this door, my men will not use you gently.'

And then she recognised the voice, and just for a moment she shivered with horror, for she knew this man would be as good as his word. 'Go to hell, Monsieur de Foucarmont,' she said.

She heard his voice no more. Instead came a hard blow on the door, and the sound of splintering wood. They were using axes. The door was oak too, and strong, but it could not last forever. And now she was aware of more blows coming from the rear of the house. They were attacking the door there also; and far from being safe, Lucy and Mrs Vane in the kitchen were in grave danger.

I can do nothing about that, she thought. More blows pounded on the door, which shivered against the iron bar that held it. Then the blows ceased.

Silence fell, cold and shivering. Mrs Chaytor looked for Rodolpho, but could see no sign of him. Hopefully he had gone to join his mistress in the kitchen; chicken-hearted he might be, but the sight of Rodolpho would surely be a deterrent.

'Mrs Chaytor,' said the menacing voice again. 'I will ask you once more. Open the door and let us enter.'

'Why?' she demanded. There came the desperate thought that if she could stall for time, someone might notice the attackers and raise the alarm. 'Is it revenge on me you seek? If so, tell me, and I will come out. But let the others alone.'

'Pleasant though it would be to pay you back for the harm you did me last year,' said the voice, 'it is not you I seek. This is your final chance, Mrs Chaytor. Open the door. If you do not, then your body and your life are forfeit to my men.'

'No,' said Amelia. The horror had gone; ice-cold anger flooded over her now. 'I warn *you*, Foucarmont. You set foot in my house at peril of your life. Get yourself gone,' she repeated, 'or face the consequences.'

Outside the front door there was laughter. 'How amusing,' said Foucarmont. Another axe slammed into the door and she jumped, then looked down to the priming of the pistol. Emma, crouched opposite her with knives in hand, was absolutely still, her eyes fixed on the door. The pounding blows from the rear of the house continued.

One panel of the door broke, an axe blade shining through. It was withdrawn; another blow followed, and the axe punched through again. Then the entire panel gave away, cold air rushing into the hall from outside. An arm clad in a black coat reached through, fumbling for the bar. Mrs Chaytor raised the pistol, but Emma hissed and held up a hand; wait.

She waited, heart pounding.

The bar was lifted. More blows rammed the door wide open, the console table sent sprawling. A fresh blast of air fluttered the candles, one of which went out. A dark cloaked figure strode into the hall, axe in hand.

Amelia Chaytor raised her pistol and fired. The man saw her and dodged; this saved his life. The ball meant for his heart struck him instead in the side and he shouted and staggered back, dropping the axe and clutching at his wound. Another man pushed through after him, raising his own pistol. Faster than thought he fired at Amelia; the ball brushed her hair, and buried itself in the wall behind. Even as he fired, Emma Rossiter rose like a coiled spring and threw her first knife. A brief flash in the candlelight and the man howled, clutching at his arm. The second knife hit him high up in the chest and he recoiled, stumbling back through the door. The third knife was aimed at the man Amelia had shot; he saw her arm go back to throw, and dived back through the doorway too, the knife whistling over his back. Emma threw back her head and screamed, an ululation of triumph and anger that rang for a moment in the hallway, and then she lowered her head, panting, and picked up the next knife.

From the rear of the house came a different kind of scream and then a crash, a clang like a pot overturning, followed by a man's long howl of agony. It went on and on, fading away as the source of the noise retreated. Running as fast as her skirts would allow, smoking pistol still in hand, Amelia hurried to the kitchen to find half the floor covered in steaming water and Lucy and Calpurnia standing in the other half, lady and housekeeper clinging to each other and shaking.

'What happened?'

'A man broke in. It was Mrs Vane's idea,' said Lucy. 'We filled pots with hot water from the copper, and when the man came through the door, we threw them at him. We hit him, too.'

'We certainly did,' said Calpurnia. 'He ran away screaming like the devil.' Then both women burst into tears.

There were noises at the front of the house. My God, I haven't reloaded the pistol, Amelia thought, and hurried frantically back to the hall, where faces were peering through the wrecked door. But they were kind faces, worried faces; the faces of her neighbours, roused by the shots. Jack Hoad was the first man in, waving away the thin veil of powder smoke.

'Blind me,' said the fisherman, staring at the scene. 'Are you all right, ma'am?'

'Yes, we are all safe. Hoad, it was the Frenchman, Foucarmont. I shot him, but he escaped. He must be out there somewhere.'

'We'll go after him. Blind me,' said the fisherman again, looking at her in admiration. 'If you ever fancy a little excitement, ladies, come along with us on the next run. I'd like to see you two with a Preventive man in your sights.'

Chapter 16

The Pieces Fall Into Place

By the time the rector arrived in St Mary fifteen minutes later, the entire village had been roused. A small crowd had gathered around Sandy House, spilling across the garden. Lanterns made haloes in the swirling fog. The first person to spot the rector was Tim Luckhurst, the landlord of the Star, carrying two wooden planks and a hammer.

'There you are, reverend! We sent for you, but Mrs Kemp said you had gone out with Josh Stemp.'

'What happened?'

'That goddamned Frenchman came back, with a gang, that's what happened. They tried to break into the house.'

'Dear God! Are the ladies safe?'

'Safe and well,' Luckhurst said, smiling. 'Mrs Chaytor showed them off, right enough. She's a right plucky one, ain't she? Do you know, she actually shot the Frenchman when he tried to come in?' Luckhurst gestured to the shattered front door. 'I offered to bring her and her cousin over to the Star, but she won't have it. So we're repairing the doors. Just a temporary job, to tide her over until she can get a joiner in to make a new one.'

'What became of Foucarmont?'

'He got away, but the lads are on his trail. With Josh not here, Jack Hoad took charge. They're out there on the Marsh now, hunting him.'

Miss Godfrey and Miss Roper were there too, twittering. Hardcastle calmed them and then entered the house, stepping over the splintered oak littering the floor. He found all four women in the drawing room. Lucy was sitting on the settee, very still, her face white as chalk; Calpurnia, red-eyed, knelt beside her with her arms around Rodolpho. Emma stood calm and still as a statue by the fire. Amelia was at the sideboard pouring large measures of brandy. Wordlessly she offered one to Hardcastle.

'Are you all right?' he asked quietly. 'All of you?'

'A little nerve-shattered,' said Mrs Chaytor, 'but I expect we will recover very shortly. Here, Lucy dear, drink this. No, do not get up. You have had a terrible shock and you must stay still.' She turned to Hardcastle. 'Your sister was very resourceful,' she said, 'and both she and Lucy were very brave. Miss Latimer showed an aspect to her character that I did not know existed. Rodolpho, I am sorry to say, did not cover himself in glory. We found him hiding under the dining room table, and had to practically drag him out.'

'Oh, but he was very frightened,' said Calpurnia, hugging the still shivering wolfhound.

Hardcastle put down his brandy. 'You are certain it was Foucarmont?'

'I heard him, and saw him. I shot at him too, but I only winged him. I must be out of practice. Normally I shoot straighter than that. Marcus; he didn't come for me.'

Hardcastle turned and looked at Emma, still motionless. 'The secret of New Hall,' he said quietly. 'How did he know she was here?'

'I don't know. Lucy has been entirely faithful, I am certain of it.'

'Foucarmont must have traced her to Lydd,' he said, completely forgetting Calpurnia was in the room. 'He must have doubled back almost at once to the Marsh, leaving Clavertye to continue the hue and cry in Sussex. If he discovered she had left Lydd, he might well have worked out why. I think he has been hunting for both her and Samuel, and Parker and that man of his will have been looking for signs too.'

'The man with the broken nose!' Mrs Chaytor said suddenly. 'He was there tonight. He will be badly injured now. Emma hit him twice with her knives.'

The rector blinked. 'I suspect one of the local servants at New Hall happened to mention that Mrs Chaytor had a young woman house guest,' he said. 'The valet Steele heard this and put two and two together, and got a message to Foucarmont.'

'Will you question Parker again?'

'No one will ever question Parker again.' He told her what had happened and she listened, her blue eyes intense.

'Foucarmont has had a busy day,' she observed. 'What do we think? Is Foucarmont then the mastermind behind this plot, whatever it is?'

'Lord Clavertye referred to Foucarmont as the lynchpin. But he has never played that role before. He was the thug of the crew, the killer, but he took his orders from another. Perhaps things have changed ... Or perhaps there is another lynchpin out there, someone we have overlooked.'

He looked at her more closely. 'Thank God you are safe,' he said quietly. 'Are you quite certain you want to stay here? If not the Star, you could go to the rectory.'

She smiled at him. 'Why? Do you think we cannot look after ourselves?'

'I don't think anyone can doubt that. Will you keep my sister here for a while longer? There is something I must do, and then I will come and escort her home.'

At New Hall the windows blazed with lights. William Rossiter came out into the hall while the footman was still taking the rector's hat and coat and gloves. 'Is something wrong in the village?' the young man asked. 'We heard what sounded like gunshots.'

'There has been an attempt at house-breaking,' said the rector. 'The intruder was warned off. Is Mrs Parker here?'

He saw the young man's face change. 'What is it? Uncle Joe went out at midday, and we have not seen him since. We're all rather concerned.'

'I must speak to Mrs Parker,' the rector said quietly. 'Take me to her, if you please.'

The family were gathered in the drawing room: Jane Parker seated on a settee, round face clouded with worry; Laure in a long red gown standing by the fire, Edward, her brother, seated with one of the London periodicals tossed on the floor beside him. He rose as the rector entered the room.

'Mrs Parker,' said the rector, kneeling down and taking her hand in his, 'I fear I have dreadful news for you. There is no easy way to say this. I must tell you that your husband is dead.'

He heard Laure gasp. Edward took a step forward and then stopped. Out of the corner of his eye, Hardcastle noticed that the young man's boots were muddy. Jane Parker gazed at the rector for a long time, her hands folded in her lap, firelight glinting off her greying hair.

'Dead,' she said finally, in a soft voice. 'Oh, dear.'

'What happened to Uncle Joe?' asked William.

'He had been struck a heavy blow on the head. If it is any consolation, death must have come quickly.'

'A blow on the head! How did it happen? Did he have a fall?'

'The coroner will determine the facts in due course, Mr Rossiter. But I think it entirely likely that your uncle was murdered.'

They all stared at him in silence.

'Oh, dear,' said Mrs Parker again, in a voice gone very small. 'What shall I do now?'

She was stunned by the news. Hardcastle had seen it before, people who simply cannot take in the magnitude of what they have heard, and only slowly begin to believe it is real. The only thing to do in such cases was to give people time to let the truth sink in, and then be ready to help them when the full force of grief hits home. Parker was in league with enemy agents and had ordered a murder, but at the moment that did not matter; what mattered was the woman before him, whose life had been shattered in a moment.

'Mrs Parker,' he said gently, 'we will make every effort to discover what happened to your husband, and to see justice done. That too will be scant consolation, I know.'

'No, no,' she said, and her voice grew a little stronger. 'I very much hope you do find the man who killed my husband. It would be a great pleasure to see him hang; whoever he is.'

Nonplussed for a moment, the rector looked at her. 'Then I must begin by asking all of you when you last saw Mr Parker,' he said.

'I think I was the last to see him,' said Edward. 'It was just after midday. He was putting on his coat, and I asked him if he was going out. He said yes, but did not say where.'

'Did he have any appointments today? Did he receive any messages?'

All shook their heads.

'Mr Parker had a valet named Steele. Is he here?'

Mrs Parker studied him for a moment. 'Why should you want to see Steele?' she asked, her voice soft and puzzled.

'He might know something of his master's plans,' the rector said.

'But Steele is no longer in my husband's employ. Joseph dismissed him yesterday evening.'

'Oh? Why?'

'Joseph caught him pilfering. Several pairs of gold cufflinks and a ring had gone missing, and were found in Steele's possession.'

'Had Steele been in Mr Parker's service for a long time?'

'Nearly twenty years.'

'It must have come as a great shock to find such a faithful servant had betrayed his master.'

'Oh, yes. It was a very great shock.'

'Have you any idea where Steele went after his dismissal?'

They all shook their heads. The rector turned to William. 'I would be grateful if in the morning you would allow me to ask a few questions of your servants. They might know something that will help us track Steele down.'

William stared at him. 'Do you mean to say Steele might have had something to do with Uncle Joe's death?'

'It is possible. An unhappy servant always makes a bad enemy. Mrs Parker,' he said gently, 'please be assured of my deepest sympathies. I shall pray that God watches over you and sends you consolation in this time of great sorrow. I shall return tomorrow to see how you are faring.'

'It is good of you to trouble,' said Jane Parker. 'I am grateful for your prayers, but I am perfectly well, I assure you. But now, if you do not mind, I think I will retire.'

The men bowed as she rose, walking slowly to the door and then out, and they heard her footsteps on the stair. The rector turned to Edward. 'Are Mr and Mrs Rossiter away from home?'

'Why, yes. They returned to London three days ago.'

'I see. You were out earlier. May I ask where you went?'

Edward looked startled. 'Oh; I went riding.'

'It is hardly weather for riding.'

'So I discovered when I went outside. I came back quite quickly, I assure you. How does this concern you?'

'Mr Rossiter, I am investigating a case of murder and espionage. Everything involving members of this household and the wider community is of concern to me. Did you see anything of importance while you were out and about? Any suspicious persons, any tracks, any movement?'

'I saw absolutely nothing,' said Edward. 'And now, if you will forgive me, I shall go and see that my aunt has everything that she needs. I do not think she should be alone at the moment.'

He bowed and left the room. That left William, silent with astonishment, and Laure, pale and biting her lip. She too looked at the door.

'I will take my leave,' said the rector, and he bowed in turn. 'Look after your aunt; she will need your strength.'

'Of course,' said William. 'But . . . reverend, why would anyone want to kill Uncle Joe? I know he dismissed Steele, but that does not seem sufficient reason for murder.'

He was the first person in the house to ask why Parker had been murdered. 'I will discover what happened and who is responsible,' said the rector. 'Of that, you may be assured.'

The rector was up before daylight, and as soon as he had dressed he took his pistol from his desk, put it in his pocket and walked down the road into the village. The morning was bitterly cold, the fog continuing thicker than ever; every tree and stone and blade of grass was rimed with frost.

Outside the front door of Sandy House, timbers nailed hastily over the splintered panels, Joshua Stemp stood with a fowling piece cradled in his arms, blowing on his hands to keep them warm.

'We'll keep watch until the volunteers come,' he said. 'There's another of our fellows around the back.'

'Has Hoad returned?'

'Came back about an hour ago, and went off to get some sleep. They tracked the Frenchies a couple of miles to the south. Jack reckons there were four fellows, and he says one of 'em at least was bleeding like a stuck pig. But they lost 'em along one of the sewers. Pity we don't have Lord Clavertye's bloodhounds.'

Four would make sense: Foucarmont, the two men who had been with him at Camber, and Steele, whom Mrs Chaytor had identified as being one of the attackers. What had really happened to Steele? It would seem obvious that he was the go-between, the carrier of messages between Parker and Foucarmont. But had he stood idly by while Foucarmont killed his master? Or had he been one of the killers?

'Are the ladies still asleep?'

'So far as I know. Is it true she pinged Foucarmont?' Stemp chuckled. 'She's quite a lady. I bet old Bertrand would like to shake her hand.'

THE RECTORY, ST MARY IN THE MARSH, KENT.
11th February, 1797.

By express.

My lord,

It is my duty to inform you of two incidents that took place last night. The first was the death of Mr Joseph Parker of Boston, brother-in-law of Mr Rossiter and resident at New Hall. The corpse was found at the ruined church at Hope. The assistant coroner concurs with me that Mr Parker was murdered. He had been struck from behind with a bludgeon, in the same manner as the young woman who was killed at New Hall.

The second incident was a violent assault on Sandy House, the home of Mrs Amelia Chaytor. Fortunately the attack was driven off, and the lady herself suffered no harm. Mrs Chaytor positively identified Foucarmont as the leader of the attackers. It is my view that Foucarmont also murdered Mr Parker, with whom he has been having clandestine dealings for some time. Mr Parker's valet, Steele, was one of the gang that attacked Sandy Hall, and may well be complicit in the murder of Mr Parker.

Foucarmont and Steele were both wounded in the attack on Sandy House, as was at least one other man. Using the authority you have delegated to me, I am instructing the East Kent Volunteers to conduct a new search for he and his gang.

I await your further instructions,

Yr very obedient servant,

HARDCASTLE

The Rectory, St Mary in the Marsh, Kent.
11th February, 1797.

By express.

My dear Mr Rossiter,

It is my sad duty to inform you of the death last night of your brother-in-law, Mr Joseph Parker. I have informed

Mrs Parker, who is in the care of her family. I shall of course render her all the assistance and consolation in my power.

I must also inform you that there is a distinct possibility Mr Parker was murdered. The coroner's inquest, which will convene in a few days' time, will undoubtedly confirm this. I have begun my investigations, and I will keep you apprised of any progress. Meanwhile, if you would favour me with an interview on the next occasion you are in St Mary, I would be most grateful.

Please accept my very sincere condolences on this event. I know Mr Parker was not just your sister's husband; he was also an old friend and comrade in arms. You will feel his loss keenly, I am sure. If I can be of any assistance or support to you, please do not hesitate to seek me out.

Yr very obedient servant,

REV. M. A. HARDCASTLE, J. P.

Captain Austen arrived at mid-morning, and was shown into the rector's study. The rector rang the bell and Biddy appeared at once, curtseying as usual. 'Will you take coffee?' the rector asked him.

'Thank you, but I won't stay. Your man Stemp told me what has happened. What are your orders, sir?'

'I will have coffee,' the rector told Biddy, and she bobbed out, closing the door behind her. 'Foucarmont has three men with him, some of them badly injured,' he said to the captain. 'Foucarmont himself has also been wounded. They were last spotted heading south. My guess is they will try to get to the coast somewhere between Dungeness and Camber, and get away by boat. The French have used that route before.'

'They will have a head start on us,' warned Austen.

'I know. This is merely a precaution, in case they decide to stay in the country after all. I will breathe more easily if I can know for certain that Foucarmont has left England.'

Austen nodded. 'And Samuel Rossiter?'

'You may cease your search for him. I have a feeling Samuel Rossiter will be found when he wants to be found.'

'Perhaps. We are not the only ones looking for him, though.'

Hardcastle looked up. 'What do you mean?'

'That fellow Edward Rossiter has been out looking for him too. I saw him two days ago, riding down one of the tracks near Newchurch, and didn't think anything of it. But we spotted him again yesterday afternoon. He had dismounted and was bent over looking at something in the track – so intent he didn't hear us until we were almost on top of him. I asked what he was doing, and he said he thought his horse might have thrown a shoe. But then he started asking questions about the search, where we had looked, whether we had seen any signs of our fugitive. All very casual, as if he was making polite conversation, but he listened intently to every word I said. Why should he want to find this Samuel fellow?'

'I don't know,' said the rector.

Austen bowed and departed. The rector sat down behind his desk, staring at the flickering coal fire and thinking about Edward Rossiter. Biddy knocked and came in with his coffee, and he sipped it and then blinked a little in surprise. 'This is excellent coffee,' he said. 'Please give my compliments to Mrs Kemp.'

'Oh,' said the little maid, and blushed. 'I made the coffee, reverend.'

'You did? It is very good. But I am surprised Mrs Kemp allows you the freedom of her kitchen. That is normally her exclusive domain.'

'If you please, sir, and I hope you won't mind, but I begged Mrs Kemp to put her feet up for a while, and let me look after things. She's not a young woman, you see,' the girl said anxiously, 'and she gets so tired sometimes. I hope I have done right?'

'Of course, Biddy, and you are a good girl to be so thoughtful.'

The maid curtseyed and departed, and Hardcastle sat and counted in his mind. Coffee, answering the door to visitors, serving meals and drinks; four times out of five, when he rang the bell, it was Biddy who answered.

A slow smile spread over his face. 'Mrs Kemp,' he said aloud. 'You sly old fox!'

He called at New Hall later that morning to see how Mrs Parker was faring. Laure came out to meet him, clearly troubled.

'Aunt is resting. Do you wish me to call her?'

'No, please do not trouble her. Tell her I called, if you will. How is she?'

'I do not think she slept much, if at all. She is very withdrawn, and speaks very little.'

'That is natural.'

'Reverend, this is all so dreadful. I heard too about the attack on dear Mrs Chaytor. Is it possible that the two events are in some way connected?'

'It is possible.' He would not tell her more, not while he felt unable to trust anyone at New Hall, Mrs Chaytor's assurances about Laure notwithstanding.

Back at the rectory he was restless, so much so that he could not sit still. The fog had largely cleared, and he put on his coat and picked up his stick and whistled for Rodolpho. The dog, apparently unscarred by last night's terrors, bounded across the fields with his usual glee, barking at birds. The rector tramped down to the sea and climbed the dunes, standing and glaring at the coast of France just visible in the thin remaining haze.

He returned home in time for dinner, which he shared with Calpurnia. He had not seen her yet today; she had, as usual, risen very late. 'How are you feeling?' he asked her as they sat down.

'Well. A little fatigued. The events of last night were a great strain for all of us. Have you seen Mrs Chaytor or Miss Rossiter?'

'They are resting— What did you say?'

'That's who Miss Latimer really is, isn't it? You and Mrs Chaytor talked about her in front of me,' said Calpurnia in slow-kindling wrath, 'as if I was an idiot incapable of understanding.'

'I don't recall that we mentioned her name.'

'You called her Emma. And even if you hadn't, I can put two and two together,' snapped his sister, 'and add up to four. Now Mr Parker has been killed, and Monsieur de Foucarmont is on the run. But you are still no closer to knowing what it was all about, are you?'

'I hardly need you to tell me that,' he said sourly.

'You need to find out what the secret of New Hall is. That must be your utmost priority. If you can find that, the rest of the mystery will unravel. I think you should interrogate the Rossiter family, all of them. One of them must know what the secret is.'

The fact that he had come to this conclusion himself made her deduction and intervention all the more annoying. 'Calpurnia, keep your nose out of this. I have warned you before about prying into my business. This is not one of your blasted novels, this is real life.'

'Oh, I know, Marcus. I experienced real life at very close quarters, last evening. My life was in danger too, do you not recall?'

He threw up his hands. 'Yes, of course. I apologise.'

She subsided a little. It was, in fact, the first time he had ever apologised to her, and she was savouring the experience.

'I have had another thought,' she said.

'Yes?'

'I said some time ago that you have been living on your own for too long. That is the reason, I am quite sure, why you are so ill-tempered and irritable. A woman's touch would soften you. I think you should consider marrying.'

'*What?*'

'You should take a wife. Find someone who will bring some light and sweetness into your dour life. In fact, I don't think you need to look very far. There is a very suitable candidate already on your doorstep.'

'Oh, dear God.'

'I think,' said Calpurnia, pursuing the thought inexorably to its end, 'that Mrs Chaytor would make a most excellent wife for you, Marcus. I think you should consider very seriously making her an offer of marriage.'

Perhaps fortunately, there came a knock at the door. 'It's a runner from Captain Austen, reverend,' said Biddy, appearing in the door and curtseying.

Fuming, the rector went out into the hall and found Austen's man waiting. 'Captain's compliments, sir, and he says to tell you we've tracked the French across to the southern coast,' the man said. 'They came out about a mile east of Camber. There were marks on the beach that showed where they had dragged a boat down to the shore and cast off. They must have had the boat hidden in the dunes.'

'In case they needed to make a rapid escape,' said the rector. 'Did all four men board the boat?'

'Looks like it, sir. The tide was coming in, but we could see enough of the footmarks to show that no one came back up the beach. It seems certain they've gone.'

'So Foucarmont has gone,' said the rector, half to himself. 'That's him done with . . . until the next time.' And there would be a next time, unless he could work out what that subtle, clever and violent man had been up to, what had drawn him over and over again to Romney Marsh and New Hall.

Not wishing to see his sister again, he retired to his study and poured a glass of port. No sooner had he done so than the door knocker sounded again. 'For pity's sake,' he growled, 'what now?'

'What are you scowling at?' asked Amelia Chaytor, coming into the study.

'You will not believe this. My idiot sister has suggested that I make you an offer of marriage.'

'Us?' said Mrs Chaytor, opening her blue eyes in surprise. 'Married? What an appalling idea.'

'I thought you would think so. But I do not know whether to be relieved or offended by your reaction.'

'A little of both in equal measure is probably the best course. I have had a letter about the Rossiters.'

His irritation vanished. She opened her reticule and handed a folded piece of paper to him in turn.

WOTTON HOUSE, WOTTON UNDERWOOD, BUCKINGHAMSHIRE
7th February, 1797.

My dearest Amelia,

It was a very happy surprise to receive your letter after such a long interval. Anne is delighted that you are in correspondence once again, and joins me in insisting that you keep your promise to call on us either in London or in the country as soon as possible.

You have asked me about the Rossiters. I am deeply curious to know the reasons behind your inquiry, but I shall respect your confidence. The Rossiter family is Dutch in origin. Nikolaus Roseter was a prominent member of the suite of King William when he crossed to this country in 1689. Like the Bentincks and other Dutch families, he served the king loyally and was rewarded with positions and land. There were large estates in Ireland, as well as lands and properties in various parts of England. He became very prosperous, though questions were asked as to exactly how that prosperity was obtained. At one point he was accused of smuggling, but as he continued high in the favour of King William and, later, Queen Anne, he was never prosecuted.

His son William Rossiter nearly encompassed the family's ruin. The young man embraced various forms of radical and anti-Hanoverian politics, culminating with his joining Prince Charles Stewart's venture in 1745, along with his two sons. He escaped proscription after the revolt was suppressed, but only at the cost of a very heavy fine, which wiped him out. The Irish estates and most of the other properties were sold. Rossiter himself died two years after the rebellion.

Both his sons migrated to America, I believe with the hope of recouping the family fortunes. However, James

Rossiter also continued in his father's footsteps by associating with radicals. He was known to our authorities before the revolt broke out as an agitator and trouble-maker. He went on to become one of our most dangerous opponents during the war.

This is where my curiosity about your request is piqued, because Rossiter's radical leanings have not dimmed. His politics are firmly Republican; that is to say, unlike the Federalists, who are largely Anglophiles and support good relations with Britain, he is of that faction that favours a *rapprochement* with France and an alliance of the two revolutionary powers, France and America, against Britain. I am told in confidence that his presence with the embassy is an annoyance to Mr King the ambassador, who is a strong Federalist, and believes Mr Rossiter was appointed to his suite to act as a spy for the Republicans.

You are quite correct; he is very charming in person and does his best to make himself agreeable. However, I think Anne summed him up very well the other day. When you invite him to dinner, she said, count the spoons afterwards!

I trust this information will be of some use to you, and remain wildly curious about the purpose behind your request. Idle female gossip! You! There was never such a thing.

I remain yours fondly,

WILLIE

'It all fits together,' said the rector. 'Foucarmont is not the lynch-pin. Rossiter is.'

'And Parker and Foucarmont were the tools he used. Do you recall what Captain Austen said? Rossiter was the smooth one, who didn't get his hands dirty. Parker was the one who wielded the bludgeon, or pulled the trigger.'

'And now the bludgeon has been used against Parker. Did Rossiter sanction that killing? Did he order it? Did he realise his old friend Parker might be about to betray him, and decide to dispose of him?'

'Rossiter is in London,' Amelia reminded him.

'Then someone here is carrying out his orders.'

'Steele?'

'It is possible. It would appear that he has fled along with Foucarmont.'

She nodded. 'He could hardly stay here, given the number of holes that Emma put in him. Someone would be bound to ask questions. Who else do you think is involved?'

'Who else would he trust? It must be another member of the family. His wife we can rule out; Mrs Parker also. That means one of the young people, Edward, William or Laure must be involved.'

'We can rule out Laure too, I believe.'

'Then it is one of the young men. I must investigate them, and I will, whatever Lord Clavertye says. Edward, to outward appearances at least, is his father's loyal supporter. But let us not forget that William abandoned his own father to join his uncle. He shares Rossiter's political views; does he also follow Rossiter's orders?'

'Allow me to play devil's advocate for a moment,' she said. 'Foucarmont has retired, presumably to France. All his men are dead, rounded up, or fled with him. The plot, whatever it is, has been foiled. Rossiter no longer has any reason to be at New Hall, and I would bet that the rest of the family will return to London within the week. Why now do you wish to stick your head into the hornet's nest? Why not simply let them go?'

'Because whatever drew them to New Hall remains there,' he said. 'And as long as it does so, Foucarmont and Rossiter will be tempted to return. And if they do, then you and I and many others will be in danger once again. We must settle this matter, completely, once and for all, or we will know no peace.'

The knocker on the front door sounded yet again. 'It is like Piccadilly today,' the rector said sourly. They heard Biddy draw the bolts, and then she shrieked like a banshee. 'Come quickly, reverend, sir! God love you, come quickly!'

They hurried into the hall. Calpurnia rushed out of the dining room behind them and stopped dead, her hand to her mouth. There, standing in the doorway, muddy and exhausted with broken manacles hanging from his wrists, was Samuel Rossiter.

Chapter 17

Return, Reunion, Return

'I must apologise for my appearance,' the young man said, his voice slurred with fatigue.

'Come inside. Quickly.' The rector slammed and barred the door and then pressed Samuel down into a chair. 'When did you last eat?'

'Two days ago.'

'Biddy, bring food. No: first, fetch a blanket. And something hot to drink.' Beneath his ragged coat, Samuel was shivering. 'There is something I must tell you,' the rector said. 'Emma is alive.'

Samuel's head shot up and his eyes, dark and intense, fixed on the rector's face. Then he nodded slowly. 'I knew it must be so,' he said. 'Forgive me for doubting your word, sir. But the more I thought about it, after we spoke, the more I knew she must be alive. I knew I would have felt it in my heart if she had died.'

'Is that why you escaped?' asked Mrs Chaytor.

'Yes ... I decided to come here, and beg the reverend to help me find her. But they were searching for me everywhere, so I had to hide. Then the search stopped, and I thought it would be safe to approach him.' He looked from one to the other. 'Where is Emma?'

'She is at my house,' said Mrs Chaytor, 'very close by. I will fetch her.'

The young man looked at his muddy clothes and the manacles on his hands. 'I do not want her to see me like this.'

'Then let us get you fed and cleaned up,' said Calpurnia briskly, coming forward. 'Come into the kitchen where it is warm. No, don't worry about the mud, Biddy will clear that up. Let's see you fed first, and then I will find some of Marcus's clothes for you. They will be a little large, but they will suffice. Marcus won't mind; will you, Marcus?'

This was said meaningfully; the rector shook his head. Clucking, Calpurnia drew the young man away to the kitchen. Mrs Chaytor looked at the rector and raised her eyebrows.

'She is angry with us for not telling her about Emma,' the rector said. 'She has decided to push her way into this affair again, no doubt so she can collect material for another of her ghastly books.'

'She is already involved, to a degree,' Mrs Chaytor pointed out. 'I shall go and fetch Emma.'

Half an hour later, Samuel Rossiter had eaten and changed into coat, baggy breeches and thick wool stockings. Calpurnia brought him back to the drawing room, wrapped in a heavy blanket, and placed him in a chair next to the fire. Biddy, skipping with excitement, answered the door when Mrs Chaytor knocked, and ushered her and Emma into the drawing room.

Brother and sister stood for a moment, gazing at each other. 'Aracoma,' breathed Samuel.

'Oh, Holeskwa!' the girl cried, tears glistening in her dark eyes. They embraced, clumsily because of the manacles still dangling from Samuel's wrists. There were tears on his face too, and Calpurnia dabbed at her own eyes with a handkerchief. Hardcastle and Amelia stood quietly, watching while brother and sister clung to each other, speaking softly in a language only they could understand. They held onto one another like shipwrecked survivors in a storm, clinging to their hope of salvation. They had endured great hardship and great sorrow; but so long as they had each other, Emma and Samuel would survive.

Gradually they released each other, and the storm of emotion receded. Emma, wiping her eyes, turned to the rector and reverted back to English. 'What do we do now?' she asked, striving to remain calm.

'First, we need to remove those manacles,' said Hardcastle. 'I will send for someone who can do so, and we will have them off you as soon as possible.' Filing through manacles was well within Joshua Stemp's range of skills. 'Tomorrow, I will see the deputy lord lieutenant and ensure that all charges against Samuel are dropped. You will then be free.'

'A moment, sir, please,' said Samuel. 'I am glad you believe me innocent, but there is still a murder to explain. Emma is alive – so who was killed at New Hall?'

They had forgotten that he did not know. 'It was Sarah,' said Emma softly. 'You remember, she used to clean at the house where we stayed? I hired her to come with me.'

'Sarah! Oh, how terrible! She was such a kind and gentle person. But who would want to kill her? And why?'

'Because someone thought she was you,' the rector said to Samuel. The young man looked confused, and Hardcastle said, 'I did not tell you earlier, but Miss Freebody was wearing men's clothes when she was attacked. This is a tragic case of mistaken identity.'

'Someone thought Sarah was me ...' said Samuel slowly, repeating the rector's words. 'That means I am responsible for her death. It is because of me that she was killed.'

'No!' said Emma. 'I am at fault. It was I who asked her to come with me, and placed her in danger.'

'And that means you are both still in danger,' said Calpurnia. 'Until the secret of New Hall is known, neither of you are safe. Whoever tried to kill you may well try to do so again.'

The rector opened his mouth to rebuke his sister for interfering, and then realised she was right. Parker was dead, Foucarmont and Steele had gone, but that did not mean the danger was over. 'You have already run great risks for us,' Emma said. 'If we are in danger, so are you. Samuel and I can go to London. We would be safe there.'

'That, you most certainly would not be,' said the rector. 'The men who tried to kill you know where you were staying in London. They found you once, and they would find you once more, quite easily; and in London, murdering you would be much simpler than here on the Marsh. My sister is right. Neither of you is safe until we know the truth about New Hall and the killer of Sarah Freebody is caught. You had better stay with us: Emma with Mrs Chaytor, and Samuel can remain here at the rectory.'

'You are kind,' said Emma simply. She paused, and they could see her thinking hard. Then she turned and looked at Samuel. 'I too have no wish to place you in danger,' the latter said.

'Let me worry about that,' said the rector.

A moment passed, and then both young people nodded. 'We trust you,' said Samuel. His face was drawn and thin, but he looked far less desperate than he had on arrival.

They did not linger for long. Samuel was swaying with lack of sleep, and Calpurnia insisted he must be put to bed. Emma went to help her, and together they half carried the stumbling young man upstairs. 'I have an idea,' said Mrs Chaytor to the rector. 'I want to introduce Emma to Laure.'

He stared at her. 'That rather obviates the point of keeping them in hiding.'

'My dear man, the people who matter already know where Emma is; that is why they tried to kill her. And how long do you think Samuel's presence at the rectory will remain a secret? I think it is time we forced the issue. Let Laure meet Emma and then tell the rest of her family about the meeting. We shall know by their reactions which of them we can trust and which are in on the plot.'

'It means taking a considerable risk,' said the rector.

'I know. But as Emma says, we are already taking risks. This affair has dragged on for too long. It is time we drew it to a conclusion, and saw justice done for Sarah Freebody.'

'Do you wish to know what I think?' the rector asked.

'Of course.'

'I think you would make a better justice of the peace than me.'

Lord Clavertye arrived mid-morning. 'I have Samuel Rossiter in my custody,' Hardcastle said. 'He came to the house last night and turned himself in.'

'Well done, Hardcastle! I knew the man would surrender eventually.'

'Save your congratulations, my lord, until you hear what I intend. We were all mistaken. Emma Rossiter is alive and well. The woman who was killed at New Hall was her servant, and the murderer was not Samuel. He did not arrive on the scene until several days later. One of the family, probably Joseph Parker, was behind the murder; whether committing it or ordering it to be carried out, we have yet to determine. It was then a case of mistaken identity; the murderer attacked the servant, who was dressed in men's clothing, in the belief that she was Samuel Rossiter. He is innocent, and I intend to release him. I must ask you to drop all the charges against him.'

Hardcastle had been prepared for an explosive reaction, but it did not come. Instead Clavertye nodded.

'Very well. And what of the charges of espionage and trafficking with Foucarmont?'

'When you interview the young man, my lord, I think you will see that these charges too are without foundation. You could speak to him while you are here, if you wish.'

One of Clavertye's virtues was that he knew how to lose gracefully. He nodded again. 'And Parker's death?'

'It is very likely that he was killed by Foucarmont the same day that the latter attacked Sandy House. Foucarmont had learned that Emma was sheltering with Mrs Chaytor; she was the target of the attack.'

'And now it seems Foucarmont has escaped. So, where does that leave us?'

'It leaves us with the Rossiters,' said the rector directly. 'Specifically, with James Rossiter, who I am convinced has been directing this entire business. The original plan, whatever it was, has failed, but it does not mean that Rossiter will not try again. He will return to New Hall very shortly, I am certain, to attend the inquest and funeral of Parker. While he is here, I intend to interrogate him closely, and if possible, get to the bottom of this affair.'

'You think Rossiter may be a murderer?'

'Rossiter is the planner, the brain behind the plot. Others did the killing. I am not ruling out the possibility that his son or his nephew may have had a hand in the murder of either Sarah Freebody, or Joseph Parker, or both.'

'Why?'

'Because they are hiding something,' said the rector. 'Something so important that it transcends blood and kinship. And anything in which Foucarmont is involved represents a threat to Britain. Will you give me your consent to investigate this matter fully?'

Clavertye thought for a moment. 'Officially, no; the sensitivities are too great. Unofficially, carry on, but go carefully. If Rossiter decides to call on his interests, we could both be in trouble. The Duke of Portland wields a great deal of influence in this country.'

'I am aware of that, my lord. But if I find evidence connecting James Rossiter to murder and espionage, will you give me your support?'

Clavertye looked him in the eye. 'It will give me very great pleasure to do so,' he said. 'And now, let me have a word with Samuel Rossiter.'

An hour later his lordship was away to London, where he would doubtless make what capital he could out of his role in the hunt for Foucarmont. It was nearly time for morning service, but as Hardcastle crossed the road to the church, a thought struck him. He turned and walked into the village and knocked at the door of Stemp's cottage. Stemp himself answered the door.

'What can I do for you, reverend?'

'I have a task for you, Joshua. I need someone to look again at the New Hall cellars, someone with a better eye for such things than myself. I need to know if there is anything unusual about them, any signs of secret doors or compartments that could be opened.'

'Jack Hoad's the man for that. I'll talk to him.'

After matins, the rector walked down to New Hall and knocked at the door. It was young William Rossiter who came down to see him this time. 'Aunt Jane is asleep. Laure is sitting with her.'

'Then I shall not disturb her. But do please tell her I called.' He looked at the fair-haired young man. 'As we are private, Mr

Rossiter, I should quite like a word with you. Might you spare me a moment of your time?'

'Of course, sir. Does this concern my uncle's death?' William asked.

'Indirectly, yes.'

'Then ask whatever you like. I'll help in any way I can.'

They sat in the big drawing room, the fire crackling in the grate. 'Would you begin by telling me what led to the rupture with your father?' the rector asked.

William looked surprised. 'How did you know about that? Oh, Laure, I suppose,' he said, looking pained. 'It was all over politics, you see. I was six when the revolutionary war ended, too young to know much about it. Our family, father and mother and myself, moved to Montréal. Mother died a few years later, and I went to stay for a time with Uncle James and my cousins in Boston. I heard all about the war and how heroic Uncle James and Uncle Joe had been. They said very little themselves; it was Eddy, my cousin, who told me most of it.'

'Edward is older than you?'

'Oh, yes, seven years. But he's always been very good to me. He's a great gun; more like a brother than a cousin.'

'And you heard his story and felt sympathy for your uncles' cause?'

'America is wonderful. There is such freedom there, such hope for the future. We have the beginnings of a great country,' he said enthusiastically. 'It really is a new world, in every sense. We've thrown off the shackles of Europe. No more constraints of monarchy or religion to hold us in our places and tie us down. We're free to imagine our own future and create a new nation based on principles like equality and justice.'

The words sounded like something Hardcastle had heard someone else say, but there was no doubting the young man's sincerity. 'But your father felt otherwise?'

'Father changed after Mother died. He lost interest in the world around him. He kept harking back to the past, back to the days before the revolution; that was all that interested him. To him, the revolution was nothing but destruction and strife. He couldn't see that was the price that had to be paid for freedom.' William paused, his handsome young face suddenly sad. 'We had a quarrel; well, a series of quarrels. And four years ago, I stormed out, announcing that I was off to live with Uncle James. I was fifteen then, too young and stupid to realise what I was doing. Father cut me off, for which I don't blame him. But I never saw him or spoke to him again. Now I regret that, very much.'

'But you continue to hold true to your beliefs.'

'Of course. I believe in America and its future. I just wish I hadn't lost Father along the way. Maybe that too is the price that must be paid. But I'm not happy about it.'

'What did your father do during the war?'

'What a lot of folk did: kept his head down and waited for it to blow over. Mother once told me that at the beginning of the Revolution, Uncle James tried to persuade him to join the American cause. Father refused and they had a violent quarrel. I don't think they ever spoke again.'

It was time for a change of tack. 'Did your father ever mention his earlier marriage? Or the children born to his first wife?'

'Not once. It was a bolt from the blue when they showed up in Boston. I say, reverend; do you think he really married the lady?'

'We shall find out in due course. Certainly their two children believe he did. But regardless of marriage lines, they are still your brother and sister.'

'Gosh,' said the boy in sudden wonder. 'I suppose that's true, isn't it? It hadn't occurred to me before. I suppose I just accepted what Uncle Joe said, that they were trying to squeeze money out of the family.'

Perhaps you should spend more time thinking for yourself than listening to what others say, thought the rector. Aloud, he asked, 'Did your father ever talk about New Hall?'

'Sometimes, especially after Mother died. He was quite sentimental about the place. That's why I wanted so much to come here, you see. But Uncle James and Uncle Joe weren't too keen at first.'

'Did your father ever mention a secret in connection with the house? Something to do with the cellars?'

'If he did, I don't remember it. What's so remarkable about the cellars? I've been down there a few times. There's nothing to see.'

'William, think carefully. Did your Uncle Joseph ever discuss the cellars? With you or any other member of the family?'

'Not in my hearing,' said the young man, shaking his head.

'Did your uncle ever meet with anyone here? Did he have appointments out of the house, or did anyone call on him at New Hall?'

'No, I don't think so. Or if he did, I never noticed. Apart from church, he rarely left the house at all; he wasn't a great one for exercise. If he wanted something, he usually sent a servant out to get it.'

The rector nodded. 'Thank you for your time, Mr Rossiter. Pray do not trouble; I will see myself out.'

He walked home through the drizzle, thinking hard. William Rossiter was a callow and ingenuous young man with a great deal to learn about life. He was an idealist and a romantic. Could he also be a murderer? Men killed for political ideals; over in

France, they had been killing them off in thousands, all in the name of liberty. On the face of it, William seemed an unlikely conspirator; he was too young and too naïve. But, it was also possible that he was an expert at dissembling.

'I came directly I received your note,' said Laure Rossiter, smiling. 'Your message was most mysterious.'

'I am so glad you could come,' said Mrs Chaytor. 'And here is the object of the mystery. Laure; may I present your cousin, Miss Emma Rossiter.'

'Goodness,' said Laure softly.

She and Emma stood still for a moment, studying each other. They were both tall; one fair and green-eyed, the other with rich, curling brown hair and deep, dark eyes.

Then Laure turned to Mrs Chaytor. 'But if this is Emma, who was killed at New Hall?'

'A young woman named Sarah Freebody,' said Emma softly. 'She came from London with me, as my servant. The person who killed her thought she was my brother.'

'But your brother has been charged with the murder.'

'No longer,' said Mrs Chaytor. 'The charges against him have been dropped. He is free, and is staying at the rectory with Reverend Hardcastle.'

'Goodness,' said Laure again.

'Perhaps we should all sit down,' said Mrs Chaytor, ringing the bell. 'Lucy? Bring us some chocolate, my dear.'

They sat, and Laure looked at Emma. She still seemed a little dazed, but she was rallying. 'Why, you are quite lovely,' she said on sudden impulse. 'And you look so much like us.'

'I have the Rossiter chin,' said Emma, raising her chin slightly and smiling again.

'We are all cursed with that,' laughed Laure. 'One of our ancestors must have had a jaw like the side of a ship.'

Lucy arrived with the chocolate.

'Tell me all about yourself,' instructed Laure, and Emma obliged, recounting again the history of her life. Laure was fascinated by her cousin's time among the Shawnee. 'One hears of these things, of children being taken away and reared by the Indians and then finding their way back to civilisation years later,' she said, 'but I have never actually met anyone who had that experience. Oh, poor Uncle Nicholas! It must have been so terrible for him.'

'Did you know nothing at all about us?' Emma asked, visibly saddened.

Laure shook her head. 'Uncle Nicholas was far away in New York. I remember he visited Boston a couple of times, but we didn't know him at all well. I remember his writing to tell us that he had married – that was to Aunt Hannah, William's mother – and then almost immediately thereafter came the war and the rupture between he and Father. The first I heard of you was when Uncle Joseph said you had come to Boston.'

Laure looked directly at the other woman. 'I know I should not speak ill of Uncle Joseph now that he is dead. But I thought the way he treated you and Samuel was horrible. Had I my way, you would have been welcomed into our home.'

'Thank you,' said Emma. 'That is good to know. For our part, we never wished to be a burden to you. We only wanted to be part of a family.'

'Well, so far as I am concerned, you are part of our family. Cousin Emma! What a nice ring it has to it.' She paused. 'Need I keep your presence here a secret?'

Emma looked at Mrs Chaytor. 'You may tell the rest of your family, of course,' said the latter.

'May I ask what brought you to St Mary?' asked Laure.

They had discussed beforehand what she would say if this question were asked. 'Father made a will, in which he left New Hall to Samuel and me. We did not know about the earlier will, leaving the house to William.'

'Oh! That complicates things,' said Laure. 'I am sure William knows nothing about this either.' Her brow wrinkled. 'What can be done about this?'

'I do not know,' said Emma. 'There is a lawyer looking into matters, so we shall have to wait to see what he says. For the moment, it has been good to come and see the house where our father had once lived, and to visit the grave of our grandmother.'

'You have seen *grand-mère*'s grave? Would you visit it with me? The two of us together?'

'It would be my honour to take you there.' Emma looked at Mrs Chaytor. 'May we go?'

'Of course.' In Laure's presence, Emma was as safe as she could ever be. After the two young women had gone, Mrs Chaytor sat and stared at the window for a while, conscious of a little prickle of emotion.

They were cousins and now, perhaps, they were on their way to becoming friends. At least something good had come from this affair.

That evening, a big coach drawn by a team of horses came up the road from New Romney. It did not turn into the drive at New Hall but came on through the village, turning through the rectory gates and pulling to a halt outside the front door.

James Rossiter was shown into the rector's study a few moments later, limping and leaning heavily on his stick. He looked tired and unwell; the rector thought he seemed older than when they last met. 'I thank you for your letter,' he said, as

Biddy was dispatched for refreshments. 'I came as quickly as I could upon receipt of the news. Have you seen my sister?'

'She is distraught, of course, but I think her niece and nephews are a great support to her. How has Mrs Rossiter taken the news?'

'Badly, I fear. It has made her quite ill, so much so that I prevailed upon her to stay in London while I travelled down here. This is a damnable affair, I must say. Do you have any idea who might have perpetrated this crime?'

'There is no doubt in my mind as to who the killer was,' the rector said. 'Parker was killed by your old comrade in arms, Camille de Foucarmont, who learned that Parker had spoken to me and feared he was about to betray your plot. But of course, you know this already.'

'I left St Mary nearly a week ago, reverend,' Rossiter said, 'and I have been in London or travelling ever since. And I do not understand this talk of plots, or your reference to the man Foucarmont.'

'You knew Parker was a weak reed. Before you left, you advised Foucarmont to dispose of Parker if he became unreliable.'

'Dispose of him! This is my brother-in-law, one of my oldest and dearest friends! Reverend, I don't know who you have been talking to or what your imagination has dreamed up, but such a suggestion is an insult!'

The rector studied the other man for a few moments, letting the silence drag on. 'I don't propose to waste time bandying words with you,' he said. 'Mark this, and mark it well. I know about the connection between yourself and Foucarmont. I know that he came to England with his men in response to a signal from yourself, a message sent most probably from London after your arrival there. I know that you and Foucarmont have been engaged in a plot against the British realm. I lack only the details of that plot, and I will have those soon enough.

'Two people have died; one an innocent servant girl, the other your brother-in-law. Others have been grievously hurt. Attempts have been made to kill both Samuel and Emma Rossiter, as well as Mrs Chaytor. On your orders, Foucarmont spread mayhem across the Marsh, and no doubt intended to extend his activities further across the country, before our forces finally drove him off. I give you fair warning now that I intend to see you prosecuted for these crimes.'

Another long silence fell while the two men stared at each other across the rector's desk, Rossiter's eyes dark with impending violence. So threatening did he appear for a moment that Hardcastle tensed, half expecting to receive a blow.

'I do not think so,' said Rossiter.

'You seem very sure of yourself.'

'Of course. Have you forgotten that I am protected?'

'I know that you are a member of the American ambassador's court. I also know that he dislikes you, and thinks you are spying on him for the Republicans. I believe he would cut you loose without a qualm.'

'Perhaps. Or perhaps he would do anything to avoid a scandal that might threaten America. News that a member of this embassy had been consorting with a French agent might well turn the British people against the ideas of closer ties with my country, don't you think? And you forget too that I have the interest of the Duke of Portland. I am untouchable, reverend. Nothing you do or say can harm me.'

Rossiter leaned forward a little. 'But all this talk is academic because you have no evidence. You have a theory, most ingeniously constructed, but that is all. There is not a shred of evidence to show that I have been in correspondence with Foucarmont, or that I have been involved in any activities against the interests of your country. Nor is there any evidence whatever to connect me with the two murders. So, I wish good luck to you, rector. You will need it. And now, I will take my leave.'

They rose. 'You are wrong,' said the rector. 'I will prove you wrong.'

'It amuses me that you should think so. Please, remain where you are, reverend. I will show myself out.'

Chapter 18

The Secret of New Hall

The inquest into the death of Joseph Parker was held in New Romney on Tuesday 14th February. The witnesses were Dr Mackay, the boy who had found the body, Joshua Stemp and Hardcastle. The jury took less than a minute to reach a verdict of unlawful killing.

James Rossiter attended the inquest along with his son, Edward, and nephew, William. He sat looking straight ahead at the coroner throughout the hearing, his face unchanging. Only at the end, when the coroner offered his condolences to the widow and all the family, did he move, nodding his head once in acceptance.

Gloom hung over the Marsh. Grey clouds rolled steadily overhead, spitting occasional bursts of cold rain. It had been days since anyone had seen the sun. In the dim light, Hardcastle returned to the rectory to find Samuel sitting beside the drawing room fire, listening politely while Calpurnia explained the plot of her latest novel. The rector retired to his study and opened a bottle of port. There are some things, he thought, that flesh and blood should not be called upon to bear.

He did not drink much, despite the call to do so, because he knew he needed to keep a clear head. He sifted through what he knew so far, making brief notes as he did so. Rossiter had made his intention clear; he would carry off the entire matter with a high hand, pretending that nothing threatened him or his family. Well, thought the rector wryly, from his point of view, nothing has. He knows I have no evidence, and even if I had, he would still be beyond my reach. He is one of the mighty and the powerful, who may do as they please and whom the law cannot touch.

That thought roused him to slow anger. 'I *will* prove you wrong,' he said aloud.

But how? Annoyingly, Calpurnia had been right once again. Until he knew what lay concealed at New Hall, he could not come near the truth. He thought about the instruction he had given Stemp about the New Hall cellars: quite dishonourable, entirely illegal, but about his only remaining source of hope.

Wednesday dawned even colder and more gloomy than the day before. At the appointed hour, the rector crossed the road to the church, robed in the vestry and then went out to wait for the funeral cortege. The coffin came, transported slowly by wagon from New Romney, followed by the family, dark in mourning, Rossiter leaning heavily on his stick and puffing a little. Once, Laure put out her arm to steady him. Jane Parker was beside him, supported by Edward, her face pale and blank. Their servants followed quietly behind.

In that moment, the rector ceased to be an officer of the law and became wholly a clergyman; intent on the people before him and the ritual of remembrance and consolation he was about to perform. As the coffin reached the lychgate, he raised his hand.

'*I am the resurrection and the life, saith the Lord,*' he said, his deep voice ringing a little in the cold churchyard. '*He that believeth in me, though he were dead, yet shall he live; and whosoever liveth and believeth in me, shall never die.*'

Throughout the funeral the widow sat unmoving, staring at the coffin. Only at the end, as the coffin was lowered into the ground, did she break down. Helpless, flooded with tears and moaning softly with pure, shattering grief, she was helped from the churchyard by her son and nephew. Hardcastle looked up, and met Mrs Chaytor's eyes.

At the end, he offered his hand to James Rossiter and said quietly, 'Believe me, sir, I am truly sorry for your sister's pain. I shall pray that God sends her consolation and peace.' Rossiter walked straight past the rector's outstretched hand, not speaking.

Two hours after the funeral, Joshua Stemp called at the rectory.

'It was easy enough,' he said. 'We reckoned most of the servants would be at the church, so we called round with a basket of fish. I knocked at the kitchen door and offered my wares for sale, and then kept 'em busy while Jack nipped down and had a look around. The cellars are dry and sound, there's nothin' unusual about them. No doors, no compartments, says Jack, and if he says so, then I reckon we have to take his word on it.'

'Damn,' the rector said. It had been a faint hope, but it was all he had.

'There's something else, though, reverend. There's something not quite right about the house itself.'

'What do you mean?'

'It's the rear wall. Part of it's in the wrong place. Or more likely, the inside wall is.'

The rector stared at him, baffled.

'You remember that passage that runs across the back of the house?' asked Stemp. 'From the kitchen, behind the staircase to the breakfast room? I remember thinking when we searched the house: part of that passage seems narrow. Nothing like as well made as the rest of the house. And then when I was outside, I saw that the outer wall and the inner wall aren't even close to each other. I reckon that inside wall is a false wall. And you know what that means.'

'You will have to enlighten me.'

'A false wall means a hiding place,' Stemp said patiently. 'Could be something like a priest's hole, or a door to a passageway or a stair. My money's on a stair.'

'A stair . . .' Revelation came in an instant. 'By thunder, that's it! The "secret of the cellars" that Emma's father told her about; it's not *in* the main cellars. The secret is that *there is another* cellar!'

'It's an old trick,' said Stemp, nodding. 'One range of cellars for legitimate use, another hidden away, where you hide the run goods.'

'And New Hall was built by smugglers. It all fits.'

'Now all we need to do is find out what they're hiding down there,' said Stemp. 'What do you reckon it is, reverend? Gold? We could go back at night and try a break-in.'

'With the house full of servants, and Rossiter doubtless expecting us to try just that?'

'I suppose not,' said Stemp wistfully. 'Gold, though . . .'

'Contain your larcenous instincts for a moment, and think. Rossiter has failed in his purpose for the moment. He will try again. But what will he do next? I'm convinced that he and his family will withdraw to London and let the fuss die down while he plans his next move. Once he has gone and the house is closed up, *then* we can enter and search.'

Stemp looked horrified. 'But surely he'll just take the gold with him to London?'

'It depends how much there is. A large amount of gold is not easy to transport. But in any case, I do not think the cellars of New Hall contain gold. I think something has been hidden at the house for a long time, perhaps since the last war, waiting for its moment. Rossiter won't move it, whatever it is – not unless he fears it is about to be discovered.'

'So what do you intend to do, reverend?'

'Stay quiet for a few days, until the family and servants have all departed. Let Rossiter think we have given up. The more confident he is that we have done so, the more likely he will be to leave everything as it is.'

That evening after dinner, a surprise caller came to the rectory. Edward Rossiter was shown into the study.

This was opportune, as the rector very much wanted to talk to Edward, but between the inquest, the funeral and his pastoral duties, he had not yet had time to do so. Slender and neat, Edward was dressed in his mourning clothes. The flash that had been apparent about him on earlier occasions was quite gone. Sober too was the expression on the young man's face.

'Thank you for receiving me, reverend, and do please forgive me for calling unannounced. If this is an inconvenient hour . . .'

'There is no inconvenience at all. How may I be of service?'

'I've been doing a lot of hard thinking since Uncle Joseph died,' Edward said quietly as they seated themselves. 'I share his politics, his and Father's, and I always regarded Britain as the enemy. But this event has brought me up short.' He looked steadily at Hardcastle. 'I was just a boy during the war, only thirteen when it ended. I thought it was all romantic and exciting, Sons of Liberty and men going out to fight for freedom and equality. It's always been a bit of a game to me, really. But now, with Uncle Joe getting killed . . . It's no longer a game, is it?'

'It never was,' said the rector quietly.

'No. I realise that now.' Edward drew a deep breath. 'As I say, I have been thinking, and I am determined to put all that foolishness behind me, and do something decent and useful with my life. And I . . . well, I came here to make a confession.'

'Oh? A confession to a priest, or to an officer of the law?'

Edward was wry. 'I think I will leave that to you to decide . . . It was I who told Uncle Joe that Emma and Samuel Rossiter were in London. I spotted them in the street. I hadn't met the girl, but I had seen Samuel when he came to the house in Boston. I looked twice, as you would, but there was no mistaking them. They have the Rossiter jaw, you see.' He rubbed his own chin. 'I'm the only one in the family who seems to have missed out on it.'

'And what led you to inform your uncle?'

'Believe it or not, I was trying to protect Cousin William,' said Edward. 'Uncle Joe believed Samuel was after William's inheritance. I worked with Uncle Joe in his chambers, so I thought it was my duty to inform him of anything that might be connected with William's estate. So, I'm the one who put Uncle Joe onto the scent, and I reckon I know what Uncle Joe did next. He went around to try and frighten them off, and then when that didn't work and they came down here, he sent Steele after them. It must have been Steele who coshed that poor servant girl and killed her.'

'How do you know she was a servant?'

'Laure told us the whole story after she met Emma. I realised then what had happened, and knew I was responsible. If I had said nothing Uncle Joe would have been none the wiser. Look here, reverend; if I am liable in law in any way, as an accomplice or something; well, tell me. I'll take the penalty, whatever it is.'

Hardcastle considered this. Edward's father would of course use his connections with the home secretary, and nothing would happen. Did Edward know this? 'You could hardly be expected to foresee what Mr Parker would do once you told him you had seen Samuel and Emma. You should have informed me when you realised that Steele might have committed the crime, of course. Though in fact it hardly matters as I came to the same conclusion. In law, you have nothing to fear. As for your conscience,' he said quietly, 'that is for you to decide. Had you come forward sooner, Samuel would have been saved from gaol, and from days of cold and hunger as a fugitive on the Marsh.'

Edward looked troubled. 'I know. I've thought the same, often, and I despise myself for inflicting that on him.' He looked around suddenly. 'Is Samuel here? Laure said he was staying at the rectory.'

'Yes.'

'Do you suppose ... Do you think he would consent to see me? I'd like to apologise, if he would accept it, and see if we can make a fresh start. When Laure told me she had taken Emma by the hand and called her cousin; well, I was quite deeply moved. I should like to do the same with Samuel, if he'll forgive me.'

The rector regarded him for a moment, and then nodded. 'I will ask him. But if he says no, you must promise to abide by his decision.'

'Of course.'

Hardcastle rose and went out. He returned after a couple of minutes. 'He has agreed to see you. Come this way, if you please.'

Samuel Rossiter still looked tired and worn, but hot food and Calpurnia's kind care had clearly restored him a great deal. Calpurnia herself stood to one side, smiling fondly.

Edward bowed as they were introduced, then walked up to the other man and stopped and looked him in the eye. 'You and your sister have been deeply wronged by our family,' he said directly. 'I would like to help put that right, if I can. My uncle and father behaved very badly, and I did nothing to prevent them. I regret that deeply. When I found out what had happened to your sister and that poor servant girl, and then how you were arrested and chained up, I was stricken with remorse.' He forced a smile. 'When word came that you had escaped, I even went out and looked for you myself.'

'Why did you do that?' Samuel asked. His manner, unsurprisingly, was guarded.

'I thought if I found you before the soldiers did, I could help you somehow; get you food, or smuggle you into the stables at New Hall and give you a hiding place. It was all a bit mad, I suppose. But I thought you needed to know that at least one person in our family actually does feel that you are kith and kin, and wants to help you. Cousin Samuel, if I may call you such; it is asking a great deal, given what you have suffered. Can you see fit to put the past behind you, and join us in making a new start?'

'If you can make such a noble offer,' said Samuel, visibly relaxing at Edward's words and breaking into a smile, 'it would be unkind of me to refuse it.'

The two men clasped hands, and the relief in Edward's face was plain to see. Calpurnia gave a little cry of delight and clapped her hands. 'Two more cousins, reconciled! Laure and Emma are already fast friends, and now this! Oh, Marcus, is it not splendid?'

'It is indeed,' the rector said gravely. 'I congratulate you both, my young friends, on your courage and generosity of spirit. But what will your father say?' he asked Edward.

'Father does not know I am here,' said Edward. 'And in any case, he departs for London once more first thing in the morning. Now, that gives me a thought.'

He looked at Samuel. 'Aunt Jane keeps mostly to her room at the moment. That leaves we three of the younger generation,

Laure my sister and my cousin William; your half-brother, come to that. Now that we have found the two missing members of our family, we would very much like to be better acquainted with both of you. Therefore, would you and your sister do us the honour of calling on us tomorrow evening? I know that my cousin would be delighted to host you. Do please say yes.'

'Yes. We should like that very much.'

'Well, that is perfectly splendid,' said Edward. He bowed again, and then to Calpurnia and then the rector. 'Would you, reverend, and you, Mrs Vane, care to join us also?'

'Surely this should be an occasion for family alone,' the rector said, surprised.

''Tis true, but the two of you have done so much to help our cousins, and we should like to express our thanks.'

'Then it gives us great pleasure to accept,' said the rector. Calpurnia beamed at Samuel.

'Good. Now that is arranged, I shall take my leave,' said Edward, smiling. 'Your servant, ma'am. Reverend, thank you so much for hearing me and offering me your advice and consolation. And as for you, cousin, and all of you; until tomorrow.'

Thursday, 16th February. At first light, wheels rumbled on the drive at New Hall and the big carriage rolled out and turned away south towards New Romney and the high road to Ashford, and London. The rector, walking Rodolpho in the meadows north of the New Sewer, watched it go. He wondered what lay behind Edward's spur-of-the-moment invitation. He wondered too why William had made no move to come and meet his cousins. Perhaps he did not share the views of Edward and Laure.

At three in the afternoon, Joshua Stemp came to the rectory. Bill Hayton, the old shepherd, was ill again; a combination of marsh fever and drink, Stemp reckoned. Whatever the cause, he was in a bad way. Stemp's wife had gone out to look after the old man, taking a pot of soup, but Stemp thought his condition might need more than that.

'He cannot survive many more of these attacks,' the rector agreed. 'We must send for Dr Mackay, I think.'

'I can easily inform him, reverend. I'm on my way to New Romney now.'

The night of the full moon was past; in another ten days or two weeks, the smugglers would be making another run. Stemp was doubtless on his way to New Romney to meet his fellows and plan the event. 'Be so good as to do so,' the rector said. 'I will go and assist Mrs Stemp, and sit with him until the doctor arrives.'

He put on his cloak and his stoutest boots, and picked up his hat and gloves and stick. Anticipating a lengthy visit, took a lantern and tinderbox. 'I am sorry,' he said to Calpurnia, who came out to see what he was doing. 'But I may be detained for some while. If I do not return in time for the *soirée*, kindly make my apologies to the Rossiters.'

'Oh, Marcus, it is a shame. It will be so lovely to see all the young people together.'

'There will be other occasions.'

'Take Rodolpho with you. He will be company for you, at least.'

He whistled to the dog and the two of them departed, walking out across the flat Marsh, the grasses swept by the incessant wind. Clouds were building up to the southwest, charcoal coloured and livid with impending rain.

Old Bill Hayton was unconscious on his bed, feverish and muttering in his sleep. Mrs Stemp, a bright woman who managed

Stemp himself and their two fractious young daughters with an ever-capable hand, looked up as the rector came in, stooping under the low beams. 'He's not at all well, reverend. I haven't been able to get any soup into him.'

Hardcastle sat down by the cot and felt Hayton's forehead, burning and dry. 'The doctor is on his way,' he said. 'I'll stay with him, Mrs Stemp, if you want to get back to your girls.'

'That's kind of you, reverend.' Mrs Stemp departed, leaving the soup. Hardcastle sat on, listening to the old man's fevered whispers and the whistle of the wind. Presently Rodolpho began to whine; looking out, the rector realised it was raining. He called the dog inside, and Rodolpho lay down, gave a grateful sigh, and went to sleep.

Dr Mackay arrived at the fall of dusk, wet and disgruntled. He checked the patient carefully, then opened his bag and took out several glass bottles. 'Will you fetch me some water?' he asked the rector.

Hardcastle found a can of water and poured some into a tolerably clean bowl. Mackay added a small measure from one of the bottles. 'Belladonna,' he said. 'It should relax him and lower the fever a little. Help me to get it down him.'

Together, they opened the old man's jaws and spooned the tincture very slowly into his throat. Mackay next took a cloth and soaked it in vinegar from another of his bottles and began to wipe the patient's forehead. 'How long before this takes effect?' the rector asked.

'Who knows? It might be a few hours, or it might be all night. Or it might be never.' Mackay looked up. 'If you want to get along, I'll stay with him.'

'I will remain for a while.' They sat on, waiting. After a couple of hours it seemed that Hayton's fever was less fierce and he had begun to breathe a little more easily.

Outside, the rain was drumming down hard. 'I shall take my leave now,' said Hardcastle. 'Thank you, doctor. It was kind of you to come so far. Send your bill to me, as usual.'

'You may be sure of it.'

He lit the lantern, hearing the wind and rain increasing. He whistled to Rodolpho and stepped outside, wrapping his cloak around him. His hat brim dripping with water, the wolfhound trying unsuccessfully to take shelter behind him and stepping on his heels, he strode back down the track towards St Mary.

The rector was about a quarter of a mile from the village when he saw something glowing on the horizon through the rain. For a few moments he was puzzled, but then the glow increased and he was in no doubt. Somewhere in St Mary in the Marsh, a building was on fire.

'Welcome,' said William Rossiter, and he bowed stiffly to Calpurnia Vane and Mrs Chaytor, and then even more awkwardly to Samuel and Emma. 'We are very happy to have your company.' His tone of voice, Mrs Chaytor thought, was rather less welcoming than his words.

'Yes,' said Edward. 'It is a great pleasure to have you all here, to be sure! Only, where is Reverend Hardcastle?'

'He was called away to attend a sick man,' said Calpurnia. 'Poor Marcus, he is a martyr to his work. He is forever being called out, for one reason or another.'

'What a shame,' said Edward, and he laughed a little.

'Perhaps I should begin,' said Laure. She too looked nervous. 'William, Eddy, may I present to you our cousin Emma? I am sure you will be as glad as I was to make her acquaintance, and welcome her to the family.'

'Well said, dear sister,' said Edward. 'I too am glad to introduce our other cousin Samuel, Emma's brother. I've only met him the once, but he is a splendid fellow and I am sure we are all going to get on very well.'

William gave another stiff bow, but said nothing. His attitude to Samuel and Emma was markedly cold, in sharp contrast to that of his cousin. Samuel bowed too, smiling tentatively. 'And this is my sister Laure,' said Edward. 'You must thank her especially, cousin Samuel. It was her courage in going against our parents' wishes that led to this reunion of our family. I doubt Will and I would have had the mettle to do it ourselves. Odd how the ladies in the family often turn out to be the strong ones, isn't it?'

He bowed to the two younger women. William was staring at his cousin. He is puzzled, Mrs Chaytor thought; he does not understand something. Come to that, neither do I.

A footman appeared in the doorway, bowing. 'That's everything loaded, sir.'

'Good,' said Edward. 'You can be on your way.'

'It's getting dark, sir.'

'Never mind, it's a good road from New Romney. You can make Tenterden tonight, if you push on.'

The footman bowed again, looking sulky, and departed. Edward poured glasses of Madeira and handed them around. Emma smiled, her eyes glowing. She wore dark clothes, as they all did, but there was no mistaking the happiness in her eyes. She had wanted to be part of a family, she said. Now, at last, she was. She crossed the room to William, smiling still.

'I am very pleased to meet you,' she said. 'I have often thought of this moment.'

'Indeed, ma'am,' he said, and he gave another stiff little bow, his manner not at all welcoming. The young woman continued to smile, but now her eyes too were puzzled.

'You appear to be packing up,' said Mrs Chaytor. Her own inclusion in the party had come at the last minute; Laure had written a sweet little note, begging her company, and she did not feel she could refuse. But she was still perplexed by the purpose of this gathering, on the eve of the family's departure.

'It is most sad,' said Laure. 'We are to depart in the morning, it seems, and all the hired servants have been sent off today. We shall make do with a cold collation for supper, but they have left us some excellent claret to wash it down. I do wonder how they came by the claret? After all, this country is at war with France.'

'It has been smuggled in, silly,' laughed Edward. 'Didn't you know? This whole area is full of smuggling; am I not right, Mrs Chaytor?'

'It is an important local industry, to be sure,' Mrs Chaytor said drily.

Edward laughed again. 'Even this house was built by smugglers. That's why it has so many cellars.'

'What, this house? Do you mean to say our ancestors were smugglers?' asked William, suddenly showing some animation.

'Of course. Didn't you know? It's part of our history, old fellow.'

'Ah!' said Emma, smiling. 'Now at last I understand! Father told me there was a secret about the cellars of New Hall. That must be it. The cellars were used for smuggling.'

'So Uncle Nicholas told you about the cellars, did he?' said Edward. 'He would have known all about them, of course; he lived here longer than my father did. So he will have told you the other secret too?'

'Oh, that,' said William. 'That's moonshine. We looked everywhere when we first moved in, didn't we, Laure?'

'We did.' Laure turned to Mrs Chaytor and explained. 'There's an old fable that there is a second set of cellars, secret and hidden away. Will and I looked for them, as he says, but we found nothing.'

'Really?' said Edward. 'You looked too?'

'Oh, for hours. If there are really any hidden cellars, they must be so well disguised that no one will ever find them again. Perhaps the secret died with Uncle Nicholas.'

'Father spoke of a secret door,' said Emma, and Samuel nodded. 'But he never said where it might be.'

'A secret door!' said Calpurnia. 'Oh, how exciting! I very much want to include a secret door in my new novel. I have been racking my brains to understand how such a door might work. Come, what does one need for a secret door?'

'A door, of course,' said Samuel, smiling at her enthusiasm. 'And a passage behind, or a stair down to the cellars.'

'Exactly! So where in a house like this might there be room for a concealed stairwell or a passageway? Oh, Mr Rossiter, this is exciting! Shall we have another look for it? It would be a splendid game!'

'Oh, do let's, Will,' said Laure, laughing. 'It is our last night here; we might not get another chance.'

'Have you tried the library?' asked Calpurnia. 'The walls of the library are panelled, and panelling is always an excellent place for hidden compartments. It features in many novels.'

'I did check it quite thoroughly,' said William. 'But I am not certain the walls of the library are thick enough to admit of a staircase. What about the morning room?'

They fell to speculating; Edward wandered restlessly around the drawing room, tapping the walls from time to time. Mrs Chaytor watched them for a while, still uncertain as to the real purpose of the evening.

'There is one wall you have not thought of,' she said finally. 'That of the rear passage, behind the stairs. It is a most substantial wall; I noticed as much from the outside. I thought it was perhaps part of a much earlier structure, when they built walls of greater thickness.'

'Oh! Let us go and look!' cried Calpurnia, her enthusiasm bubbling over.

William, his earlier hesitation quite gone, and Laure led the way out of the drawing room, Edward behind them carrying a candle in each hand. Mrs Chaytor followed them all, watchful. They walked down the kitchen passage beside the staircase. At the end of the passage was a blank wall. To the left, a door gave way to the kitchen; to the right, another passage ran behind the staircase and around it, leading to the morning room and breakfast room.

The wall that faced them was smooth plaster, quite blank. 'I can see nothing,' said Calpurnia.

'I can,' said Samuel, pointing. 'There is a very faint line, just there.'

William took one of the candles and bent down for a closer look. 'So there is. I wonder how we missed it before? Now, how does it open, do we think?'

'There must be a spring or a catch somewhere,' said Samuel.

William knelt down and ran his fingers around the skirting boards, slowly. Suddenly he stopped. 'I think I've found it! Let's see what happens . . .'

He pressed with his fingers. There was a sudden click, and a little panel in the wall sprang open to reveal a keyhole. The young people gave a concerted cry of delight, Edward joining in.

'How exciting!' said Calpurnia, and they all agreed. 'Now if only we had a key.'

They stood and stared at the keyhole. An odd expression passed over Edward's face. 'I wonder,' he said. Reaching into his waistcoat pocket, he drew out a black key and held it up in the candlelight. 'I wonder,' he repeated slowly.

'Where did you get that?' asked William. His tone was sharp.

'Father gave it to me, before he departed for London,' said Edward. 'He never said what it was for.'

'Why would he give it to *you*? This is after all my house, not yours!'

'It was just as he was leaving. I don't think you were around, old fellow. There was nothing to the matter; he just said he thought the key should stay here. I put it in my pocket, and never gave it a second thought, until now.'

William continued to look unhappy. 'But you're quite right, it is your house,' said Edward. 'Take it, please. See if it fits, if you like.'

Slowly, William took the key, knelt and inserted it in the keyhole. There was another, louder click, and the panel swung open to reveal a doorway opening onto a dark stair. A draught of cold musty air blew upwards. Calpurnia gasped, and clutched at Samuel's hand.

'So it wasn't moonshine after all,' said William thoughtfully. 'Well. I think I would like to see the secret cellars of my house. Do any of you care to join me?'

'Oh, yes!' said Emma, full of enthusiasm. 'And Mrs Vane; surely you will join us? The stair is narrow and rough, but Samuel will help you.'

'Oh, I will come too!' said Laure, following. At the head of the stair, Edward turned to Mrs Chaytor and bowed. 'Shall we join them?'

Mrs Chaytor looked down the dark stair, and then back at Edward, who was smiling blandly. She met his eyes, searching his gaze, but there was nothing to be read in his face. Reluctantly, she gathered her skirts, stepped through the doorway and began to descend the stair. Edward followed close behind her.

These cellars were large, much larger than the others. As she stepped from the bottom step to the brick floor she saw there were at least ten vaulted rooms running nearly the length of the house.

And then she saw, too, the real secret of New Hall. The cellar rooms were full. Long wooden crates lay piled on the floor, beside bundled shapes under canvas. And behind them, stacked from floor to ceiling in row after row, ton after ton, were dozens of wooden kegs of gunpowder.

Chapter 19

The Courage of Rodolpho

'But what is all this?' said William, his eyes wide. He turned on Edward, the candle flickering in his hand. 'What are these things? Why are they hidden in my house, with me knowing nothing of it?' Samuel and Emma were blank-faced with incomprehension; Calpurnia stood with her hand to her mouth.

'What is this place? It is an armoury,' said Edward. He moved forward and kicked one of the wooden crates, holding up the second candle. 'That holds twenty Charleville muskets packed in grease, and there should be about a hundred more crates like it. There's some boxes of spare flints somewhere too, and musket balls.'

He pulled aside the canvas cover of one of the objects, revealing a cannon barrel lying on the floor. 'That's a bronze six-pounder. Not much use like this, of course, but a good joiner and wheelwright between them can build a gun carriage in a few hours. There's enough down here for two batteries, with shot and bags of grape. And of course, enough powder to start a small war. Which,' he said reflectively, 'is exactly what it was meant to do. Will, old fellow, don't stand too close to those powder kegs with your candle, I beg you.'

'You knew . . .' said William. 'You knew all along this was here.'

'I did,' said Edward. 'I've known about this place for years. Father and Uncle Joe let me in on the secret a long time ago.'

Mrs Chaytor turned to him. 'Who put this here?'

'Do you remember 1779?' asked Edward. 'A big French and Spanish fleet came up along the south coast of England, carrying an invasion army.'

'I remember,' said Mrs Chaytor. 'It caused a panic at the time. But the fleet was driven off by bad weather, and then the Royal Navy intervened.'

'It was a near run thing, though, wasn't it? If those French troops had got ashore, there wasn't much to stop them marching on London.'

'And what is the connection between that incident and New Hall?' she asked.

Edward laughed and took a step back. Just at his shoulder there was a small wooden cupboard, fixed to the wall. A length of something that looked like thin rope hung down beside it. 'My dear Mrs Chaytor, New Hall was vital to the invasion. My father and uncle planned the whole thing, along with a cousin of ours, Camille de Foucarmont. Yes; the very same whom you shot the other night. He was already rather displeased with you, by the way; he'll be even more angry now. Monsieur de Foucarmont came over to America with Lafayette, and was involved in spying work; that's how he met Father and Uncle. He described the plans to invade England, and Father at once suggested the secret cellars at New Hall would be just the thing for their purpose. The plan was to have plenty of ordinance on hand, you see, when the French landed, so they could replace lost or damaged muskets and munitions without having to ferry them from France.'

'So Foucarmont returned to France and smuggled the weapons into the cellar, using directions given by your father,' said Mrs Chaytor.

'Exactly so, ma'am.'

'And at the end of the war, left them here in case they should be needed again.'

'Again, you are correct,' said Edward, smiling. 'It is ingenious, is it not? An entire arsenal of weapons hidden under the noses of the British authorities, ready for use at a few hours' notice. And so now, with France and Britain at war again, Foucarmont came back to see if the weapons were still there.'

'Why?' said William. 'To support a French invasion?'

'No; to start a revolution in England. There are many Englishmen who sympathise with the republicans in France, and think it is high time this country had a revolution of its own. You may even have met some of them, Mrs Chaytor. With French backing, they would rise up against the government. Foucarmont would supply them with weapons from this armoury. An army of Free Englishmen would march on London, overthrow the king and proclaim a constitution.'

'Of course they wouldn't,' said Mrs Chaytor. 'They would be swatted away like flies by our own army. But that did not matter, did it? They would distract the government in London, which would be forced to send soldiers to Kent. And every man deployed here would be one soldier less to send to Ireland, where the French intend to land their invasion army. This was to be a diversion. Foucarmont and Parker and your father were quite content for a thousand, two thousand of their allies to die in Kent, if it brought victory in Ireland.'

'And you!' cried Laure. 'You're part of this, aren't you? My own brother, my father, my uncle! This monstrous scheme; you intend to help carry it out!' Beside her, Samuel and Emma remained absolutely still. Mrs Chaytor could see them from the corner of her eye; like her, they were watching everything around them with deep intent.

'But we're at peace with England now,' said William. 'The English are our friends!'

'Don't be a damned fool!' snapped Edward. 'Between republics and monarchies, there can never be peace! Look at France, at war with half of Europe! The kings and queens and emperors will never be happy until the republics are crushed. The only way to deal with them is to crush them in turn. Fight fire with fire! The war is not over, and will never be over, not until one side or the other has knelt in abject surrender.'

'Then what has this to do with us?' asked Mrs Chaytor. 'You brought us down here by design, of course. The suggestion of a family reunion, with a few carefully chosen additional guests; the game of searching for the hidden cellars; the charade with the key; you have prepared all this very carefully. But to what purpose? Why did you want us to see all this?' and she gestured to the weapons.

'Well, Mrs Chaytor; perhaps I hoped to recruit you all to the cause. My sister and cousin are loyal Americans, surely. Samuel and Emma have no reason to love this country. And you, Mrs Chaytor; you are an intelligent, free-thinking woman. Surely you espouse the cause of freedom? Surely you understand that monarchies have had their day?'

Samuel and Emma had stirred a little at the mention of their names. 'That is not so,' said Emma. 'We have been more kindly treated in this country than where we were born.'

'And I am a loyal subject of my king,' said Calpurnia stoutly. She was shivering a little; she too could sense the tension in the air.

'This is nonsense,' said Mrs Chaytor coldly. 'You summoned us here because you thought that we, along with Reverend Hardcastle, might already have learned about the arsenal.'

'What? I knew nothing of any of this!' cried Laure.

'Ah,' said Edward, 'perhaps you did, and perhaps you didn't. I couldn't take a chance, you see. You and William wandering around tapping the walls and floors; what did you really discover, I wonder? And who did you tell about it? You have become very friendly with Mrs Chaytor; what secrets might you have passed on to her? And William, you had a long talk with that interfering busybody the rector; what did you tell him? And my dear new-found cousins; what did you discover, rummaging around the house before we arrived? Mrs Vane, you are the rector's sister, you share his house and you have an inquisitive mind; my guess is that whatever he knows, you know as well.'

'Clearly you believe that we have betrayed your secret,' said Mrs Chaytor. 'We have not, but I doubt you will believe us. What then do you intend to do with us?'

'Surely you must have guessed by now, Mrs Chaytor,' said Edward in tones of reproof. 'Why else would I have brought you down to the cellar?' And he opened the little wooden cupboard, reached inside it and pulled out a double-barrelled pistol, which he raised, cocking both hammers.

'For God's sake!' said William.

'Eddy!' screamed Laure. 'You cannot do this! I am your *sister*!'

'Oh, God, don't I know it, and don't I hate it! Look at you, with your books and your music and your intellectual pretensions, trying to pretend how pure you are. Not for you the dirt and the muck of politics and war, oh no; you're too pristine for all that, aren't you? I show you the weapons that will bring freedom to this country, and what do you say? *Oh, this monstrous scheme!*' he mimicked. 'You make me sick,' he shouted at her and she recoiled, taking several steps back, her face white with horror and fright. 'You make Father sick too, and Uncle Joe! They tried to marry you off, get you out of the way, away from us, but again, no, you're too prissy to marry anyone who isn't perfect. You're a damned burden! A nuisance and disgrace to the family, and I'll be glad to see you dead.'

'And you,' continued Edward, rounding on William. 'You *talk* well, don't you? You parrot all the fine phrases about liberty and equality and the brotherhood of man, but you're not prepared to get your hands dirty either, are you? You're quite happy to preach revolution as a shining idea, but let someone show you its dirty face, and you quail away. You think war is some kind of chivalric quest, with rules, and honour, and courtesy to beaten foes. You'll never make a warrior because you don't understand that a battle is only over when your enemy lies dead with your knife in his heart. You're weak, cousin,' he said venomously, 'weak and feeble and useless. I've done with you.'

Betrayed by the man whom he had idolised and emulated, William Rossiter exploded into anger. 'You bastard!' he shouted, starting forward with raised fists, only stopping when Edward aimed the pistol at his head. Slowly, sullenly, William lowered his hands. Amelia Chaytor watched Edward's face, and saw the affable veneer bubble and crack, and the hate and madness come pouring from his eyes. She saw Samuel and Emma watching him too, their eyes steady. *I know the look on their faces*, a little corner of her mind whispered. *I have seen it before, in hunting hawks.*

'Weak, as I said,' observed Edward. 'The rest of you will note that this pistol is primed and loaded. Should you think of doing anything stupid, like challenging me, two of you will die. Decide among yourselves who those two will be.'

'None of us will challenge you,' said Amelia quickly, in case either of the young men – or Emma – should think of doing so. Calpurnia stood rooted to the spot. 'But as you appear to know all the details of the plot, Mr Rossiter, perhaps you can tell me something. Who killed Emma's servant? Parker? Or was it Steele, the valet?'

Edward looked at her, hefting the pistol a little. He was enjoying himself, delighting in the power he had over them all. *He too parrots fine phrases about liberty*, she thought, *but underneath, he is just a bully who likes killing people.*

'I don't see why not,' he said after a moment. 'None of you will leave this cellar anyway, so no harm will be done. I killed her. We put Steele to watch the rooming house in London, and when he reported that two men had left and taken post for Kent, I assumed one of them was Samuel. I followed them here and slipped into the house on Christmas afternoon. I spotted a black man going upstairs, and assumed that I had Samuel in my sights. I thought of shooting him, then thought better of it and used a club instead.

'I thought he was dead,' Edward said, almost accusingly. 'He, or rather she, should have been. The black bitch must have had a bloody hard head. Anyway, I went back to check to see whether the secret door had been opened, and then had a look around to see if I had left anything behind that might give me away. When I came back, the body was gone. I went outside and found her lying in the pond, clearly done. But I had also heard horses leaving, so I knew I had to get away before whoever it was came back.

'I returned to London feeling quite satisfied; a job well done, I thought. You can imagine my surprise when I opened the paper and saw a woman had been killed. So, I assumed I must have disposed of my dear cousin Emma instead. Never mind, I thought, one down. Time to finish the other later.'

'You are a murderer,' said Laure in a whisper.

'Oh, do shut up,' said Edward in irritation. 'I am quite tired of listening to you.' Laure stood still, her face suddenly wet with tears; Emma came up and put an arm around her, still staring unblinking at Edward. Her body freezing cold, Mrs Chaytor gave a shiver that had nothing to do with temperature. She wondered if Edward had any idea what he was facing.

'You have overlooked one thing,' said Samuel, speaking for the first time since they had entered the cellar. 'Reverend Hardcastle knows as much as any of us. If you kill us, he will discover the truth.'

'Yes, I had intended for Hardcastle to be here as well,' said Edward. 'But never mind; I'll take care of him later. I doubt that drunken old sot will give me much trouble. Once he is dead, all the loose ends will be tied up.'

'There is another thing you have overlooked,' said Mrs Chaytor. 'There are six of us, and you have only two shots in that pistol.'

'Oh, Mrs Chaytor. You are an intelligent woman; use your imagination! The gunpowder, don't you see? Of course, thanks to you and the rector, the plot is compromised. Foucarmont has had to retire to France, and the rising is called off. There will be other chances, but meanwhile, things in Romney Marsh are a bit too hot. Volunteers and Preventive Men prowling around, that damned interfering fool Clavertye poking his nose in; and of course, that old soak Hardcastle managed to stumble quite close to the truth. He confronted Uncle Joe, and convinced him the entire plot was about to be discovered. Uncle Joe got the jitters, so badly that we had to silence him in case he decided to blab. I told Steele to find Foucarmont, and they did the job between them. But the problem still remains. Sometime, probably very soon, someone will stumble across this armoury. We cannot let all this material fall into British hands, and it is too risky to move it, even by night. So, we will destroy it. And, along with the weapons and the powder will perish the witnesses who know the secret.'

'I see,' said Mrs Chaytor, her voice calm. 'And these are your father's orders?'

'No, no. He merely told me to get rid of the arsenal. Blowing it up, and you along with it, was a little stroke of genius of my own.'

'No,' said Laure in a small voice. 'No, Eddy, you cannot do this.'

'I can,' said Edward. He held the pistol in his right hand and the candle in his left. Now he gestured at the length of thin rope. 'This is slow match, a hemp cord soaked in saltpetre. When I light this end, the flame will run along the rope until it reaches the powder. It's called "slow match", but it will reach the other end quite quickly, within a couple of minutes at most. That will give me time to get out of the house and get clear.'

'What about your aunt?'

Edward laughed. 'Auntie Jane is a good soldier, like me. She has been in on this affair from the beginning. Like Uncle Joe, she has been one of Father's loyal lieutenants for years. She knows of my plan, and is already out of the house, waiting for me. In the commotion, we'll get away. As far as anyone else knows, we'll have left the house long before the explosion.'

He truly is mad, Mrs Chaytor thought. One could not detonate five tons of gunpowder in the middle of Romney Marsh without someone starting a formal investigation. The servants would know that there were still people in the house when they left, and eventually some of them would talk. But by then, for the six of them, it would be too late. Horrified, she watched as Edward touched the candle flame to the slow match. It caught light, hissing like a little snake, and a ball of flame began to travel up the cord towards the ceiling.

'The slow match was laid long ago,' said Edward conversationally, 'so that the armoury could be blown up quickly if there was a threat of discovery. There was a fear that if the match was laid along the floor, damp would seep in. So they found a way of running it behind the bricks above the ceiling. It is quite ingenious. What a pity you will not be alive to appreciate it.'

'No,' cried Laure, sobbing. 'No, no!'

William, Samuel and Emma all stood watching Edward, their bodies tense, waiting for any chance at all. None came.

'And now,' said Edward cheerfully, 'I fear I must leave you. Farewell. Enjoy the rest of your lives.'

From overhead came the sound of a slamming door, and the unmistakable noise of a key turning in a lock and being withdrawn.

'Auntie!' called Edward sharply. 'Are you still here? You must get out, my dear. I've lit the slow match, and I am coming up directly to join you.'

'You will stay where you are!' shouted Jane Parker. 'I have locked the door and taken the key. Stay down there and burn, you evil whelp, and suffer all the agonies of hell!'

The ball of flame was nearly at the ceiling, out of reach.

'Aunt Jane!' shouted Edward, suddenly desperate. 'Please! Let me out!'

'Let you out? Why? You killed my husband! I loved him, and you killed him, and I *hate* you! Damn you!' she screamed with fury, '*Damn you!*'

Edward began to panic. His forehead was suddenly wet with sweat, his lips parted, his chest heaving.

'No!' he screamed. 'I never touched him! It was Foucarmont!'

'Murderer and liar! You lured him out to that church! You and Steele between you! You killed him, and now you'll die too. *Die!*' she shrieked.

In the cellar, the slow match was working its invisible way towards the powder. Mrs Chaytor looked at Samuel and saw the look in his eye. She nodded and turned to William, standing with a candle in one hand. 'Throw me your candle,' she hissed.

Whatever else William Rossiter might have been, he was not weak. He tossed the candle lightly to Amelia, flame arching in the air. Edward saw the movement and fired on instinct, smoke and flame spurting from the pistol; the ball, fired wildly, flew into a ceiling arch, dislodging a shower of brick shards.

Even as the pistol fired, Samuel sprang. Like a tiger, he landed on Edward's shoulders, dragging him to the floor, sending the candle hurtling away. Edward fought to raise the pistol and fire the other barrel but William, coming close behind Samuel, kicked it out of his hand so that it spun across the floor. Edward fought furiously, swearing and spitting. 'Lay him out,' said William.

'He's your cousin!' said Samuel, pinning Edward's arms behind his back.

'He's no kin of mine,' said William grimly, and he balled one big fist and slammed it into Edward's jaw. The other man's head rolled back and he sagged senseless to the floor.

Emma was already climbing up the stacked kegs of powder, and now she began to hurl the uppermost kegs to the floor. 'What is she doing?' gasped Calpurnia.

'Looking for where the slow match comes down from the ceiling,' said Mrs Chaytor. 'Quickly, come.' She ran into the next chamber and started to climb. The room was almost entirely dark. Her shoes slipped and she stopped and wrenched them off, then climbed in stockinged feet up the face of the ranks of barrels. She grasped the topmost and pulled it away; gunpowder is not especially heavy and she dislodged it without difficulty. It crashed to the floor and broke open. Calpurnia could not climb, but she had found a long pole with a twisted spike on one end, which Mrs Chaytor vaguely recognised as some sort of device for artillery, and she used this to hook the upper rims of some of the gunpowder kegs and haul them crashing down.

The air was full of dust and stank of sulphur. The ceiling was visible now and there was no sign of the slow match. They hurried into another room where William was working like a madman, lifting kegs over his head like Hercules and hurling them down, and another where Emma and Samuel were working quickly and efficiently together. One of them had found Edward's candle and lit it, leaving both candles together in the passageway that ran along the front of each cellar; that thin wavering light was all they had to go by. The next cellar had not yet been touched. Again, Mrs Chaytor climbed the stack while Calpurnia used her worm to pull the kegs down to spill on the floor. Laure was there too with some sort of rammer in her hands, bashing at the topmost kegs and knocking them down with surprising strength.

'There it is!' screamed Calpurnia.

Ten feet from Mrs Chaytor's reach, where the ceiling arch came down to meet the wall, was a small black hole. Out of it, like a snake coming out of its lair, ran the thin dark rope, coiling through the shadows down over the rearmost kegs. Desperate, she pulled up her skirts and crawled across the kegs, tearing her gown on the iron rim of one. She grasped the end of the slow match and tugged; nothing happened. 'I need a knife,' she screamed.

There was a shout from below, and William Rossiter scrambled up to her with a penknife in his hand. He saw the match and reached up to the ceiling to cut it away, throwing the end out into the passageway, away from the spilled powder. As Amelia slithered down to the floor with a bump, wrenching her ankle, Emma and Samuel came flying into the room and began hauling more kegs away. Heart pounding, Amelia watched a bright ball of flame appear in the dark hole, run down the short remaining length of match – and stop.

Emma screamed, that same ululation she had let out the night Sandy House was attacked, and William whooped. 'Come on! We can bash the door down!'

They ran for the stair, Amelia still barefoot. William, the strongest, went up the narrow stair first. He hit the door with his shoulder, hard. Nothing happened. Again and again with increasing desperation and anger he rammed the door, which refused to give. 'Aunt Jane!' he shouted. 'Open up and let us out!'

Silence. There was a sudden smell of smoke in the air. 'Please, Aunt Jane! Let us out! We've done nothing wrong!'

'Oh, dear God,' said Amelia suddenly.

William stopped, and then they all heard it: the crackle and spit and roar of fire. Jane Parker, not content with trusting to the slow match, had made sure of her night's work by setting the house on fire.

By the time the rector reached the village the source of the flames could be clearly seen. New Hall glowed like a torch beyond the trees. Heart in his mouth, he ran heavily down the street. Of all the nights for this to happen! Stemp and Hoad and many of the other men of the village would be away in New Romney. But there was Luckhurst, coming out of the Star to gaze in astonishment at the flames.

'Tim! Collect everyone you can, and bring buckets! We'll use the water from the horse pond.'

Luckhurst shouted a response and began to run along the street, banging on doors. The rain still slanted down, driven on the stiff wind, but it was easy to see that the fire was increasing. Panting, the rector carried on towards New Hall. The gates stood open; he ran up the drive, seeing the windows of the library and drawing room glowing orange with fire. Several windows had cracked and fallen and flames were beginning to lick up the walls. Ivy on the wall beside the library flared and flamed and died. Sparks flew up in clouds, disappearing into inky smoke.

The front door was wreathed in curling smoke. Desperate, followed by the dog, Hardcastle ran around the north end of the house and through the gap between the house and stables. He saw at once that there would be no need for Luckhurst and his bucket brigade; the ground floor of the house was an inferno, only the kitchen so far spared. Flames licked up in some of the first floor windows as well. He ran towards the back door next to the kitchen, hoping against hope that he could bring out anyone who might still be alive. A dark shape moved before the door. Firelight gleamed off the pistol in her hand.

'Stand back!' said Jane Parker, in a voice harsh with rage and grief and madness. 'Come a step nearer, and I will kill you.'

On the stair the smoke was thick now, and William was coughing as he continued to smash against the door, yelling hoarsely for his aunt. 'Let me take over,' said Samuel. His brother nodded and slid down the stairs in search of cooler air, hacking and retching, while Samuel silently pounded his shoulder against the door. In the cellars themselves the smoke was visible now, and it was growing warmer. Edward still lay unconscious on the floor.

'We do not have long,' said Emma.

They did not have to ask what she meant. Sooner or later, and probably sooner, the fire would burn through the floor timbers overhead, and they would start to crash down onto the brick vaults. Sooner or later, the weight of the timbers would cause the brick to give way, and sparks and burning debris would cascade down onto the gunpowder. Many barrels had been broken, and loose gunpowder lay everywhere. A single spark in the wrong place could mean the end.

Steadily, rhythmically, Samuel attacked the door. Her feet in her shredded stockings crunching on grains of powder, Amelia searched for something, anything, they could use to pry open or chop down the door. Her hand, groping in the dim light, found something metallic; a hammer.

'Here!' Passed from hand to hand, the hammer went up the stair to Samuel at the top. They heard the thunder of metal on wood as he began to pound at the oak planks, and their spirits lifted for a moment; but still the door remained unyielding. The smoke and heat increased still further.

At the far end of the cellar, away from the area where they had been searching, the ceiling gave way and burning timbers crashed down onto the floor, followed by a shower of sparks.

Calpurnia Vane began to scream.

'Let me pass,' said the rector. Rain fell steadily around him, hissing in the flames. His heart thundered in his chest and he could feel the pain in his lungs. 'There may be people in there whom we can save.'

'There is no one there.'

The thunder of a hammer gave her the lie. Someone was trapped inside, pounding to get out. 'Mrs Parker,' the rector implored, 'I beg you to let me in. Can you not hear? There are people in there, fighting to get out. Please.'

'Let them burn!' snarled the woman, and as the rector stepped forward her finger tightened on the trigger. 'I mean it! One more step and I will kill you dead! I've done it before, and I'll do it again, so aid me God!'

The pounding continued, and then the screaming started; a long shriek of utter fear. The rector tensed, ready to attack with his stick and knowing that he stood little chance of succeeding. He was too late.

Rodolpho too had heard Calpurnia scream. The hiss and roar of the flame struck utter terror into his heart, and without the presence of the rector he would have fled long ago. But now he heard the voice of the woman who had rescued him and given him complete and unstinting affection, and he had no choice. In the single bravest action of his young life, Rodolpho gathered himself and sprang, snarling, at Jane Parker.

The pistol barrel moved, and spat flame. Rodolpho shrieked, twisting in the air and crashing down on the cobbles; he rolled over once, still squealing, and then lay with thrashing legs trying to rise but unable to stand. The rector took one long step forward and smashed the useless pistol from Jane Parker's grip, and ran past her into the house.

He located the sound of the hammering without difficulty. 'The door is locked. Who might have the key?' he called through the door.

'Mrs Parker,' shouted Samuel. 'We are almost out of time, sir.'

The rector ran back to the courtyard. He had never struck a blow against a woman before, but now he picked up Jane Parker and shook her like a rag doll.

'Where is the key? Tell me at once, or I will break every bone in your body, one at a time.'

'No!' screamed the woman, and she clutched at the reticule at her belt.

The rector ripped it away from her and shook it; the key fell out onto the cobbles. Jane Parker made a grab for it; the rector hurled her away, seized the key and ran back past the whining dog into the house. The key slid into its hole and the door hissed open. Samuel Rossiter stumbled out, then turned at once to pull the others up, Laure, Emma, Calpurnia, Amelia Chaytor, and last of all William, dragging the unconscious body of his cousin behind him.

'We need to get away from the house,' panted Amelia. 'Quickly.'

'Why?' He was gasping too.

'Gunpowder. Lots of gunpowder.'

In the courtyard there was another scream; Calpurnia knelt over the body of Rodolpho, sobbing uncontrollably. 'Oh, my baby!' she cried. 'Oh puppy, no!'

Samuel knelt beside her, his fingers searching the wound. Beside him, the kind woman who had nursed him and fed him and read him her books – the wondrous, magical stories of faraway lands that he loved so much – was crying with shattering grief, oblivious to the danger. 'The wound is not mortal,' he said to her. 'I think it is only the leg. We will take him away and heal him together, and he will be as good as new.' And with great gentleness, he lifted Rodolpho's enormous weight onto his shoulders and began to run. Amelia and Emma lifted Calpurnia to her feet and pulled her after them. The rector searched wildly for Jane Parker but could see no sign of her. Then he heard the sound of shattering timber as the floors caved in, and he too began to run.

Halfway down the drive the escaping group met Luckhurst and the first of the bucket brigade. 'Get everyone back,' gasped the rector. 'Back to the village. Stay away from the house.' They obeyed him without asking why, hurrying back down to the gates. Just as they turned onto the main road there was a red flash behind them, followed by a shattering roar as the rear elevation of the house collapsed, and then another larger flash and a boom like the end of the world as five tons of gunpowder began to explode.

Chapter 20

The Ashes of the Past

Outside in the street there was a steady ripple of sound, the clop-clop-clop of hooves and rattle of iron-rimmed wheels on cobbles blending into a single dull rumble. It seemed strange to hear such sounds again, after so long on the Marsh, where ordinarily the loudest noises were the cries of birds and the incessant sound of the wind.

Ordinarily ... if you could erase from your memory the sound of five tons of gunpowder blowing up, or the pounding of roof tiles and chimney pots and bricks falling around you like hail.

Miraculously, none of them had been hit by falling debris as they fled the explosion. The bucket brigade had all escaped serious harm too. Even more miraculously, Jane Parker had been found wandering next morning behind the stable block; cold, wet, dazed and deafened but otherwise physically unharmed. The condition of her mind was something else entirely.

Now, the rector and Mrs Chaytor sat in chairs on opposite sides of the coal fire, listening to the sounds of London around them and waiting until they should be called. The room itself was silent, apart from the gentle hiss of the fire. Voices could be heard in the office next door, a gentle murmur only, the words inaudible.

A door opened. An attendant, white-wigged in blue breeches and coat, bowed. 'The Foreign Secretary will see you now, sir.'

Hardcastle and Mrs Chaytor rose. 'Just a moment, ma'am,' said the attendant, holding up a hand. 'I'm afraid you can't go in. No ladies allowed, that is the custom.'

'Don't be ridiculous,' said Mrs Chaytor. 'Go and tell Lord Grenville that Amelia Chaytor is here.'

The attendant hesitated, then bowed and withdrew. He was back in a moment, looking chastened. 'If you would accompany me, ma'am, sir?'

In the next room another fire burned, keeping out the late February chill. The walls were lined with shelves of books interrupted by massive oil paintings in gilt frames. A small group of men sat or stood around the fire. One, a tall aristocratic man in his late thirties with brushed-back dark red hair, turned and then hurried forward to greet them, smiling. He bowed and kissed Mrs Chaytor's hand.

'Willie,' she said fondly. 'It *is* good to see you again.'

'Amelia,' said William Wyndham Grenville, Baron Grenville and Foreign Secretary of Great Britain. 'My dear, are you well? You are recovered from your ordeal?'

'Quite recovered, thank you.'

'I am so sorry that you have been dragged into this business.'

'I'm not,' she said smiling. 'You know me, Willie. I have a nose for trouble.'

'That you most certainly do. Come, please be seated. And you must be Reverend Hardcastle. Welcome, sir, and thank you for coming.'

There were four other men in the room, two of whom needed no introduction. One was Lord Clavertye, the silver hair at his temples glinting in the firelight. The second, sitting silently before the fire with one hand resting on his ebony walking stick, was James Rossiter. The third was a wigged man in his late fifties with sharp nose and bulging double chins; the fourth was a balding, heavyset man in his mid-forties.

'His Grace the Duke of Portland,' said Lord Grenville. 'His Excellency Mr Rufus King, ambassador of the United States of America.'

King bowed. 'Your servant, ma'am. Reverend.'

'Very well,' said Grenville briskly. 'We are all busy, and I do not propose to waste time. Lord Clavertye has already briefed us on the essential facts of the situation. My lord, have you anything to add?'

Clavertye shook his head. 'Reverend Hardcastle was much closer to this affair than myself. My account relied heavily on information provided by him.'

'Of course. Reverend, is there anything further you wish to say about this matter?'

Hardcastle looked at Rossiter. This time the other man looked straight back at him. His face might be tired and strained, but his eyes were strong and challenging.

'I should like to begin with a question,' said the rector. 'May I ask after the health of Mrs Joseph Parker?'

It was not the question Rossiter had been expecting. 'There has been little change,' he said at length. 'She is in the care of a doctor who specialises in nervous disorders. He warns that it may be a long time before she recovers. If at all.'

'I am truly sorry to hear it,' said the rector. 'She has suffered enough already, as have many others of your family. I shall pray for her.'

'Thank you,' said Rossiter. The irony in his voice was faint but unmistakeable.

'If there is one thing about this case that disturbs me more than anything else,' the rector said, 'it was your apparent willingness to sacrifice anyone, including the very closest members of your family. Your sister. Your daughter. Your nephews and niece. Your brother-in-law, whom you once called your old friend and comrade-in-arms. All of them were to be allowed to die, for the sake of your cause.'

Rossiter stirred a little, stretching out his bad leg. 'Every man should have a cause he is ready to give his life for,' he said. 'Otherwise, life is not worth living.'

'Speaking as one who was nearly immolated in the name of your cause,' said Mrs Chaytor, 'I would beg to differ. But it was never *your* life that was in danger, was it, Mr Rossiter? Instead, you sent others to the pyre.'

'I had no idea that either my son or my sister would commit the acts they did,' Rossiter said coolly. 'I admit I favour the republican cause in France. What of it? So do many in America, and so do no small number of people here. During our war of independence, I met a French officer and discussed plans for an invasion of Britain. I also offered him the services of my family home to assist that invasion. Again, what of it? Both we and France were at war with England. My action was entirely legitimate.'

'But you came to this country as a member of an embassy, whose aim was to establish peace between our two nations,' said Grenville, his face hard. 'And while a member of this embassy, you connived at murder and espionage and engaged in a plot that could have endangered the security of this realm. Those acts, Mr Rossiter, were *not* legitimate.'

'Fine words, my lord. But you cannot prove them.'

'Speaking as an officer of the law,' said Lord Clavertye, 'I think we can. Your son boasted about the entire affair before a number of witnesses, including your daughter, your nephews, your niece and Mrs Chaytor. There is more than enough evidence to commit him to trial for capital crimes. And I believe we should have no trouble proving a case against you as an accomplice to intended murder, at the very least.'

Clavertye looked at King. 'Unless, of course, the American minister wishes to extend his protection to Mr Rossiter and his son?'

'I have no particular desire to do so,' said King shortly. 'I accepted Mr Rossiter as a member of my embassy unwillingly, but in good faith. I assumed that even though our political views are very different, he would join me in working for the greater good of the United States of America. What he has done instead is to jeopardise the future of everything our government has worked for over the past ten years. I will remind you all that Congress has yet to ratify the treaty negotiated by my predecessor Mr Jay and your government.'

In plain words, the rector thought, King is throwing Rossiter to the wolves. Rossiter looked at Portland, who waved a hand.

'We have already discussed this,' the duke said to Grenville.

There it was: five words that would save Rossiter and his son. Behind the scenes, the bargain had already been made. Portland had exercised his interest; some day, in return, he would do an equal favour for Lord Grenville.

'We have discussed it,' said Lord Grenville shortly. 'Though to tell the truth, your grace, I am more minded to heed the words of Mr King. We need the American treaty. If we are to carry on waging war against the French Republic, as it looks as though we now must, then we need American trade and commerce. I am hopeful also that the day will come when American warships fight alongside ours on the high seas against the French navy.

'I accept your words, Lord Clavertye. But his grace has recommended that Rossiter not be prosecuted, and I support him.'

'Thank you,' said Rossiter, and he looked at the rector, his hazel eyes full of amusement.

'However,' said Grenville firmly, 'you will not be permitted to remain in this kingdom. When the ships begin to sail again in spring, you will depart on the first available vessel, along with your wife and son. Until that time, you will not leave London. Your every move will be watched and your correspondence will be intercepted and read, the contents shared with the American ambassador. The same restrictions will apply to your son, Mr Edward Rossiter. Mrs Parker will be allowed to remain in England until such time as her condition allows her to travel, upon which event she too will be deported.'

He looked hard at Rossiter. 'Is that quite clear?'

'Perfectly clear, my lord.'

'Have you anything to say in response?'

'Only this. What happened on Romney Marsh is only the beginning,' said Rossiter. 'More will come after me; my son, many others. We will not rest until our cause is won. You fine gentlemen speak about peace between Britain and the United States; agreements, treaties, alliances. But there will never be peace between your kingdom and our republic. How can there be? We are opposed to each other in every respect. Our nation is built on the principles of freedom and equality, yours on the basis of oppression and the slavery of the poor. Your king and his minions hate us and wish to witness our destruction. We feel the same about them.

'So, it is war to the death between our nations. We will not rest until we triumph. This war began with a British army marching into Lexington. It will end when a republican army marches down Whitehall. Then, Britain will be free. And only then, gentlemen, may we begin to talk about a true and lasting peace.'

In the silence that followed, it was the rector who spoke first. 'You are wrong,' he said. 'I can quite understand why people once felt as you did, in the heat of battle. But those days are past. You think the war is still being fought, but you are quite wrong. Down in the street there are young Americans who have begun to recognise what all of us ought to have known all along: that we are one people. Britons and Americans, we are kin. We share many things: our language, our faith, our love of liberty; for you are wrong, Rossiter, liberty is one of the cornerstones of this country. We have fought before to preserve it, and we are fighting again to preserve it now, from the blood-stained tyranny of the French Directory. And the things we share are far greater, far more powerful than the things that divide us.

'I think you know this. I think you know you are trying to hold back the tide, and that is why you are willing to go to the extremes you do; insane, evil extremes, to breathe life and fire back into a conflict that has already died.

'There is no life left there, Rossiter. The ashes are cold. Go back to America, and make your own peace, with God, and with your conscience, if you have one. You are done.'

Outside, the four of them were waiting, the little quartet that had become inseparable in the days following the burning of New Hall: Laure, William her cousin, and the twins, Samuel and Emma. Looking into their young faces, fresh with cold, bright with promise, the rector felt suddenly very old; but he felt also the stirrings of hope.

'It is done. They will be sent home in the spring. No action will be taken against them.'

'I am glad,' said Laure. Of the four, it was she who still bore the marks of sadness in her face. 'I have broken with them, but I could not bear to see them punished. I want to make an end to it all, and start anew.'

'What will you do?' the rector asked her.

'Remain in London for a time,' said Laure. 'Mrs Chaytor's friend Lady Grenville has kindly invited me to stay with them. I have friends here, and I think I shall be happy.' Her eyes strayed for a moment to Mrs Chaytor.

'And the rest of you?' the rector asked. 'I am sorry, William, that there is nothing left of New Hall.'

'I think I am quite glad there is nothing left of New Hall,' said the young man. 'I've seen about as much of the place as I ever want to.' He smiled. 'We've reached a settlement,' he said.

'Oh?' said Mrs Chaytor.

'Father had land in Canada as well as England,' said Samuel. 'William has renounced his interest in the English estates, and Emma and myself will transfer our interest in the Canadian estates to William.'

'They're worth about the same,' said William. 'Better still, I'll have an income of my own, and don't have to take a penny from my uncle. It works out all around.'

'And you two?' the rector asked the twins.

'I think we shall stay in England,' said Emma. 'I have taken Mrs Chaytor's advice. There are people doing good work here. I shall join them.'

'And I too,' said Samuel, and he smiled. 'I will call from time to time, to visit Rodolpho.'

Rodolpho was at home at the rectory, recuperating under the devoted care of his mistress. Come spring he would be up again, bounding over the Marsh with ears and tail flapping, being frightened of rabbits. 'You know you are both welcome, at any time you care to visit,' said Mrs Chaytor. 'The door will always be open.'

She and Hardcastle left the four young people, busy planning and rebuilding their lives. 'I think we did something rather good by bringing them together,' said Mrs Chaytor.

'I agree. The four of them are living testimony to the notion that good will always win out over evil.'

'I would not go quite that far. But I agree they give one hope.'

'Hope?' he said, looking at her as they walked down the street. 'It is good to hear you talk about hope.'

'And it is good to hear you talk about good triumphing over evil. I always assumed you were as cynical as me. How fascinating to think that we can still learn new things about each other.'

'Indeed, I learn new things about you all the time,' he said, smiling. 'For example, I did not know until recently that you fished.'

'And I did not know that you were a playwright. I have been meaning to ask you; were any of your plays ever staged?'

'Yes; one.'

'Oh? Tell all, I beg you. What was it about?'

'It was a satire, entitled *Of Men and Manners*. It was intended as a biting yet witty critique of modern times. I fancied myself as a kind of theatrical Hogarth, ridiculing the pretensions of our leaders in Parliament and the Church and exposing the vice that lies beneath the surface of genteel society.'

'Goodness, all that in one play! How long did it run?'

'One night. To be strictly accurate, not even that.'

'Oh, dear. Did the audience boo and hiss?'

'At first. Then, midway through the second act, they set fire to the theatre. My career as a playwright ended at that moment. You are coughing. Are you all right?'

'It is nothing, I assure you. A little touch of catarrh, that is all.'

'Mrs Chaytor,' he said severely, 'I know you well enough by now to know when you are lying.'

'Indeed,' she said. 'And *that*, my dear, is precisely why I would never marry you.'

Afterword

As in *The Body on the Doorstep*, we have rearranged the details of St Mary in the Marsh to a considerable degree. The rectory is located east of the church, in the field to the north of the present-day Star. The Star itself has been moved a little further south. Sandy House and New Hall are both entirely invented. We have been a little more faithful to detail about New Romney, though we have made allowances for the fact that the village was then much nearer the sea. The ruins of the church of All Saints Hope can still be seen, though they have decayed considerably since the events portrayed here.

The winter of 1796–7 was an exceptionally harsh and bitter one. At one point, the cold was so intense that three of the standing stones at Stonehenge were toppled by frost. Easterly winds drove the British blockading squadrons off their station and allowed the French navy to escape from Brest, its ships loaded with soldiers for an intended invasion of Ireland. Fortunately or unfortunately, depending on one's point of view, bad weather prevented the French army from getting ashore, and the entire force returned to Brest.

The threat of invasion remained, however, and even as the rector and Mrs Chaytor were meeting the foreign secretary, French troops were landing at Fishguard in South Wales. They surrendered a few days later.

A week after the Fishguard incident, Lord Clavertye had a very public falling out with the Duke of Portland. His lordship then departed the Whig bloc and was accepted into the ranks of the moderate Tories under the patronage of Lord Grenville, with the promise of the post of attorney-general when next it should fall vacant. Lord Clavertye devoted a great deal of time and effort to trying to find out why the Duke of Portland was willing to go to such lengths to protect James Rossiter. He never succeeded.

Edward Austen, later Edward Knight, continued his career as a gentleman landowner in Kent, eventually becoming high sheriff of that county. No one dreamed he would one day be overshadowed by both his brother, an Admiral of the Fleet, and his little sister, who went on to become one of the best-known novelists of all time, eclipsing even her early mentor, Calpurnia Vane.

William Rossiter returned to America, where he embarked upon a career in politics. He was later elected a United States Senator for the state of Maine, making a name for himself as a passionate opponent of slavery and a strong advocate of close relations between Britain and America.

Laure Rossiter remained in London, indulging in her passions for music, books and ideas, going on to marry an impecunious composer and musician somewhat younger than herself.

Samuel and Emma Rossiter also remained in London, where they lived in a modest house in Marylebone and worked for the abolitionist cause. Together, they paid for a handsome headstone to mark Sarah Freebody's grave in St Mary in the Marsh, and later named a mission house for impoverished former slaves in her honour.

Mrs Cordelia Hartbourne's novel *The Lighthouse of Vavassal* was an immense success. Serialised in *The Lady Magazine*, it was then issued in book form and reprinted twenty-one times.

Rodolpho made a full recovery and continued to live happily at the rectory. And yes; he remains frightened of rabbits.

The rector and Mrs Chaytor will return.

Acknowledgements

The first book was a step into the unknown; now comes the 'difficult second album'. We are deeply grateful to all those who have supported us through both books, and given thoughts, feedback and advice.

Pride of place must go to Dr Annie Gray, who generously shared her vast stock of knowledge about eighteenth-century food, especially Christmas dinners, and reviewed the first chapter for us. Many thanks are also due to Tricia Stock, Sam de Reya and Ivor Lloyd for helping with information about the appearance of corpses. (If you have not yet read the book, don't worry; dead bodies do not feature on the Christmas menu. Not quite.) Of course, any errors about either food or bodies are ours and not theirs!

Crucially important in our research was the work of historians of people of African origin in Britain in the periods before the twentieth century. The work of Malisha Dewalt, who maintains the wonderful Twitter and Tumblr feed entitled *Medieval People of Colour* www.medievalpoc.tumblr.com/ (tag line: "Because you wouldn't want to be historically inaccurate") has provided numerous images and ideas that informed our writing. Historians such as Miranda Kaufman, David Olusoga and many others – whom we found by using a variety of resources including the excellent www.blackbritishhistory.co.uk/ – also provided very useful books, articles and websites. The *Black Georgians: the Shock of the Familiar* exhibition at Brixton's Black Cultural Archives was a particularly enjoyable way to increase our knowledge on the subject.

On Romney Marsh, Liz Grant at the Kent Wildlife Trust Visitors Centre near New Romney has been great source of knowledge and support; thanks in particular for pointing out the scarlet pimpernels. Sadly, we couldn't use them in this book, but they will feature another time. The staff at The Rye Bookshop have also been keen supporters (if you're ever in Rye, go in and buy something). Mary's Tea Room in Dungeness continues be our cake provider of choice when working on the Marsh. Don't laugh. For writers, cake is important.

Thanks to members of the two book groups from Ashwater in Devon, who listened to us reading parts of an early draft of the book, gave us a reception and good feedback. And some wine. Oh, and more cake, too.

To all at Bonnier Zaffre, thanks again for your support and hard work in taking our book and making it into something special. Particular thanks go to Kate Ballard for her detailed and painstaking edits – thank you again, Kate, don't know how long it took you, but the wealth of detailed ideas you provided was very much appreciated – and Jon Appleton for his careful copy-editing. Thanks to Emily Burns for all her work on publicity, to Georgia Mannering for her marketing skills, and special thanks to Kate Parkin for her support and for being there.

Our friends who do artwork for books often complain, with entire justification, that people don't give enough credit to artists or designers. Let us help put this right, and thank Nick Stearn and Head Design for a superb cover. People are still telling us how much they like it. Hopefully, the book lives up to its cover.

One a similar note, thanks to Gary Beaumont for the updated map, floor plan and family tree, and apologies for having to decipher our handwriting. Rachel Richards at Chameleon Studios has continued her great work on the A.J. MacKenzie website. We are fortunate to have such talent at our fingertips in a small Devon village.

Special thanks also to our wonderful agents, Heather Adams and Mike Bryan from HMA Literary Agency; probably, the best literary agency in the world. Your comments, advice and support for the book – and above all, your never-failing patience – have been, as ever, invaluable.

And thanks once again to our family and friends, whose enthusiasm and support has meant the world to us. You were kind enough to say nice things to us after reading the first book in the series. Hopefully, you'll still be speaking to us after you read this one.

West Devon, 2016

Turn the page for a sneak preview of the next mystery for Reverend Hardcastle and Amelia Chaytor, *The Body in the Boat* . . .

1

Ships in the Night

On a moonless night in high summer, a small boat lay drifting in the English Channel, rising and falling slowly on the long low swells. A single man sat on the rowing bench, hands resting on the oars. Every so often he dug the oars into the water and rowed a few strokes, keeping the boat on station against the current. The oarlocks were stuffed with rags to stifle their sound, and the boat was almost silent as it glided over the black water. Mostly, though, the man simply sat, and waited.

The night sky was clear and beautiful. Stars flamed in their thousands, flickering against the deep blue of midnight. In their midst, the Milky Way glowed like the vault of heaven, arching from horizon to horizon. There was no other light save for the faint spark of Dungeness lighthouse, shining four miles to the south. A light wind blew gently from the north, rippling the water a little.

The man in the boat paid no attention to the stars. He sat staring east, listening and watching, his attention focused on the dark sea. They must come soon, he thought. In a few hours, dawn would arrive, and the cloak of night that hid he and his boat would be dispelled.

On the heels of the thought, there came a ripple in the shadows to the east. The man stirred. He pulled a small spyglass from his coat pocket, raised it to his eye and focused. There, black against blackness, was a small ship, a cutter creeping along under a single jib. The man in the boat puffed his cheeks and exhaled with relief. *About bloody time*, he thought.

The cutter drew closer. The man in the boat cupped his hands and gave a soft hail. 'Finny! Say voo?'

A moment, and then a voice sounded low over the water from the ship. '*C'est moi, bien sûr. Où êtes-vous?*'

'Heave to. I'll come to you.' He dug in the oars again.

A few minutes later the boat was alongside the cutter, hulls bumping together in the long swells. 'Yorkshire Tom', said a shadowy figure in the cutter. He spoke good English, though with a rasping north French accent. 'It is good to see you, my friend. All is well?'

'All quiet, Finny. Are we on?'

'As agreed, in two days time. We'll come a little before high tide, as usual. Here are the manifests.'

An oilcloth packet was passed over. Inside it, the man called Yorkshire Tom knew, were lists of the consignments that would be smuggled across the Channel: tubs of gin, casks and bottles of brandy, bolts of silk and lace, bales of tobacco: comforts and luxuries which were heavily taxed in England. Every item on the manifests had been ordered and spoken for, some by local shopkeepers in Kent, others by middlemen and negociants who would transport the goods to London and arrange their sale there. That was nothing to do with him; the task of men like Finny and Yorkshire Tom was merely to get the cargoes across the Channel and safely ashore.

'You have the downpayment, of course', Finny added.

'Of course.' Yorkshire Tom reached into the boat and pulled out a heavy canvas bag that clinked a little. 'Twenty per cent', he said, handing the bag across to the cutter, where eager hands grasped it. 'Rest to follow on receipt of the goods.'

'*Bon.* I will inform *Le Passeur*. The location is the same? St Mary's Bay?'

'Yes. Look for the usual signals.'

'And the Preventive Men?'

'The revenue cruiser went down the Channel yesterday. She'll be down Brighton way until next week. We've arranged a distraction for the land guard, but if they do come near us, Clubber will have enough men to deal with them.'

'Then all is well.'

Yorkshire Tom nodded in the dark. '*Le Passeur* will be in charge of the boats. What about Bertrand? Will he be there?'

The man called Finny chuckled. 'Bertrand does not want to see you. Does he still owe you the money?'

'He does', said Yorkshire Tom. Finny chuckled again. All the smuggling communities on both sides of the Channel knew that Bertrand owed this debt, and why.

'I saw Bertrand's lugger this evening', said Finny, conversationally. 'He set out from Wimereux just after sunset, shaping a course west. On that heading, I reckon he was making for Dungeness.'

Yorkshire Tom swore. 'What's that blasted lubber up to now?'

'I have no idea. We do not see each other socially.' Finny was from Ambleteuse, while Bertrand was from Wimereux; the French smugglers, just like the English ones, had their local rivalries. 'I must go', said the Frenchman. 'It will be light soon. *Au revoir*, Tom.'

The man in the boat waved and dug in his oars, pulling away from the cutter. Dim in the darkness, he saw her mainsail run up, and then another jib; she turned, gathering way, and vanished into the night. Yorkshire Tom, who also answered to the name of Joshua Stemp, rested on his oars for a moment, thinking about the man called Bertrand.

Six months ago, he had done the Frenchman a good turn, helping him escape from an English gaol and recover his ship. The price for this favour had been clearly agreed. But since then,

Bertrand had been elusive. Stemp's inquiring messages had gone unanswered. When Stemp himself went across to Wimereux, there was no sign of Bertrand; his colleagues claimed that he had gone away to visit his dying mother. Or was it grandmother? They had not been certain.

'Dungeness', Stemp muttered to himself. 'What would that daft French bugger be doing down at Dungeness? Who is he meeting there?' Did Bertrand perhaps have a new English business partner? If so, Stemp wanted to know who it was. He dug in the oars again and bent his back, turning the boat south and rowing steadily across the quiet, rolling sea.

High above, the stars shimmered in their cold, distant glory. The coast of Romney Marsh lay low to his left; he could just make out the tall tower of St Nicholas, dark against the starlight. From time to time, he stopped and turned to scan the sea ahead through his spyglass.

An hour passed. The gleam of Dungeness lighthouse was brighter now. Dawn must not be far away. Stemp turned to look ahead once more, and at once drew in his oars, letting the boat rest on the gentle sea. Through the glass, he could see a shadow against the stars; a dark rectangle, the lugsail of a ship perhaps half a mile away, crawling over the sea in the light breeze. He stared hard at the sail. This was not Bertrand's ship. In fact, he was quite certain he had never seen that particular rig before.

Even as he watched, a light flashed from the ship's deck, a lantern briefly uncovered and then covered again. The signal was repeated. Stemp strained his eyes, looking for an answering signal from the shore; he saw none. But the ship's captain must have been satisfied, for the sail came down. The lugger drifted on the current now, her bare masts and yards dark lines against the faint sky. Cautiously, Stemp dipped his oars and rowed a little closer.

Another sound came to his ears; the creak and splash of oars. Another rowing boat was coming out from shore. Again, Stemp strained his eyes through the spyglass, seeing the silhouette come out of the night. He studied the boat, and then went still.

He knew the boat, and he knew the man who owned it. All the boats built along this coast were of the same design, with high thwarts and pointed prows, but equally, every one was built by hand and each had its own unique character.

This particular boat belonged to man called Noakes, a boatman from Hythe. Like Stemp himself, Noakes was a smuggler; but even in that unruly fraternity, he was regarded as a violent and dangerous man. Stemp suspected him of murdering at least two men, possibly more, although no charges had ever been brought against him. He focused the spyglass on the man at the oars. There: that bulky shape, driving the boat over the water with powerful strokes, that surely was Noakes in person. Instinctively, like a man trying to ward off danger, Stemp crouched a little lower in the darkness.

The boat moved up alongside the lugger. Voices called quiet greetings. Stemp continued to study the ship. She was broad in the beam, and judging by the way she rolled on the swells, of shallow draught. From the rake of her masts and the angle of her yards, he was certain she was not French. Dutch, perhaps? He had seen ships out of Rotterdam in the past, and they looked a little like this.

He looked again. There were gaps in her bulwarks too; gunports. This ship carried cannon.

Something was being lowered carefully into Noakes's boat, something long and heavy. In the darkness, Stemp could not see clearly what it was. He watched the silhouettes of the men on deck, talking and gesturing to Noakes. Then the lugger hoisted her sails and turned away east, sailing close to the wind. Noakes watched her go for a moment, and then began to row again, heading straight back to shore.

Cautiously, keeping to a parallel course, Stemp followed. They were not far from Dungeness now, no more than half a mile from the point, the lighthouse a stone finger rising from the empty wastes around it. In the east, the light was growing. Pink streaks began to flush the sky, the waves below reflecting patterns of rippling pale and shadow.

The air grew hazy. Fog rose, feather white from the water. In a matter of minutes, the sunrise and the coast were both out of sight. The lighthouse faded and vanished. Visibility fell to perhaps twenty or thirty yards. Cold and clammy, the fog settled on Stemp. Sweating though he was from his exertions, he still felt the chill bite into him. A gull mewed, its cry muffled in the thick air.

Up ahead more gulls were wailing. Something had disturbed them; Noakes, perhaps, landing his boat. Stemp turned towards where he thought the sound was coming from and rowed on, slowly, straining his ears. Now he could hear the sea on the invisible shore, waves breaking with a soft thump, foam hissing on the beach, then the rattle of stones as the receding waves dragged the shingle after them.

Ta-whoom . . . sheeeee . . . ratta-ratta-ratta-ratta-ratta.

Ta-whoom . . . sheeeee . . . ratta-ratta-ratta-ratta.

The beach loomed out of the mist, a steep bank of shingle in front of him. Stemp ran his boat ashore with a grate of keel on stone and stepped out, dragging the boat up onto the beach. His boots crunched on the stones with every step. The fog hung like a grey cloak, hiding everything. Still the sea hissed and rattled.

Ta-whoom . . . sheeeee . . . ratta-ratta-ratta-ratta.

'*Ee-ow! Ow! Ow! Ow!*' Something hurtled, shrieking out of the mist and nearly hit Stemp's head before veering off sharply, still wailing in alarm. He started violently, reaching for his knife. Then he realised it was a gull, lost in the fog like himself. He cursed, then stood working out what to do next.

He thought Noakes might have landed a little way to his left. Slowly, with deliberate steps, he set off down the beach. The shingle crunched beneath his boots. The wind rose gently at his back and sent ghostly shapes of fog spinning around him, clutching at him. His heart thudded hard in his chest. He was sweating and cold. The fog reeked of the sea, filling his nostrils. The clumps of sea kale that grew out of the shingle were black in the dull light. *Crunch, crunch, crunch* went his boots, and the sea continued its hissing rhythm, sinister in the fog.

Ta-whoom . . . sheeeee . . . ratta-ratta-ratta-ratta.

A dark shape in the fog ahead, a low lump on the beach. He crouched down, drawing his knife. A gull cried mournfully overhead, setting his stretched nerves still further on edge. He wiped the water from his face and moved forward slowly, crunching. The outlines of the dark shape hardened and he saw Noakes's boat, deserted. Indentations in the shingle showed that the boat's owner had climbed the beach and gone inland. Stemp waited for several minutes, listening for any sound of his return, but beyond the sea and the nerve-shredding cries of the gulls, all was silent.

He walked forward to the boat. He listened again for a moment, then stooped and drew back the boat's canvas cover. Then he stood stock still, staring.

Lying in the bottom of the boat was a coffin.

Tingling with tension, Stemp studied it. The coffin was plain, of dark wood with carrying handles on either side. The lid was securely nailed down, either to protect the cadaver inside or, more likely, to prevent the smells of corruption from escaping. It had been a little damaged in its recent handling; splinters had been knocked out of one corner. Stemp wondered, briefly, where it had come from, and whose body was inside.

Stemp was not a superstitious man, and he had been in the presence of death before, many times. But here, on this lonely fogbound beach, with the sea hissing and rattling and the dark sea kale glowing like devil's eyes against the pale shingle, the hair stood up on the nape of his neck. He drew the cover back over the boat, concealing the coffin, and backed away. His hands were shaking. He no longer cared who the body in the boat was. He only wanted to get away from this place before he was spotted.

Too late. *Crunch, crunch, crunch* came distant to his ears. Invisible overhead, a gull screamed a warning.

Panicked, Stemp turned and ran back towards his boat; but the thing pursuing him ran faster still. He heard the footsteps drawing closer and closer, the rattle of shingle louder and louder; cornered, he wheeled knife in hand, and out of the fog came an immense shape, its size magnified by the dim light, bounding on four legs across the shingle. It was a mastiff, a huge one, black fur matted with damp, jaws dripping long strings of slaver. When it saw him, it skidded to a halt and then stalked forward slowly, hackles raised, eyes mad with violence, growling deep in its throat. The dog threw up its head and barked loudly, twice.

Stemp cursed. He stepped backwards, still facing the dog, knife held well to the fore; not that the knife would be much use against the mastiff. One leap, and it would throw him backwards and pin him, then rip out his throat. And now he could hear more running steps, the dog's master coming in response to its call. He continued to back away, his eyes never leaving the dog, until he bumped against his own boat.

Crunch, crunch, crunch. The running footsteps were only a few yards away. Still watching the dog, Stemp heaved the boat into the water, then scrambled over the thwarts. The mastiff rushed after him, teeth bared and ready for the kill. Stemp stood up in the boat, an oar in his hand. He flailed at the dog, then pushed against the shingle to drive the boat into deeper water. Balked, the mastiff raged at him, dancing up and down the line of the water snarling and barking. After him, out of the drifting fog came a big man with shaggy dark hair, carrying a knife of his own. His seamed face and broken nose were dark with rage.

'*Yorkshire Tom!* Get back here, you bastard!'

'Go to hell, Noakes', said Stemp, breathing hard.

Noakes roared at him, baring yellow, gapped teeth. 'Damn you! What're you doing down here? This ain't your patch!'

'I could say the same about you.' Stemp sat down on the bench, slammed the oars into their locks and dug into the water, pulling hard.

'Get back here, I say! Get back here!' The boat carried further from the beach, and Noakes snarled. 'Nah, that's it! Run away, you bloody coward!'

Stemp gritted his teeth and pulled on the oars again. 'I'm coming after you, Tom!' Noakes shouted, slashing the air with his knife. 'I'll finish you, by God I will! I'll cut your heart out, you son of a whore!'

'Go bugger yourself', said Stemp. It was not the most original insult, but it was all he had energy for. Then the fog swirled again and the beach was hidden from view, and all he could hear was the complaint of the gulls and the mad snarl of the dog. Weary with relief, he turned the boat north towards home.

Want to read
NEW BOOKS
before anyone else?

Like getting
FREE BOOKS?

Enjoy sharing your
OPINIONS?

Discover

READERS FIRST
Read. Love. Share.

Get your first free book just by signing up at
readersfirst.co.uk

For Terms and Conditions see readersfirst.co.uk/pages/terms-of-service